Because she was a pro, Kay wouldn't entertain the notion that fate played a role in the field of nursing. Kay always did her best, against the odds—or with them. And she was convinced that it was her work, not fate, that turned the tables on a patient in need of help.

But then there was the time that Cass, Kay's lover from the past, appeared on the scene of a rescue flight and returned with her to the hospital.

"Still working a gosh-awful job aren't you, Kay?" he asked as they walked through TRU's reception area. Then he took her arm as they paused in the corridor. He still had the power to make her feel wanted and loved and secure. His big frame and handsome face still turned female heads, she noticed, as they talked in spite of the passersby. And Cass seemed to love her still, after all these years.

Suddenly, Kay wanted to cry. "I have to get back to the unit, but I'll see you later," she said. Then she walked swiftly away from him, knowing that he watched her until she turned the corner to the nurses' lounge and out of sight.

In the days that followed, Kay's conviction about fate would be put to an even greater test. . . .

NTRAUMA NURSE

BY PATRICIA RAE

ZEBRA BOOKS
KENSINGTON PUBLISHING CORP.

ZEBRA BOOKS

are published by

KENSINGTON PUBLISHING CORP.
475 Park Avenue South
New York, N.Y. 10016

Printed in the United States of America

DEDICATION

To

Mildred and Howard

FLORENCE NIGHTINGALE PLEDGE

I solemnly pledge myself before God and in the presence of this assembly, to pass my life in purity and to practice my profession faithfully. I will abstain from whatever is deleterious and mischievous, and will not take or knowingly administer any harmful drug. I will do all in my power to maintain and elevate the standard of my profession and will hold in confidence all personal matters committed to my keeping and all family affairs coming to my knowledge in the practice of my calling. With loyalty will I endeavor to aid the physician in his work, and devote myself to the welfare of those committed to my care.

CHAPTER I

Kay was thinking, Wouldn't you know on Marsha's first day off in eleven days this would happen? Two events had to evolve to cause her to be winging swiftly eastward high above the city as nurse in charge of Ranger I, St. Luke's flying medivac unit. First, the accident had to occur in the first place. Second, it was Marsha Walsh's day off. Walsh was nursing supervisor of Trauma Receiving on day shift and was usually in charge of the medivac unit's emergency flights. Kay, next in command as Trauma Recovery's charge nurse, was in charge of emergency flights on day shift when Marsha was off duty. Luckily, Kay had had two years of training in the trauma units at St. Luke's which included occasional emergency flights in the medicopter, referred to by hospital staff affectionately as the Ranger.

Still, she was scared.

While the Ranger clattered, drumming steadily eastward, the pilot, Jerry Bergdorf, was singing loudly, ". . . So there's an old flame burnin' in yore eyes. . . ." Kay and her assistant, Anita, were busy checking emergency equipment and supplies, anticipating what they'd need once the victim of the accident was aboard. What had the dispatcher said? Gunshot wound to the

7

chest. It was eight o'clock on a Monday morning. No way a ground ambulance could reach the scene of the accident through freeway traffic during the rush hour and get back to the hospital in time to save the victim of a gunshot wound to the chest. But the Ranger could.

"Was it a gunfight or something?" Anita asked loudly over the sound of the copter's engines as she laid out a sterile pack of syringes on the anchored-to-the-wall Mayo stand. "Somebody mad at somebody else?"

Kay was glad Anita was along to help instead of one of Trauma Receiving's nurses. Dr. Kreel had ordered Anita to go on this flight in order to give her more in-flight experience; because after Kay, Anita was next in command, so to speak, in Trauma Recovery.

Kay shrugged. "All I know is it happened on the parking lot of Hersheal High School and the boy who shot him was his friend."

"Some darned teen-agers playing cowboy, probably," Anita said.

Jerry was singing, "For kissin' cousins don't stop with kissin' anymore. . . ."

Kay uncoiled the green plastic tubing from its sterile package and pushed the flared end onto the oxygen spigot. She had already checked the portable respirator, cardiac monitor, suction, and defibrillator, *God forbid*. Teen-ager. Kay thought of her twelve-year-old son, Russell, and felt her skin prickle with apprehension. She laid the oxygen mask on the Mayo stand, tested the oxygen in the tank attached to the wall by turning the valve on, then off.

The Ranger, painted blue and white on the outside, looked like any helicopter, but within its roomy, wide-windowed interior was one of the most sophisticated

8

compact emergency rooms in existence. The Ranger could accommodate two patients, a critical-care team, a pilot, and a passenger. It contained special critical-care equipment such as the defibrillator, cardiac monitor, neonatal isolette, respirator, and oxygen tanks. All emergency supplies such as IV fluids, plasma, medications, and dressings were contained in a compact cabinet behind the passenger's seat. Behind the pilot the radio transmitter was located and afforded ground-to-air and air-to-ground communications between the Ranger and Comstat, St. Luke's dispatching center.

"There we are. Down below," Jerry said. "Poe-lice have set flares. Even cordoned off an area for us. Usually I beat the poe-lice to the scene when it's called in by a layman, don't I, blue eyes?" Layman was Jerry's term for anybody not wearing a uniform. "Hold on to your hat, lady," he sang, "for this kiss is gonna blow yore ever-lovin' top. . . ."

Down the copter drifted—slowly, slowly. From the large, blue-tinted windows in the copter's cabin, Kay could see the blacktopped surface of the school parking lot with its yellow lines, rising to meet the vehicle as she snapped the catch on her shoulder harness. There was a crowd standing outside the ring of flares. Kids.

"What time was this accident called in?" Anita asked, snapping on her shoulder harness for the landing.

"Dispatcher said the accident occurred at 7:45. He received the call at eight," Kay replied gripping the emergency flight bag in her hand; and glancing at her watch, she added, "It's 8:10."

"Jeez, the kid's probably dead by now," Anita said.

Kay only gave her a don't-say-that look and held to the side bar to steady herself as the Ranger jostled them briefly as it settled on the pavement.

"MFI," said Jerry to the Ranger's communications center, "Ranger I. Just touched down in Hersheal High parking lot. Four, Comstat."

Kay's pulse thudded in her ears as Jerry cut the rotors, not stopping them, only slowing them. She unlatched the shoulder harness, threw the latch on the door, and scrambled out into the bright, airless early-morning light. When Anita had leaped out also, they pulled the stretcher from the cabin and ran crouching below the slowly whirling rotors to where four policemen were huddled in a circle on the pavement. The usual crowd that always stood around every accident was being held back by other policemen, and one of the young officers watched as the nurses approached and shouted, "Where's the doctor?"

"No doctor," Kay heard Anita say as they elbowed their way through the ring of policemen on the ground.

An officer stood aside and Kay fell to her knees beside the victim.

The victim. "Victim" was the first word one learned to use in Trauma Receiving. In Trauma Receiving one learned to use the word "victim" instead of patient. "A victim becomes a patient, Carlton, only if he lives and is transferred upstairs to Trauma Recovery," Dr. Kreel had told her during her first days of orientation to the trauma units.

"My God! A shotgun blast to the chest and they only send nurses?" demanded the young officer with gray eyes.

The victim was indeed a teen-ager—maybe fifteen— dressed in faded blue jeans and green T-shirt, now covered with blood, too much blood. The officers had cut

10

away the T-shirt and Kay could see his torn chest, the muscle tissue of the right chest wall and right upper arm torn away. He was still conscious; respiration was labored and rapid. He was also cyanotic. Definite open pneumothorax, air being sucked into the right lung through the open wound, collapsing the lung.

First things first. *Plug the hole in the chest.* Anita, having pulled the Vaseline-coated abdominal dressing pack from the flight bag, tore open the pack, slapped it on the gaping wound, quickly, while the boy was exhaling—one quick application of the dressing, none too gently. To secure it Kay applied wide adhesive tape over it quickly. Then her fingers traced the blood-covered skin on his chest. Crepitus on the left, air bubbles under the skin, air escaping from the left lung also, but slowly. Tension pneumothorax. As dangerous as the open kind.

As Kay took her stethoscope quickly out of her bag, she looked up at one of the teen-aged boys standing between two officers and asked, "What's his name?"

"God, she asks his name," she heard the irritating young officer exclaim.

"Bobby," the freckle-faced boy replied. "Bobby Cross."

The victim's name is Bobby. From the periphery of her hearing, Kay became aware of the story spilling out of Bobby's two frantic friends who stood shaking and pale among the policemen. Bobby had planned to go hunting over the weekend and borrowed his friend's shotgun. He met his friend on the parking lot before school to take the gun; didn't know it was loaded. Shell must have been jammed in the chamber. Bobby's friend was putting the gun into the back seat with Bobby watching from the opposite side of the car. *Bam!* Gun went off knocking out one of the windows and catching Bobby in the chest at a range of six feet.

While Kay was assessing Bobby's injuries, she was also talking to him, not aware of what she was saying exactly, only that she was trying to reassure him that he'd be all right. Soon they would give him oxygen and he'd be able to breathe better. . . .

With her stethoscope she listened for breath sounds in the damaged right lung. As she suspected, there were none. The right lung was collapsed. The blast had torn away part of his chest wall; there was blood and air in the pleural cavity of the lung—the space between the two membranes lining the walls of the thoracic cavity and the lung itself. The collapsed right lung was probably compromising the left lung and the heart as well. And besides that . . . breath sounds in the *left* lung weren't all that audible either. . . . In fact, it appeared that the left lung was damaged also. A quick neuro check determined that there was no indication of damage to the spine.

But there was too much blood. Bobby was losing consciousness. Anita had gotten a vein, started an IV in his left arm. Heck of a lot of good it would do Bobby with no lungs, Kay thought desperately.

Anita had applied a pressure dressing to the arm wound and Kay, snapping the stethoscope from her ears told her, "Start the plasma first, and get the mast pants on him." Then she stood up and said to the policeman nearby, "Help her get him onto the stretcher and into the mast pants." She forgot to say "please."

". . . Nurses," she heard the young policeman say as she ran for the Ranger. But she was thinking that the plasma would replace some of the blood loss and the mast trousers—a device resembling the inflatable splint—

12

would exert pressure on the veins of the lower extremities to aid the returning of blood to the heart. Both plasma and mast trousers were aids to prevent shock. She hoped frantically that they worked.

"I put a blanket on him, but—" a young girl shouted to her from nearby.

Kay leaped into the helicopter and snapped to Jerry, "Got Comstat? I need a doctor. Got one yet?"

"Kreel hisself, blue eyes, and standin' by," Jerry drawled and flipped the switch on the radio transmitter. "Comstat, this is Ranger I. Dr. Kreel? You've got a blue-eyed nurse wants a chat."

Kay had no time for pleasantries. She pulled the earphone headset on and glanced at the built-in radio transmitter behind Jerry's seat. "Dr. Kreel?"

"Here!" came the trauma director's deep voice over the headset.

"It's a massive chest wound. Teen-age boy, fourteen, fifteen. Definite open pneumothorax on the right and I think there's damage to the left lung also. He's lost a lot of blood. Don't think he's going to make it, Dr. Kreel, but we've got plasma going and we plugged up the chest wound on the right."

"O.K., Carlton. Now take a deep breath and give it all to me very carefully," the doctor said.

Kay was already taking a deep breath. "There's a deviation of his trachea, a sucking sound . . . Dr. Kreel, I *know* an open pneumothorax when I see it."

"O.K. But now, how about the left?"

"Breath sounds, but faint and getting fainter. Subcutaneous emphysema on that side."

"Head trauma or spinal injuries?"

"None that we can determine."

13

"O.K., Carlton. I think I've got the picture. Where's the victim?"

Kay glanced over her shoulder to see Anita scramble aboard holding the plastic bag of plasma high over her head as Jerry and the policemen tugged the stretcher on board. Kay said, "Just boarding the Ranger, Doctor."

"O.K., baby, tell Jerry to make haste and you keep reading me. Vitals?"

Jerry was shutting the door, latching it. Anita, shaking violently with anxiety, was snapping the safety belt over the stretcher while Kay clamped the O_2 face mask onto Bobby's face. "Vitals, Anita!" she demanded.

Anita pumped the blood-pressure cuff already on Bobby's left arm while Kay reached over to take his radial pulse . . . no pulse. She pressed her cold hand to his neck to feel for the carotid. The carotid pulse was there, but weak and rapid.

"Eighty-two is all I get," Anita said.

"Pulse is weak and too rapid to count," Kay reported. "BP is eighty-two."

Jerry, white-faced and tuneless now, was flipping switches and throwing controls.

"He's cyanotic, breathing stertorous and rapid. He's unconscious now, Doctor," Kay said.

"O.K., Carlton. I got the picture. Listen carefully, sweetheart," the doctor began. "Since the left lung is all we have to work with at the moment, we've got to save it first. Besides, that's a tension pneumothorax and that's bad news."

The helicopter motor roared, the entire vehicle shuddered, and as the pavement fell away below, Kay thought she heard Dr. Kreel say, "Ask Jerry if he has a condom on him."

Kay blinked. "A what?"

"Ask Jerry if he has a condom on him. A *rubber*."

Kay stared at the transceiver, but Jerry, who had his headset receiver in place now shouted, "Not on the member for which it was intended, Doc. And not in any of my pockets either. Usually I am better prepared, but today—"

"O.K., Carlton. You'll have to use a finger cot," Dr. Kreel's voice said.

With tears of fury filling her eyes, Kay shouted, "I don't understand you, Dr. Kreel." She looked at the boy barely breathing now, still cyanotic in spite of the oxygen. Anita had started another IV in the same arm. "A finger cot?"

Anita looked up at Kay. "He's gotta be drunk," she said, "or full of shit."

The doctor said, "Carlton, trust me. Have you got a finger cot or not?"

"No!" she shouted red-faced. A finger cot was a small rubber device which resembled a prophylactic condom, but which fit over the finger for the purpose of inserting rectal suppositories.

"O.K. You'll have to resort to a rubber glove, Carlton. Cut the index finger off a rubber glove," the doctor said, "and cut a hole in the other end."

Kay rummaged in her flight bag, came up with a package of sterile rubber gloves, tore open the package, tore open a package containing sterile scissors, and snipped off the index finger of one of the gloves, while Dr. Kreel continued to intone over the helicopter's communications system. "Have you a syringe with an eighteen-gauge needle?"

"Yes."

15

"A rubber band, perchance?"

Kay froze. "Rubber band?" She and Anita stared at each other again. Then Anita, remembering the rubber band she used to secure her hair in a short ponytail at the back of her neck, pulled it off with one quick movement. Not very sterile but—

"Yes!" Kay said.

"Great. Carlton?" Dr. Kreel said blithely. "You're going to decompress that left lung."

"Oh no!" Kay said. The procedure which Dr. Kreel was suggesting she do was not one usually performed by a nurse.

"The pleural cavity is filling with air and the left lung is slowly collapsing," said Dr. Kreel. "As I said, that's a tension pneumothorax."

"Attention who?" asked Jerry.

Dr. Kreel ignored that. "The left lung has already collapsed, as you know, Carlton. You don't have a choice, baby."

Kay swallowed while Jerry said, "Nerves of steel, don't fail me now!"

"O.K., Carlton. Now remove the syringe from the needle, that eighteen-gauge needle, and rubber-band that finger onto the hub of the needle. You see, it should act like a flutter valve. It should let air in, but not let it out. O.K.?"

Hastily, Kay did as she was instructed, understanding that if she did enter the air-filled pleural cavity, the device she was concocting should decompress the left lung.

As Dr. Kreel's handsome bass voice continued to give directions, Kay carefully inserted the needle with its ridiculous rubber finger between two of Bobby's left

16

anterior ribs. She was aware of how cold his skin was—too cold. "Carefully now," the doctor was saying. "When you go through the pleura, it'll sort of snap."

In the fog of fear surrounding her, Kay saw nothing but the pink hub of the needle slowly getting closer to the boy's white skin where the point had pierced between the two ribs as she pushed. Then, she felt the snap like the feel of a needle piercing a vein, only more pronounced. "I think I did it," she cried joyously. "The flutter valve's working!" She saw Jerry genuflecting extravagantly.

"Good, Carlton. Great!"

Anita had placed the diaphragm of her stethoscope over Bobby's left chest, and now smiled at Kay. "Breath sounds loud and clear."

Kay said, "Breath sounds loud and clear in the left lung now, Dr. Kreel."

"Terrific! Jerry?"

"Hello!" the pilot answered.

"Anticipated arrival, man."

Jerry consulted his wrist watch. "Eight forty-five!"

There was silence for a moment. Then Dr. Kreel's voice again. "Vitals?"

"Vitals!" Kay snapped to Anita.

"BP is seventy," Anita said loudly. "Can't find a pulse. Respiration still shallow, rapid, stertorous."

Kay reported the observations to Dr. Kreel.

He replied, "Tell Wilson to force that plasma in with pressure."

"She is, doctor."

"Tell her to force it in as fast as she can and keep hanging more."

Kay repeated the instructions to Anita.

"Now, Carlton? You did great with the flutter valve,

but wipe that pretty grin off your face, sweetheart. The victim's too far from the hospital yet so I gotta tell ya you'll have to insert a chest tube on that bad right side, baby."

"Chest tube? Me?" Kay and Anita stared at each other in horror. "I can't," Kay said finally.

"Yes, you can. You've got the trocar, the tubing, and the suction."

"But I still can't!"

Insertion of a chest tube was *certainly* never performed by a nurse and it was always done in the operating room with the patient under anesthesia, most generally, and under sterile conditions, and always by a doctor—

"You don't have a choice, Carlton. That open pneumo will compromise that other lung and the heart as well, and the kid's too shocky to last."

So Kay, with eyes shut, indicated to Anita to hand her the sterile thoracotomy pack. Inside would be the trocar and all the equipment she would need. It was a set meant to be used only by a doctor on the scene of the accident, or by one in the helicopter.

"Carlton?" came the doctor's voice over the headset. "I'll tell you every move to make and you do it," he crooned. "You can. You're special. You girls are all special. Didn't I tell you before? I don't let the fainthearted work on my trauma team, and you aren't fainthearted."

The doctor's voice was coddling now, soothing. The director of St. Luke's Trauma Receiving and Trauma Recovery units babied his nurses, the other hospital personnel complained. TR and TRU nurses were even more prima donna than ICU nurses. And that was pretty darned prima donna.

18

Trembling, Kay followed Dr. Kreel's directions exactly, swabbing the site of insertion with Betadine—swiftly—using a sterile Betadine-saturated swab enclosed in its own packet; making the small incision with the scalpel—she had never actually used a scalpel before—inserting the trocar slowly, slowly, meeting an obstruction, giving the trocar a slight twist. . . . And listening to Dr. Kreel's voice, she imagined him hunched over the microphone in Comstat's booth, his dark, curly hair always unruly; blue, blue eyes that turned black when he was angry, which wasn't very often, but if he was, look out; married, mid-forties, father of six young children, not very handsome to look at, but making you feel as if he was. His voice—gentle, stroking, almost sensual—making her feel that inserting a chest tube was the simplest thing in the world, making her feel confident, making her forget that the procedure, if done wrong, could kill Bobby and that she could be sued, her license taken away, that—

Suddenly, there was a snap and blood and air rushed into the tube attached to the trocar and into the Evacuset suction container attached to the wall of the copter. Anita checked quickly to see that the suction pressure gauge was still on "low."

Kay said, "I think I did it! I—there was the snap, and blood—" Then remembering what she should do next, she pulled the headset down around her neck, bent over Bobby's chest, plugged the stethoscope earpieces in her ears, put the diaphragm of the instrument to the right side of Bobby's bloody chest, and listened.

She smiled and almost wept. "There're breath sounds," she said. "When the suction hesitates, I can hear breath sounds. In the right lung! There're breath sounds in the right lung, Dr. Kreel."

"Sure there are, Carlton. Didn't I tell you you girls were special?" said the doctor.

But Bobby wasn't out of the woods yet. His blood pressure was eighty-four over twenty when the Ranger landed on the helipad at St. Luke's. He had been given three pints of plasma and continued to bleed profusely from his chest and arm wounds in spite of the pressure dressings.

The Trauma Receiving team was there on the helipad waiting, bending beneath the whirling rotors as Jerry threw open the hatch. White-clad, muscular arms reached for the stretcher and drew it out, attaching portable O_2 to the O_2 cannula, a portable suction machine to the chest tube. Orderlies and nurses and one doctor rushed the stretcher down the ramp to Trauma Receiving, Dr. Kreel's own emergency room for trauma victims, carrying the IV bag of Ringer's lactate and the half-full bag of plasma, the suction meter, the portable oxygen tank. Kay and Anita stepped out of the helicopter, and only then did they notice that their blue-green jumpsuits were soaked with blood.

"Jeez," Anita said staring at Kay's flight suit. "That was hell and we didn't even know it."

"*I* knew it," Kay said as they began to walk toward the white brick building. It was the worst call she had ever made. Usually her emergency flights were simple—a heart attack, or a precip delivery, a stroke. The flights to accidents did not happen often because the ground ambulances were usually able to reach the victims, but on the few accident calls she had participated in, there had been nothing as serious and bloody as the one they had just completed.

Both nurses were still trembling a little as they entered Trauma Receiving, the huge pneumatic doors sighing open for them as they stepped onto the black pad outside. Within, they saw that the stretcher bearing Bobby Cross was being wheeled directly to the trauma surgery suite. They caught a glimpse of Dr. Kreel already in surgical greens, surrounded by other members of the surgical team, ready to take over where the flight nurses had left off—ready to try to save Bobby's quickly fading life.

CHAPTER II

In the wing adjacent to the trauma units at St. Luke's, in OR number four of the general surgical suite, Syd was watching a rare kind of surgery. It did not happen often, but St. Luke's was a progressive hospital; its associated private psychiatric unit one of the most modernized and innovative in the country. There, the staff earnestly tried to help the mentally ill. They questioned patients and families, probed into backgrounds, puzzled over symptoms, spent sleepless nights studying and wrestling with diagnoses. They experimented with new drugs, hypnotized when necessary, and performed psychic surgery occasionally. No lobotomies ever.

But they used the highly meticulous electrode-implantation method on hopelessly ill temporal-lesion epileptics to relieve their symptoms, and hoped it worked.

Jesse Mann, cruelly nicknamed Boogy, lay on the operating table awake. Six microminiaturized electrodes were being implanted in the left temporal lobe of his brain by neurosurgeon Edwin Cash. Mann, normally a congenial enough truckdriver, had been experiencing sudden onsets of violent behavior due to the temporal-lobe lesion. The tumor had been removed two months ago, but the resulting scar formed by the operation produced the same abnormal electrical impulses in the brain that the lesion had, causing psychomotor epileptic seizures simultaneously with violent behavior. No medication helped. Now, Mann lay quietly; sedated, but awake. He could not feel the electrodes being implanted in his brain, for the human brain itself contained no pain receptors. A tiny electric pacemaker the size of a quarter would be implanted under Mann's scalp and when abnormal brain waves began, the pacemaker would fire, intercepting the abnormal waves and, hopefully, preventing the seizures and the violent behavior.

The electrodes were being inserted manually, but with the guidance of a computer and telescreen mounted on the OR wall—a device that Syd, a psychologist, could not begin to comprehend.

Dr. Cash was wearing special goggles through which he peered into a sophisticated, two-lens microscope, which reminded Syd of a television camera, hanging down from the ceiling over the head of the patient. Cash was using miniature instruments one could hardly see.

The operating room smelled of Betadine prep and the disinfectant which housekeeping personnel used to clean the equipment and mop the gray-tiled floor. The walls were covered with green ceramic tile. Four tables of surgical instruments lay bared of their green, sterile drapes; stainless-steel instruments were laid out neatly—unused—and askew—used. A clock on the wall, round, white, and unmistakably correct, ticked almost inaudibly. The anesthesiologist, comfortably surrounded by monitoring equipment and reinforced with resuscitation devices, was taking vital signs continually, measuring central arterial pressure through a catheter inserted

23

into the patient's left arm, a prophylactic measure taken to detect impending shock should it begin to occur.

One scrub nurse and two circulating nurses seemed glued to the floor, dressed in surgical greens, gowned and masked, eyes riveted to the hole in Mann's skull. They seldom saw this kind of surgery, fascinating, innovative, and brand-new. Syd could feel their awe, the thrill of this new experience, their tension of expectancy.

The computerized screen on the wall, a mini CAT scan, with its multicolored squares in the shape of a brain, barely distracted Syd. It wasn't the procedures that most interested him. It was the experiment that Cash had agreed to do for him—a harmless experiment and a rare one.

Mann had been referred to St. Luke's psychiatric wing because of his sudden onsets of violent behavior which were increasing in frequency and intensity. Syd was a psychology professor at the university, but had been doing studies now for eighteen months on memory. Inherited memory. His baby. His idea too.

If a single molecule of DNA's product, RNA, could carry a genetic code of 10,000,000,000,000,000 bits of information, why couldn't it carry bits of memory? If potential high IQ was inherited, why not memory?

Psychics, psychoanalysts, and other pseudointellectuals tended to attribute the pre-life memories of certain hypnotized individuals to the reincarnation theory. Syd did not believe in reincarnation. The memories described by such individuals were inherited by genetic code from their great, great, great—

"Dr. Carlton," said Dr. Cash now, "we are about to proceed with the memory experiment. Please step closer, but be careful not to touch anything, please."

24

The female surgical assistant glanced at Syd and said, "You forget, Dr. Cash, that Dr. Carlton was an R.N. once."

"Indeed?" said the neurosurgeon. "Well, that carries no weight with me, Miss . . . er . . . Dr. Donald. I don't hold nurses to be anything special as some of my most distinguished colleagues do. Naturally, I speak of Kreel. At least I don't mollycoddle them so that I can have them under my thumb. Dr. Carlton, you were wise to shed that dull rag of a profession and take your Ph.D. in something else. And you, Dr. Donald, as a woman, were certainly wise to go for an M.D. instead of wallowing around in the nursing profession."

Syd's black eyes flicked to the scrub nurse, the circulating nurse, then to Dr. Cash. "My wife is charge nurse of Trauma Recovery," he said simply.

Dr. Cash stood on one foot; then shifted his weight to the other and back again and said, "My apologies, Dr. Carlton."

"And without nurses you and Dr. Donald might have to carry a few bedpans, Dr. Cash," he said stepping close to the operating table. Syd never was one to mince words or worry about his own popularity.

The neurosurgeon took a deep breath. "With the scalpel of my own tongue I incise my own formidable hide. I withdraw my comments, with apologies to all concerned and beg forgiveness; this is not one of my better days." He glanced at the nurses and added, "Forgive me, girls, and accept my apologies, everyone."

They nodded and Syd said, "Accepted."

He stood beside the anesthesiologist looking through a four-inch hole cut neatly in the top of Mann's skull, down at the glistening gray-white matter of the brain—a giant, gray raisin with its wrinkles, fissures, convolutions, and lobes.

The modern way to implant electrodes was to insert them through the skull without doing a craniotomy, an opening of the skull. But a previous CAT scan had revealed a small frontal lobe lesion which had to be removed surgically. They were all awaiting the word from pathology as to whether it was benign or malignant.

Meantime, the anesthesiologist had brought Mann up out of deep anesthesia after the surgical removal of the tumor, and had removed from his trachea the endotracheal tube through which the anesthesia had been administered.

"Mr. Mann," said Dr. Cash now. "Can you hear me, Mr. Mann?"

Mann's lips, dry from hours without fluids and from the usual injection of atropine, were stuck together, but pulled apart when he said softly, "Yes."

"I want you to tell me what you see, hear, smell, or remember as you experience it. Understand?"

Before surgery, the possibility of doing the experiment had been explained to the patient and he had agreed to it both verbally and in writing. Hopefully, in his sedated state, he still remembered what was expected of him.

Dr. Cash touched the electric probe to the brain now; a tiny trickle of electricity teased the surface. It was not known exactly where memory lay within the brain. On the surface only? Deep inside also? Localized or all over?

Mann laughed suddenly.

"What are you laughing about, Mann?"

"My dog, Rocket. He's pulling Mrs. O'Rourke's wash off the clothesline," Mann said in a falsetto voice. "Looky, looky. Here, Rocket, come on, boy!"

Syd glanced at the OR nurses as they laughed. "Ask him who he is," Syd suggested to the neurosurgeon.

"Who are you?"

"Name's Jesse Mann."

For the next thirty minutes, Dr. Cash moved the electric probe a micromillimeter at a time in the best-known "memory center" of the brain, eliciting brief memories from Jesse Mann's childhood, adolescence, and adulthood, with Jesse vividly recounting his experiences and with Dr. Cash repeatedly asking, "What's your name?" And always the patient replied, "Jesse Mann."

In those moments, Jesse Mann remembered nothing of a past he had not lived. No genetic memory was elicited by the electrical stimulation. But the experiment proved nothing, of course. For memory was thought to be spread all over the brain in codes or a code not yet understood, located in every lobe, not just in the so-called "main center." And there were theories that memory was more than an electrical process; that it could be a chemical process also. And where would genetic memory be localized if it *were* localized?

Syd kept going back in his mind to the tired old experiment performed by McConnell when he taught a flatworm to recoil from a flashing light, chopped the worm up into microscopic pieces, injected the pieces into other untrained flatworms, and found that most of the injected flatworms would recoil from a flashing light. Chemical memory. But you couldn't minimize the possibility of electric impulses being involved. The electric-probe experiments stimulated the memory; no doubt about that. Chemicals had been known to do the same thing.

Syd did not believe in instinct. Instinct was genetic memory—a *learned* response; even in animals. If somebody could prove that every human being carried inside his brain a certain amount of genetic memory from his ancestors, that might explain certain kinds of mental illness, certain unexplainable phobias, learning disabilities, genius. Observe a litter of kittens raised in the same household. One kitten might be a bundle of nerves, skittish, afraid of everything. Another, an easy-going, soft-soaper. Both kittens are from the same mother and raised in the same environment, but had different sires. One sire was an alley cat chased frequently and maybe severely injured once by a dog. The other sire spent most of his days sleeping in a sunny window in an old lady's house. Genetic memory. No doubt in Syd's mind at all.

But, in the past eighteen months no volunteer student hypnotized by Harry Wyatt, his associate, had demonstrated an ancestral memory. Not yet.

Maybe hypnotism wasn't the way to elicit it. Apparently electrical stimulation wasn't either. Everybody experienced flashes of genetic memory once in a while, but what he and Harry needed was one of those rare individuals one read about occasionally in the psychiatric journals, a person who had an unusually large memory bank of genetic memory when under hypnosis. An unlikely happenstance.

Syd graciously thanked Dr. Cash now and took his leave as the neurosurgeon began to replace the bone flap in Mann's skull. In the doctor's lounge Syd removed the surgical mask, cap, gloves, gown, and conductive booties.

Outside in the sunshine he sauntered toward the parking lot. For some reason the hospital's front lawn reminded him of the campus of UTE where he had taught the spring semester two years ago. And today, the day itself, reminded him of that spring afternoon when Kay had come running to him in her white uniform, running while he stood frozen to the spot not believing his eyes, yet seeing her face and knowing she'd come to him at last—and forever. His.

His love for her had existed for years before that moment, when he had worked as a nurse beside her, through the pain of her first husband's death and her subsequent frustrations and indecisions, through two other suitors hopeful for her hand—the cowboy and the photographer. And now, two years later, if anything, he loved her more.

Why did sunny days remind him of Kay? Or for that matter snowy days or fall nights and summer evenings? And why did he want to share with her everything he saw or heard or thought or experienced? Such a mystery. Yet, it wasn't a mystery. It was simply because she cared—at least until lately. And he loved her.

As Syd started the four-year-old white Cutlass and backed out of the parking slot, his mind went back to that day in May two years ago, when she had come to him breathless, a plaque in her hand taken from the supervisor's office, which read, A FRIEND IS A PRESENT YOU GIVE TO YOURSELF.

At that time, her ten-year-old son, Russell, had had two weeks of school left before his summer vacation; so moving Kay and Russell to the city, where he was to take a position as associate psych professor, was put off for those two weeks. Meantime, Syd managed—well, not absolutely, but he *almost* managed—to keep his hands off. Actually they didn't have intercourse for almost a week—until they could locate their birth certificates and get their blood tests done and secure what Russell had called their "driver's license." Then there was a quiet ceremony by a justice of the peace; a justice of the peace because, much to their surprise, none of the three clergymen they contacted would marry them without two weeks of counseling, which they thought was absurd for two mature people in their thirties, and they hadn't had time for it anyway.

Quiet, whispering, warm nights they had spent in a room next to Russell's in Kay's apartment, doing everything on the floor because the bed squeaked. He remembered Kay's snickering when he raised up once and nearly cracked his skull on the night stand; his tender, frustrated ministrations to her when she got a cramp in her foot during a crucial and very heavy moment of their love-making.

But the days when Russell was at school . . . ah, those long, warm, brilliant days . . . the packing . . . the trip to the city and to Uncle Ben's big Victorian house where they were to live. And Kay, Russell, and Ben had hit it off right from the start, a complete integrated family from the beginning.

That first night at the house when she had suggested that he carry her over the threshold of their bed-room . . . and he had fallen with her onto Great-grandma Carlton's big, four-poster bed, the old slats of which gave way with a thundering crash. At first, they had lain laughing, slowly getting more serious as they had become more aware of each other's bodies . . . then making love, the best yet, and spending the night in that caved-in bed with the headboard and footboard tilting inward dangerously. Kay with beautiful eyes damp with love and tears of ecstasy . . . Sydney, old buddy, he thought now, damned if you're not getting poetic!

Regrettably, they'd never gotten to take a honeymoon—or, as Russell had called it, a "field trip."

Syd was smiling now as he pulled into his parking slot outside the psych building. He switched off the engine, got his briefcase out of the back seat, got out of the car, locked the door, and started toward the building. Yep, it was a beautiful day.

Inside, he unlocked his office door on the second floor, went in, and checked the mail he had laid on his desk earlier but hadn't had time to look through—two bills for office supplies, two catalogs from office-supply stores, a card or something from the J. C. Whittenburgs, no telling what that was, and then . . . a hand-addressed envelope in a scrawl he did not recognize. He sat down in his chair, and as he opened the letter, something teased his consciousness with a twinge of . . . expectancy. His intuition proved accurate. The scrawl was almost illegible, but to Syd the message was invaluable. It read:

Dear Proffesor Carlton,

Sir, I've got a cousin who goes to your university and from him I heard about your interest in memory and your experiments. Now I don't hold with witchcraft stuff or anything like that and I don't have a collige ejucation, but I have had some strange flashes of memory that I can't explain. At first I told my friends about it and I kind of think they think I'm a bit daft. But I've read stories about this kind of thing and am wondering if I might be reincarnated or something. If so, I sure as hell had a much better life then than I do now.

Anyways, my cousin, Jeffrey Stone, says you might

be interested in intervueing me in case you want to hypmotize me or whatever it is you do. Since I'm curious about myself and why I have these memory flashes I'd do it for no pay. I only want to solve a mystery that's damned near driving me crazy.

So please write and let me know one way or the other.

Yours very truly,
William Royce Ballew

Syd took a deep breath, let air out between his teeth. A crank letter? A hoax? Or a true Ballew walking memory bank?

Whatever. It was too good to be true. And too good to pass off as a prank. He took his Bic pen in hand, a sheet of stationery from his desk drawer, and smoothed the sheet in front of him. Billy Roy, old buddy, he thought, you're going to get a letter from Dr. Sydney Carlton by return mail.

And as he penned the "Dear Mr. Ballew" under his own dignified, engraved letterhead, something told him that without a doubt, this was the break he'd been waiting for.

CHAPTER III

Trauma Receiving and Trauma Recovery were only five years old. Fathered by Dr. J. Braxton Kreel, general surgeon, St. Luke's had given birth to the trauma units and had agonized with the same birth pangs all important new medical innovations seem to suffer. But finally, after years of hard labor, the trauma units were delivered. And not by any physician or board of directors, but by a philanthropist of the city, named Kessler.

When Reuben Kessler's grandson, Kelly, was brought into St. Luke's emergency room after being involved in a motorcycle accident, J. Braxton Kreel and his special trauma team snatched the teen-ager from the very jaws of death using Kreel's controversial diagnostic treatment techniques, his special surgical expertise, and the very implicit recovery orders which he imposed on the existing ICU staff. Kreel had preached the benefits of a separate trauma unit with specific trauma diagnostics for nine years, since he had interned in Maryland under a cardiovascular surgeon who had preached the gospel that traumatic shock was the most subtle and lethal killer on earth. Kessler had known about Kreel's ambition, and when Kelly not only lived but was released from the hospital with no permanent disabilities, Kessler gave a sigh of relief and donated to St. Luke's, four million dollars for the specific purpose of creating the hospital's own trauma units, its own communications center, and its first flying medivac unit.

Nobody had agonized with the birth of the trauma units more than Dr. Kreel; not even the hospital board. The main obstruction to the units' birth had been the usual lack of funds; and there had been the usual balking, braying, and backbiting of jealous colleagues and politicking administrative board members. But alas, what else could an administrative board do with four million dollars donated to St. Luke's for the express purpose of delivering the twin trauma units, other than build and equip the trauma units? So they did and delivered them into the hands of their father, whose idealistic seed had germinated somewhere in the entrails around the emergency room, OR suites, and the intensive care units for nine years.

Trauma Receiving resembled most modern emergency rooms, but included four adjacent surgical suites of its own. It also housed Comstat, a communications center which had a tie-in with all ambulance services, fire departments, and police headquarters within a hundred-mile radius, and was manned by a dispatcher on duty twenty-four hours a day. St. Luke's owned the one helicopter. It was truly a lone Ranger. Now that the trauma units with their flying emergency room had attracted much positive notoriety to St. Luke's—not to mention more patients—the board hoped to have two, maybe three helicopters based at St. Luke's someday.

The city's fire department ambulances were equipped with the latest emergency equipment; their firemen were highly trained and invaluable in their service. But when accidents happened on freeways, stalling traffic to where a ground ambulance could not reach the scene of the accident, or in inaccessible places, or out somewhere on the vast and rugged rangeland of the hill country, it took the lone Ranger to get to the scene of the accident or the emergency in time to save lives. The Ranger wasn't used *instead* of ground ambulances, but in *addition* to them. Luckily, the ambulance services and the fire department maintained the same respect for St. Luke's and its helicopter unit as St. Luke's trauma department had for the fire department and the ambulance services. There was none of the friction of competition among the hospitals either. People at St. Luke's attributed that bit of camaraderie to easygoing, blue-eyed, drawling, good-natured Dr. Kreel, who seemed to remind everybody of a middle-aged Ben Casey of TV fame. And besides, Kreel loaned his expertise out to other hospitals in the area who were willing to try his methods. The Ranger carried patients not only to St. Luke's, but to other tertiary trauma units as well—and it was available for emergency flights or convenience flights to and from other hospitals. The Ranger created more good will than Santa Claus, the board members claimed jauntily.

Trauma treatment began in the Ranger or one of the city's ambulances, and was continued in Trauma Receiving at St. Luke's. If surgery was necessary, the hospital contained four special trauma surgical suites, and from there the victim was taken directly to the special Trauma Recovery Unit.

To Kay, Trauma Recovery was very much like the ICU she'd worked in for four years in Preston General Hospital. There were eight private cubicles in a row on one side of the unit across a hallway from the nurses' station, and a small kitchenette, the linen room, and the "dirty" utility room. From the nurses' station a nurse could see into all eight cubicles; but if privacy was required, as when a patient was given a bed bath, the nurse could pull a drape to separate the room from the hallway.

There was an outside window in each room and each room contained its own medications cabinet, its own Emerson respirator, and, at the foot of each bed, a chart stand. Instead of the patient's chart being kept at the nurses' station, it rested—open—on the stand at the foot of the bed. Each room was absolutely self-contained and ideally each patient had his own nurse.

Kay coordinated and supervised the care basically as she had done in the ICU at Preston General. She was only moderately busy most of the time, which allowed her time to visit with the patients. She was also free to go on emergency calls as she had done yesterday when she and Anita had gone out in the Ranger to bring back the shocky, bleeding, dying Bobby Cross.

Today, Bobby was lying in a semicomatose state, attached to the Emerson respirator via a tracheal opening at the base of his throat called a tracheostomy. When Bobby arrived at Trauma Receiving, Dr. Kreel had already notified his favorite thoracic surgeon, Mahil Daizat, who mended the boy's battered lungs after extracting twenty-two buckshot from them—leaving more in than he took out—along with several pieces of splintered bone from his shattered ribs, and microscopic bits of glass from the car window. Since the first infusion of two pints of plasma until the present moment, Bobby had consumed sixteen units of whole blood. He had regained consciousness at 6:05 that morning, but remained lethargic and disoriented.

Entering his room now, Kay smiled at Anita who had been assigned as Bobby's nurse on day shift, and went to his bed. She checked the chest tubes, two on the right side of his chest draining the pleural cavity of blood and fluid, and one on the left. The two right chest tubes were still draining bright-red blood which fluctuated with inspiration and expiration and slowly moved down the tubing and dripped into a flask on the floor. The left chest tube was draining a watery, pinkish fluid into an Evacuset suction canister on the wall near the head of Bobby's bed. The left tube would be removed in a day or two.

Bobby's skin was warm and dry, which was good. According to the readout under the cardiac-monitor screen which was mounted on the wall over the head of Bobby's bed, his pulse rate was 102, high, but not abnormally so for a postsurgical patient. On the same screen where the electronic blip bobbed up and down representing the electrical activity of Bobby's heart, the arterial-blood-pressure blip undulated, corresponding roughly with the heart blip. It appeared normal. Kay looked over at Anita.

"All signals are go," Anita said returning her smile.

They'd saved a life—at least so far; at least until an infection set in or pneumonia, or shock again, or a dozen other horrors that lurked around the weakened resistance of a trauma patient.

Bobby's right arm was swathed in bandages. The initial assessment made by Kay and Anita at the sight of the accident had proved to be correct—no fractures, only torn muscle and vessels—but the wound would be a long time healing.

"Heard from the abdominal yet?" Anita asked coming to stand beside Kay at the end of the bed.

Kay shook her head. Anita, a petite, flaxen-haired blonde with a neat sprinkling of freckles across the bridge of her nose and cheeks, was an energetic twenty-eight-year-old who tended to take on more of the patient load than she should. Kay knew Anita wanted the care of the abdominal trauma which Trauma Receiving had admitted early that morning, an hour after they had come on duty. Kay hadn't heard the nature of the trauma or its cause, only the brief report over the telephone from Marsha Walsh in Receiving that the woman had been admitted with bruises and contusions, that the abdominal tap had proved positive and the victim was being wheeled into surgery. That had been three and a half hours ago, Kay noticed consulting her watch.

She had just checked Room Three after Mr. Parsons had been transferred out to the third floor. Housekeeping had been called, had cleaned the room and all its equipment with disinfectant, had wiped every surface including both sides of the mattress, the entire bed, the window sills, sink, meds cabinet, monitoring equipment—everything—with disposable cloths saturated with disinfectant.

Lula Hailey, Trauma Recovery's only black nurse, usually took it upon herself to keep an eye on housekeeping personnel when they cleaned the patient rooms. As an ICU nurse at another hospital, Hailey had once observed an epidemic of staph in the ICU and subsequently maintained a healthy respect for it. Mention staph and Hailey's eyes would roll and always she'd say the same thing. "Lo-ord, you get staph in here, and honey, you got hell on wheels!"

But Hailey needn't have worried. Housekeeping people were meticulous and thorough. Walk on one of their freshly mopped floors while it was still wet and you got a thorough scolding. Those, who were careless when they tossed paper towels at the wastebasket and missed, were told about it. Whoever spoke with a bit less than total respect to one of the housekeeping girls got a personal visit from the director of housekeeping. This same meticulous care had been the rule at Preston General, too. Kay had often thought that some doctors and nurses should be that conscientious about cleanliness.

So Room Three was gleaming: its lavatory scoured, bedrails and equipment polished, and bed freshly made with stark white linen; all waiting for the abdominal trauma patient which she had assigned to Anita's care.

Satisfied that the equipment for the new patient was set up and the rest of the room was in order, Kay went to Room Five. Barney Werger lay on his special mattress, gazing placidly at the ceiling. She always had a few laughs with Barney. He turned his head as she entered his room, his big, pockmarked nose aimed right at her face, and as she approached the bed he said, "This injury presents more problems than I care to think about. Suppose this bag breaks while I'm with a girl? I mean, *if* I'm ever to function with a girl again."

Embarrassed, Kay placed her hands on the bedrail. "It won't break."

"So how do I . . . make love to a girl with this thing on me?"

An interesting question. Kay wanted to laugh as she thought, They don't teach you in nursing school how to answer a patient who's worried about his colostomy bag

39

breaking during the act of love-making. She knew that although Barney was attempting to joke, he was naturally disturbed. And he had every right to be.

He was an actor by profession. He had made his living for years acting in one of the local dinner-theater groups and in the city's little-theater productions. "How do you make your living, Mr. Werger?" Kay had asked when he first had come into the unit two days ago. "Meagerly," he had replied. The nurses soon learned that Barney was very serious about his acting career, worked at it constantly, had acted in several off-Broadway productions as well as in local theater groups and dinner-theater tours around the country. The nurses in Trauma Recovery suspected it wasn't his acting ability that kept him so consistently employed, however, but the fact that he was incredibly ugly and still maintained a sense of humor.

In the first place, his nose was huge. He should be on Broadway playing a continuous role as Cyrano de Bergerac, Kay thought. His face was red, and totally and deeply pockmarked. He had wiry brown hair as curly as Hailey's and his eyes, a gorgeous violet blue were, alas, bugged. Whoever happened to meet Barney in the dark would scream just to look at him, everybody said.

Anita had seen him in several little-theater plays in town and told the other nurses that Barney usually played the heavy. But with an unusual twist. His sense of humor, coupled with the audiences' fascination with his ugliness, swayed them to favor the villain rather than the hero. Everybody loved Barney, and that was what had gotten him into trouble.

Two days ago, Barney had gotten caught in the dressing room of one of the actresses with whom he had

40

been working—by the actress's husband who had suspected the pair of clandestine meetings and had come prepared to catch them in the act. He did. When the husband kicked open the door of the dressing room, Barney jumped up, turned his back, and proceeded to bend over to yank up his trousers. The husband aimed a sawed-off shotgun and caught Barney exactly in the center of his buttocks as if his anus had been a bull's-eye; the result was a quick, bloody and painfully humiliating trip for Barney to St. Luke's Trauma Receiving. Seven hours of patchwork by Dr. Kreel and a colostomy saved Barney's life. Dr. Kreel hoped the colostomy was temporary, that the lower bowel would eventually reestablish peristalsis and heal. Kreel had severed the injured descending colon and brought the end of the functioning portion to the surface of the abdomen forming an abdominal anus through which Barney would defecate. The injured part, he repaired in the hope that eventually the sensory nerves would be reinstituted, the injury heal, and peristalsis be restored. Then he would suture the colon back together. But first, plastic surgery was necessary to re-form a normal anus where it was supposed to be, along with the building up of a normal-appearing buttocks.

The worst damage that had been done by the scatter shot, aside from that done to Barney's pride, was to the caudal nerves—the nerves which fan out from the end of the spinal cord just below the last lumbar vertebrae. This damage had paralyzed Barney from his perineum to his feet. Dr. Kreel hoped that eventually the damaged caudal nerves would regenerate and reestablish communication between the spinal cord and the perineum so that Barney's ability to perform coitus would become possible again. But Dr. Kreel doubted that Barney would ever walk again.

"How's the pain?" Kay asked, checking under the sheet to see if the skin around the colostomy bag attached to the stoma in Barney's abdomen was clean and dry.

"Excruciating. And I've got a morbid curiosity to know what kind of behind Dr. Kreel built me."

"He didn't build one, Barney. He only patched. Don't you remember he told you that he'll bring in a plastic surgeon in a week or so?"

Barney looked up at the ceiling again and contemplated it silently while Kay checked the hemovac drainage. The tubing was inserted into the perineum and drained the injured area of blood and fluid. The other end of it was attached to the hemovac, a vacuum system which resembled a squashed accordion. The tubing was draining a pinkish fluid today, not the bright-red blood it had drained two days ago.

"That beats all, you know," Barney said.

"What does?"

"I've heard of plastic noses and plastic arms and legs, even plastic ti— I mean, plastic breasts, but I've never heard of plastic buns."

Kay flashed him a smile and said, "Well, you have now."

He shook his head in wonderment. "It's amazing what medical science can do these days," he mused. "Can you imagine? I'll bet I'm the only man on earth who'll have a plastic behind."

"You didn't answer me about the pain, Barney," Kay said and bit her lip to keep from laughing, for it really wasn't a laughing matter.

"Yes, I hurt all right."

42

"Be specific," she said hoping there might be some feeling returning to the groin area, in the perineum.

"It's my abdomen, Carlton. If you're hoping I have pain in the 'tain't, I don't. It's dead."

"'Tain't?" she dared to pursue.

"The place between what's male and where I used to evacuate my bowels."

Kay took the bait, accustomed to playing Barney's straight man by now. "O.K., why do you call it a 'tain't?"

"It's simple. It ain't one and it ain't the other," Barney said.

Hailey was standing in the doorway listening and fell all to pieces because when she laughed, all her limbs seemed to become disjointed. Even Kay had to laugh so she left the room to Hailey, for Barney was her patient. "'Tain't," Kay heard her say. "I thought I'd heard it all, Barney, but that's a new one."

The wide, pneumatic doors of Trauma Recovery sighed open as Kay left Barney's room, and four orderlies came wheeling in the green-draped gurney from surgery. She helped them pull the gurney into Room Three where they used the roller to get the patient onto her bed. A roller was a neat device constructed of four long rollers about three inches in diameter which were attached to each other. One nurse could slip the roller under a patient while another nurse tilted the patient to her side. Then they could lay the patient on the roller, pull her from the stretcher to the bed, tilt her again to her side, and remove the roller without disturbing any tubes, catheters, or IVs.

Kay hung the two IV bags on the sliding IV pole which hung down from a track on the ceiling, while one of the orderlies hung the unit of blood over on the patient's left on another IV pole. Hailey had appeared and was hooking the nasogastric tube to the suction meter on the wall. Jan, who'd been with Mr. McPherson in One, hooked the drainage tube coming from under the abdominal dressing to a suction meter on the opposite side of the bed.

Kay noticed that the patient, a young woman about her own age, had bruises and contusions on her breasts and face. One of her eyes was swollen shut, the tissue around it blue and black. Kay looked up quickly, questioningly at the anesthesiologist standing on the other side of the bed.

Bodecker, the freckled female anesthesiologist with flaming red hair, glared back at her, her thin lips pressed tightly together—speechless.

Kay frowned. "What on earth happened to this patient?"

Bodecker glared back and said, "You'll find out soon enough. Dr. Kreel is mad as hell."

Will I ever get over being shocked at the injuries that come in here? Kay wondered with a growing suspicion in her mind. The suspicion and its attending anger demanded an answer. "What—"

"Her colon was lacerated in two places. Her spleen was ruptured. Dr. Kreel had to do a splenectomy on her. When you do your check on her, Carlton, you'll see there are bruises all over, the son of a bitch." Then Bodecker snapped her mouth shut lest she say something else the patient might hear. "You've got a heck of a mess on your hands is all I've got to say," she said at last; then turned and strode out of the room.

Kay, Jan, and Anita stood, a still life of inactivity, all of them realizing what Bodecker meant. "My God," Anita breathed.

Kay had just opened her mouth to ask if the orderlies

44

had left the patient's chart when Dr. Kreel exploded into the room. Still in surgical greens, cap, conductive booties, with the surgical mask dangling under his chin, he threw out, "Vitals!"

Jan had attached the arterial line to the monitor on the wall and was still adjusting the stopcock. Kreel fixed his icy blue eyes on the screen; his face relaxed somewhat when he saw the near-normal arterial-pressure curve on the screen, a light-green electronic blip leaving a light-green line behind, going across the screen to disappear on the right, only to reappear on the left.

Kay said, "Pulse 110, respiration is twenty-two."

Kreel stood a moment, mouth tight, expression unreadable, and abruptly turned to Kay with a jerk of his head toward the hallway. She followed him to the nurses' station across from the rooms and he stood a moment, his mind apparently elsewhere.

"What happened to this patient?" Kay asked.

Dr. Kreel did not answer for a long moment. Then, abruptly, he looked at her, his face reddening, his eyes black and awful with anger. "We don't know. Her . . . her goddamned husband says a pile of bricks fell on her. Bricks, hell, Carlton," he said turning to her. "It was his goddamned *fists*." Kreel studied her horrified astonishment; then turned abruptly and left the unit.

His fists!

Kay took up the patient's chart somebody had left on the desk and sat down slowly.

The nurses' station was an oval-shaped laminated desk with built-in cardiac monitor from which the nurses at the desk could monitor all eight patients in TRU. The monitor setup was the same as the one in the ICU she had worked in at Preston General, except the monitors here

45

were newer and contained a memory readout. One could push the memory button and get a reading on monitor patterns that had appeared moments, even hours before. But at the moment her interest was more on the chart than on the monitors.

Leola Parkman, age thirty-four, had been admitted to St. Luke's Trauma Receiving unit at 7:36 that morning. She was unconscious upon admittance. She had sustained numerous fresh contusions on the abdomen and chest. There were numerous other contusions located on various parts of her body which were in various stages of resolution, or healing. The usual abdominal tap had been performed in TR; a small incision had been made below the umbilicus and a small catheter inserted into the abdominal cavity. Using an attached syringe, a small amount of fluid was aspirated. The tap proved to be positive; both blood and intestinal material were found in the abdominal fluid. Leola was rushed to Trauma OR Number One where two lacerations were repaired in her ascending colon, and her ruptured spleen removed.

In a fury, Kay picked up the receiver of the telephone and asked the operator to give her Trauma Receiving. Marsha Walsh answered.

"Marsha? This is Kay in TRU. What in the world happened—"

"I know what you're calling for, Kay," Walsh interrupted. "You've got Leola Parkman, haven't you. Ever seen the like? I'll bet Kreel was still fuming when he came into TRU. You should have seen the husband. Brought her in and he was scared to death, telling us a stack of building bricks fell on her. They must have fallen on her last week, too, for all the old bruises we found." Marsha Walsh went on with her story, barely catching

46

her breath. When asked politely, Mr. Parkman had been unwilling to leave the trauma room where they had begun the initial assessment of Leola's wounds. So Dr. Blasingame, the young resident in charge of Trauma Receiving, suspecting the nature of Leola's injuries, finally ordered Parkman from the room telling him if he didn't leave, he'd call the security guard. Parkman left reluctantly, only to cause a commotion later outside the trauma surgical suite, saying the doctors were lying to him and that they'd not taken his wife to surgery at all.

"He's guilty as the devil," Walsh said. "If you'll look outside your door, Kay, I think you'll see Pasternak stationed out there."

Pasternak was the day-shift security guard for the south wing of St. Luke's. The south wing contained the critical care areas: emergency room, surgical ICU, medical ICU, CCU, and the trauma units. Pasternak was fascinated by CPR's. Everybody was, but Pasternak was more so; he was in awe of them. He never failed to show up when a CPR was in progress—just in case, by some fluke or other, he might catch a glimpse of the mysterious thing that went on. It was a joke with the critical care staff and the CPR teams that if you ever needed Pasternak you should call his office. But if you ever needed him *stat*, call a CPR.

". . . Because somebody as crazy and guilty as Leola's husband, would just as soon burst into the unit as not," Marsha was saying.

Kay was angry, like everybody else who had seen Leola—suspicious and angry. "Did Leola ever gain consciousness before surgery?" she asked.

"Yes. And when I asked her what happened, she only shook her head. Kay, it's the old story of the beat-up

47

wife; scared to tell on the bastard husband. Scared and maybe she even *wants* to protect—"

There was a click and the operator broke in on the line. "Is this Trauma Recovery and Trauma Receiving?" she demanded.

Kay said yes.

"Hold, please, for an emergency call from Dr. Kreel."

When Dr. Kreel's voice came on the line it had moderated from its previous controlled fury to the soothing steady tone he used during emergencies. "Carlton?"

"Yes."

"Walsh?"

"Here!"

"Girls, we've got an emergency call from Benson Community. An infant in trouble needing our newborn ICU and we need the Ranger stat. This isn't a regular pickup and delivery; this is an emergency. There's no ground ambulance there within forty miles, so we're elected. Walsh, be sure to take the isolette. I'll be in contact."

Kay hung up the receiver, rushed to Room Three, informed Anita she was in charge of TRU while Kay was gone, glanced at the new patient, pale and still unconscious, and then at Anita who answered her inquiring look. "All vitals are stable," Anita said.

So Kay rushed out of the doors of TRU, past Pasternak, the security guard—a big, hairy ape of a man anxious to take on the next son of a bitch that tried to give any trouble—down the corridor to the stairs and down the stairs to the first floor and into Trauma Receiving's corridor. No need to change into the flight suits this trip because this wasn't an accident call; but she'd pulled on her lab coat.

As Kay hurried through the corridor she passed the surgical suite on one side and the five trauma rooms on the other. Near the outside door was the waiting room on one side and the TR reception desk on the other. Kay overtook Walsh just as she was pushing the isolette out the pneumatic doors to the outside.

As they ran up the ramp with the isolette, Kay said, "Hear any more about the baby we're going after?"

"No, only that it's a newborn and it's in a heap of trouble. And Dr. Paine sent word to us that we are about to see something we've never seen before."

A newborn in trouble. They'd gone after a newborn in trouble before, because of St. Luke's Ranger and its superior newborn ICU. There was something about a newborn in trouble that made their feet go faster, their minds think clearer, and their hearts beat faster.

The Ranger's motor was already clattering, *clop-clop-clop,* its rotors whirling, stirring up dust, leaves, and debris, stinging their arms and faces.

As they pulled the isolette aboard the Ranger, Jerry—his flattop haircut flatter, the parentheses around his mouth deeper—was at the controls. "Benson Community, girls? What's at Benson Community we want?"

"Newborn in trouble," Kay said as they shoved the isolette against the side of the copter. Newborn in trouble, she thought, but there *couldn't* be anything they hadn't seen before.

CHAPTER IV

But Kay was wrong. And the others—nurses, doctors, medical personnel—who thought they'd seen everything, were wrong.

In the isolette, a small enclosed chamber on wheels which was designed to provide optimal temperature, humidity, and oxygen for the newborn, baby boy Harrison now lay, his tiny chest retracting severely, his nostrils flaring in an effort to take in the air he needed to live in a hostile world into which he had been so cruelly pushed two hours and twenty minutes earlier. He was pink. But if someone were to take him from the isolette with its oxygen, he would quickly become cyanotic, beginning with his fingers and toes, and then spreading to his arms, legs, and over his entire trunk within seconds. But neither Kay nor Marsha would take him from the isolette now.

As Ranger I clattered and roared eastward toward St. Luke's at a speed of one hundred forty miles per hour, both Walsh and Kay were silent. The sight of the tragedy, labeled by its arm band, *Baby Boy Harrison*, had silenced even Jerry. And the nurses could only watch and stare and hope they wouldn't have to resuscitate the infant.

Kay was thinking how strangely people behaved when

50

faced with an unknown, a deviation from the norm. Even the charge nurse of Benson Community's newborn nursery, who met them at the hospital's ER door with the infant in an isolette, said, "Take him out quick and get him into your own isolette. I don't want *his* death on my conscience."

And the pediatrician, young, blond, and already full of experience, said, "But if God is good, the poor kid will die before you get him into St. Luke's."

When Kay and Walsh saw the infant, they hesitated and drew back with *Oh my God!* on the tip of their tongues. It was Kay who overcame her revulsion first; she plunged her hands into the isolette, took the child up, and laid him in their own isolette.

"No, not head down for this one, nurse," said the pediatrician. "Head up so his diaphragm doesn't press on the lung and heart."

"What kind of—" began Marsha softly as Kay switched the child around so that his head was elevated slightly above his trunk on the tilted mattress of the isolette.

"One of the trilogies. Chromosomes paired up wrong, I guess. I've seen several of the chromosome abnormalities, but none of us here at Community have ever seen this. It's not even in the textbooks. He's undoubtedly got a heart defect too. Maybe a dozen heart defects. Who the hell knows?"

Kay checked the oxygen and the temperature setting of the isolette again while Marsha took the baby's birth records and tube of cord blood from the nurse; then they wheeled the isolette to the waiting helicopter on Community's parking lot.

Now they could only hope and watch and wait. They

51

hoped the infant wouldn't convulse or stop breathing or become more cyanotic, and they stared, because baby boy Harrison was a monster.

His tibiae, the bones in the lower parts of each of his legs, were missing. His feet were attached where his knees should have been. He had no radius or ulna on either arm. His hands were attached where his elbows should have been. His head seemed normal in size and shape, but his hands were short, their fingers stubby, and each thumb was near the wrist like those of a child with Down's syndrome, like those of a Mongoloid child. In addition, he had an extraordinarily hideous cleft palate and lip.

The nurses had thought they'd seen it all: infants with spinal meningocele—herniated masses of spinal tissue protruding from their backs—and hydrocephalic babies with heads three times normal size, newborns with encephaloceles—brain tissue protruding from the backs of their heads—chromosome abnormalities which made monsters from the sperm and ovum of normal parents. But they hadn't seen it all. Probably they never would.

For a brief moment each of the nurses in Ranger I wondered if they should make an effort to help baby Harrison live. Then they saw him open his eyes; his tiny, abnormal fist moved to his mouth to suck his fingers. And they both knew they'd do everything, use every bit of their skill and knowledge in emergency nursing to help him live as long as he was in their care.

Marsha had been reading baby Harrison's chart, and looked up at Kay. "The mother is young, in her twenties, normal in every way. She was on no drugs, doesn't smoke or drink. Father's young and on no medications. Smokes, but not excessively. Nothing like this on either side of the family." She let the chart fall back into her lap. "Why?"

Kay shook her head. "How many times have you asked 'Why?' since you became a nurse, Marsha?" she queried almost irritably.

Trauma Receiving's charge nurse turned her face away and looked out the window of the Ranger. "I'm taking Valium four times a day. I drink a nightcap every night to help me sleep. Next, it'll probably be sleeping pills to help me sleep and then an upper so I can wake up. What's the attrition rate in ICU, Kay?"

"Two years last I heard."

"It's only nine months in trauma units all over the country. How long did you work in ICU where you came from?"

"Four years, not counting a couple of years I worked part time before that."

"And you've worked almost two years in Trauma Recovery. Boy! Are you ever overdue for burn out!"

Kay looked out the window now, saw the white brick building in the shape of an E below—St. Luke's. "Yes, I know," she said.

The attrition rate would have caught up with Kay years ago if it hadn't been for Syd. It was the beautiful moments they shared that made the impossible things at the hospital tolerable. On the evening of the day she and Marsha Walsh brought baby Harrison from Benson Community to St. Luke's, she sought Syd's always-available ear and his eternally eager affection. He was always gentle. One of the most endearing things he did was to take her face in both his hands and kiss her long and gently, almost tentatively, again and again; then his hands went up into her hair and his kisses became longer

53

and less gentle, and Kay responded with her own, and their passion soared and soared until it climaxed with two quiet, simultaneous explosions. Occasionally, though, the slats gave way and Great-grandma's fourposter bed with its new Posture Firm mattress crashed down resoundingly on the old oak floor. The house shook a little, the old rafters snapped, the light fixture overhead with its crystal prisms tinkled, a step on the stairway creaked. Then all was silent.

It amused Kay and Syd that when the bed fell in with a crash, neither Russell nor Uncle Ben ever inquired about the noise or why it had occurred.

As always after it happened, they held each other laughing, snickering, locked in each other's arms, Syd's hard, firm body damp and spent, her soft one warm and clinging, her hair spread across the pillows askew. And settling down into the mattress together—for it wouldn't do to attempt to repair the slats now—they sighed, smiled, and contemplated their situation; then intoxicated with love, they laughed quietly some more.

Tonight, Kay settled her head upon his chest, damp, the black hair tickling her nose. Her chestnut tresses were spread over his left shoulder as he rested his chin on the top of her head.

"Feel better?" he asked.

She nodded. She'd really spilled everything to him tonight, about making the trip from Benson Community with the pitifully deformed infant, confronting the pediatrician at St. Luke's, experiencing disappointment over the assortment of attitudes demonstrated by the nursery nurses there.

When Kay and Marsha had wheeled the isolette into the newborn nursery, Dr. Paine, Chief of Pediatrics, had

54

screwed up his face and said what everybody else wanted to say but didn't, "Oh, my God!"

He was in his mid-thirties, short of stature, partially bald, and bifocaled. In his five years of practice, he'd seen Mongoloids, club feet, spina bifida, hydrocephalics, missing limbs, cleft palates, and dozens of other freakish maladies with which infants were born, but never this. Never this deformity.

As the doctor stared, a nurse with whom Kay was not acquainted looked down into the isolette and then up at the doctor. "Are you going to call Dr. Pugh?"

Dr. Paine held his grimace for a moment, the nurses knowing he was weighing the possibility of whether to call the cardiologist or not. Then he said, "I guess I have to, don't I?"

Pugh was particularly proficient in open heart surgery on infants and children. The nurses knew without asking that Baby Boy Harrison had a congenital heart defect, demonstrated by cyanosis when not under O_2 administration, and Kay, Marsha, and the four nursery nurses knew Dr. Paine was weighing one crime against the other; do nothing and let the hopelessly deformed child's condition slowly deteriorate until he mercifully died? Or call in Pugh, the cardiologist, and Dr. Daizat, the thoracic surgeon, and get started on lifesaving measures that would only cost the young father and mother a lifetime debt and which would eventually prove to be of no avail? Even if the infant survived, probably he would be mentally deficient. At best, he would go through life severely handicapped.

The crowd around the isolette grew. White-uniformed nurses joined the surgical-green group. Everybody on the OB floor was coming in to view the monster. Meantime, baby boy Harrison sucked enthusiastically on his fist, his blue eyes seeming to look everybody straight in the face. Although he appeared to be distressed at what he saw, his distress was due to the efforts he had to make to breathe.

"Jesus Christ," breathed one nurse from OB, and she turned away and left the nursery abruptly.

"He's probably got hyaline membrane disease too," offered a nursery nurse.

"The kind thing to do is put him in one of NICU's isolettes and—leave well enough alone," said a nurse from labor and delivery.

Kay had looked at the ring of faces around the isolette, faces showing pity, disgust, curiosity, awe, horror, nothing. She was not usually outspoken, but some instinct within her caused her to become suddenly furious with all of them, caused her to overreact in a kind of dramatic rage that would have caused Barney Werger to applaud.

"The kind thing to do is what we as nurses gave an oath to do," she said passionately. "Have you forgotten?"

There was a hostile glare or two from the other nurses, but she didn't care. "And Dr. Paine? Aren't you committed to saving lives? Any life? Or is that Hippocratic oath limited only to the lives of people without deformities?"

With that she turned abruptly and left the nursery, tears of rage and shame in her eyes—shame for medical personnel everywhere who would not fight for a life. But as she turned down the corridor toward Trauma Recovery, she saw through the huge window of the nursery Ursala Meuller, the buxom, raven-haired charge nurse of St. Luke's newborn nursery, taking the baby out of TR's isolette. She had knocked on the window to get

56

Kay's attention, and now pointing to the baby, placed him in the nursery's own sophisticated isolette. Ursala winked and shook her fist in the direction of the doctors and other nurses to show Kay that *she*, at least, would see that Harrison had the best of care. Then, as Kay stood watching, Ursala wheeled the isolette into St. Luke's newborn ICU where the nurses were committed to saving lives.

Later that day Kay had gone into the nursery again to see Harrison. A screen had been set up in the newborn ICU around Harrison's isolette to prevent visitors on the outside of the big windows from gaping at the baby. Ursala directed Kay to put on a clean scrub gown over her uniform and don a surgical mask before she went in to see the baby. Deformed infants usually have defective immune systems—nature's way of disposing of them, one of the nurses had suggested—and every precaution was being taken to prevent the transmission of disease from the outside to the newborn ICU.

Harrison was still in NICU's special isolette and still naked; the vernix, or white cheesy substance with which most babies' skins are coated at birth, still stuck in the folds of his skin. Someone had installed a tiny nasogastric tube through his left nostril through which he could be fed a formula, or more probably, to check for any fistulas or stenosis in the esophagus and stomach. His cardiac activity was being monitored by a device similar to that used on adults; small disks had been placed on his chest and leads ran from the disks to the monitor.

Tomorrow, Ursala said triumphantly, Harrison was to undergo open heart surgery. Chest x-rays and a cardiac catheterization and angiograms—dangerous tests for a distressed infant, but Harrison had survived them—had revealed that he had a heart defect called transposition of the great arteries.

"Let the bitches say what they want," Ursala told Kay as she pounded her own buxom chest. "But me? Harrison will get the best. Just you wait and see, Carlton. They think just because he hasn't got all his parts and don't look like you or me he should die? Start with that kind of attitude and what you got? Another Auschwitz! But this time they take all people that are abnormal, maybe people missing an arm or a thumb and run them through the gas chamber."

Ursala was overdramatizing the situation, of course, but she had a point. What she was saying was that baby boy Harrison had as much right to have lifesaving measures done for him as if he had two normal arms and legs.

"Then after that will go the mental deficients. All Mongoloids—*poof!*—into the chamber. Dr. Paine says if Harrison lives what a terrible burden it will be on his parents. What does he know? I got an eighteen-year-old kid that's normal in every way except he's a sex maniac. Got five regular girl friends. Eighteen years old and he's a sex maniac! All those magazines with naked girls, and he smokes pot and gives me hell. I should trade him in for a nice, happy Mongoloid!"

"Can I hold Harrison?"

Ursala's face softened. "Only if you put on sterile gloves. I say nobody holds Harrison without gloves. Not even the sons-of-bitches doctors." The newborn nursery's charge nurse went to a dressing cart, secured a package of gloves, opened the packet, and held it out. Kay snapped on the gloves and Ursala said, "Now sit on the stool, honey; it's easier on the back."

Kay sat down on the stool and reached inside the isolette through two flap-covered holes in its side. When she touched him, Harrison blinked awake, screwed up his face, and began to cry—a normal, newborn-infant cry. Kay smiled, lifted him up, held him within the isolette in both her hands, rocked him, rocked him. His hideously deformed mouth closed and he seemed to be listening, listening, as she rocked him.

"Ah, Harrison is not a mental deficient," Ursala said softly as she watched over Kay's shoulder. "All his reflexes are normal and look at that face. Another Einstein is what he is."

Kay had never gotten acquainted with Ursala before. She'd seen her in the corridors and in the cafeteria, and a couple of times when she and Walsh had brought a distressed infant to the newborn nursery from another hospital. Once Ursala had rushed into TRU with a personal crisis. As she had been walking down the corridor she became puzzled by the stares of hospital personnel. She looked down at the front of her shirt, which seemed to have been the focus of their stares, and discovered that the nipples of her very prominent breasts were showing very plainly through her scrub top. Red-faced and breathless she ducked into the nearest place of concealment which was TRU. She showed the nurses there her plight. She had put on a brand-new kind of bra that morning, she said, "And just look what it doesn't do!" she had fumed.

It was Hailey who had come up with the solution. Stick a couple of round Band Aids over the nipples. Ursala went into the nurses' restroom in TRU, applied the Band Aids, and came out smiling. Hailey's solution had worked!

Ursala was German-born, thirtyish, built thick and bosomy. She had the chin and jaw of a prize fighter and her lips turned in forming a thin line of a mouth. Except for her recalcitrant jaw, Ursala's face was almost attractive.

"Tomorrow, open heart surgery for Harrison by Drs. Pugh and Daizat. Maybe Dr. Hishu will do surgery on the lip and palate too. Then with his heart all fixed up, Harrison will grow up to be another Albert Schweitzer, just you wait and see," Ursala crooned.

After Kay left the nursery, she went back to TRU. Bobby Cross was fully awake now and already running the nurses ragged. There was no one worse to have as a patient in critical-care areas than a teen-ager. They were full of mischief, humor, despair, hope, impatience, a vertitable potpourri of emotions and attitudes, and the nurses never knew what they would face when they entered a teen-ager's room.

Bobby could not speak because a tracheotomy had been performed on him, an incision made in the trachea for the purpose of inserting a tube to which the respirator tubing was attached. The respirator was breathing for him. Once Bobby had become fully conscious, it had taken the nurses several hours to convince him to relax and let the respirator do the breathing for him. The machine was set to keep his lungs partially inflated, acting as a splint for his fractured ribs.

To have been so critically injured so recently, it amazed the nurses and doctors that Bobby was so alert so quickly, that he was no weaker than he was. Once he discovered that he couldn't talk but could write, he wrote volumes. In report that day, the nurse from the eleven to seven shift swore he should have an instructor from a medical school to sit by his bed just to answer questions.

He had one ready for Kay.

When she walked into the room and asked how he was feeling, he placed his hand on his chest and frowned. Then handed her a note he'd already written. It said, "When can I have visitors?"

Kay thought, Oh boy. Wouldn't you know? She said, "Visitors are rarely allowed in here, Bobby. And then it will have to be someone in your immediate family. No friends yet."

He was already scribbling again. "Why?"

"Because when you've sustained a trauma, you're susceptible to infection, so we don't expose you to any. In here, if we let a visitor in, we have to make a path for the visitor with screens from the door to your room."

He dropped his hands in despair and turned his face toward the window.

"If you like, we'll carry notes from you to your family and friends in the waiting room. But for a while, we'll have to bring back messages verbally on account of the risk of infection."

Bobby smiled and nodded.

Kay's concession to the lonely teen-ager was a mistake. For Bobby was popular in school and had many friends and had been writing volumes to his friends and family all day. "The other nurses hate me," Kay told Syd later.

After she left Bobby, she went to check on Barney. He was dozing when she quietly entered his room. Hailey was adjusting the CVP line. As she had explained to Barney earlier, CVP stood for Central Venous Pressure. A small catheter had been threaded through a vein into the upper right side of his heart and connected at the other end to a water manometer mounted on a portable

61

IV pole. CVP readings were important for monitoring circulating blood volumes, so that the doctor could determine whether the patient was receiving too much or too little IV fluids. She did not add that an overload of fluids in the bloodstream could cause too much strain on the heart and no trauma patient needed any more strain on his heart.

Barney opened his eyes, pointed his nose at Kay, and smiled. Had nature been kinder and given Barney an average-looking face, his smile would have caused him to become handsome. "Hello, Carlton," he said. "Are you back, or am I having hallucinations?"

"I'm real. How have you been feeling?"

"Rotten. I've never had any experience at feeling rotten before and I'm not sure how I should react. I've never been sick since I had my childhood diseases. Not even a head cold. It doesn't make me feel very good knowing I'm in a sort of intensive care unit, and that this is where they put people who're on the brink of eternity. It's either go upstairs to the trauma ward from here, or down into the basement to the morgue. Hell, this place is the hospital's purgatory. Who's praying to get me sent upstairs? Lit any candles for me, Carlton?"

Kay removed her hands from Barney's bedrail and placed them folded on the bed beside him. Barney was beginning to experience that peculiar type of depression the doctors called critical-care-itis. It happened with cardiac patients, stroke patients, any critically ill patient who, up until the depression phase, had denied the seriousness of his illness and either sought oblivion in long bouts of sleep, or joked as if nothing serious had happened to him. Kay recognized that Barney was alert enough now to realize his close brush with death and to know he was not yet "out of the woods"; to realize that he was not immortal after all. It must be a horrible feeling, she thought. The denial stage of a critical illness was more comfortable than this depression stage, but the depression stage did represent a step toward the patient's acceptance of his own condition, a critical step forward as he walked the mental tightrope between acceptance and despair.

She replied, "There're candles lit all over your room, Barney." She indicated the four IV bottles hanging, one of Ringer's lactate, one containing an antibiotic, another a unit of packed blood cells.

Hailey raised her brows and with a sweep of her hand indicated the cardiac and arterial monitor, the CVP line, the foley catheter.

Barney looked at each piece of equipment and each bag of IV fluid, then said with the old one-sided grin, "Yeah, but think this stuff carries any weight with the Big Doctor in the sky?"

Hailey replied, "It must, Barney, 'cause it's done sidetracked many a person headed for the basement; I can guarantee you that."

Perhaps Hailey shouldn't have mentioned the basement, because Barney regressed suddenly to denial again. He shut his eyes tight and smiled. "It just occurred to me. What a sensation I could be as a male stripper! I can just see my name on the lighted marquee; SEE THE SINSATIONAL BARNEY WERGER, THE ONLY MALE STRIPPER IN THE WORLD WITH A POLYETHYLENE DERRIÈRE!" While Hailey laughed and Kay smiled, Barney added, opening his eyes to look at Kay, "It'll attract millions. Wait'll I tell my agent."

Moments later, still smiling, Kay had entered Leola

Parkman's room. Leola had sufficiently awakened from the anesthesia now to be aware of what was going on in her room. Her soft brown eyes followed Kay as she approached her bed. The nurses in TRU had little experience with battered women, because it wasn't often that one needed intensive care. But in a recent hospital in-service course, which every R.N. at St. Luke's was required to take, the nurses were told that a recent hospital census showed that two percent of the adult female patients admitted to St. Luke's were victims of marital violence, and that the percentage was increasing each year. The social worker who had held the in-service classes told the nurses that only very recently had the public recognized the existence of the problem. Until recently, wife abuse by a male partner was thought to be a family problem and not a concern of the community. Battered women showing up at the ER or the doctors' offices were treated and released. No doctor wanted to become involved in a "family" dispute. Even the clergy, when approached for help by a battered woman, urged her to go back home and "try her best to make the marriage work." But lately shelters for battered women were springing up in cities all over the U.S., the social worker said, and so she had come to offer the in-service course on abused women to the nurses at St. Luke's, to make them aware that there was help for their patients outside the hospital environment.

Leola was sedated when Kay saw her for the second time that day, because she was having trouble tolerating the nasogastric tube in her throat. The tube passed through her left nostril and her nose to the back of her throat, then down the esophagus to end in her stomach. Its other end was attached to a suction meter with intermittent suction; this caused her gastric contents to move an inch or so up the tube toward the suction cannister on the wall each time the meter clicked on. When the suction clicked off, the fluid stopped flowing. The nasogastric tube was meant to keep Leola's stomach empty of excess secretions in order to prevent nausea, but the tube itself caused her to gag over and over again.

She was also afraid; but unlike Barney, she was not afraid of death in the Trauma Unit. Her eyes traveled not to the equipment in the room, but beyond the room, out into the hallway, past the nurses' station toward the big doors that led into the hospital corridor. The nurses had seen her fear. They knew but could not tell her yet that a big, burly security guard was stationed outside the door for her protection.

A battered woman in the hospital made everybody uncomfortable. It was always a touchy situation and one in which the nurses and doctors might feel more hostility toward the abusive husband than did the victim herself. The social worker who had held the in-service class told the nurses, "It's a waiting game. You don't push the battered woman to tell you about what happened to her. You wait for her to drop a hint. Always be ready to listen; that's the first rule."

In the meantime, the TRU nurses sensed that the strategy at this stage in Leola's recovery was to show her they cared about her physical welfare, and that they were concerned with her mental distress. They just couldn't do anything yet but care. And it seemed to be enough— for now.

When Kay left Leola, Anita was placing a cool washcloth on the patient's head and throat to help assuage her nausea.

The other two patients in TRU remained stable.

One was the philosophy professor from the university, a fifty-two-year-old red-headed man whom Syd knew only as a "stuffed shirt." He had been in an automobile accident four days ago in which his liver had sustained damage and his tranverse colon had been perforated. Dr. Kreel had given him a temporary colostomy. In fifteen days or so, depending on how quickly the injured colon healed, Dr. Kreel would operate again, attach the two ends of the severed colon together, and hopefully, the professor could evacuate his bowels normally for the rest of his life.

His name was Dr. Moriah Worley, and he conversed very little with the nurses. TRU was not conducive to any intellectual deliberation as far as he was concerned. He preferred the privacy of using the urinal without aid, of washing his own private areas during his bed bath—in spite of the excruciating pain the movements caused him—and begrudged the interruptions to his meditations when the nurses had to change his IVs or check his vital signs. He refused to use his nurse call bell to summon help, and only when the pain in his abdomen became unbearable, which it frequently did, would they hear him complain. His complaint always began with a long, loud, drawn-out "I" that rose higher and higher in pitch then dropped off to a soft, clipped, "hurt." If the nurses didn't respond instantly, they heard another "I—hurt."

Then there was the dignified, white-haired, hook-nosed little old fellow from the nursing home who'd wandered out the door of the home and as a result of a fall down a ravine, had suffered multiple fractures; three in the right femur, one in the ulna and radius on the right side, and four fractured ribs. Usually a person with only fractures would be sent to surgical ICU, but due to McPherson's age and the fact that he had a hemolytic disease, the orthopedist wanted him in TRU. McPherson was even more uncommunicative than Dr. Worley, because he didn't know anything. At least if he *did* he wouldn't admit it.

"How do you feel, Mr. McPherson," Kay asked when she visited him the last time before she left that day.

"I—don't—know," he answered in his usual staccato cant, not looking at her. He never seemed to look at anybody.

"Feeling any pain?"

"I—don't—know."

"Do you know where you are, Mr. McPherson?"

"I—don't—know."

"You're in St. Luke's Hospital, Mr. McPherson. You fell down and broke some bones, but you're going to be fine now. O.K.?"

"I—don't—know."

Who did? Sometimes Kay decided she didn't know anything either. On the other hand, she was aware that her experience as a critical-care nurse had made her more knowledgeable about many aspects of medicine than most nurses and some doctors, and that awareness tended to make her a bit vain. She wallowed in the security of her knowledge. From the beginning of nursing school eleven years ago she had stored away every experience, good and bad, in the expanding files in her brain, vowing to herself that someday, someday, she'd write a book about all the things she'd seen and experienced.

Now, reliving the day just past, and running the events in TRU through her mind, she listened to Syd snoring softly beside her. She grew drowsy after a while and finally slept. She dreamed that Harrison climbed out of his isolette and went waddling out into the hospital corridor with Ursala running after him shouting, "Come back, you little monster. Trying to escape us, eh? You're going to have surgery and live, buster, whether you like it or not. Me, Ursala, I'll see to that. Come back, Harrison, come back and *live*, you little bastard!"

CHAPTER V

"Harrison had a transposition of the great vessels,"
Dr. Daizat began. It was always he who would take the
time to explain to the nurses different procedures and
treatments. He was taking time to explain to them now
the surgery that had just been performed on Harrison.
The other three doctors involved were hovering over the
babe in the NICU. "The problem was simply this: the
aorta, the main artery in the body, was attached to the
right chamber of the heart, and the pulmonary artery was
attached to the left chamber. As you know, those vessels
are supposed to be the other way around."

The thoracic surgeon was standing at the nurses' desk
in the newborn nursery. Surrounding him were the
nursery nurses and Kay, who had been summoned by
Ursala to hear the surgeon's explanation. He was drawing
the transposition on a prescription pad as he explained.

"Here's why this particular congenital heart defect
caused Harrison to become cyanotic. The right ventricle
or chamber of the heart kept receiving from the body
blood with used-up oxygen which made the blood bluish
in color, and it kept pumping it right back to the body. The
left ventricle kept pumping red, oxygenated blood to the
lung and from the lung it returned back to the left

69

ventricle. The red, oxygenated blood was never getting to Harrison's body because it kept circulating to the lung, then back to the heart, then to the lung again. And the deoxygenated blue blood was never going to the lung to be oxygenated; it just kept going to the body and coming back to the heart to be pumped back to the body." Daizat looked up at the nurses to see if they were understanding. Satisfied that they were, he went on, "Harrison would have died at birth except he was lucky. The hole between the two upper chambers of the heart, which every normal fetus has, did not close at birth as it should have, and therefore it allowed a little oxygen to seep into the right upper chamber. Since we administered O_2 in high concentrations, enough refluxed back through the hole to the right chambers to be pumped through his body to keep him alive." The doctor looked up from his drawing on the nurses' desk again to see if the nurses understood. They nodded in unison.

Daizat was small and swarthy, with a bushy black mustache and snapping brown eyes. He had never gotten rid of his slight Mideast accent, though he had resided in America for over twenty years.

"In the fifties, sixties, and early seventies," he went on, "in infants with this defect, we did a shunt procedure when they were only a few days old. We transposed the arteries to correct their position later at about the age of two. Lately, we've perfected the pump oxygenator—or as some call it, the heart-lung machine—to such an extent that now we can perform the total procedure, provided the infant is not premature and is strong. And this is what we did for Harrison."

"Explain to them how the pump oxygenator machine works," Ursala said.

Daizat smiled quickly. "The pump oxygenator kept Harrison's blood circulating while we worked on his heart. His blood went from his subclavian vein to the oxygenator, was oxygenated, then returned to his body through his femoral artery. The machine was acting as an artificial heart and lung while we were working on his own heart."

The nurses smiled at each other because Daizat was so enthusiastic about the procedure.

"We succeeded," said Daizat, "because our pump oxygenator is highly sophisticated and Harrison was strong and not premature. Besides, all indications are that Harrison is a fighter. He's a right plucky little fellow; mad as hell—pardon me, ladies—when he woke up out of the anesthetic. And as you have seen, Harrison is bellowing at the top of his very good lungs because he is hungry." Daizat shook his head. "The cardiologist did not need me much after all. Harrison has good lungs."

Indeed, Harrison hadn't stopped bellowing since he'd been returned to NICU. He hadn't had anything by mouth since his birth and he was angry about it.

Moments earlier, Kay had watched him in the open crib of the newborn ICU from the outside window. He was crying loudly, his stumpy arms and legs pumping furiously as he bawled.

"Any more questions?" the doctor asked.

Kay said, "This isn't your specialty, Dr. Daizat, but has anything been said about correcting Harrison's extremities? I mean, is there anything that can be done about his arms and legs?"

The doctor shrugged. "Not to my knowledge. If Harrison lives, and we give him only a forty/sixty chance, he'll have to go through life,"—he shrugged—

"a freak."

"Ah!" erupted Ursala. "Don't call him a freak. Put a long-sleeved shirt on him and pants, and who's to say he hasn't got all his bones? So he walks with a waddle. So what?"

"So he is severely handicapped," the doctor replied. "No dexterity of the limbs. What happens when his arms grow longer? He couldn't even feed himself."

"About the forty/sixty chance," Kay said. "Is the higher percentage in his favor?"

The doctor pulled off his surgical cap, ducked his head, shook it, and said, "No. Sixty he won't survive, forty he will."

Harrison's cleft lip had been repaired while he was still under anesthesia. His cleft palate would be repaired in a year or so, if he lived. In the meantime, a plastic prosthesis had been fitted into his mouth over the opening where the palate should be so that his food and liquids could not reflux out his nose. With his new repaired heart, Harrison, who had everything against him in the beginning except parents who wanted him to live and a medical and nursing team who were determined that he should, now had a chance at life. Twenty years ago, he would already be dead.

Knowing Dr. Daizat as she did, Kay was certain that from a respiratory standpoint Harrison would get the best of care.

Daizat called himself a Persian, but like Abigail Jones, the critical-care nursing supervisor, told her once, "Persian? He's an Arab. Nothing but an Arab. But smart as the dickens and as kindhearted as Santa Claus. Kinder. You never lose faith in Daizat."

Someone tapped Kay on the shoulder. It was Ursala

handing her a mask. She jerked her head toward the newborn ICU. "Take this. Get a gown. Let's go make sure the other doctors are doing their business."

Smiling, Kay eagerly tied on the mask, took the ugly, faded but clean gown Ursala handed her, slipped her arms into it, wrapped it around her, and tied it at the waist.

The newborn ICU contained special apparatus for infants in distress, the same as the adult ICU. Here, two premature infants, or premies as the nurses called them, lay dozing in isolettes against the wall. Three open cribs with warming hoods were lined up against another wall; two were unoccupied, the third was surrounded by gowned, gloved, and masked doctors. Kay recognized Harrison's pediatrician, Dr. Paine, among them in spite of his disguise; and the plastic surgeon, a Taiwanese named Hishu, who would soon be visiting Barney Werger in TRU; and Dr. Pugh, the cardiologist. Kay could only glimpse Harrison through the transparent face tent fixed over his head, but she could see the tubing of the microdrop IV infuser coiling down from an IV hung over the warming hood and slipping into a tiny vein in Harrison's scalp. A feeding tube had been inserted through an opening in his abdomen and probably went directly into his small intestine. He even had a chest tube—small but just like an adult's—draining the chest cavity of blood and fluid and running into a small flask attached to the lower part of the warming crib. The monitor attached to the wall above the crib was monitoring his heart and blood pressure. A rectal probe had been inserted into his tiny rectum and a lead coiled from the probe to a temperature gauge on the wall.

Harrison was awake. He had stopped crying, but the unhappy look on his face showed everybody he hadn't forgotten that he was hungry. He was thirty hours old and still nobody had fed him. He sucked his strange, stubby fingers noisily when Dr. Paine removed the face tent and he contemplated the masked giants he could suddenly see looming over him.

Dr. Paine glanced over his shoulder at Ursala and said, "Get me a Foley catheter. We'll need to monitor his urine output because of the surgery." Another tube for Harrison.

"Oops, too late," said Dr. Hishu. The doctors jumped back just as Harrison let go with a stream of urine that arched neatly over the side of the warming crib and sprinkled the front of Dr. Paine's gown.

"Shit," Dr. Paine mumbled while his colleagues laughed and cheered.

"Take *that*, for not giving me anything to eat," said Dr. Hishu.

"Ah, it's what you get," Ursala told Dr. Paine. "You should have catheterized him in the operating room." But she fetched the sterile catheter package. Dr. Paine ignored her, peeled off his gloves, and took the sterile ones from the package she held open to him. He snapped on the sterile gloves, took the sterile swab from its package, held Harrison's tiny penis in his fingers, and swabbed it; then he took the catheter and threaded it into the baby's male organ until a small amount of yellow urine appeared in the tubing. The doctors cheered again, but Harrison screwed up his face again and began to cry. Oh, the indignations one suffers in the hospital, he seemed to think.

"I'm surprised there was any urine left." Dr. Pugh laughed.

Then their shoulders came together blocking out

Kay's view of the baby, so she waved her hand to Ursala and left the NICU.

Sixty/forty, she thought going back to TRU. Sixty he'll die, forty he'll live.

In TRU, Jan, a big-boned Swedish girl who was relatively new to the unit, and Hailey and Anita came out of their rooms. "How's Harrison?" they wanted to know.

"How's Harrison?" had become the most asked question in the entire hospital since the infant had been admitted thirty hours ago. Kay told them. Sixty/forty was how Harrison was.

When they went back to their patients, Kay sat down at the nurses' desk to try to sort out the various reactions she had observed from the doctors and nurses concerned with Harrison's welfare. The doctors were trying to save him—they really were—because that's what they were committed to. But they weren't very enthused about it. Some of the nurses weren't either. Why go to all that trouble and expense to save a freak? All that financial burden on his parents! And so on, and so on. In effect, that's what they mouthed, but surely none of them believed their own words. And they'd all fight if they had to, to keep Harrison alive, wouldn't they?

"I don't feel good about Bobby."

Kay looked up from the latest intake and output records which she had pulled over in front of her, but which she hadn't done anything with yet. Anita's freckled face showed bright, guarded concern.

"Why?"

"His BP is up and so is his temp."

Kay and Anita regarded each other. Having worked together for eighteen months, each one had begun to know pretty well what the other was thinking most of the time. Anita's thoughts now were disturbed.

Kay laid down her pen, rose, and crossed the TRU hall to Bobby Cross's room.

The nurses in Trauma Recovery knew that there were several kinds of shock—all fatal. Among those most familiar to the nurses in the Surgical Intensive Care and the Trauma Recovery units were cardiogenic shock, which involved pump failure, and hypovolemic shock which involved severe blood loss. In TRU the most feared kind of shock was septic shock, caused by bacteria. It presented, in its very early stages, opposite symptoms from the other kinds of shock. In TRU, nurses had to recognize early signs of septic shock and report them to the doctor immediately to prevent it from progressing.

During the past thirty-six hours, Bobby Cross had progressed from what the supervisors called "critical condition" to "serious." That morning, earlier, Bobby had been alert, smiling, indicating he wanted a sip of water, scribbling notes. All his vital signs had been normal. As Kay entered his room now, she could see the difference in his face. It was flushed. When she clamped both hands on his arm, it felt hot to the touch. One glance at the monitor showed a pulse rate of one hundred six. He was drowsy.

"Hey, Bobby," she said. "Sleepy?"

His blond lashes fluttered as he fixed his glazed eyes upon her.

"Sleepy?" she asked again.

He nodded slowly, eyelashes fluttering. She went to the foot of his bed where the chart platform rested like a podium. The vital-sign sheet told a mute story. Vitals the first three days in TRU were taken hourly for a reason; a trauma patient's condition could deteriorate in an hour's time. Bobby's temp had risen from 101° to 103.8° in one and a half hours. Pulse rate had increased from ninety-eight to one hundred eight, BP from 112/90 to 142/80. The difference between the systolic blood pressure and the diastolic pressure was widening. Always a dangerous symptom, this indicated a deterioration in the effectiveness of every heartbeat. His respirations were more shallow and rapid than they had been earlier. Kay knew what the Foley catheter bag would tell her, that his kidney output was normal. In any other kind of shock, it would have dropped.

In order to take an arterial blood sample from the arterial line in Bobby's arm, Anita had to have Kay's permission. Anita asked the mute question with only a raised eyebrow and Kay had only to nod. Anita took the sterile arterial tray, opened it, and removed the glass syringe while Kay filled a paper cup full of ice from Bobby's water pitcher.

The arterial line in Bobby's arm was a small catheter which had been threaded into an artery and was kept patent, or unclogged, by a minute infusion of heparinized IV solution. The arterial line not only fed into the brachial artery to determine arterial blood pressure, but provided a ready access, by way of a small faucet called a stopcock, for the nurses and respiratory therapist to obtain a sample of arterial blood for blood-gas studies. Blood-gas studies revealed the pH of the patient's blood and that showed how well the blood was being oxygenated.

Anita took a five-cc syringe from the supplies drawer near Bobby's bed and drew up a small amount of heparin from a vial. The heparin was used to prevent the blood from clotting before it was taken to respiratory therapy.

She removed the needle from the syringe, fitted the point of the syringe into the stopcock, and turned the valve. The syringe filled with bright-red blood. She turned off the valve, withdrew the syringe, capped it, and plunged it into the glass of crushed ice which Kay had set on the bedside table for her.

Next, Kay hurried to the nurses' station and dialed the lab. Electrolyte studies would be needed, and a complete blood count and blood cultures must be done. Stat—immediately. She held the receiver of the telephone to her ear with her shoulder while she pushed the zero button on the dial with one hand and reached for the lab slips with the other. When the hospital switchboard operator came on the line, Kay said, "Page an orderly for TRU, please, and page Dr. Daizat for TRU also. And dial the lab for me, will you?"

After she had asked the lab tech to come to TRU stat to draw a blood sample, she hung up the receiver and took Bobby's nameplate from the little rack on the desk. She placed it in the stamper and stamped the requisition slip for arterial blood gases and another lab slip on which she checked CBC, Culture and Sensitivity, and Electrolytes. When the telephone rang seconds later, Anita was there with Bobby's latest vital signs on a slip of paper. It was Daizat on the phone so Kay reported Bobby's vitals and stated the other important observations she and Anita had made as well. She glanced at her wrist watch. It was noon and time for lunch. She was thinking that the orderlies would probably be in the cafeteria and reluctant to leave their meal to run errands. She'd have to be sure one showed up promptly because it wouldn't do to hold the blood sample very long. The longer the blood sat before the studies were done the less likely the

78

respiratory therapist would be able to obtain a correct reading.

"I—hurt," came Dr. Worley's voice from Room Four.

Dr. Daizat was saying, "I'll be in TRU in a few minutes." Kay thanked him and hung up the receiver.

"I've got vitals to do on Leola," Anita was complaining. "And I'm behind on my nurses' notes. Now Dr. Worley's starting up. Why doesn't he ring the bell like everybody else?" Anita threw up her hands in dismay.

"I'll give him an injection if he's due," Kay said.

Ding. The nurses' call bell sounded and the light came on over Barney's door.

Oh boy. It was going to be one of those days. It never failed. Hailey was at lunch and Kay knew Jan was busy changing a dressing on Mr. McPherson's leg. Anita was behind in her work and everything was starting to happen at once.

"I—hurt," Dr. Worley sang again.

Kay hurried across the TRU hallway, and paused at Barney's door. He looked over at her and grinned. "Does that guy down the hall think he's got a patent on hurting?"

Kay smiled in spite of the pressure she was beginning to feel. She put her hands on her hips. "Barney, what do *you* want?"

"A shot for pain."

"Let me help Dr. Worley first. Then I'll get to you. He asked first."

"Louder too," Barney said as he folded his hands together over his abdomen to wait patiently.

She went to Worley's room to check his chart which lay open on the stand at the foot of his bed. She scanned his medication record to see when he had had a pain shot last. He had received no pain shot since 1:10 that morning, so Kay said, "Dr. Worley, I'll have your shot in a second." He nodded once and looked up at the ceiling.

All meds were kept in each patient's med cabinet except for the narcotics. These were kept in a locked narcotics cabinet behind the nurses' station. Kay hurriedly went to it, pulling the key out of her pocket on the way. At the desk, she recorded the withdrawal of the seventy-five mg of Demerol on the narcotics slip and went to Worley's room. With a great show of dignity, he rolled over and allowed Kay to bare his right gluteal area—more often referred to as the hip—and there she injected the medication. He nodded a thank you and Kay recorded the injection on the medication sheet on his chart.

12:08P—Demerol 75 mg. IM R gluteal. KC

Then she went directly to Barney's room and checked his chart.

"Nurse."

It was Dr. Daizat out at the nurses' station and Kay knew what he wanted—her. Daizat was kind, but he invariably preferred to speak with the nurses in charge; whether it was the charge nurse of the floor or ICU or TRU, he always preferred to direct his instructions to the charge nurse.

While Kay stood with the empty syringe in her hand, the doctor's order for pain medications for Barney in her mind, Dr. Daizat began to list verbally everything he wanted done: lab work, a reading on the CVP— Kay glanced at Anita who had been standing at the nurses' desk, and as Daizat went into Bobby's room, Kay told her,

"I've called in that lab work already, but will you help him check that CVP?"

Anita agreed to help with the CVP and Kay, having gone to the narcotics cabinet a second time, unlocked it. But her mind went blank. What *was* the med order for Barney? Demerol 75? No, that was Dr. Worley's order. Darn. She wasn't sure now. Exasperated, she slammed the narcotics door shut and locked it again.

"I—hurt," came from Dr. Worley's room.

Gritting her teeth, Kay paused at Worley's room. "Dr. Worley, you've had a pain shot. That's all we can do for now." Then she bit her lip because she'd lost her temper and said, "The shot hasn't had time to help yet; just give it a little time, O.K.?"

Worley did not reply, but only blinked up at the ceiling.

In Barney's room, she checked his chart again. She'd been right the first time. His pain medication order was for Demerol 75 mg, the same as Dr. Worley's.

"Thought you did that once, twinkle toes," Barney offered as the pain tightened his facial muscles into a grimace.

"I did, but I got sidetracked and forgot the order," she said as she left his room.

Since Anita was assisting Dr. Daizat in checking Bobby's CVP line, Kay took the tubex of Demerol from the narcotics cabinet and locked it.

"Kay?" It was Jan in Room One.

Kay paused at the door to Room One on her way to Barney's.

Jan, only six months new to TRU was not quite confident enough yet to proceed on her own sometimes, and Kay, carrying Barney's pain med, went to her. Jan

81

had just lifted the dressing from Mr. McPherson's unfractured right leg. The dressing had covered an open laceration in the side of the leg. The wound, which should have been healing, looked swollen and angry. Kay nodded. "O.K., Jan. I'll call Dr. Markowitz. Meantime, go ahead with the usual dressing change." Then she looked over at McPherson. "Leg hurt, Mr. McPherson?"

"I—don't—know."

"Aw c'mon, surely you know if you hurt," Jan said raising her head to look at him.

McPherson did not reply.

Kay checked McPherson's vital-sign sheet. No elevation of temperature yet, but if the ankle was becoming infected, he would have an elevation in temp soon.

When she left McPherson's room, she almost ran smack into Dr. Daizat. He smiled. "Have the blood-gas results on Bobby come back yet?"

Kay's eyes went to the Styrofoam cup still sitting on the desk top. The blood hadn't even been picked up yet by the orderly. "Uh, I'll call," she said, not saying *who* she was going to call. She hurried to the desk and dialed the operator again and had her page an orderly for TRU. To her relief, however, an orderly came through the TRU door at just that moment, looking innocent. She picked up the blood-gas requisition slip and the cup of melting ice containing the syringe. "Get this to respiratory therapy stat," she said none too politely. About ten minutes had lapsed since the blood gas was drawn and it was probably still O.K.; at least she hoped so. Now that orderly would go tell somebody in respiratory therapy that the nurse in TRU sure was a grouch.

Kay turned from the orderly to see Dr. Daizat coming

out of Bobby's room again. "I'm got to do another cutdown on Bobby," he said shaking his head. "That CVP reading can't be right."

Hailey, just coming back from lunch, paused and listened as Dr. Daizat continued, "Get me a cutdown tray, please, and we'll proceed with that if you'll assist me."

By then Kay was flustered. "Anita can help you."

Daizat shook his head. "It will take two of you. Bobby's becoming delirious, I think."

"I—hurt," announced Dr. Worley.

Kay turned to Hailey, handed her Barney's syringe of Demerol, and said under her breath, "Give Barney this, will you?" and rolled her eyes to show how exasperating things had become. Then she hurried toward the dressings cabinet for the cutdown tray. Hailey would have to check the medication record again in Barney's room to be sure of the med she was to give. Nurses did not take another's word about type and dosage of medication. They always checked for themselves. They took every precaution. They checked and double-checked and checked again.

As Kay snatched the cutdown tray from the cabinet, Dr. Kreel entered TRU happily, blithely unaware of the nurses' tension. "Hello, hello," he said maddeningly. "Busy? How's the kid you picked up yesterday, Carlton?"

"Harrison? He survived open heart surgery today," she said as she hurried past him and into Bobby's room. No time for pleasantries today. Dr. Kreel would probably complain to somebody that TRU nurses certainly tended to become moody. Well, Hailey could assist him in checking on Barney.

83

Carefully, she placed the cutdown tray on Bobby's over-bed table, pulled off the tape that held the sterile drapes together, and pulled back the corners revealing the tray with its sutures, scalpel, prep, dressings, and catheter tubing. Dr. Daizat was washing his hands at the sink in Bobby's room and Anita was arranging the new CVP setup on the portable IV pole at the side of the bed.

Kay poured the Betadine prep into the sterile glass bowl in the cutdown tray and opened the package of sterile gloves for the doctor.

"I—hurt," came Dr. Worley's voice from Room Four.

Dr. Daizat was snapping on the sterile gloves and said, "Why doesn't that patient ring the nurses' call bell?"

"I don't know," Kay said.

The doctor sat down on the revolving stool which Anita had rolled into the room for him, dipped the sponge into the prep, and began to swab a space on Bobby's right arm. He looked up at Anita. "Well, why does he shout like that?"

Anita shrugged. "*I* don't know."

"Does he have something against bells?"

Kay paused, seeing that Daizat was looking at her. "I— I just don't *know*."

Kay and Anita stared at each other then. They had worked so long together both of them knew what the other was thinking; that they were sounding like Mr. McPherson. They both had to work very hard to keep from giggling. It was easier to catch the giggles when they were under pressure than at any other time, and nothing irritated a doctor more; because when nurses giggled, the doctor invariably thought they were giggling at him. Sometimes they were.

While they bit their lips and tried to keep from

laughing, Dr. Daizat, intent on his business, took the syringe from the tray, drew up a small amount of one-percent lidocaine from the sterile vial, and carefully, slowly, injected it into Bobby's arm. When the needle pierced his flesh, Bobby tried to fling his arms about, but Anita was ready for that and held him still. "Ah, just a stick, Bobby, and then you won't feel any more pain. O.K.?" the doctor said.

Bobby did not respond, but Daizat kept talking as he worked. Taking up the scalpel he said, "Just got to make a small hole," which he did very deftly with the scalpel and sponged the blood that trickled freely from the wound with a sterile four-by-four sponge. "Then we need to find a nice fat vein," he said as he dipped his gloved finger into the one-inch incision. "Aha, like the fishing worm we use to catch the catfish with, eh?" He brought the slithery, gray-white vein up between the red edges of the incision and secured it from slipping back into the depths of the arm with the shaft of the sterile scissors. Then, taking the scalpel, he glanced at Kay. "Ready with the catheter, Carlton?" She did not have to answer, for he saw that she was ready to rip open the sterile package containing the catheter. One deft nip with the scalpel slit open the vein and Kay had the pack open. While the doctor clamped off the vein, he reached for the catheter, unclamped the vein, then threaded the catheter into the vessel quickly; a bloody job for a second or two, but he quickly took several stitches to close the vein over the catheter, several more to secure it to Bobby's skin, and to close the wound. Meantime, Anita had hooked the CVP tubing to the hub of the catheter and now flushed it briefly. Dr. Daizat peeled off his gloves, paused, and squinted at the CVP manometer as she ran the water into the setup.

"Ah," he said at last. "You see? This is better. The old site was getting clogged. Now. How about those blood-gas results?"

"I'll check again," Kay said hurrying from the room. She called Respiratory Therapy and Buddy said he was on his way with the results in person because Daizat was sure to need a change in the respirator settings.

As she was hanging up the receiver, Pasternak, the security guard, entered through the pneumatic doors. Reverently he stood inside like some new arrival at the pearly gates. "Sssst," he said crooking his finger at Kay. "Miz Carlton?"

Kay paused and raised her brows.

Pasternak stabbed his thumb over his shoulder in the direction of the door. "It's that maniac husband of the poor lady, Parkman," he said. "He's insisting I let him in. Said he had somethin' to tell his wife. I told him that nobody, not even family, were allowed to visit in here and if he had a message I'd be glad to deliver it." Pasternak paused and licked his lips. "He got real mad. Said he was going to have her discharged. I told him to go ahead, but I doubted that Dr. Kreel would allow it. He went off saying to hell with Dr. Kreel."

Kay didn't know what to do, but she was too busy to be frightened. "You'll still be outside the door for a while, won't you?" she asked.

"Oh, you bet. I'll be there. Brought my lunch even. You don't have to worry. But I just wanted to warn you in case I get called away or something. And you can tell Dr. Kreel about it."

"O.K., thanks."

Pasternak gave an O.K. sign with thumb and finger, clicked his tongue, and went back through the doors of the unit.

Seconds later, Dr. Kreel sauntered out of Leola's room and Kay reported to him what Pasternak had just told her. Kreel's eyes narrowed. "Well, don't worry, Carlton," he said in that infuriatingly soothing tone he used in emergencies. "If I see him I'll have a talk with him—and keep my hands in my pockets so I won't beat the living hell out of him." Then Kreel sauntered on into Bobby's room to greet Dr. Daizat and see what was going on in there.

Lot of help he was; but nurses in TRU knew they were sitting ducks. TRU was at the end of the trauma wing. A thing the nurses in TRU feared was that someday, some narcotics thief would slip in, hold them at gunpoint, and take narcotics from the cabinet. They were so isolated anyone could do it, leave, and not be seen. It had never occurred to the nurses until now that anyone could use the same technique to steal a patient.

More uncomfortable about Leola than ever, Kay went into her room to check on her. She was asleep so Kay left the room quietly and went to check on Dr. Worley. He was sleeping peacefully at last. The doctors had both left the TRU together and all was settling down again it seemed. She went in to see Barney.

When she entered his room, Hailey was studying her wrist watch, waiting for Barney's temperature to register on the thermometer in his mouth.

"Hi," Kay said brightly. "Feeling better?"

He shook his head. "Nope," he said around the thermometer.

"Shot not help?"

"What shot?"

Oh, the gradual look of horror that stole into both

87

nurses' faces!

Kay said slowly, "Hailey . . ."

Hailey's mouth had dropped open gradually.

Casually, slowly, expressionlessly, both nurses strolled out of Barney's room and beyond his hearing.

"It was Dr. Worley I gave the shot to," Hailey said. "You told me *Worley*. Didn't you?"

"I said *Barney*—at least I think I did. . . ." Kay covered her face with her hand. "I just *gave* Dr. Worley an injection."

Hailey said, "You said—I thought you said Worley, and it was Worley that was yellin'. I just . . . I assumed . . . Oh *shit*, Kay!"

Kay took her hand from her face and placed it on Hailey's arm. "Look, Hailey. Everything's going to be fine." Then she hurried to Barney's room. "Uh, Barney, Hailey will get your injection now, O.K.?"

"Promises, promises," Barney said smiling.

Kay went back to Hailey who was still standing petrified in the TRU hall. "You didn't *check*, Hailey? I recorded Worley's injection on his medications record. I gave him 75 mg of Demerol."

"I saw that, but I thought you'd recorded the injection before you had time to give it, and things were so busy— and it was *him* that was yellin'."

It was a misunderstanding. And Dr. Worley had gotten twice the Demerol that was ordered. It was, of course, an overdose. Kay went to the telephone and had Dr. Kreel paged. Kreel answered immediately and she told him that Dr. Worley had just been given two injections of Demerol 75 within a five-minute period of time. Kreel was silent. It was that silence that a nurse dreaded more than any ranting or raving the doctor might do. But Kreel laughed. "How the hell did that happen, Carlton?"

"A misunderstanding of directions," Kay said not understanding Kreel's amusement.

"Are you sure you didn't just get tired of his yelling?"

"Dr. Kreel—"

He laughed heartily. "O.K., O.K. Give him Narcan, four-tenths of a milligram IV now and another four-tenths in thirty minutes."

As Kay injected the Narcan into Dr. Worley's IV tubing, she explained to the drowsy Ph.D. that this was a new medication. She kept reasoning to herself that 150 milligrams of Demerol wouldn't kill him; but still it was an overdose. A medication error of that kind could be lethal; something she had dreaded since the beginning of her nursing career, something every nurse feared horribly. When she turned to leave the room, Worley, smiling for the first time since he'd been admitted to TRU, high and euphoric on Demerol said, "Thank you, thank you. This is the first time I've been comfortable since I came in here. Thank you, thank you," he said. "Tallyho, my dear."

Tallyho nothing, Kay thought as she slunk out of the room. Within thirty minutes the Narcan would have washed all of the Demerol out of his system and Dr. Worley would be hurting again.

She would have to instruct Hailey to take his vitals every ten minutes, too, for the next hour or so. Not only that, she and Hailey would have to fill out an incident report explaining how the error had occurred, what measures they had taken to remedy it, the results, and how the error could be avoided in the future. It was a humiliating document, a report made out in triplicate: one for the critical-care supervisor, one for the nursing administrator, and one for the nurses' own files—forever. As she'd heard other nurses say, *Secretaries could erase their typos, sales clerks could void their errors, business executives could correct their mistakes, and doctors didn't make any. But the nurse?*

Hailey didn't like it either. She was noticeably solemn. She'd made a mistake because Kay hadn't made her instructions clear. Kay blamed the confusion in TRU on the lack of help. Too many critical patients for only four nurses. But both nurses were aware they were at fault when it got right down to it.

Barney, however, having received his pain shot at last, was feeling nothing. He opened his eyes and smiled as he watched Kay approach his bed. "Guess what?" he asked.

Kay did not feel like joking with Barney, but she folded her hands together on his bed and forced a smile. "What?"

"Once when I was performing for the little theater in a play called "Of Mice and Men," I sat down on an upholstery tack sticking up out of a chair. Right there on stage in front of everybody. I jumped up and made some sort of comment—I forget what now—that brought the house down."

"I'll bet," Kay said smiling across the bed at Hailey. But Hailey wouldn't look at her. Hailey was pouting and would continue to pout for the rest of the day—maybe for a week.

"It just occurred to me," Barney went on. "I'll be a famous actor on Broadway with my polyethylene behind. I'm in a very serious play. I 'happen' to sit on a tack and

90

pop my beind. Ta-dahhhh! The most celebrated fart in history."

Kay bit her lip to keep from laughing and Hailey smiled in spite of herself as she kept studying the IV tubing with which she was fidgeting.

"Say," Barney said yawning, "I never did learn to swim. With my new backside, think I'd float?"

Kay replied, "Go to sleep, Barney. When you've had your shot, you begin to get indiscreet."

"Sorry," he said grinning. "I don't mean to talk naughty in front of you ladies, but you've got to admit, I can't discuss *my* handicaps without becoming a little indiscreet."

Going home Kay ran the events of the day through her mind. Harrison was still doing O.K. after his surgery and Ursala had given him his first tube feeding. Bobby Cross's respirator settings had been adjusted to improve his blood gases and new antibiotics had been hung for him, but his vital signs still remained unstable. Leola had remained quiet and untalkative the rest of the afternoon. Dr. Worley was complaining of pain again. And when she'd checked on Mr. McPherson, she had gotten the usual, "I—don't—know."

Over and over she kept running through her mind the things she hoped she had done; she wondered if she'd checked all the meds given—to miss giving a patient his medication could cause a recurrence of a symptom, or the lowering of his serum antibiotics. Had she remembered to count narcotics with the charge nurse of the upcoming shift? Yes. A narcotic missing meant the hassle of finding where it went and caused embarrassment. So nurses going off duty always counted narcotics with those coming on duty. Charts cosigned? If not she'd hear about it from the next shift, also an embarrassment. Intake and output records double-checked? If she'd forgotten to check one, and one of the nurses on her shift had failed to record an I and O, they'd all get chewed out by the doctor. Doctors' orders checked off? They'd better be or some patient might miss a medication or treatment unless the upcoming shifts caught it. Incident report filled out by her and Hailey, signed, and handed to the nursing supervisor? Yes. Horribly, embarrassingly, yes.

And what about Bobby? Had they caught the shock syndrome in time? And would the efforts of Drs. Daizat and Kreel save him from septic shock? Would Harrison be dead by morning? Was Dr. Worley really safe now from the overdose of Demerol? Tune in tomorrow for the next episode of General Chaos! Same time, same channel . . .

Suddenly the flashing light in her rear-view mirror caused her to glance at her speedometer. She was only doing thirty, so what—

She pulled over to the curb blushing, tired, soaked with perspiration in spite of the station wagon's air conditioner.

The policeman took his time getting out of the squad car and approaching her window. She rolled it down with tears of rage in her eyes and said, "I was only doing thirty!"

He smiled patiently, gray eyes flashing. "In a twenty-mile-per-hour school zone, though, lady. Driver's license, please."

As Kay fumbled in her purse and handed him her license, he said, "You went right through the flashing yellow light in a school zone. That's bad, lady." He squinted at her. "I see by your uniform you're a nurse. Well, I guess you had your mind on something else," he said as he vigorously wrote up the traffic ticket on his pad.

"Yes," she replied faintly. "I guess I had my mind on something else."

CHAPTER VI

"All I said was 'Why aren't we having steaks?'" explained Syd spreading his arms wide.

Uncle Ben sat a moment puffing on his pipe regarding Syd, then offered, "But she came home tired. And she was out of sorts because she got a traffic ticket for speeding."

Syd stared at Ben a moment, then sat back down in the chair. He had risen moments earlier when Kay jumped up from her chair and ran from the room. "Speeding? *Kay?*"

"Doing thirty in a school zone," Russell offered tonelessly as he bit into his grilled-cheese sandwich. "Besides, you can't have steak every day, Dad."

"I don't even *want* steak every day. I just thought we always had steak on Thursday," he said. His dark-eyed gaze went to the ceiling as if he could look into their bedroom above.

"You're in your mid-thirties and already set in your ways," Ben said. "She has a demanding job, Sydney. Comes home exhausted and then has to cook for three men."

"Two. Russell's still a lad."

"He eats like a man," Ben said. "I still maintain we should hire Olga to cook on the days she comes to clean, at *least*. Anyway, go on up and apologize."

"For what? All I said was I thought we were having steaks for dinner." Syd was angry and out of sorts himself. He'd met William Royce Ballew, the welder who claimed to have had flashes of memory; had interviewed him that day for the first time. The man had seemed sincere.

"It's like this, Dr. Carlton, *rrrrrr*," Ballew had said. "I'll be driving down the street—say, from work. Suddenly, I'm going down this here dirt road with trees growing over it, *huge* trees. I can see the horses' heads bobbing in front of me. Then all of a sudden I'm back on the paved street again *rrrrr*."

The flashes of memory which Ballew claimed he had experienced were interesting and too good to be true. In fact, they were so good they sounded more like hallucinations than genetic memory. They probably were, because they were too vivid, too pronounced, too damned convenient.

Ballew looked like a blacksmith, a wheezing, big, musclebound, hairy, bear of a man with a huge paunch— from his belly up. From his belly down he looked like Mickey Mouse. Spindly legged. He reminded Syd of the cartoon characters in the evening newspaper; only this character was real. He was fiftyish, bristly jawed. Ballew did not smoke; he chewed, which did not explain why he growled as he walked or talked or did anything that took a bit of effort. After every statement he made, his breath drained away to a low growl as if his vocal chords were located in his chest instead of in his throat. "It's like this, Dr. Carlton, *rrrrrr*. I'll have on my goggles and I'll have lifted this red-hot rivet with my tongs, see? *Rrrrrrr*.

And suddenly, I'm a-chinkin' mud between these here rough logs on some god-da—I mean, on some sort of old-fashioned cabin, *rrrrrr.*"

The reason Syd was so out of sorts was because when he had called his associate, Harry Wyatt, on the telephone to see if they could set up a hypnotic session with Ballew for the next day, Harry claimed he was down in bed with the flu. "The flu or a floozy?" Syd had demanded irritably. "I swear, Syd, I'm so sick I couldn't come in and interview a reincarnated Marilyn Monroe," Harry claimed.

Ballew had something to say about that when Syd told him of Harry's illness. He had nudged Syd in the side and said, "What you perfessers need, son, is some meat on your bones like me. You bookish fellers are too soft. No exercise. Me, I exercise eight hours a day at my job, *rrrr.* Never sick, *rrrrrrr.*"

Now Syd looked over at twelve-year-old Russell, Kay's son by her first husband. Russell was glancing at him sullenly, but not saying a word. He looked at his own Uncle Ben. Ben only puffed and kept watching him expectantly through narrowing eyes.

Well, maybe he had been tactless. Syd shoved himself away from the table and strode out of the kitchen, through the little-used dining room to the entry, to the foot of the stairs. There he paused, looked up, then began his ascent.

Kay was dressed for bed. At six in the evening, dressed for bed already, in a lightweight robe trimmed with blue lace. She'd let her beautiful chestnut-colored hair down and had brushed it out, leaving it shimmering. She was sitting on the cushioned window box looking out the window across the rooftops to the north, where on a clear day, one could see the rolling green mesquite and cedar-covered hills of the Texas hill country. When he entered, she turned to look at him. Kay had large blue-green eyes, framed by soft brown lashes. Her complexion was blemishless but pale, and Syd was surprised to notice the dark smudges beneath her eyes and the almost imperceptible parentheses around her mouth that spoke of an inner tension that she would not talk about. He remembered, in that instant, her "patient voice" the one which she used to speak to her patients, a low, soft voice with a lilt, her voice that soothed and never jangled the nerves and yet gave evidence of concern and a belief in a better tomorrow at the same time.

He loved Kay with a passion that was painful, always had. And now during their two years of marriage, it had not changed. He came to stand beside her. "Uh—I didn't mean that I didn't like grilled-cheese sandwiches," he offered.

Her full lips pressed tighter against her teeth and she said nothing.

He fingered the lace trimming on the sleeve of her robe. "You're not feeling well, baby?"

She took a deep breath. "I feel fine."

He stood a minute in silence. Then, "You dressed for bed early and you didn't eat dinner."

She looked up at him slowly. "I'm tired. I had a bad day."

Syd sat down on the seat beside her. "How's—Harris?"

"Harrison?" she said. "The doctors give him a sixty to forty chance he won't make it," she replied.

"How's Bobby Cross?"

97

"Trying to go into septic shock, we think."

"And how's the patient whose husband beat her up?"

"The same."

Syd still fingered the lace on the front of her robe. "Kay, aren't you letting the trauma unit get to you a little?"

She fixed her eyes upon his face. "Maybe."

"It's not worth it. I've always encouraged you to continue to work, haven't I? Because you love it so. But you've been under the gun now for six years."

"And you're my psychoanalyst telling me I should resign?"

"Kay, you only had a two-week break between ICU at Preston General and St. Luke's trauma unit. No honeymoon. No vacation—"

"I can't quit. There's nobody to replace me. We're short of people in the units. And besides, we couldn't get along unless I worked. Not on your salary. Not—" The words escaped her before she realized she was speaking instead of thinking them.

Syd flinched almost visibly, then stood a moment looking down at her.

She shook her head as tears came to her eyes. "I'm sorry," she said looking out the window again.

He backed away from her then, toward the door, and when she looked back at him she saw that his eyes had turned black with anger and his hair was standing up in places, two things that always happened when he was upset. "We could do fine on *just* my salary, Kay, and you know it. Our rent is free and Ben shares expenses. You're working because you want to work, because you have to have an outlet for your emotional energy. You need constant assurance of seeing your efforts rewarded. And that's O.K. But TRU offers about as many failures as it does rewards. And you've developed an ego problem, baby, since you started working in TRU. You've got a skill few people in the world have and you think you're indispensable. Well, you're not."

She nodded angrily. "Thank you. I needed those words from you just now, Syd. Thanks a lot," she said sarcastically.

"Nobody's indispensable, Kay," he said and turned on his heel and stalked out the door slamming it behind him.

She threw the cushion at the door halfheartedly, and then went to the bedside table where she had put the plastic bottle of Valium. Four years ago when her husband, Ken, had died in the crash of a private plane, Dr. Patton had prescribed Valium for her. She'd never had the prescription filled. But last month after a week of almost sleepless nights, she'd asked Dr. Kreel to prescribe a tranquilizer for her. He obliged, saying blithely for her to take it only before bed, not when she was on the job. She hadn't yet succumbed to the need of it.

But it was there, a little help, maybe, if she needed it in the middle of the night sometime, on one of those nights when she woke up soaked with perspiration after she had dreamed of dragging some bleeding man to the helicopter while parts of arms and legs were being strewn behind, or of the helicopter plunging suddenly to the ground in a burst of flames with Ken screaming— Or after she had dreamed of doctors screaming at her or after any of the other nightmares that came sometimes following a harrassing day at the hospital.

She pulled back the bedspread and the top sheet and crawled into bed. It was still daylight outside. Her eyes went toward the window. She missed her friends at Preston General: Shirley, now married; Mary Jane, now a grandmother; Hap, in whom Dr. Ellis had recently diagnosed cancer of the liver, and Sally who had crocheted her a black shawl as a going-away present. And Janey Engleman, her nursing supervisor. Kay still believed her to be one of the best nurses she had ever known. She missed Dr. Pappas and his petulant smile, Dr. Spatik with his quirks, even bored Dr. Ellis and ambivalently likable Dr. Pirruth—Dr. Pirruth, alone again in his practice after his associate, Dr. Longley, had died a year before Kay had left Preston. . . .

She thought of Hugh Boyett, the plane-crash victim the doctors had pieced back together and the nurses had nursed back to health, the patient who had become her friend, more than a friend. *How free are you, Katy?* Free enough. *But not for this crippled man who adores you?* No, Hugh. I'm sorry.

She looked up at the old, high ceiling, the chandelier that used to be gaslighted. And there was Cass, a visitor who fell in love with her, the only man besides Syd whom she had ever let make love to her since Ken's death. Cass, with his promise of a bright future: *I'm not the poor country hick you think I am. I'm not braggin', Kay; I just want you to see that you'll never have to work again.* And when she finally turned down his proposal: *Time, Kay. It just takes time.*

It occurred to her once or twice to wonder what her life would have been like if she had accepted Cass. No hospital work; that's for sure. *You'll be so busy . . . ridin' a horse over the range and enjoying the great outdoors, you'll never even think of a hospital.* Cass, I can't ride a horse. *You'll learn. I'll teach you. Four thousand acres of range* land . . . a herd of registered Herefords and a herd of Brahmans . . . miles of rolling hills covered with cedar, Kay.

But she had loved Syd instead. And loved him now even more. Syd, with his intense love for her and his passion for life, his curious genius.

She slept after a while, and when she finally felt him crawl into bed beside her, it was dark outside. He made no noise and moved as little as possible so that he would not wake her. She lay very still lest he know she was awake and try to touch her, to speak to her. She was too tired for that now. Better that they both rest, and maybe tomorrow they'd feel better about everything. She supposed they couldn't feel much worse.

Report happened three times a day when each shift's charge nurse gave report to the nurses of the upcoming shift. There was an overlap of shifts of about twenty minutes or however long it took to report on all the particulars about each patient, their lab work, new treatments, new developments, good and bad. The overlap also encompassed the time it took the nurses to recount hospital gossip or call down invectives upon the heads of some grouchy, arrogant, or negligent physicians. If a doctor ever cared to take his popularity pulse among the nursing staff, all he would have to do was secretly listen to the change-of-shift report on one of his patients. In TRU, report was given in the kitchenette because patients were less likely to overhear the nurses' remarks there: the Kardex, a tablet of capsuled information on each patient, was their guide.

The morning after Kay and Syd's argument, she stood listening to Ginger Manning, charge nurse of the eleven to seven shift, give report on Leola Parkman whose problems seemed to require three times as much time as reports on the other patients.

"Dr. Kreel doesn't understand a man beating his wife," Ginger was saying, "but as you might guess, he doesn't understand her silence about it either. He thinks she ought to spill the beans on her husband; then get a court order against him."

"Fat chance," Grace Yancy said as she stood with arms folded over her ample bosom. "I'll bet if Parkman ever *did* get put in jail for assault and battery because of beating her up, she'd be the first to take up a collection and bail him out."

Yancy didn't understand Leola either. Leola had spoken very little to the nurses her first week in TRU and answered their questions only briefly and hesitantly as if she were carefully measuring every word, thinking through every answer. Her primary nurses, the ones who were usually assigned to her care on each shift, had all reported to the others the same observations: that Leola seemed politely distrustful of them, that she avoided most conversation that touched upon her personal life.

Grace Yancy was the only L.V.N. in TRU. Once an army nurse in the Korean war, Yancy claimed she'd seen all the "blood and guts and human indignity there is to see." When she came to TRU to work a year ago, she took over the severely traumatized patients without batting an eye. Yancy was built like a tank and just as formidable. There hadn't been a patient in TRU yet Yancy couldn't bully into doing what was best for him. Getting surgery patients to turn, cough, and deep-breathe in order to aerate their lungs was one of the hardest chores nurses in TRU or the surgical floors had, but Yancy never failed to elicit their cooperation—until she met Leola.

When Ginger had assigned Yancy to Leola on her third day after admission, Yancy had barged into the room and bellowed, "Now lookee here, youngun'. Suppose you try turning over and coughing for me eh?"

Leola's response to Yancy on that occasion, and other occasions after that, was to burst out crying bitterly.

Yancy could handle stubbornness in a patient, or fear or ignorance or even violence, but she couldn't handle tears. Yancy sniffed now and rocked back on her heels. "You get nowhere with her," she said. "That son of a bitch has broken her spirit." Yancy glanced toward Room Three. "She really doesn't care whether she lives or dies."

Ginger continued report. "Anyway, you know Kreel respects women. At least he gives us nurses credit for having a few brains. But we also know he's a bit condescending. Calling us sweetheart and baby and stuff like that is condescending, puts us on a level with little kids."

Pam, the youth of the two shifts, said sagely, "If it isn't your husband or boyfriend that's calling you honey or sweetheart, it's condescending."

The nurses all nodded in agreement. It was one of their frequent philosophical pauses for thought. Ginger went on. "Well, Dr. Kreel's condescension, no matter how carefully he disguises it, is not fooling Leola. She won't talk to him at all. Even to us, she only hints about the cause of the bruises on her face and body. 'These bruises aren't the only ones I've had in my life,' she says. Things like that. Now Kreel came in this morning about five o'clock and told me to pass the word on to the other shifts that Leola will be moving out to the floor in a week or so

103

and if we're going to make any progress getting her to tell on her husband, we'd better do it quick."

Pam raised her hands. "So what do we do? Try sodium pentothal on her like a truth serum?"

"Dr. Cash, you know him," Ginger went on, "nosing into everything Kreel does, heard about what Kreel told us and he came by and told me that Leola's marital problems are none of our business."

"Cash is a nerd when it comes to women," Anita said. "Of course it's our business. As citizens of the human race it's our business. Next time Parkman beats up on Leola, he'll probably kill her. We've got the opportunity to do something about it with Leola here in our care. It's now or never."

"But she won't talk. You ask her any personal questions and she starts getting evasive," offered Jan.

"You can't push," said Hailey standing on Ginger's other side with her arms folded, shaking her head. "No-oooo, ma'am, you just can't push."

"I don't like nursing-care plans in TRU," Ginger went on, "except what we decide among us verbally. And I say we need to make every effort now to find out why Leola has allowed the abuse and why she doesn't confide in us."

Kay said, "I discussed Leola with Syd several days ago and he says it's guilt."

Ginger looked up at Kay quickly. "Guilt!"

"That Leola feels she deserves to be beaten," Kay said.

Ginger laid the Kardex in her lap. "What else does your hunk of a psychology professor husband say?"

The nurses laughed and Kay said, "Guilt because she isn't as good a wife as she should be. Maybe she doesn't fix his meat loaf the way he likes it or something."

"Meat loaf!" exclaimed Yancy about to go off on one of

her tangents. "I'd fix his meat loaf for him. I'd put my big number-nine shoe right up—"

Ginger interrupted, "How does Syd think we should proceed with Leola?"

Kay said, "Slowly. But something just occurred to me." She looked up at the asbestos-tile ceiling a moment, the same kind of ceiling her patients contemplated many hours a day every day. Then she told the nurses that several days ago, Leola had asked her if she was married and Kay had told her about Syd and that they had been married only two years; that she had been a widow before that. Leola had begun to show more than ordinary interest in Kay's personal life, but their conversation had been interrupted by the telephone at the nurses' desk and Kay had had to leave the room. She said now, "We're taught in nursing school never to talk about ourselves to the patients, to always turn the conversation back to the patient. But I wonder sometimes—"

Ginger said, "You know, Kay? I think I follow your line of thinking."

"So do I," Hailey said. "Think it'll work?"

Anita said, "We won't know till Kay tries."

"We're taught in nursing school to never talk about our own problems or personal life to a patient," Ginger mused, "but I wonder just how many things like that we've been taught need to be ignored once in a while." She filled her cup with more coffee from the carafe on the warmer. "But, naturally, you have to be careful when you bend the rules."

"Bend the rules?" Yancy said. "Hell, we bend the rules all the time. Dr. Kreel likes to say, 'There're no absolutes in medicine.' Well, there're no absolutes in nursing either."

The nurses all nodded in unison.

It was an hour after report before Kay was able to visit Leola. She began checking the IV hanging on the IV pole above Leola's head and said, "Guess what my husband gave me for an anniversary present two weeks ago. Did I ever show you?"

The head of Leola's bed was rolled up all the way so that she could look out the window of her room. She brought her gaze from the window to look at Kay. "No, what was it?" she asked softly, her natural curiosity overwhelming any inhibitions she might be feeling.

Kay showed her the beautiful, thin, quartz wrist watch encased in a gold bracelet.

"Oh," Leola breathed touching it gently. "Isn't it beautiful?" She smiled up at Kay. "It was your second anniversary wasn't it?"

Kay nodded.

"You must tell me about this handsome husband the other nurses say you have. They must have just met him for the first time, because everybody that's been in my room this morning has mentioned him. Was he really a nurse once?"

Kay had to smile at how the nurses had all paved the way for this particular conversation, unable to resist getting in on the act. "Yes, he was an R.N.," she told Leola. "He worked evenings as a nurse and went to school during the day to earn his master's degree. Then, he went on to earn his Ph.D."

"And you were a widow in the same hospital where he worked?"

"Not at first," Kay said. "When I became acquainted with Syd, my husband, Ken, was still alive."

Leola's eyes left Kay's face, went to the window, and

for one disappointing moment Kay thought she had lost interest in the conversation. Then she said softly, "I was a widow once, too."

Kay's brows shot up. "Oh?" So that was why Leola was so interested in her widowhood and in Syd!

Leola turned her face back to Kay. "I don't feel like talking about it now, but I do want to hear what happened with you."

It was hard to keep from being too cheerful or too stoic around Leola. Nurses had to practice a bit of dramatics in all their relationships to patients. With Barney, you had to be a big sister. With Dr. Worley you must be businesslike, no nonsense, and mostly silent. With Mr. McPherson you had to be chipper and try to draw him out of his escape mechanism of the "don't knows." With Bobby Cross you really had to be careful; if you were too cheerful you were a fake, too solemn you were an old sourpuss, too businesslike you were a real drag. Kay felt that nobody could perceive insincerity as well as a teenager. With Leola you had to be cheerful, soft-spoken, and patient—very patient.

So Kay, hoping the telephone wouldn't ring and that no doctor or nurse would come in and request assistance, sat down in the bedside chair, casually, as if to take a break from her routine. She began to tell about herself and Ken, her first husband—how they had grown up in the same neighborhood, attended the same high school, married at seventeen, had Russell. How she had gone to college, gotten her B.S. in nursing. Then how Ken had been killed taking a light plane up for his first solo flight. While she and Russell had watched, his plane had plunged, burning, to the earth.

Leola's eyes never left Kay's face; her thin hands

picked at the top sheet draped over her, and Kay could see the pain, the sympathy in Leola's face.

Kay paused in her story, trying to decide if she should go on. It was Leola who decided for her. "Please now tell me about your professor."

Kay had to smile while thinking, Ah, but you have to pay for the second part of the story. I've captured your interest and now there must be an intermission before part two.

"I've talked only about myself," she said. "But what about your first marriage, Leola? Were you very young?"

Leola smiled. "Sixteen."

"That's young."

"We met in high school and married. I didn't finish high school until after Carlos died. Then I went back and finished and went to college for two years. I didn't go to high school when we were married because I had to work." Leola laughed softly. "We never had any children, but we were so very happy, so very happy."

Kay listened while Leola told about her first husband's job, their tiny rented house, of both their parents' disapproval of the marriage because Carlos Vicente was of Latin American descent and Leola was Jewish. When the couple had been married three years, Carlos had contracted a respiratory viral infection and died of the complications that set in. He had waited too long before seeing a doctor.

Leola paused, as Kay had before the second part of her own story.

But the second part of both their stories was interrupted by the telephone at the nurses' station. Irritated, Kay excused herself, hurried to the nurses' desk, and answered, "Kay Carlton, Trauma Recovery."

"Kay, this is Marsha in TR. We have a thirty-two-year-old head trauma victim just brought in by the fire department ambulance. His name is Harvey Chunn. This one beats all. Gunshot wound to the head and he's in surgery now. Attempted suicide. So it's possible you could really have your hands full with him."

While Kay was listening to Marsha, she was already pulling out the pages she'd need for the new patient chart: a white page, Nurses' Notes and Medications Sheet; the Vital Sign Sheet, the Graphic Chart; the pink sheet, Doctors' Orders; and the blue sheet, Doctors' Progress Notes. The Admissions Sheet with all the patient information on it would go on the chart first when it came from Admitting, then the Trauma Receiving Admissions Sheet, the surgery report, Anesthesia Record, and the History and Physical sheets would go at the back of the chart. But would she need a chart? Victims of gunshot wounds to the head at close range seldom survived the ride to Trauma Receiving; much less often did they survive surgery.

"I know what you're thinking, Kay," Marsha said. "Go ahead and make up this patient's chart because he's going to make it. He rode sitting up in the ambulance all the way to the hospital talking to the attendants."

"You're kidding!"

"The doctor thinks the bullet passed between the two hemispheres of the brain without doing any serious damage. But he may have performed a prefrontal lobotomy on himself, in which case he'll be an easy patient to deal with because he won't care where he is, who he is, or anything else."

"And won't have any more inclinations toward suicide

or anything."

"He'll have an inclination for a big headache, though."

Kay hung up the receiver and put Harvey Chunn's chart together; then crossed the hallway to Room Two to check the equipment. She switched on the monitor, checked the suction meter on the wall, and all the while was wondering what could make a man of thirty-two so despondent that he would shoot himself.

The pneumatic doors to TRU opened, and instead of the head trauma patient, Dr. Cash, the neurosurgeon came in still dressed in his surgical greens. He flashed Kay a rare smile, and came to stand beside her at the nurses' station.

"TR called you about my patient, Harvey Chunn?" he asked as he sat down in a desk chair.

Kay, realizing that the doctor wanted to chat, a rarity with him, leaned against the desk and folded her arms on its top. "Yes."

Dr. Cash shook his head contemplatively. "I've seen everything now. This patient's a staff writer for the *Evening Globe*. You've seen his name, I'm sure. His neighbor says he's also written a couple of dramatic screenplays for television which have been shown on national network TV." The doctor looked up at Kay. "He shot himself, but he had dead reckoning—pardon the pun. It was a small caliber bullet from a twenty-two pistol; passed as neatly down the longitudinal fissure between the two hemispheres of his brain as if his guardian angel had guided it. Missed all the critical centers, passed neatly over the ventricles and the corpus collosum. I thought at first he'd performed a prefrontal lobotomy on himself, but the bullet managed to miss

110

those nerve fibers too. To extricate some small fragments of bone from the frontal lobes was all I had to do there."

Kay clasped her hands. "That's great, but sounds impossible."

"It's great, but the bullet did angle downward just enough to injure some of the optic nerves in the upper occipital lobe. In other words, it exploded out of his skull and left a three-inch hole there, injured some optic fibers which is all the brain damage I could find. I can't believe it either. Anyway, he'll be blind or partially blind. May at least have tunnel vision."

By then Jan, Anita, and Hailey had come out of their patients' rooms and were standing at the nurses' station listening.

"Does anybody know why he tried to kill himself?" Anita asked.

Dr. Cash smiled and oscillated in the desk chair back and forth as he went on. "Everybody should have a neighbor like Harvey Chunn's. The neighbor says Harvey's last two plays had been turned down by the studios. Also the chick he was living with had just run off with some other fellow. The neighbor heard a gunshot coming from Chunn's apartment next door and got the landlord to unlock the door. They found Chunn lying unconscious on the floor. She called the fire department ambulance, but by the time they arrived, Chunn had regained consciousness and refused to lie on the stretcher in the ambulance."

The doctor stood up, thoroughly amused and bemused. He said to Kay, "I'll leave orders for very careful observation of this patient, the same observations you make on any head trauma patient only more often and more detailed. There could be something I missed. Or he could develop a complication, intracranial pressure, or a hematoma. He's got a plastic plate covering the three-inch hole in the back of his skull, but once the scalp wound heals and the hair grows back you'll never know it. Has a smaller plate under the skin of his forehead. That scar will be visible the rest of his life." He smiled at the other nurses, pleased with his new patient and thinking what a great story it was to tell the other doctors over coffee in the lounge. "Anyway, girls, the resident is closing the scalp wound now and the patient should be in shortly." He turned to Kay. "I'd advise you girls to keep a very close watch on this fellow. He's despondent, and if he tried it once, he could try it again."

"Oh boy," Jan said.

Dr. Cash smiled at Kay and held out his hand. "You the little nurse that's married to Dr. Carlton?"

She nodded and handed him the Doctors' Orders sheet.

"He's really worked up a very difficult project for himself, honey. And very interesting. Where'd he get that inherited-memory idea of his?"

"It's his own idea," Kay replied.

"Has he done much research on it?"

"Some."

"Does he have a government grant for the research?"

"No."

"Well, who knows, maybe he'll dig something up yet. Does he work very much on it?"

Kay's mouth tightened. None of this was any of Cash's business. "A few hours a day."

Seeing that he was getting nowhere with his questions, Dr. Cash turned and went to the doctors' booth where he would dictate his operative notes into the dictaphone and write his doctor's orders.

*   *   *

Harvey Chunn was admitted to Trauma Recovery at 12:05. His head was swathed in dressings, his eyes were swollen almost shut, the tissue around them blue-black. He stared up at the ceiling while the nurses placed the cardiac-monitor leads on his chest and took his admitting vital signs. Chunn was awake and his brown, crisp, neatly trimmed beard moved as he tried to speak. His voice was hoarse from the endotracheal tube that had been placed in his trachea for the administration of anesthetic. His nose was packed with gauze to prevent further bleeding from it due to the severe blow to his head.

His cardiac monitor showed a fast but steady rhythm. His blood pressure was slightly below normal. Kay rolled up the head of his bed about twenty degrees, Anita adjusted the monitor as Jan checked the IV injection site. Hailey was recording the amount of urine in the foley catheter bag which the orderly had hung on the side of the bed near the floor. Kay was surprised that Chunn didn't have a nasogastric tube. Head trauma patients, like other trauma patients, usually had NG tubes installed before they came into the unit, to help prevent nausea and vomiting. Vomiting could cause intracranial pressure which—

"My eyes."

Kay looked up from the vital-sign sheet to Chunn's face.

"My eyes—" he said softly.

Anita froze and looked at Kay. Hailey, squatting on the floor beside the foley bag, looked up at Anita. Jan paused at the door of the room just as she was about to leave, and looked back at Harvey.

113

Kay went to him and said, "What about your eyes, Mr. Chunn?"

"I can't see anything but—shadows." The young man's hands, white and soft with brown curly hair on the back of them reached up and touched Kay's face. "Only shadows."

She took the hand and held it in both of hers. "Mr. Chunn, is that all you can see, just shadows?"

His brown eyes moved from one nurse to the other, then over to the window and back to Kay's face. "Only shadows," he said softly. Then he smiled grimly. "The phantoms of things to come."

"Sir?" Kay said leaning closer.

"Forget it," he said and closed his eyes.

"Mr. Chunn, is that all you see?"

He nodded, eyes still closed. The nurses looked at each other, each sharing a fraction of his despair, his fear of the unknown, each realizing that here in their care was a young man who *suddenly* could not see.

Since he was conscious, the nurses were able to elicit important responses from him in their initial neurological assessment. Kay watched and supervised, comparing these results with the small bit of information she had on his chart from Trauma Receiving.

When Jan asked Harvey to open his eyes, he responded; to turn his eyes back and forth, he did. "No oculomotor deficiency noted," Kay wrote in the admitting nurse's notes. He answered their questions drowsily, but appropriately. He could grip their hands, move each limb, wiggle his toes. The pupils of his eyes reacted instantly and evenly when Hailey shined the flashlight into them. Kay recorded the results of every step in the neuro check. So far, all Harvey had suffered was a hole in the back of his head, a smaller one in front, and a couple of swollen black eyes and a bloody nose. And partial blindness.

The nurses would make the same assessment every hour for twenty-four hours and then twice a shift for however many days Dr. Cash ordered it to be done.

Harvey felt more comfortable lying on his back with the pillow fixed so that it did not press on the wound at the back of his head. The nurses talked to him, fluffed his pillow, fussed over him as they always did over a new patient, and all the while he did not speak unless asked a question. In fact, he seemed bored with the whole thing.

After Harvey Chunn's admission, Kay was at the nurses' station arranging the anesthesia record which the anesthesiologist had just delivered when he went in to check Harvey's level of consciousness. Dr. Kreel sauntered into the unit, glanced at the doctors' booth where Dr. Cash still sat speaking into the dictaphone, and over at Harvey's room. With hands in his pockets he looked at Harvey, then over at Kay. "Dr. Cash going to put in an NG tube?" he asked.

"I don't know," Kay answered. "I haven't gotten anything but the routine admissions neuro check yet."

"Did he say anything about an arterial line?"

"No." As Kay watched out of the corner of her eye, Dr. Kreel sauntered on into Harvey's room. Kay glanced at the doctors' booth. Dr. Cash had seen Kreel go into Harveys' room and sat watching as he dictated. Kay's eyes then turned to Anita directly across the hallway in Leola's room. Anita had seen Kreel and Cash and had raised her brows at Kay in a silent question.

Presently Dr. Kreel sauntered out of Harvey's room, paused, looked at Kay, snorted, shaking his head in disbelief—no doubt at Cash's stupidity—and sauntered out of the unit.

Moments later Dr. Cash came out of the booth, his brows lowered, tossed the doctors' orders onto the desk in front of Kay, and left the unit without a word.

Hospital gossip suggested that Cash was jealous of Dr. Kreel's trauma units. For many years Cash had tried to have a portion of the hospital funds directed to the establishment of a neurological ICU but had not yet succeeded. The fact that Kreel, a relative newcomer to St. Luke's, a virtual *youth* in medicine, had succeeded in establishing two trauma units, galled Cash deeply. The fact that the funds for the units were donated for their establishment didn't placate him one bit. Kreel knew about Cash's jealousy, and besides that he had no little amount of disdain for Cash's lack of knowledge of trauma medicine. Cash in turn had great disdain for Kreel's radical methods. All the nurses knew the two doctors disapproved of each other's methods, because each one had berated the other to the hospital personnel. As far as the nurses knew, neither one of them had slandered the other to his face yet. Nothing like having a little friction between doctors to add to the tension of a critical-care unit.

Before Kay left for work that day she went by the nursery to check on baby boy Harrison. Outside the nursery, she was able to look through the uncurtained plate-glass windows at him, because the nurses in the nursery had forgotten to put the screen around his crib when they opened the drapes for visiting hours. She smiled to see Harrison still lying in the open crib in the NICU, without a couple of his tubes. An oxygen cannula was now installed in his tiny nostril, the feeding tube and Foley catheter had been removed. None of the other apparatus seemed to be bothering him. His tummy was full and he was sleeping soundly.

It was visiting hours in the adjoining OB floor and the usual flock of visitors was gathering at the nursery windows. While Kay stood there, she derived some insight as to what Harrison's future would be like.

A teen-ager near her said, "Mom, look! Quick! What's the matter with that baby over there?"

"Oh look, George," said a new mother in a blue satin robe. "That poor little thing over there with all the tubes. What's the—? Look at his legs!"

"My God! It's missing part of its legs—and arms too!"

Its! Furious, Kay rushed into the nursery and saw why the nurses had forgotten to screen Harrison. They were watching and listening to Ursala having a mild spat with Dr. Paine at the nurses' desk.

"Let the mother hold the kid. He's got to know somebody cares," Ursala was saying.

"You care, I care, we *all* care," Dr. Paine said tiredly as he scribbled on a chart, not looking at her.

"But nobody cares like the mother. We can put them in the isolation nursery. Let her hold him in there."

Dr. Paine lowered the chart and looked at her. "The kid's got a defective immune system and *I'm* not going to be responsible for his catching something and dying. It's too early to allow outsiders to hold him."

"Outsiders! The mother's an outsider? Too early. Too early. We let the mothers with the premies hold theirs. Why not Harrison?"

Sighing, Dr. Paine pulled off his mask and started peeling out of the gown he had put on over his suit.

"Those premies have a helluva better chance of survival than Harrison," he said. He threw the gown into a canvas bag which was standing near the outside door for that purpose. As he left the nursery hurriedly, Ursala looked at Kay red-faced, raised her hands to the ceiling, and dropped them.

It was easy to be angry with Dr. Paine because he seemed hardhearted, as if he didn't care one whit about the babies and children he was committed to helping. But Kay couldn't forget the story she had heard once about Dr. Paine. Several years back after he had spent a particularly bad day, performing six appendectomies on children within a twelve-hour period of time, the pathology lab gave him its reports on the six appendixes. Three of the appendixes had pieces of peanuts lodged in their swollen lumen which had caused the inflammation. Dr. Paine, in a mounting fury, had stalked out of pathology and through the lobby on his way out of the hospital. As he strode past the vending machines in the lobby, he paused, went back, picked up the big JOHN'S SALTED PEANUTS machine, carried it to the outside door, and tossed it out onto the pavement.

Ursala's face was still red as she watched Dr. Paine leave the nursery. "Ah, what does he know?" she said. "A damned man is what he is."

Kay, tying her gown around her waist said, "Dr. Daizat been in?"

"Yes," Ursala snapped and went with Kay through the door to NICU and to Harrison's crib. Ursala felt his diaper and bent to retrieve a dry one from the stack on the shelf beneath the warming crib as Kay pulled the rolling screen to Harrison's crib. Ursala raised up and looked at her. "Today I asked Daizat, 'Is Harrison going

118

to live do you think?' What does he do? Shakes his head and walks away. So what does that mean, that he thinks Harrison will not live, or that he doesn't know?" Ursala paused, threw up her hands again. "Ah, what does he know anyway? It takes a woman to feel that Harrison will live. You and me, Kay. We know. We feel it in our bones that Harrison will live, and we'll fight for him. It's up to you and me." Ursala flung her hand in the direction of the other nurses in the newborn nursery. "They fight for nothing but a bigger paycheck and they're afraid of the doctors. Now stand aside, while I take off Harrison's wet diaper. Because if I know him, he'll aim right for the front of your gown with his built-in water pistol. And his aim is very good, eh, Harrison?"

Ursala's voice chirped on, speaking of their certainty that Harrison would live, but before Kay left the nursery seconds later, she did not miss seeing the tears in Ursala's eyes.

Now, trudging down the corridor toward TRU, she paused and looked out the corridor windows and saw that rain had begun to fall, pounding upon the streets and the walks and on the hoods of cars on the parking lot nearby. She thought about the evening before, about her argument with Syd, how she had hurt him, how bad they had both felt about the argument.

"You're not indispensable, Kay," he had said. But he was wrong. He just didn't know. But Ursala knew. Dr. Kreel knew. And Marsha Walsh. And Anita, and Thompson, the nursing director; and maybe Leola. And Barney and Bobby Cross and . . .

CHAPTER VII

"What you need, son, is to eat rare beefsteak once a day like me, *rrrrr*. Do you know how I got these muscles? Worked on the docks unloading freight at the port of Houston for twelve years, *rrrrr*. That's what both you perfessers need. To eat rare beefsteak and work on the docks a few years. It'll make hair grow on your chest, *rrrr*."

Harry Wyatt laughed. "Yes, Mr. Ballew, you're probably right. But now, let's talk about you."

Syd and Harry shifted in their chairs again, amused and both knowing what big Billy Roy was thinking because he'd already expressed it once; that if Harry would grow more hair on his chest, he wouldn't have to prove to the ladies how much of a man he was by growing hair on his *chin*. By now, after their third interview which had included careful history-taking of Ballew's entire life, and as much of his ancestral background as he could fetch up out of the muddy back roads of his memory, they felt that they knew him pretty well. Between the two of them they'd been able to check out enough of his background this past week to agree that he wasn't an escaped convict or an ex-mental patient, and that except for occasional exaggerations, he'd told them the truth about himself. Syd and Harry had documented every detail of Ballew's conversation, recorded every word during their last three interviews, and Ballew was becoming impatient with all of it, ready to get on with the "hypmotizin', son, so I can find out who I used to be, *rrrrr*." For Ballew was convinced he was reincarnated, that he used to be a duke or a count or maybe even a king back over in the old country hundreds of years ago. And if he was, he sure as he—, sure wanted to know who and what.

Now, Harry explained to Ballew what hypnotizing was and asked him again, for the sake of the record, if he understood what was being done to him and why.

"Why sure, Perfesser, you done told me all that and I've been chewin' the fat with you boys for a week now. So let's get on with it, *rrrrr*."

"Very well, Mr. Ballew," Harry said. Then he turned to Syd. "Is the recorder running and in good order?"

Syd gave Harry the O.K. sign.

"All right," Harry said looking back at Ballew.

They were sitting in a room that had once been a classroom but which had recently been designated and furnished for group-therapy sessions. One could sit on one of the metal folding chairs that were arranged in a semicircle around the metal desk, or on a cushion on the floor. The room was one of many moods because its white plaster walls were the victims of group rape by the art students of Oil Painting 202. The walls displayed psychedelic paintings, modern art—renderings of disturbed minds, in Syd's opinion. Harry, however, appreciated the art more, explaining to Syd that *anybody* could paint a picture of what one *saw*; it was what one *felt* when one looked at something and how it was rendered

121

from the interpretation of one's own mind that made it contemporary art. Syd hoped he never met the artists in the dark sometime. *He* might become the victim of rape. The fact that one mural faintly resembled a nude woman reclining on God-only-knew-what did disturb Syd. He thought, If that's how the artist interprets a woman's nude body, he should be locked up in a state mental institution in the ward for the criminally insane.

Outside, the rain that had begun to fall four days ago was beating down steadily, heavily. Flash-flood watches were in effect for the area and Syd found himself wishing Kay was at home and safe. He hoped the rain would let up before morning.

Ballew was sitting in a high-backed leather chair with his feet propped up on the desk, with Harry sitting in the desk chair facing him. Syd was behind the desk manning the recorder and the pen and paper on which he hoped to describe Ballew's facial expressions or any physical changes that might accompany his vocal recital.

"William Royce Ballew," Harry began in a natural tone of voice. "You are very tired. You're tired because you worked all day welding ornamental iron grates. Eight hours you worked—"

"Ten, son. Guess you forgot I got up at five o'clock this morning, *rrrrrrr*," Ballew informed him.

Harry looked stunned for a moment, but Syd had to give him credit that it was only for a moment, and he resumed his intonations. "You worked hard and you are very tired. You came here at three o'clock directly from work and your arms are heavy with fatigue, so-oo-oo heavy, William, and you're so very tired all over. So tired and so sleepy."

After several moments of Harry's persuasions about

122

how tired Billy Roy was, the big man's chin began to sink into his bull-like neck, deeper and deeper until chin and neck merged, and then as the jaw slackened and the big mouth hung open, the chin and neck sunk upon the big chest and the lids of his small blue eyes drooped, sagged, until they covered the eyeballs entirely. His arms hung limp at his sides, his boots slipped off the desk, the jolt never waking him, and Billy Roy began to snore softly. *"Rrrrrrrrr."*

This was what Syd had waited for, for three years—this—a likely candidate with whom he could probe into genetic memory. He had wanted this since the study for his thesis on genetic memory had begun for his doctorate. And yet, incredibly, he found that he wasn't overwhelmed with the prospects at all. His mind kept going back to Kay, and he kept wishing he were home. He felt uneasy about her. His interviews with Ballew and the evenings after classes checking Ballew's background had kept him away every evening for a week. For five years he had craved that blue-eyed little nurse in Preston's ICU and being married to her these past two years hadn't lessened that craving a bit. He wasn't away late in the evening, but Kay, having to get up in the mornings at five o'clock in order to be at St. Luke's at a quarter to seven, had to be in bed by ten P.M. and she was usually asleep or nearly so when he got home in the evenings. Syd found himself wondering how long it had been since they'd made love. He decided it was before their last argument, maybe a week before the night he came home and blurted out that he thought they were having steak for dinner.

I can't quit work, Syd. We couldn't make it on your salary. . . . You've got an ego problem, Kay. . . .

Damn. Why hadn't he just kept his mouth shut. It was

true, she did think she was indispensable to St. Luke's, but he shouldn't have told her so. Their relationship had been cold ever since. He felt his hair standing on end as he wondered if it was possible to lose her now that she was his—because of his thoughtlessness, lack of attention. Syd's dark eyes fastened on Billy Roy's face again as the big man roared, "Mama, Johnny's got my scooter and won't give it back."

Harry had urged Ballew's subconscious to go backward into time, into his childhood, reviving old forgotten experiences. And tonight, Harry would take him back to the moment of his birth. Ballew, like other subjects he and Harry had studied, was so vulnerable to hypnotic suggestion he would probably have no problem remembering his childhood. To help him remember his own birth was a wild hope, something almost rare, but Harry would proceed as if it were expected that he should. Not only would he urge Ballew to remember his own birth, but his existence as an embryo too. All that in today's session. Then tomorrow, or maybe the next day, he'd take him back in time *beyond* his birth—if those cells in his brain contained genetic memory as they desperately hoped. There wasn't one chance in ten million it would happen, but Ballew might be the one in ten million.

This session was the beginning of the experiment he had been waiting for, no doubt about it; but somehow, amazingly enough, Syd just didn't seem to give a damn.

The final decision as to whether Ranger I should go up on a mission fell ultimately to the pilot, Jerry Bergdorf, who, for safety's sake, adhered religiously to visual flight rules. In VFR there were minimum visibility standards to be taken into consideration, plus wind velocities, and other weather conditions. While Jerry stood beside Comstat's control booth and pondered the weather, Kay and Marsha Walsh were shrugging into their neat, green, one-piece jumpsuits in the nurses' lounge, just in case.

Rain had fallen steadily for five days. Flash-flood watches had been in effect since noon the day before. Tornadoes had been reported in counties to the south that morning, and clouds hung dark and heavy over the city. An almost constant rumble of thunder rattled St. Luke's, vibrating the floors underneath the nurses' feet as they zipped up the jump suits.

"You realize," Marsha was saying as she twisted to view her behind in the mirror over the stainless-steel sinks against the wall, "that these suits are the sexiest uniforms in the entire hospital?"

Kay shrugged into her shoulder bag, the one that held most of their first-aid equipment, and smiled. "I know."

"You know, but you couldn't care less. I don't blame you. How'd you ever *meet* that good-looking husband of yours anyway?"

"I'll tell you sometime," Kay said, "but right now, we'd better get over to Comstat."

"Yeah. People like you make me sick," Marsha said, but she smiled because she was mostly just joking and because she liked Kay. She opened the door of the lounge for Kay, saying, "You've got the best job at St. Luke's on the best shift and, except for the supervisors, I'll bet you've got the best pay of anybody on the nursing staff. You go home to a big house to a handsome hunk that has brains as well as looks. You even have a kid." Marsha threw up one of her hands in mock exasperation. As they hurried down the corridor toward Comstat, she went on, "When I was your age—ahem—only three years ago, I

125

was a floor nurse on an alcoholic ward, married to a big ugly oaf, and had tried for years to get pregnant without success. That's my luck. That's why people like you make me sick."

They came to stand beside Jerry who had his flight cap in one hand and was tapping the window ledge of Comstat's booth with the fingers of the other.

"Well?" Marsha asked him.

Jerry was whistling a tune and he paused. "I dunno yet. I'm waiting for an update on the weather north of here."

"Well, what poor slob is out there hanging by a thread between life and death waiting for your decision?" Marsha asked.

Jerry sighed. "He's an old fellow, I gather. Cowboy or something who's had heart trouble for years. Sounds like he's had a heart attack out in an isolated section of ranch land some ten miles or so off highway 183. The fellow who was with him called in on a CB from his pickup truck and got in contact with a trucker on the highway."

"But why does he need us?"

"Can't get across a crick in the pickup. Bridge is washed out and the crick's full bank to bank. He's somewhere close to where the San Saba flows into the Colorado River, and every crick and arroya in that area is bank to bank. Can't get any ground ambulance through."

Kay was apprehensive about going up in weather like this, but she also felt sorry for the heart-attack victim. Since working in ICU, heart-attack victims were special to her.

Jerry said, "I told Cal to see if Dallas or Fort Worth's CareFlite units could pick him up. Waco's closer, but they've got heavy rain." Jerry shook his head. "I hate to risk us, the patient, and the Ranger in this. Fact is, I won't unless this rain lets up and the visibility improves."

Cal, the day-shift Comstat operator rapped on the window to get Jerry's attention. Jerry opened the door of the booth and Kay and Marsha leaned close to hear what he was saying. "Dallas and Fort Worth are socked in, Jerry, with ground fog. Visibility there is less than a tenth of a mile."

"How far north does the fog go?"

"Starts in patches near Waxahachie, the highway patrol says, and has spread into all counties north. South we've got heavy rain. Looks to me like we're just about as well off visibility-wise as anybody."

Jerry looked at the nurses. "Rain has let up some," he mused. "And the weather bureau says visibility is half a mile. I reckon I'm game. What do you girls say?"

Kay and Marsha looked at each other. Marsha said, "Jerry, I'd trust your piloting blindfolded." Then both of them looked at Kay.

She shrugged. "I can't keep from thinking about the poor man with the heart attack."

Jerry pulled on his billed cap, genuflected, and said, "Let's go."

The directions to the sick man had been given to Comstat by the trucker who had pulled off the highway when the rancher had contacted him via his CB radio. Comstat instructed Jerry to follow highway 183 out of the city going northwest. Visibility was indeed half a mile and Kay felt more fear than she dared show. Flights like these, when difficulties were thrown in, reminded her that Ken had been killed in the crash of an airplane which had taken off from the runway but had not gained an altitude of more than one hundred feet. The Ranger was higher than that now. She was also remembering Hugh Boyett, a patient in ICU who had crashed his light plane; he had been brought to Preston General, and had had to be pieced together by surgeons and nursed back to health from the very brink of death. It was Hugh who had taken her for her first flight in a helicopter; at the same time, he had taught her not to be afraid of adventure, to try whatever she wanted to do, to overcome her fear of doing it.

Now her fear of going up in the Ranger when added risk was involved was quelled because of a stronger instinct than fear, an instinct that demanded that she help the unknown man marooned in a remote section of Texas hill country in a downpour. Instinct. Syd said the only real instinct was that from the reptilian brain, the brain from which evolutionists claimed the human brain had evolved. And even that instinct of the reptilian brain was an accumulation of memories, Syd maintained. Why then did she and Marsha and other nurses and doctors sometimes risk their own lives to save others? Or people like Jerry with no medical training, who did the same thing? Maybe it had nothing to do with instinct after all. Maybe it was just concern for someone in trouble, or maybe it was an effort to placate a nagging conscience. Or as some people thought, maybe it was just stupidity.

The Ranger shuddered with the gusts of wind. The medicopter had been constructed for minimum engine noise within its cabin, but the roar of rain and engine noise combined caused its occupants to have to shout to be heard. The rain washed down the cabin windshield, and the Ranger's wipers were barely adequate. Marsha was clinging tightly to the bar on the side of the copter and Kay's fingers were digging into the palms of her hands. The fact that Jerry was only whistling tunelessly instead of singing was evidence enough that even he was worried about weather conditions.

They were flying low, but not so low as to become tangled in the electric wires, following the highway. It was noon, but the day was so dark the vehicles on the highway were using headlights. The highway looked like a river; its sleek, shiny surface undulated with the swells and dips of the countryside and meandered between cedar- and mesquite-covered hills. A small town, probably Briggs or Watson, slid by below. Streetlights had come on; traffic there was slow.

Kay discovered that she was biting her bottom lip due to her tension so she leaned back against the seat and tried to relax. Above the din and roar she heard Jerry say, "Four, Comstat, we've just come to farm road 1025. Repeat directions."

The instructions over the transceiver from Comstat must have been garbled because Jerry had to ask twice for Cal to repeat the directions. Jerry glanced over his shoulder at Kay. "Hold on; I've got to buck a headwind, girls, and things are gonna get bumpity."

They nodded as Ranger swung its tail to the east and headed west along a paved farm road flanked on either side by barbed-wire fencing. The Ranger shuddered and bumped and jarred like an automobile on a bumpy road and Kay found herself wishing she were sitting in front of a fire, even the one from the gas logs in the fireplace in the living room of Ben's house, the house that was to become Syd's when Ben died, according to his will. *That's why you ought to take an interest in redecorating it, Sydney. Kay has a knack for that kind of thing and I'd like to see it repapered and painted and fixed up before I die, though I don't plan on dying for a dozen or so years yet.* Kay wished she were with Syd and Russell and Ben, drinking hot chocolate in front of that gas-log fireplace right now. When she shut her eyes, she could feel and smell Syd, Syd whom she loved and had missed so much this past week. Partly her fault, partly his. He hadn't been home much in the evenings. She understood that. She understood what his work meant to him. And to be truthful with herself, she hadn't been home either. Her mind had stayed at St. Luke's with Harrison, still recovering nicely from his terrible surgery. And with Barney. And Harvey. And Leola . . .

". . . You see," Leola had confessed the next day after she had begun to ask Kay about her first marriage, "the reason my first husband died was because I did not insist that he go to see a doctor. I *knew* better. Oh, why didn't I make him go?"

Guilt, Syd had guessed and he had been right. Leola was feeling guilty that she had not made her first husband go to a doctor. The result was that when he did go, it was too late—too late—and he had died. "I was absolutely useless as a wife when he became sick," she told Kay.

Over the past five days Leola had revealed more and more about her second marriage. Guilt-ridden Leola had met Carl Parkman and had fallen in love, vowing that she would give him children, would take care of his house, cook his meals, go to work to help make ends meet. But Parkman did not want her employed outside the house. He told her a woman's place was in the home and expected the house to be perfect, his meals on time. When the three children came, Leola took great pains to see that his peace and solitude were not disturbed. He had no patience with crying children.

Ah, but Leola had broken off her story there. During the last few days Kay had felt that it was time to approach her about the causes of the old bruises on her body. "Leola," she had begun, weighing each word carefully, "when you came into the trauma units there were old bruises on your body as well as new ones." She simply made the statement and did not ask the question.

Leola had flashed her a quick look and replied softly, "I'm clumsy. Always falling and bumping into things."

Kay had felt that all the TR nurses' careful preparation had gone down in defeat, that Leola would never admit her husband's brutality. But this very morning she had said, "You're always so pleasant, Kay. I guess you must be very happy at home." She had smiled. "I would be happy too if only Carl—if I weren't always"—she had paused, but finally added softly—"afraid."

Dramatic moments in TRU were invariably interrupted. At that moment the telephone had rung and Marsha had summoned her to prepare to board the Ranger for an emergency flight.

Jerry was talking in a monotone now into the transceiver mike and Kay looked at Marsha; both realized that they were nearing their destination. They peered out the windows on either side of the copter and at first saw nothing but the soaked landscape, lakes of water standing in low places between cedar-covered hills; a river not far below, probably the Colorado, out of its banks, boiling, rushing, churning to the southeast carrying with it uprooted trees and debris. They flew over the river going westward, over more sodden range land, and a creek of rushing water, also out of its banks. Then they saw the white pickup truck and a man waving a piece of white

131

clothing back and forth.

Jerry glanced back and mouthed the words, "Hold on." Hold on! Neither of them had ceased to hold on since they'd left St. Luke's.

The Ranger hovered over a clearing for a moment; then, shuddering, lowered itself to the ground.

After Jerry cut the rotors, Kay unlatched her harness and threw back the latch on the door. Marsha went out first, then Kay. Jerry pushed out the tarpaulin-covered stretcher. They ran slipping and sliding through pouring rain carrying the stretcher, which was light when there was no victim on it. It was designed to be carried to the scene of the accident and rolled away from it with the victim. Kay was wondering how they'd manage to roll the stretcher today in the mud.

They approached the pickup truck where the man, his clothing soaked to the skin, stood, shouting, "He's over here in the truck!"

Kay ran up to the truck, slipped, and almost lost her footing, but the man in the cowboy hat caught her arm. She looked up to thank him and stared. *Cass!*

I'm not the poor country hick you think I am. I'm not braggin', Kay. I just want you to see that you'll never have to work again. . . . You'll be so busy . . . ridin' a horse over the range . . . you'll never even think of a hospital. . . . Four thousand acres of range land . . . Time, Kay. It just takes time. . . .

"My God! Kay!"

In a moment of time that seemed an eternity, but which was only a second, they stared. It had been three years since she'd seen the man she had almost married, the one who had promised her so much. He had not changed, except that perhaps the creases at the outer

132

corners of his eyes were deeper. He shook his head in disbelief, pushed his hat back on his head, and said, "I don't believe it!"

But Kay said, "Is it Ike in the truck, Cass?"

He came to himself. "Yes."

Marsha was already attending to Ike Salter in the cab of the truck when Kay climbed in. Ike, his friendly face twisted in pain, saw her. A look of recognition registered on his face instantly, and he was able to say, "Kitten!" before he lapsed into unconsciousness.

So Ike, a friend, became once again Ike, the patient. Kay felt for a carotid pulse and found it. Luckily, Ike wasn't fibrillating, but his slow pulse indicated a heart block.

"Marsha," Kay said digging into her bag, "I know it's against the rules to give more than four-tenths milligram of atropine until we have him on the monitor, but I know this man. He had a temporary pacemaker once because of third-degree block. I'm betting he's got it again. I'm going to give him six-tenths now and worry about it later."

Marsha only paused. "O.K., kid. Whatever you say."

Atropine should speed up the pulse and keep Ike alive until a pacemaker could be inserted at St. Luke's. His slow pulse indicated that the electrical impulses generated in the upper chamber of his heart weren't getting to the lower chambers fast enough so that the heart could beat at a normal rate. Marsha was tying the rubber tourniquet onto Ike's upper arm and Kay palpated a vein. With a prefilled syringe of atropine in hand, Kay found the vein, inserted the needle, and drew back the plunger until blood appeared above the hub of the needle into the syringe, indicating that she was in the vein. Marsha released the tourniquet, and slowly Kay injected the

133

atropine. Marsha then felt for the carotid pulse, and shouted over her shoulder for Jerry to bring the stretcher closer. Jerry never left the Ranger unattended at the scene of an accident, but in this instance there was no crowd of people to worry about and the girls needed help.

Marsha said to Kay, "O.K., he's up from about forty to fifty. Let's get him out of here."

The nurses stepped back as Jerry, with Cass's help, lifted Ike out of the truck and onto the stretcher. Rain soaked them all as they whisked the stretcher away, rolling it through the mud toward the helicopter. It was not until Ike was inside the Ranger that Cass shouted, "I'm coming, too."

The nurses hesitated because it was against the rules to let a passenger ride in the Ranger with a patient. But in this case, Cass was stranded and had no way out. Rules were to be broken. Marsha motioned him aboard and commanded him to take the seat in the front next to the pilot.

Cass was swift to obey.

By then Kay had pulled open Ike's shirt and stuck the three adhesive disks from each of the monitor leads onto his chest. On the small monitor on the emergency defibrillating unit attached to the side of the copter next to Ike's stretcher, the electronic blip, representing the electrical impulses of his heart, registered bradycardia, a slow pulse of fifty; not bad, but not good either. The PR interval was wide, indicating a first-degree block, and a premature ventricular contraction—or PVC—alerted them that the ventricles, the lower chambers of the heart, were trying to compensate for the slow beat by initiating the beat themselves. That was an ominous sign and a danger if it were allowed to increase. Marsha got the prefilled syringe of lidocaine from the bag, just in case, hoping it wouldn't be necessary to use it. Kay was palpating a vein in Ike's arm again. Marsha had hung an IV of Ringer's lactate, attached the indwelling catheter needle to the tubing, run fluid into the tubing, and held it ready when Kay reached out her hand. Kay took the needle and plunged it into the vein; she released the tourniquet, and IV fluid began to drip from the bag and move slowly through the tube into Ike's vein. A life line had been established now in case it was needed.

With a more nearly normal pulse rate established due to the effect of the atropine, Ike regained consciousness; his eyelids fluttered and he mouthed the word, *Kitten,* the nickname he had used for her three years ago.

"Hi, Ike. Are you lonesome for your old pacemaker?" Kay asked smiling and holding his dear hand.

He smiled. "Not me," he said slowly. "My ticker. Needs a—" He winced. "Needs a *re*charge, I reckon."

Marsha was injecting a small amount of morphine sulphate slowly into the IV tubing to alleviate some of Ike's pain and anxiety, though she didn't want to inject very much because of his slow heart rate. Nobody but Ike, and perhaps Cass, knew that his anxiety had been alleviated already, only moments ago when he had recognized the little nurse with the touch of a butterfly's wings.

Only once did Kay glance up to see Cass turned halfway around in the seat to watch. She was surprised to note the Ranger had already lifted off and was headed for St. Luke's. Cass asked how Ike was, and it was Ike who signaled an O.K. to him with his thumb and finger.

But Ike wasn't O.K. The premature ventricular contractions showed wide and ominous on the monitor

135

screen again. Five in one minute constituted a need for lidocaine. They did not want to give it in Ike's case because a ventricular beat was better than no beat at all. On the other hand, a run of PVCs usually preceded the fatal ventricular fibrillation. The PVCs Ike was having now were warning signals and were only about two per minute. A standing order for nurses on call for cardiac patients was to defibrillate for ventricular tach if the patient was unconscious. Ike wasn't. But Kay was thinking that it would be better to correct the heart by defibrillator rather than to knock out v. tach (which was what a run of PVCs was) with lidocaine. It was a nursing judgment they might have to make.

So Kay told Marsha, "Better that we use . . ." she nodded her head toward the defibrillator, "than the lidocaine if we have to. Do you agree?"

Marsha answered by checking the voltage indicator of the defibrillator, just in case. Kay continued to hold Ike's hand in both of hers.

She loved almost all her patients, but once in a while one came along who became a friend. Ike was one of those. How old was he? Three years ago he had been sixty-eight. He'd be seventy-one now. He had been engaged to be married then, and looking down, she saw the wedding band on his hand and pointed to it.

Ike grinned through his pain-set face and nodded.

She tried not to let him see her glance at the monitor, but she didn't need to anyway. In ICU, CCU, and Trauma Recovery, nurses developed a peripheral vision which could keep a monitor screen in view most of the time.

Jerry had Dr. Pugh on the Ranger's transceiver now and Kay pulled the headset on. She knew what information the cardiologist would want and said, "Dr.

Pugh? The patient's pulse rate was forty-two and steady when we got to him, but we injected sixth-tenths of atropine intravenously and the pulse is now fifty. He's having occasional PVCs, about two per minute, but they're perfusing. I know this patient, Doctor. Three years ago he had a temporary pacemaker installed for a ten-day period because of third-degree block. He's alert now."

"Terrific, nurse. Now don't give lidocaine. Those PVCs are helpers right now since they're perfusing. Good work. Do what you have to, but be conservative in this case. Know what I mean? You were right to go with the six-tenths of atropine, though. If there's a change, I'll be here. O.K.?"

"Right. Over." Kay pulled the headset off and let it hang around her neck. She exchanged a look of mild triumph with Marsha, her smile communicating that Dr. Pugh had thought they had made the right decisions so far.

Kay got a brief glimpse of Cass's face now. The old look was there—his love for her still showed, she saw that plain enough—and there was no wedding band on his hand, she noticed. She felt uncomfortable under his gaze, incredulous, too, that she should be meeting him again on the one chance in a hundred million, and like this. Surely he had seen the rings on her finger and there would be no resumption of any relationship between them. Yet she was certain they were both remembering the one irrational lapse she'd allowed during her period of grief after Ken was killed, Cass carrying her from her patio to the bedroom. . . . He had been so kind, so safe, and with him she had felt so secure. Only she did not love him; she had loved Syd instead, and still did.

Still holding Ike's hand, she looked up into Cass's face not three feet from her own. Marsha must have sensed their familiarity or seen Cass's expression. Kay was aware that Marsha was alert to something even more dramatic to her than the helicopter rescue of a heart-attack patient.

"That wasn't your ranch was it, Cass? Isn't yours in Hill County?" Kay asked.

In his hand Cass still had the handkerchief with which he had mopped the rain water from his face. Smiling, he handed her another one, folded and ironed neatly. "To wipe your face with, Kay. You look as if you just stepped out of the shower."

Their faces turned red simultaneously. Kay hadn't been aware that her flight suit was soaked and stuck to her body, that her hair was sticking in wet spirals against her face. Still blushing, she took the handkerchief and wiped off her face. Marsha had been mopping hers with a dry washcloth and upon seeing Kay accept the handkerchief from Cass, looked down at the washcloth in her own hand and tossed it disgustedly to the back of the cabin.

"We were on Ike's ranch. I was visiting him when the rains started, helping him get his cattle to safe ground. We had half a dozen hands helping us yesterday. Got some stranded cattle to a safe place. Cattle are stupid, you see, worse than sheep. They'll stand and drown in a low place while all they have to do is head for high ground."

"They had drifted south along with the wind," Ike offered.

"Only thing wrong with that, on Ike's south section there were arroyos and canyons. Took five days to round up the herd and head them west to higher range land. The men rode on back to Ike's homestead, but Ike and I stayed overnight at a friend's place. We started back to

138

his ranch house today, not knowing the bridge over Gladstone Creek was washed out.''

"Then poof goes the ticker," Ike said now drowsy from the morphine.

Kay was still aware that Marsha had not missed the look on Cass's face as he talked to her, or her silly blushing. She knew what Marsha was thinking: *How can anybody have two men like Syd and this rancher interested in her in one lifetime? It isn't fair! It just ain't fair!*

Kay saw the flashing beacon ahead and below, the beacon next to St. Luke's helipad. A glance at the cardiac monitor showed her that Ike's pulse was slowing down again to forty-eight, but he remained conscious, and the electronic configuration on the monitor, representing electrical activity between the atria and the ventricles, had not widened. Not yet, God help, not yet.

Two orderlies, a resident doctor, and a nurse, all clad in heavy rain gear, were waiting near the helipad when the Ranger touched down. Cass threw open the door of the helicopter, the orderlies reached in and pulled the stretcher from the copter, and as Cass watched, they rushed it down the ramp toward Trauma Receiving.

Kay walked with Cass down the ramp from the helipad. The rain had slackened to a light drizzle, but they were both still soaked to the skin. Water was dripping off the end of Cass's nose and hung like tears to Kay's eyelashes. At the door of TR, she paused, looking up at him, and said, "Ike will be taken to the general-surgery suite in the main building. It's on the fourth floor and there's a visitors' waiting room there. Then he'll probably go to CCU.''

Cass took hold of her arm. "And you? Do you work there?"

She shook her head and they went through the doors

of Trauma Receiving as she said, "I work in Trauma Recovery. It's like ICU only it's strictly for trauma patients. It's in this wing on the second floor, but Ike will be on the third-floor CCU. Cass, they'll probably have to put in another pacemaker."

Cass, big, sun-tanned, broad-shouldered, looked like a thunderstruck schoolboy as he smiled at her. The incredulous look that had petrified his face when he first saw her was still there, too. "I can't believe that out of the clouds this white-and-blue helicopter came. I had been standing in the rain waiting, wondering if Ike would die there in the truck and me not knowing what to do for him, wondering if a helicopter could make it through as the trucker had assured me over the CB. Then I heard it; then saw it. It was like a chariot from the gods to me then, and I guess I almost bawled. But when I saw that one of the angels of mercy was you—" He laughed briefly. "I couldn't believe it. And yet, I'll be durned if it didn't seem just right."

She only smiled.

"Still working at a gosh-awful job aren't you, Kay?" he said as they walked through TRU's reception area. Then he took her arm again as they paused in the corridor. "By choice?"

"Yes."

"Who's the lucky man, Kay?"

"Syd."

He nodded. "I thought so. He persisted where I momentarily gave up, didn't he?"

"I love him, Cass. It's as simple as that."

"Forgive me, Kay, but I don't recall it being that simple for you at the time."

He still had the power to make her feel wanted and

140

loved and secure. His big frame and handsome face still turned female heads, she noticed as they walked down the busy corridor. And Cass still loved. That was what was remarkable to her. After three years . . .

Suddenly, she wanted to cry. "I have to get back to the unit, but I'll see you later," she said. Ducking her head, she walked swiftly away from him, knowing that he stood watching her until she turned into the corridor that led to the nurses' lounge and out of his sight.

"I met Dr. Hishu, the plastic surgeon, today," Barney said to Kay when she had changed into her dry scrub clothes and gone back to TRU. She planned to check each patient before giving report to the upcoming shift. "He says since I still don't have any feeling in my yahoo, I probably won't need an anesthetic when he goes to do his remodeling job. I told him I'd remember him when I become famous. He'll go down in history as one of the twentieth century's most famous sculptors. My behind will be immortalized in plaster and marble in every museum in the country."

Kay, feeling unusually light-hearted, laughed. That only spurred Barney on.

"I've always heard about people sitting on their dead butts, but I'm the only one that has a legitimate claim to one." Barney was making his usual jokes, but Kay didn't miss seeing the despair in his eyes when he added, "On the other hand, I guess all people who're paralyzed from the crotch down have that claim. I guess I can still claim to have the only rebuilt model in history."

When she went into Harvey Chunn's room, he turned his handsome, bearded face toward her and grimaced. "Here you are. The others said you'd be back. I can tell it's you because I can't hear you walk. Neither your shoes nor your bones squeak when you float into my room. They say you went out in this lousy weather on a mission of mercy. What's your reward, a case of pneumonia?" He held up his hand suddenly. "And don't ask how I feel. Please observe the sign I printed which the other nurses claim they taped to the wall over my bed, and which my physician resents."

The sign was indeed there. In wavering letters it read, I FEEL LIKE SHIT.

"You see, I feel like that now," Harvey said. "I've always felt like that and I'll always feel like that in the future." He dropped his hand to the mattress. "Don't make small talk either, Kay. I *can* call you Kay, can't I? I *shall* call you Kay. I abhor the name Carlton, I don't honor a Mrs., and I don't trust nurses. Your name is Kay; I heard the others call you that. As I just said, don't make small talk about the weather or any such drivel. Do not speak to me unless what you have to say is very profound."

"You're in a lousy mood," Kay said.

"That's very profound. I can tell you are very observant."

"What made you do it, Harvey?"

"Shoot myself?" He grimaced, a wince that was meant to pass for a smile. "I missed. I actually placed the barrel of a twenty-two pistol to my head and missed." He laughed mirthlessly. "I saw a Bugs Bunny cartoon once where Elmer Fudd put a gun to his head, pulled the trigger, and missed. That's me, a real comic character right out of—"

"You didn't miss, Harvey. That's why you're here."

"Wrong. I missed my *brain*, which is what I was aiming

142

for, and *that's* why I'm here. I should be six feet under by now."

"Or a vegetable."

He grimaced again. "That's why I almost like you, Kay. You get right to the heart of the matter, don't you? Didn't they teach you in nursing school to be gentle with a patient's psyche?"

"Yes, but you're different," she said. Indeed he was. Harvey would not tolerate small talk as Leola did, or require a listening ear as Barney did, or polite silence as Dr. Worley did. And Kay was experienced enough to know it. In a way, Harvey was like Bobby Cross; he could see through farce and pretense in the twinkling of an eye, without the eye or the twinkle.

"Yeah. I'm different," he said contemplatively. "So different I can write a beautiful screenplay, a thing with a lot of history and characterization and profundity, a thing so beautiful the network studios' big asses can't even comprehend it. They'd rather show stuff that's on a sixth-grade level. If you've got an IQ over ninety and want to watch a good show on TV, forget it. Sorry, friends, the boob tube's for morons only." Harvey reached up and touched the dressing on his forehead. Kay noticed the tissue around his eyes was fading from the blue-black bruised look to gray and yellow. "Writers are supposed to be able to paper their studies with rejection slips. Not me. I use mine for toilet paper. Haven't bought a roll in years."

"Sorry."

"Sure. Yeah. Now if you're through checking to see if my ticker's still racing and my IV's infiltrating and my mind's wandering and my kidneys are drying up, you can leave, Kay, because I've just been refused a pain shot

143

because head trauma patients have to tough it out, shithead Dr. Cash says. And I seek oblivion in sleep if I can possibly manage it. Sweet oblivion. Good day."

"Sorry, you can't have a pain shot," Kay said. "Did the doctor explain why?"

"Yeah. He says it masks symptoms of complications. If my brain swells or bleeds or something I'd become lethargic, he says. If I'm already lethargic from a shot, nobody can detect the change, he says." Harvey moved his head back and forth on his pillow. "Ever have your brain on fire? It even hurts to open my mouth. I said, please leave me in peace. I choose to suffer in silence. Good day."

"See you tomorrow, Harvey."

On the way out of the building to the adjacent parking lot, Kay stopped by the newborn nursery. Ursala asked her to wait and she'd walk out with her. And while they made their way across the lot, Ursala said, "Dr. Paine says tomorrow the Harrisons can come into the isolation nursery and hold him."

"Great! What made him change his mind?"

"Who knows? And what's so great? To hold Harrison is to love the little bastard, and I was hoping the Harrisons wouldn't want him and would put him up for adoption. Then I could adopt him, the little booger."

Syd did not believe in instincts, but Kay did and she knew Ursala's maternal instincts were very strong. Harrison was lucky to have her on his side. The other nursery nurses were not sure, had not come to grips yet with their inner conflicts, whether they wanted Harrison to live or not.

Going home, she thought back over the conversation with Beasley in CCU. She had called CCU just before she left the unit and Beasley said Dr. Pugh had installed a temporary pacemaker in Ike Salter again and that his condition was stable. Ike had told every nurse in CCU that he knew Kay, and Beasley had asked her before she hung up, "Uh . . . if you know Ike Salter, then maybe you know his friend, the big, good-looking cowboy or rancher or whatever he is; do you?"

"Yes, I know him," Kay had replied. *I know him very well,* she thought.

But she decided not to tell Syd about Ike or Cass. Syd had a jealous streak in him like all husbands, perhaps, so she saw no reason to irritate him.

As it turned out, Syd was late getting home, so she didn't have the chance to tell him anyway.

CHAPTER VIII

Leola said, "Tell me about your new husband, Kay. Is he very brilliant?"

Kay sat down on the window sill and smiled. "*I* think he is."

"And what does he teach at the university?"

"Three courses in Introductory Psychology and one of Abnormal Psychology."

Leola smiled and smoothed the sheet that Kay had placed over her knees when Anita had helped her up to sit in the bedside chair. "You know, of course, that Carl will try to get me out of here soon."

Kay said, "Oh?"

Leola nodded. "The only reason he's left me in this long is he was afraid I'd die."

Kay did not reply.

"You don't believe the story about the falling bricks, do you?"

Kay studied Leola's expression, knowing Leola was also studying hers. "No."

"I didn't think so." For a while Leola was silent. Then, "He does hit me once in a while." A quick glance at Kay, then at the clock on the wall at the foot of her bed. "But it's only when I've really done something stupid.

Normally, he's a very reasonable man."

Kay felt herself getting angry at Carl Parkman again and at Leola for tolerating him. "Nobody deserves to be beaten, Leola."

The shy woman looked at her, then away again. "I did not say I was beaten."

"What do you call it then?"

Leola fell silent and Kay could not be sure whether or not she would have spoken more about it, because at that moment the telephone rang at the nurses' station. It never fails, she thought as she crossed the hallway to the nurses' desk. Jan had answered the telephone and held the receiver out ot her. "It's Thompson."

Thompson was St. Luke's nursing director and Kay had very few dealings with such a far-removed authority, so she felt some apprehension as she answered.

Thompson said, "Kay, I've got something to talk over with you. Are you free to come to the office now?"

"I think so."

"Will you then? And hurry, because I've got another conference at nine."

Thompson's spacious office was a bit more plush than the nursing director's office at Preston General, and Thompson herself presented a most forbidding appearance. She reminded Kay very much of a charge nurse she had worked under one summer in her days as a student. Thompson was tall and slender with salt- and pepper-colored hair which she had drawn back and secured in a French roll at the back of her head, just as Pragg had fixed hers. Thompson's brows, like Pragg's, were very arched, giving her the appearance of perpetual haughtiness and disapproval, the eternally raised brows being almost intimidating. Kay recalled how forbidding

Pragg had seemed to her as a student: domineering, never giving a nurse—especially a student nurse—the benefit of a doubt, or so it seemed. Kay had changed her mind about Pragg when she had become an R.N., employed by Preston General and working side by side with Pragg as her equal at last. It was funny how the formidable Pragg had proved to be a very human lady with a husband and teen-aged daughters, and with very normal doubts, fears, and hang-ups. *Kay, will you start an IV on Smith for me? Dr. Pirruth wants it started with an indwelling catheter and I don't know how to use those darned newfangled intracaths. . . .*

". . . Anita Wilson is a lesbian?"

Kay blinked. "I beg your pardon?"

"I said, did you know Anita Wilson is a lesbian?"

Kay stared at the nursing director and became instantly angry. "No. And I don't believe it."

"Then perhaps you'll believe your own nursing supervisor. Abby Jones saw Anita and her roommate kissing in the car when the roommate delivered her to work this morning. *On the lips.*"

Kay shut her mouth which had just dropped open. "That can't be!"

"But it is. I just wondered if you had suspected it or seen anything that would have made you suspect her."

"No," Kay said, her face flushing with a mixture of embarrassment, anger, and disbelief. "No, nothing."

"You realize, of course, that we can't have a person we know is a lesbian or a homosexual taking care of our patients. At least *I'm* not going to put up with them on *my* staff."

Kay, still blushing, stammered, "But—why?"

The intimidating brows rose another quarter of an inch.

"Why?" Thompson's face turned red, too, as she picked up a pencil off her walnut desk and said, "Your generation seems to accept that kind of thing. Mine doesn't and never will. Don't tell me you're one of those liberal-minded, so-called freethinkers who—"

"No, I'm not. My religious background— But what does one's sexual preference have to do with whether or not one is a good nurse?"

"It's a sickness. And if she's sick what's to keep Anita from . . . from handling a female patient in an . . . intimate way?"

Kay blushed even more, so much so that tears came to her eyes as she replied, "What's to keep any of us, male or female from doing that?" When Thompson didn't answer right away, Kay said, "We nurses had to take an oath, remember? To . . . to abstain from whatever is deleterious and mischievous, to devote ourselves to the welfare of those committed to our care."

"The Florence Nightingale Pledge also includes the oath to pass our lives in purity."

"And so we try. In spite of our human frailties, we try. Our personal integrity keeps us trying."

"Does a lesbian *have* integrity?"

"Why wouldn't she?"

Thompson leaned back in her chair quickly. Suddenly, Kay was aware that the nursing director's office was decorated in monochromatic shades of brown; walnut paneling, walnut desk, beige draperies at the wide windows, rust carpeting, rust-upholstered chairs; and on the wall behind her desk two prints hung done in various shades of brown depicting old English countrysides. "I had no idea you'd condone Anita after this," Thompson said. "I called you in here to ask you, as her closest supervisor, to confront her with this. I thought you were very . . . what do the teen-agers call it, straight? I thought you were very straight. 'Integrity plus,' your former nursing director stated in her letter of recommendation.''

"Mrs. Thompson, Anita's private life is no concern of mine—or yours either. If we started delving into the private lives of every nurse and making moral judgments, we'd probably discover that none of us are fit to care for the sick. Nor would anybody else be fit who belongs to the human race. I hate being called an angel of mercy. I'm just another human being trying to help another.''

Thompson closed her eyes tightly. "But Anita's behavior is precisely the kind that has given the nursing profession a black eye, Kay.'' Her eyes flew open. "You were quick to mention our pledge as nurses. Remember that pledge also includes the oath to elevate the standard of our profession. I'm sick of the dirty jokes about nurses. We're thought of as being a little coarser, a little dirtier somehow than any other professional. One step above the prostitute in some people's eyes. Yesterday my college-aged son received an envelope in the mail and on the envelope were the words, 'Explicit Sexual Material Inside.' I opened that envelope and it contained a catalog, a catalog of all sorts of sexual devices one could order by mail. And guess what one of those things was? A life-sized poster, an actual photograph of a girl on her hands and knees, naked except for a nurse's cap on her head.'' Thompson's almost nonexistent bosom was heaving with indignation. "I'm sick of that image and I'd think people like you would be, too.''

"I am. Truly I am.''

"Then you must agree that as long as nurses act the

part we'll be cast in the role."

"Yes, but—"

"Haven't you seen the stupid bumper stickers that say, 'Love a nurse PRN'? Or the coffee mugs that have a picture of a syringe printed on it with the words, 'Bottoms up'?"

Kay had seen those things and had been disgusted by them. But because Thompson was so vehement about it, Kay was beginning to find the whole thing amusing. She bit her lip.

"And what about the bumper stickers that say, 'Nurses do it better'?" Thompson demanded. "Any nurse who buys that and puts it on her automobile is lowering the standard of her profession and perpetuating the image that nurses are practically whores!"

Now Kay was *really* fighting to keep from smiling, not because the bumper stickers were funny—they weren't, they were disgusting—but because Thompson was overreacting, "losing her cool," as Russell would say. It was rather comforting to know that Thompson could lose her cool.

"I've heard that you nurses in ICU, and the trauma units especially, fight the image that nurses are the doctors' handmaidens. While we're on the subject, I was impressed with a statement you made at an in-service meeting once. You said you would fight for the right of an experienced nurse to make her own assessment and judgment concerning a patient's condition and to act accordingly. As a trauma nurse I guess you've done that."

"I guess I do it daily."

"You are fighting an image. Nurses have been cast in the role of doctors' handmaidens too long, and now that we are highly trained and educated professionals, we are still fighting the old image of the doctors' handmaiden. Right?"

Kay nodded. "Yes," she replied, deciding to go along with Thompson's question-and-answer game.

"Who casts us in the role of one step above a prostitute?"

"I guess the public does."

"Exactly. And who casts us in the role of doctors' dumb little handmaidens?"

"The doctors, but—"

"Precisely. And a few old-fashioned or brainless nurses. And who's going to change that image which we no longer deserve?"

"*We* must."

"We must. Excellently put. Almost poetic. But how?"

By now Kay was feeling like a fourth-grader being interrogated by her schoolteacher. "Well, as long as we think like doctors' handmaidens I guess we'll behave as handmaidens."

"But when we begin to think of ourselves as the physicians' colleagues and fellow professionals, we will behave as such, and our image can't help but change." Thompson smiled thinly. "Get my point?"

Kay touched her fingertips to her forehead. "I'm confused." As truly she was. The discussion had begun about Anita's suspected lesbianism and had ended questioning how the nursing profession was going to change its image.

"The point is, if one lesbian is allowed among us, people will find out. Then, suddenly, we are *all* suspect."

Kay was still confused. If one sheep was black, was it natural to suppose that all sheep were black? "Ah—I

152

don't understand."

Thompson leaned forward. "I really don't give a damn what other hospitals do about keeping the reputation of the nurses on their staff above suspicion. No, I *do* care, too, but I *mostly* care about my own. Are you in favor of leaving the matter about Anita as it is?"

Kay thought about that. Finally she said, "Yes."

"You honestly think we should just not say anything and let her go on as she is?"

"Anita's a terrific nurse. And if I, who work with her closely every day, have not suspected her of being a lesbian, then how is anyone else to suspect it?"

"But Abigail Jones said—"

"I know. And I'm still for leaving Anita alone."

Thompson regarded her silently a moment. "Yes, you're opinionated. Your former nursing director wrote me that, too. Very well, we'll leave Anita alone as you say. Unless her sexual preference becomes too apparent. But it's up to you, Kay, to keep a close eye on her."

Kay stood up. Almost nine o'clock in the morning and she was feeling very tired already. "What for?" she asked wearily. "What shall I watch for?"

Now it was Thompson's turn to be confused. "I . . . I don't know what for. Just . . . just be sure she continues to behave as if . . . as if she were *normal*."

As Kay left Thompson's office, she was thinking, Normal? What's normal? Anita was as sane as anybody and twice as smart as most. But Kay hadn't been honest with Thompson. She was shocked and hurt by this revelation about Anita. And somehow her respect for Anita had dropped to a new and unsuspected low.

There had been a pediatrician at Preston General whom the nurses had suspected of being gay. Gay? He was a grouch! But he must have been queer. She, like the others, had been ready to have him driven from the town, stripped of his M.D. Yet, she was *defending* Anita.

She was still confused and when she came face to face with that blithe spirit she had so staunchly defended, she couldn't look her in the eye. She had just sat down at the nurses' desk and pulled the intake and output records in front of her when Anita came to her and said, "While you were gone, Pasternak came in and said Leola's husband wanted to see her. I told him to tell Parkman that we absolutely do not permit visitors in TRU. Kay, I know Parkman is going to find out that we occasionally screen off rooms and let patients see their families. Think we should call Dr. Kreel?"

Not looking at Anita, Kay said, "I'll call him," and drew the telephone toward her.

Anita stood there and Kay wished she'd go away. "Also, Barney's really depressed," Anita went on. "Naturally he keeps cracking jokes almost like they're a reflex, but he's depressed, and I don't like his vitals."

Kay looked up at her quickly. "Why?"

"His BP is low, for one thing. Pulse is low. Temp is low."

Kay looked at Barney's blip on the cardiac monitor; pulse rate was sixty.

"It's as if he's just . . . just willing himself to die. As if he were just slowing down, running down like a"—Anita pressed her lips together, her eyes moistened—"like a damned clock."

Impossible. Still . . . "After I call Dr. Kreel, I'll come see him. Meanwhile, Anita—"

She nodded. "I know. I'll start checking his vitals every thirty minutes."

154

Dr. Kreel at first said, "Hell no, Parkman's not going to get in there and see his wife!" Then after Kay explained to him that Parkman was bothering the security guard repeatedly with requests to see her, Kreel relented. "Well, all right. But ask her first if she *wants* to see the son of a bitch. And if she does, then screen the other rooms as usual. Make sure he doesn't have a cold or some damned thing, tell Pasternak to stand just outside the unit door. And watch them, Carlton, at a discreet distance—but not *too* discreet, and then get the son of a bitch out of there."

To everybody's surprise, Loela *did* want to see her husband. So Kay and Anita screened a path from the TRU door to Leola's room. When Parkman came in, it was the first time Kay had seen him up close. He wasn't a big man—only tall, thin, sinewy, with a hard, tight, muscular body like that of a ballet dancer. He would have been handsome if it hadn't been that his entire demeanor was so intense, that the pupils of his eyes were enlarged giving him the appearance of being frightened, and that he was so obviously nervous, like a cautious cat.

As Kay explained to him the visitors' rules, he nodded repeatedly, impatiently, clenching and unclenching his fists. Then when she told him he could go in to see Leola, he tiptoed in, actually tiptoed in. *Nobody's going to believe that*, Kay thought.

She could not hear everything Parkman said to Leola. She watched out of the corner of her eyes while she pretended to work on doctors' orders which Drs. Cash and Spade had left on the desk while she was in Thompson's office. Parkman gestured wildly, glanced frequently at the nurses' station, and Kay heard the words, "hospital," "doctors," "hurt," and "stupid."

155

Then, abruptly he left Leola's room and came to stand at the desk. Kay looked up slowly.

"My wife," Parkman began, "how do I go about getting her out of here?"

Kay swallowed because Parkman scared her. "Dr. Kreel has to write an order to—"

He shook his head violently. "No, I mean out of the hospital?"

Kay moistened her lips. "Dr. Kreel still has to release her. And it'll be several weeks before he can do that."

Parkman turned his head abruptly and looked toward Leola's room.

Kay went on, "Leola is in serious condition—"

Parkman looked at her so quickly it caused her to pause. His eyes bored into hers.

"Sh-she needs close medical supervision and *will* for a long time," Kay said.

Parkman stared at her. "I'll just bet!"

"She does. Her colon . . . her large intestine was perforated, you know, and she—"

"When?"

Kay, seeing his tight mouth, his viable temper, his keen, sharp, intense eyes upon her, realized for the first time how much fear Leola must have felt of this man. "When?"

"When will she be let out of this unit?" he demanded.

"She will be in here for another week, maybe two."

He stared at her again. Then his eyes quickly went to the telephone on the desk, to the door, the narcotics cabinet, the other rooms, and back to Kay, and a smile grew on his lips. "Will she?"

Kay stared after him as he turned suddenly and left the unit. Her trembling hand went to cover her face. She threw down her pen, stood up, and went to Leola. Leola was sitting up in the bed throwing her sheet aside. Hailey went in behind Kay, knowing Parkman had left. "Now what are you up to Leola?" Hailey demanded cheerfully.

Leola's brown eyes went to Kay's face. "He'll get me out, you know. So why don't I just leave and save you nurses any more trouble?"

"You lie back, honey. Unless you just want to sit in your chair for a while," Hailey said.

"No." Leola looked at Kay again. Then her eyes widened. "He *does* hit me," she said.

Fear, so much fear in Leola's face, fear and hopelessness and growing panic.

"I know," Kay said helping Leola lie back. She fluffed the pillow behind her head.

"He hits with his fists, you know," Leola went on. "He hits the soft places—my breasts mostly, and my stomach." Her voice was trembling, loud, and her words began to tumble out hysterically, as if she were anxious to get rid of them. "When he's sober he only threatens; when he's drunk he hits—no, no, no, he hits sober or drunk; why am I lying?"

"Leola, why?" Kay demanded.

"Once I burned the roast," Leola cried frantically. "Once I was on the telephone too long when he tried to phone me. Once he said I laughed when he accused me of not loving him. Sometimes, it's because I can't . . . I can't enjoy . . . sex."

Kay was aware that Jan had come into the room now. Kay said, "But why haven't you told somebody, Leola? Why haven't you run away?"

"Who? Where? I have no family. Both my parents have died in the past six years. And the kids—I can't

157

leave them like that." She laughed hysterically. "Do you know that if I ran out of the house, just left, Carl could divorce me and get custody of my children on the grounds that I had abandoned them?"

"No!" Hailey said shaking her head vehemently.

"Yes. It's true. Ask a lawyer. You'll see. It happened to my neighbor. It's the courts!"

The nurses knew that what Leola was saying was true; they had learned that from the social worker in the in-service course on battered women.

Leola raised both trembling hands toward Kay. "It's true. If a woman runs away even to save her life and the husband files for a divorce, the courts won't give her custody of the children. I know. I know because I sat in the courtroom with my neighbor and I heard and saw it happen. Ask, Kay. Ask any woman who's tried it. The courts will give him the children even though he's emotionally sick. Ask, ask, ask," Leola sobbed and all her defenses and self-control dissolved while the nurses stared in horror and anger.

Weakly, Kay said, "There are places to go, Leola."

"There must be. God help me, there must be."

Kay was sure Leola's voice had carried to the other rooms, but she had not quieted her because she needed this catharsis. Kay looked at Hailey who was speechless and wide-eyed. "Call Dr. Kreel."

Hailey would know that Kay meant for her to tell Kreel what had happened.

When Leola's sobs subsided Kay said, "There are centers for battered women in almost every town. In fact, our city was among the first to establish a center for battered women, Leola, and we have several now. You can go to one of them with your kids. They'll protect you

158

and your children, get you a job—"

"He'd kill me."

"He won't find you."

"He'd find me. And when he did, he'd kill me."

"He may anyway if you stay with him. God knows he almost did."

"But you don't understand."

"I do, believe me," Kay said.

"No, you don't," Leola said. "You see, Kay, I love him."

Kay released Leola's arm and backed away. "How? How could you?"

"I don't know. I only know I want my marriage to work. I want to live with him. But I'm afraid of him."

Kay thought wildly, What this damned unit needs is a permanent psychiatrist; a psychiatrist for Barney because of his denial, for Harvey because of his depression, for Leola because she's crazy, and for the nurses who have to care for them all.

Leola looked up at Kay. "You think I'm crazy?"

Kay, whose own face was flushed with rage, shrugged.

"Yes, I've lost some of your regard for me, just when I was gaining, I lost."

"No."

"Oh yes. Because people don't understand that my love for a man doesn't wax or wane with every whim of his or mine. He loves me, too, believe it or not."

"I don't believe it. He needs psychiatric help."

"I know that, but he won't go. Suggest that to him and he'll beat *you* up."

Kay thought, He'll have to catch me first.

There was a long silence: the nurses and the patient were caught in a vacuum of emotion the cause of which none of them shared, though all shared the dilemma of being a woman in a man's world.

Hailey came into the room with an injection which Dr. Kreel had ordered to calm Leola. Kay knew what he had probably said: "All she needs is to get all worked up and get to vomiting or something to tear things loose. I should have obeyed my own instinct, stuck to my guns, and let Pasternak handle the situation if it got out of hand. Give her Valium 10 milligrams IV." Kay leaned against the wall while Hailey said, "I've got a shot, Leola to help calm you. Do you want it?"

Leola nodded. "Please."

"Turn over then, so I can get to your bottom. That's it. And Dr. Kreel is going to ask a new doctor to come in to see you." She gave Kay a look. Kay knew the doctor would be Dr. Spade, the psychiatrist, who had already reviewed Barney's and Harvey's cases and was planning to begin consultation with them in the morning. Spade was the one Dr. Kreel always brought in on consultation for trauma patients, who needed help in coping with their severe injuries and disabilities.

Leola winced as the needle went home. "A psychiatrist, I'm sure," she said.

Kay wasn't sure how Dr. Spade could help Leola— except that she needed to be assured she didn't deserve to be beaten. She needed help to build her self-esteem. Then, she'd need courage to change her life, to leave Parkman if necessary. And Kay had no doubt that it would be necessary.

Moments later, still shaken from the ordeal in Leola's room, Kay was hanging an IV for Hailey in Harvey's room. "I see your shadow, Kay. I heard the ruckus in the other room. Kind of makes you want to wade in and start beating up on the husband, doesn't it?"

Adjusting the drip rate, Kay said, "Sorry if it disturbed you, Harvey."

"Well, we a-lll got problems."

"Yes, we do."

"Even you?"

"I have you for a patient, don't I?"

"Now the nurse is a comic."

"I'm really not."

"No, you're a lousy comic, Kay. But then you've got a lousy job. Carrying bedpans, getting blood on your hands, handling pus, smelling every kind of odor there is."

"But I never receive rejection slips, Harvey."

He grimaced. "You really know how to put a guy down, don't you?"

"If it's necessary."

"Yeah, I'll bet you're a tall, statuesque blonde with blue eyes, a creamy complexion, and a Venus de Milo figure."

Kay bit her lip.

"Naw. The Venus de Milo's figure is too fat, and her— Well, I can tell by your shadow you aren't all that tall, but you're slender. The de Milo thing was part of my vivid imagination. But beware. People with vivid imaginations can figure out ways to do themselves in, even though they're flat on their backs in bed with no less than two holes in their heads."

"Not in here."

"Yes. Suppose I just rip out this IV?"

"Won't do anything but bleed a little where the needle went in."

"Yeah? O.K., I'll sneak somebody's scissors and cut

161

the IV line. Won't air get sucked into the tube, go into my veins and to my heart? I read that in a book."

"It won't work. Air won't go into you. Think about it, Harvey. Your heart will pump blood *out* of the tubing in your arm instead of air going in. You're not a vacuum inside, you know."

He fell silent, then said, "I can't scare you even a little bit?"

"No. You're being watched too closely, my friend."

He almost smiled. "Afraid I'll do what I threaten, eh?"

"No. We watch all our patients closely."

"But I'll find a way. I wouldn't tell just everybody this, because— Well, anyway, I'll find a way."

"Why?"

"The agony. In my brain."

"Still needing a pain shot?"

"I mean the agony there before I ever shot the hole in my sombrero. The agony of being unable to . . . to fulfill my very simple and sane ambition."

"Which is?"

"To write. To write something beautiful . . . a lovely play . . . maybe a book of poetry. Did you know I have forty-two rejection slips for my poetry?"

"I thought you used those slips for something else."

"Do you know I'm a walking reject? I was an orphan who was never adopted, a reject as a human being."

"But you can't give up, Harvey. I wish you'd write us some of your poetry."

He smiled slowly, almost wickedly. "Nice try, Ms. Psychiatrist. But it won't work," he said. "You forgot, Kay. I am *blind*."

Mr. McPherson's pulse rate was rapid, his skin was

cool but not clammy, and Jan had told Kay that his blood pressure had begun to decrease. It was nearly three o'clock and time for report, but Kay called Dr. Markowitz, the orthopedic surgeon, about Mr. McPhersons' vital signs. Dr. Markowitz gave her an order for a vasopressor to increase the blood pressure and Kay had just injected it into his bag of D5W.

"Are you feeling O.K., Mr. McPherson?" she asked.

". . . Don't know," he said slowly.

"You are a good patient, Mr. McPherson," she told him affectionately. She had always had a soft spot in her heart for the elderly patients, those who knew their time on earth was running out and yet did not panic or fight or worry as one might think they'd do in the face of eternity. She held his arm a moment, letting him know somebody cared. She knew Jan talked to him and held his hand often to let him know somebody was there trying to help. Because he might be afraid, after all. Or as he kept saying, maybe he really *didn't* know.

Sometime during the night, little old Mr. McPherson crashed. CPR was of no avail. The autopsy report revealed that a fat embolism had traveled from one of his fractures to a pulmonary vessel in his lung and had lodged there. Whether or not the old fellow ever knew he was in the hospital or even that he had broken several bones, no one would ever know.

Kay called CCU daily to check on Ike Salter, ashamed that she had not visited him, knowing he'd wonder why. So, on the third day after his admission to St. Luke's, during her lunch break, she walked through the corridor and took the elevator to the third floor. Beasley, charge nurse in CCU, let her in to see Ike. When she walked into his room it seemed that time had stood still for three years; for Ike, with the head of his bed rolled up all the way, looked up from the newspaper he was reading, whipped off his glasses as he had done so many times three years ago, and said, "Kitten! Come in here and sit down."

She had to smile. "Hi. You look chipper."

"I'm always chipper." He tapped the pacemaker taped to his arm. "Getting recharged again. But Doc Pugh says they're going to have to put in a permanent pacemaker soon."

Ike had not aged. The deeply tanned face was the same, his gray hair no grayer, the lines in his face no deeper.

"How's married life?" Kay asked.

"Beautiful. I was a bachelor too long. Didn't know what I was missing. I come home in the evenin' and Maydy has my favorite meal on, the house all fancied up." His face went solemn. "Cass says you're married."

She nodded.

Ike scratched his chin. "Well, I was hopin' . . . Ah, Kitten, you know what I was hopin'. Cass, he hasn't remarried and I bet you can guess why. But maybe it's not proper for me to talk about it."

"It's not, Ike. Because I *am* married—very, and happily."

He nodded. "I'm glad for you, but not for Cass. He keeps busy, though, makin' money, but mostly politickin'. Ran for county commissioner; got that. Now he's going to run for a seat in the statehouse and he'll probably get that, too."

"I didn't know."

"You will. He was late making the decision, but he'll make it. Wait and see. He's popular with every landowner in Texas—on both tickets. And as for big business, he knows— But you didn't come here to talk politics. Just watch the newspapers from now on, Kitten. Now!" Ike pushed the overbed table away. "Tell me about yourself—how you're doing; what you're doin'."

So Kay spent a pleasant ten minutes with Ike and went back to TRU almost wishing she were still working in ICU. Almost.

On her way back, she decided it was easy to see why laypersons got ICU and CCU mixed up. In smaller hospitals the critically ill trauma patients, heart patients, and critical surgical patients were combined in ICU. The larger the hospital, the more diversified the units were. St. Luke's was a one thousand-bed hospital and boasted a surgical ICU for critical surgery patients, a medical ICU for critically ill patients on respirators or needing special care, a cardiac care unit for heart patients—unique with its carpeted floors and separate private rooms built for ultimate quiet—and the Trauma Recovery unit. Some hospitals had respiratory and neurological ICUs as well.

Kay felt that each unit had its own advantages and disadvantages as a place in which to work as a nurse. ICU and Trauma Recovery were busier. As a nurse you had more patients to ambulate, more treatments to give, people on respirators, more medications. You were busy constantly; most of the time you were *too* busy. You rushed from the time you arrived till you left for home.

In CCU there were many hours of absolute quiet. You gave a few routine meds. And your eyes never, never left the monitor screens. You sat a lot, you got bored. Then suddenly—chaos; two patients, maybe even three could go bad at the same time. Mr. X's BP could suddenly drop out, while Mrs. Y develops crushing chest pain, and Mr.

Z crashes. CPR would be initiated, maybe two at once. There would be days when two patients would hover between life and death and you felt as though you were sitting on a powder keg that could blow up at any moment; and there were days when everybody was quiet and slept and mended and got transferred out to the floor, a promotion up the ladder of recovery.

Kay wouldn't trade nursing for any profession on earth. Critical care was the most rewarding of all the areas of nursing to her. There you frequently saved a life, often single-handedly. Ego problem, Syd had said. He was right. She'd never felt more necessary in her entire life than she did at the present time. But . . .

You could tell yourself one simple Valium had never hurt anybody. And it probably hadn't, unless it was the beginning of a long line of tranquilizers and sleeping pills. But it was the idea of having to take one—or a half of one—in order to go to sleep at night that bothered her. She had started that because she was aware she was worrying too much about things: she cried when Mr. McPherson died, she was caught up too much in Leola Parkman's problems, she worried about whether the other TRU nurses would watch Harvey Chunn close enough, whether Barney was going into a depression he couldn't shake. She was angry with Dr. Kreel for not calling in a psychiatrist for Barney, she was impatient with Dr. Worley when he yelled that he hurt. She was afraid of what Leola's husband would do. Too much worry, fear, depressing situations. Syd was right again. She was experiencing what the nursing journals called, "burnout." She knew a human being had just so much emotional, mental and physical energy. If a person's

166

work was too intense or if that person had been in it too long and didn't take measures to combat the stress effect, the result was burnout. The attrition rate for ICU was two years. Kay had spent four. The attrition rate at St. Luke's for nurses in TRU was nine months. She'd spent twenty-four.

When you began to wake up in the middle of the night in a cold sweat wondering if you had forgotten to give somebody his two o'clock medication, you lost even more sleep. You drank coffee all day to stay awake. And you either drank that glass of wine before you went to bed, or you took a half of a Valium. Most of the time one or the other would work. Sometimes it took both to work. Sometimes nothing worked.

You also got short of patience with your family, your patients, the doctors, even the weather. Your sex life was almost nil. You could talk of nothing but TRU and its patients; you longed for a day off and were miserable when it came and you ended up calling the unit to check on Barney or Harvey—everybody.

And you're always tired. Laughter doesn't come easy anymore. You jump when somebody drops something. Where you used to find fulfillment in comforting a patient, you discover it's just part of the routine.

And you've become emotionally flat—as flat as the streets on which you drive every day, every week, every month.

Syd had tried to take her out, to take her to a movie or to dinner. But she always came up with a reason not to go: she was too tired or wasn't in the mood; she wouldn't go to a movie because there was nothing she wanted to see. To the opera or a play? She didn't have anything appropriate to wear; everything she had was out of style, out of season. . . .

"I love you, Kay," he would say, studying her face with his dark, intense eyes.

"I love you, too," she would answer. But not with much feeling.

Still, she had the stamina of a bull. She knew that. So she knew she'd keep pushing on. Quit like Syd had suggested? Take a leave of absence? And leave Barney to crack his most desperate jokes to whom? And Harvey to threaten whom? Leola to rely on whom? Who would help Ursala fight for Harrison's right to live? Or be there to fight for Anita's job? Say good-by to Ike forever? How does one choose which patients to walk out on in the middle of their recovery?

You're not indispensable, Kay, Syd had said.

But wasn't she?

CHAPTER IX

"What you perfessers need is a good long stint in the army, *rrrr*. They'd make you shave off your whiskers, Harry. And they'd feed *you* lots of mashed potatoes and gravy, Sydney. Put some meat on your bones, *rrrrrrr*," Billy Roy Ballew said, and then he began his slow, measured, wheezy, rattling, "Haw . . . haw . . . haw . . . haw. . . ." He sounded like an old steam locomotive starting up, except it that it never gathered momentum.

Billy Roy was truly a researcher's dream. Syd and Harry were more than glad to provide him with Styrofoam cups to spit his tobacco juice into during their sessions. They didn't mind when he occasionally forgot and scratched his privates, or broke wind when he laughed. They laughed when he did. They didn't understand half his jokes and the other half weren't funny. But they laughed anyway, because Billy Roy was a walking memory bank.

During his first hypnotic trance, Billy Roy went back through his childhood, and much to the professors' delight, back to the moment of his own birth. He had agonized almost stoically through the entire birth trauma, only in reverse. He had begun with the twisting of his body and ended curled up on the floor in fetal position. There was nothing spectacular about that particular feat of memory, because others had experienced it before during hypnotic trances. But this was the first time that Harry had been able to elicit the birth-trauma memory from a subject.

During Ballew's second session, they began with him already in the fetal position and attempted to draw his memory back beyond his embryonic state. When Harry urged him to go back, back in time, Billy Roy lay sprawled upon the floor as if dead for so many minutes that he scared both Harry and Syd. For a period of about eleven minutes Ballew lay unmoving, and Harry was about to snap him out of his trance, when Ballew sat up. Simultaneously, the hair on Syd's head stood up because Ballew's cheeks had become sunken and he had a peculiar look on his face. It was then that Ballew began speaking in a foreign tongue without the *rrrrr* on the end of every sentence. Syd looked at Harry. Both recognized that the language Billy Roy was speaking was French. Luckily, Harry could speak a little French and understood that Ballew had asked if the ship had docked at the port of Galveston yet. Harry asked Billy Roy his name, to which he promptly replied, "M. Louis Velours."

During that same session, Monsieur Velours described the countryside around Moulins, France—in detail. Harry had just asked Monsieur Velours if he knew a countryman by the name of Ballew, when Velours' face twisted in distaste and Billy Roy started vomiting on the floor and Harry had to bring him up out of the trance. When Billy Roy woke up and saw his own emesis on the front of his shirt, it scared him. The session, having lasted only about twenty minutes, had exhausted both Ballew and Harry.

After Ballew had wiped his mouth and shirt front with a handkerchief, Harry asked him who Louis Velours was. Ballew shook his head. "Hell, I don't know. Why?"

"Have you ever been to France?" Syd asked.

They were hoping he hadn't, but Ballew said, "Yeah. When I was about twelve, me an my pa went over after my ma passed away, *rrrr.*"

"Where in France did you go?"

"Versailles, Paris, Moulins. That's where Pa's grandfather came from—Moulins, *rrrrrr.*"

Syd and Harry had exchanged delighted glances. Ah, both thought, ancestral memory. Or was Ballew only describing what he himself had seen? "Your father's name was Ballew?" Harry asked.

Grouchy because he wasn't feeling well, Ballew said, "Yeah. What d'ya think I am, a bastard?"

"Your mother's people came from France?" Syd asked hoping Velours was his mother's name.

"Ma was English. And all her people were English. Singleton was her maiden name, *rrrrr.*" Ballew ducked his head, raised it, and said, "Look fellers, I know you're trying to hep me, but I'm sick. Don't know why. Can we call it quits fer tonight? *Rrrrrrr.*"

So Syd and Harry had to let Ballew go, but they made an appointment for two days later for a third session. Meantime, they compiled their data, and while Ballew's expression and appearance were clear in his mind, Syd wrote it all down. If Ballew's paternal grandparents were Ballews and his maternal grandparents were Singletons, who was Louis Velours? Did Ballew's memory go back *beyond* his paternal grandparents?

Days later Syd was to reflect with amazement that while Harry and he had exulted over their success with Ballew, it never once had occurred to them to be awed by it; eliciting from someone, hypnotized or not, a prebirth memory was extremely rare and a phenomenon that very few researchers had been able to witness. The fact that Syd believed in ancestral memory so much himself seemed to make the phenomenon of William Royce Ballew a logical one.

They should have put him on ice, locked him up in a luxury hotel somewhere, put him under national security. Instead, they let a man worth his weight in gold, worth more to science than a thousand years of research into the inner space of man, go free to walk the streets and be subject to the same hazards to life and limb as the most worthless bum on skid row.

But now in the third session, Ballew had gotten over his stomach upset and was in good spirits. It bothered him that Harry wore a beard and wasn't ashamed of it, and that Syd wasn't sun-tanned, and that neither of them had muscles worth a marshal's belch. But he did admit that Harry was friendly, Syd was handsome, and both were pretty durned smart.

Now Harry, with his soft voice that had very little inflection to it, talked Ballew into a hypnotic trance. Harry's voice, soothing enough to put Syd to sleep also if he hadn't concentrated upon not listening, soon had Billy Roy snoring loudly as tobacco juice oozed wetly from the corners of his mouth.

Syd pressed the button on the recorder, the *Record* light came on, and he began to record the third hypnotic session of William Royce Ballew.

St. Luke's General Hospital

DOCTORS' PROGRESS NOTES

Patient   *Leola Joy Parkman*
Hosp. No.   *05621*   *Ward*   *TRU*

June 15—Behavior organization in this patient points to potential explosive excitement. Agitated depression obvious. Unwilling to cooperate this session; will try new approach tomorrow.

                                        Andrew Spade, M.D.

June 16—Attempts to encourage verbalization of anxieties unsuccessful. Will try again tomorrow.

                                        Andrew Spade, M.D.

June 17—Obviously suppressed hostility has evolved to sense of guilt, possibly relative to some unconscious sexually related fear. The usual pattern of fear of expressing hostility is threat to her security. Aggressiveness turned inward upon herself. Still uncooperative.

                                        Andrew Spade, M.D.

June 18—All attempts to communicate with this pt. unsuccessful, Dr. Kreel. I suggest you call Dr. Williams or other female psychiatrist in on this case. Thanks for consult, nevertheless.

                                        Andrew Spade, M.D.

St. Luke's General Hospital

DOCTORS' PROGRESS NOTES

Patient   Barnard E. Werger
Hosp. No.   04340   *Ward*   TRU

June 15—*Pt. suffers denial in extreme, attempts to avoid
reality of his paralysis and possible impotence.
Have attempted to impress upon him importance
of accepting his handicaps. Pt. jokes in response—denial in the extreme.*

Andrew Spade, M.D.

June 16—*Suggest transfer of this pt. from TRU as soon as
possible before denial results in complete loss of
contact with reality. In my opinion pt. is capable
of adjusting normally and a transfer to the ward
would facilitate adjustment. Will withdraw from
consult, Dr. Kreel, unless needed further.*

Andrew Spade, M.D.

St. Luke's General Hospital

DOCTORS' PROGRESS NOTES

Patient   Harvey Piedmont Chunn
Hosp. No.   06784   *Ward*   TRU

June 15—*This pt. is suffering severe retarded depression.
Hostilities probably stemming from long-standing
sexual conflicts, resulting in loss of self-esteem
which recent monetary reversals and anxiety-*

producing rejections have aggravated. Subject to your approval as amenable with head trauma, Dr. Cash, I recommend Elavil 25 mg p.o., t.i.d. Advising nurses to take extreme caution in keeping potentially lethal instruments from this pt.'s reach. This pt. requires <u>close supervision</u>.

Andrew Spade, M.D.

June 16—D.C.'d Elavil order as per your advice, Dr. Cash. Pt. suffers severe neurosis and delusional self-deprecation. Hostile and uncooperative. This pt. has history of maladjustment to new situations and should have as much TLC and psychiatric support as possible. Will stay on case.

Andrew Spade, M.D.

June 17—Little progress. Pt. hostile, uncooperative.

Andrew Spade, M.D.

June 18—Pt. hostile. Digressed during this session to giving me an <u>obscene gesture</u>. Will remain on case, nevertheless.

Andrew Spade, M.D.

"You shouldn't have done that, Harvey."

"Are you my conscience, Kay? The creep's a shrink. I hate shrinks. He asks these questions of me like I'm a psycho. I'm not a psycho. Did you hear what he asked? He asked if I had ever had any homosexual experiences. I told him, Hell, no. He asked me to reconsider my answer. I told him I didn't need to reconsider my answer; that it was the truth. He told me to reconsider the question carefully and then reply again. So I gave him the finger."

Kay bit her lip to keep from smiling. Dr. Spade was a short, cocky, very handsome man with a blond mustache, wavy blond hair, and an ego proportionately as large as the list of his female conquests, or so the hospital grapevine claimed. He thought every woman, including all the nursing staff, was secretly in love with him, Ginger from the eleven to seven shift claimed. As she said that day in report, "He has a complex. It's spelled S-E-X."

Spade had absolutely no success with Leola. He had pronounced Barney normal and progressing, although all the nurses in TRU disagreed, knowing that Barney was going downhill, even losing weight and strength. But Spade was delighted with Harvey's hostility. The nurses decided that Leola's rejection of Spade had created inner conflicts within his ego with which he was unable to cope, so he gave up her case. Barney was too clever and Spade couldn't adjust to such an abundant sense of humor. But Harvey? Ah, there was a pathological neurosis he could sink his psychiatric teeth into.

"Everybody wants to rescue me," Harvey said now turning his near-sightless eyes toward Kay. "I don't want to be rescued. What's wrong with wanting to die? The ancient Greeks were allowed to take their own lives, a thing which was considered responsible and noble. If I'm miserable and there's no hope for me, why can't I relieve my own misery, to seek oblivion?" He hit the side rail with his fist. "You tell Cash if that shrink comes in here again I'll do more than give him the finger. I never, never had homosexual tendencies; not even as an adolescent. Brought up in a dorm of boys in an orphanage and not once, not *once* did I have a homosexual experience. I'm pretty proud of that record. Then some shrink comes along and suggests—*accuses*—"

"You're actually proud of yourself for something, Harvey?"

He thought a moment, said, "I guess I am." He pondered a little more. "Really got something to be proud of, haven't I? That sexually I'm normal? That I like girls? Now ain't that nice? Pat me on the head, Mamma, I've been a good boy. Oh, get out of here, Kay." His hands went to his head, his teeth clenched, and Kay left the room wondering if Dr. Spade hadn't done more harm than good that day.

What Leola wouldn't tell Dr. Spade, she would tell Kay. Kay was the only nurse with whom she talked about it at any length. The others understood why, that Kay's second marriage seemed happy and successful, and Leola was trying to discover the ingredients of it. Leola asked more questions of Kay than Kay did of Leola.

In report that day, Leola's problems were discussed in depth. Abigail Jones, day-shift supervisor for the critical-care units, sat in on the report because among the nursing staff, Leola's problem had become theirs. They stood in the TRU kitchen discussing the fact that until only recently society believed that women's "place" was in the home. Even the nursing profession was barely eighty years old. In hospitals at the turn of the century, "trained nurses" were just beginning to be employed. And men, until recently, were considered the supreme authority in the home and in business. Even the clergy believed that if a woman was whipped by her husband, it was not a matter of concern for the churches. Even now, in many communities, violent marriages were still considered a personal matter. A decade earlier battered children began showing up in emergency rooms and suddenly battered children became a community concern. Then, with the awakening of professional pride and equality awareness in women, the battered women who showed up in emergency rooms became a concern that also spread to the community. But still there were many cities and towns with no facilities to care for abused women.

At St. Luke's a battered woman sent a prairie fire of rage through the nursing staff, and that's why Thompson had brought in the social worker from the Battered Woman's Shelter to conduct an in-service course on the subject in April. That's why TRU's nursing staff spent twenty minutes of report today discussing Leola and how they could help her.

"First," the social worker had told them in the seminar, "the battered woman must *recognize* that she has been beaten. She tends to deny it to others and even to herself."

Well, Leola had finally admitted that Parkman had beaten her numerous times.

"She often clings to the abusive husband because of guilt, dependency, or fear that she will lose her children," the social worker had said.

That was Leola too. She was bogged down in guilt because she felt responsible for the death of her first husband. Dr. Spade never had gotten her to admit that, but she had offered this information willingly to Kay.

"What we as nurses have to do next is to make her realize she owes that jackass husband nothing," Ginger said.

"She claims she's in love with him," Hailey offered.

Abby Jones looked at Kay. "Is that right?" Jones was fiftyish and freckled with a curly hairdo dyed red. Hailey said when Jones was angry, her hazel eyes could make a

178

viper turn tail and squiggle away.

Kay answered, "I'm afraid so. But I wonder if it's love or—maybe dependency and maybe gratitude that he married her and gave her children."

"One thing. Before she leaves this unit," Jones said, "you must impress on her the fact that there are shelters in this city for her and her children. If she does decide to go back to the husband after leaving the hospital, sometime in the future she'll have to run for her life and she'll know where to go, or at least who to call for help. Locations of shelters are kept secret. She'll *have* to call."

Later Jones called the welfare agency and found the number of the shelter nearest Leola's home, and Kay gave it to Leola that morning, explaining to her what it was and that if she couldn't get to the shelter, to tell them and someone from the shelter would pick her and her children up and carry them to the center.

"You realize that I have no place to keep this telephone number, don't you?"

"What do you mean?" Kay asked.

"I have no place to hide this. If he finds it, he'll call and find out what the number is. I can't hide it because he goes through all my things."

"Put it in your underwear drawer."

Leola laughed bitterly. "That's the worst place—that and the dirty-clothes hamper." As Kay felt her own face reddening, Leola told how Parkman went through the clothes hamper for signs of seminal fluid on her panties as evidence of her infidelity to him while he was at work. Leola Parkman sat in her bedside chair, calmly telling the story as if she were telling about her latest birthday party.

It was ten o'clock in the morning and Kay suddenly went a little mad. She did not excuse herself as she flew out of Leola's room into the kitchenette where Anita was pouring herself a cup of coffee. "Take over," Kay commanded and left the kitchen without any explanation. She grabbed up her lab coat from the back of the desk chair at the nurses' station, rushed through the TRU door, and out into the corridor. She ran past Pasternak sitting with his chair tilted against the wall eating a donut, ran blindly down the corridor, up the stairs, up two flights to the fourth floor and the administrative offices. She brushed past the receptionist and burst into Thompson's office.

Thompson, sitting behind her desk, looked up, astonished.

"I quit!"

Thompson pushed her glasses up on her nose. "I beg your pardon?"

"I quit. I can't stand it, Ms. Thompson!"

Thompson was an old veteran of nursing and she'd seen this reaction many times in her career as nursing administrator. It happened—oh, perhaps once a week—that a nurse burst into her office and announced she wanted to quit her job. There was a variety of things that usually caused this: a doctor yelling at the nurse, a doctor threatening a nurse, somebody with less experience getting a larger raise, the charge nurse scheduling her three weekends in a row, or seventeen days straight. Or a doctor having thrown something at the nurse—

"I've had it! I'm sick of nursing! I've seen everything! I'm tired, and I want to resign!" Kay was flushed and trembling and perspiring.

"Sit down, Kay."

Kay sat down. "When I have to control myself to keep from killing somebody, then I should quit before I *do*."

"Who yelled at you?"

"Nobody."

"O.K. Tell me about it."

"To go through her underpants, and you can't even have enough privacy to keep a telephone number and you just sit there and tell it with your hands folded—"

"Whoa. Back up. Take a deep breath, Kay, and start all over again."

Kay was normally a calm, intelligent individual, with a tendency toward being sentimental perhaps, but also possessing a ready sense of humor. All of that had vanished. Her present state had been coming on for a year. She took a deep breath and her face, which had been flushed, turned suddenly pale.

"You know about Leola Parkman?"

"Yes."

In a rush, but stammering and halting, Kay told Thompson what had just transpired that day: of report that morning, of her giving Leola the telephone number of the shelter, of what Leola said about her husband going through the clothes hamper.

Even Thompson had to lower her face into her hand and breathe, "Dear God!" But she lifted it promptly and said to Kay, "But we knew the situation was something like that, didn't we?"

"But this is too much!"

Thompson studied her a moment. "Do you feel you're overreacting to this, Kay?"

Kay was trying to hold back the flood of tears and sobs that was welling up inside. "Yes, I am. And I've been overreacting for a year now. Worse the last two months." Then it happened. Months, perhaps years of frustration, tension, worry, heartache, feelings that everything was

181

unfair and what good was it to live if all there was in the end was dying, poured forth in sobs, tears, running nose; and after a moment, ashamed and feeling degraded, she raised her face out of her hands. "I'm sorry. Do you think I'm going crazy?"

Thompson laughed gently. "No. Do you see that box of Kleenex on my desk here?"

Kay nodded.

"I keep it there always, because somebody is in here every day who needs one. Sometimes I'll have as many as three a day in here who need one. Go ahead. Take a tissue or two. However many it takes. I replace that box about once a week. More often than that during the Christmas holidays. Take some."

Kay did, blotted her hot face, wiped her nose, sniffed, took a deep breath.

"Now," Thompson said, "do you still want to resign?"

Kay said, "I don't know." Then, emphatically, "Yes, I do!"

The nursing director tapped her manicured nails on the desk top. Nurses who worked with patients were asked not to wear anything but clear nail polish at St. Luke's. Thompson's nail polish was pink. "What would you think if I rotated you to say—the surgical floor?"

Kay said, "I hate floor duty."

"Why?"

"The routine. I like the routine to be condensed. All that telephone ringing and rushing around and desk work nurses do on the floors isn't for me."

"You like total patient care better?"

"That's why I like ICU and CCU. I've worked in both."

"Your application says you worked in labor and delivery and on an OB floor too. My, you could write a

182

book based on your experiences, I'll wager."

"It's occurred to me before," Kay said smiling through her tears.

"You'd be bored in CCU after TRU, wouldn't you? Or would you like to try it there awhile? Or how about labor and delivery?"

How about the moon, Thompson? Kay thought. Anything to keep me here. "For how long?"

"Six weeks or so, I'd say. Then, I'll wager you'll be ready to go back to Trauma Recovery."

Kay shook her head. She didn't know why; she just shook her head.

Thompson, realizing that she was losing ground, thought a moment. "I'll tell you what, Kay, take three days off starting tomorrow. Then come back and give me two weeks to try to find somebody to work in TRU. You can't leave the unit now. Who would replace you?"

"Anita Wilson."

Thompson smiled wryly. "I'm sure with what Abby Jones knows, she and Anita would get along just fine. Like two fighting co— like two fighting roosters. And who would replace Anita?"

"I'd say that's your problem. I'm sorry."

Thompson's mouth tightened. "Let me ask you this favor; take three days off. Maybe by then this whole thing will blow over and you'll feel better. If not, give me a two-week notice to find a replacement for Anita and I'll move you to CCU."

Kay nodded, stood up, and took another Kleenex.

"Thank you, Kay. I'll put Anita in charge of TRU during your three days off and have Yancy fill in for Anita. I can use people from the nursing pool on the night shift. There's a couple of them who are experienced

183

in ICU that I can ask for." She smiled. "Meantime, go home, get some rest, lie in the sun, read a good book, enjoy your family."

"Thank you. I will."

"Put TRU out of your mind for a while."

Kay nodded, thinking, Sure, easier said than done. She went back to TRU feeling better but knowing actually nothing was improved. She knew from experience that Thompson wouldn't seek a replacement for her. Supervisors and directors never did until you had actually resigned. Then they asked for another two or three weeks so they could frantically find somebody to replace you, which they never could in two or three weeks.

Kay went to TRU's kitchenette and poured a cup of coffee; Anita came and leaned on the doorjamb watching her.

"Leola get to you?" Anita asked, reading her mind as always.

Kay looked somewhere just left of Anita's shoulder and nodded.

"Yeah. She gets to me, too. But I get madder at her than I do at the husband." They stood in silence a moment; then Anita said, "What have I done wrong, Kay?"

Kay looked at her, waited, decided to tell the truth. "Somebody says you are a lesbian, Anita. Is it true?"

Anita's face turned crimson. "I hate that word. But . . . I love a girl, yes."

Kay shut her eyes, opened them. "Any girl?"

"Of course not. Do you love any man?"

"Is she the first?"

Anita's defiant gaze melted under Kay's hurt one. "No."

"Then you really are a lesbian, Anita." Kay was about to cry again so she took a sip of hot coffee.

"Yes, I guess I am," Anita said with a lift of her chin. "But don't worry. I won't make a pass at you, Kay—or anybody else. I'm not a sex maniac; nor am I nuts. I . . . just love a girl. Can't you understand that?"

Kay looked at her, then shook her head. "No. I'm sorry, I can't understand."

Anita bit her bottom lip, then turned and left Kay alone in the kitchenette.

Barney said, "Dr. Kreel says as long as I'm running a low blood pressure Dr. Hishu won't do his sculpturing on my yahoo. Come give me a kiss, Carlton, and see if that helps the blood pressure."

"Dr. Kreel has given us an ultimatum to get you up in a chair, Barney. Today!"

"Oh, wow. What will I sit on?"

"Your bedside chair or a wheelchair."

"No, I mean *on what?*"

Dr. Kreel had indeed left orders two weeks ago for Barney to sit up in a bedside chair and he had refused. Then, early that morning, Kreel had commanded that the nurses get an orderly and *force* Barney to sit up. Kreel had ordered physical therapy for him also, passive leg exercises so that the muscles of his legs wouldn't atrophy. The nurses had been putting Barney's useless legs through range-of-motion exercises once a shift and the physical therapist had been coming in once a day to do more rigorous exercises for him. It would have been more beneficial to everyone concerned if Barney could be wheeled to PT once a day for extensive physical therapy. But nobody could persuade him to get up in a

185

wheelchair. And like Barney himself, everybody wondered what there was left for him to sit on. His gluteal muscles were but ragged, red, and torn bits of flesh. His coccyx was shattered, his upper thighs just barely healing, and slowly. Veins had been torn and repaired like small garden hoses; new collateral vessels had to form. Barney's testicles had been torn by the gunshot blast and repaired. One thing in his favor though, Barney couldn't feel the pain of sitting on that backside. But of course they'd have him sit on the donut, an inflatable plastic ring the size of a toilet seat, where there would be no pressure on the gluteal area except at the end of the spine with its shattered coccyx or tail bone.

"Tell Dr. Kreel thanks but no thanks."

Kay said, "Barney, he said for us to do it. And he won't take no for an answer any longer."

"I'm staying in bed. If I survive—I say *if* I survive, and Dr. Hishu creates me a new seat cushion, then I'll sit in a chair."

Barney's refusal to sit up in a chair was a development nobody had foreseen. Barney's no better than Harvey, Kay thought. He wanted to live, but he was beginning to believe he wouldn't.

"Barney, sitting up in a chair will not only help your circulation, it'll help your lungs to ventilate better, will strengthen you."

He smiled. "Nice try, Carlton, but the kind of circulation I want I'll never be able to do again. And I wouldn't dare ventilate what I want to ventilate, not in the presence of nice girls like yourself. Nope, you can't make me believe I have any future beyond this unit."

"If you were dying, Barney, Dr. Kreel certainly wouldn't order you up in a chair q.d."

"What's q.d.?"

"Every day."

"Q.d.," Barney mused. "Sounds like a degree they'd confer on a graduate from a mental institution. Barney Edwin Werger, Q.D. That stands for Queer Duck, and I don't mean the homo kind. If you say it'll help me, I'm game. When do we begin sitting up?"

"Is now all right?"

"You're the boss, lady."

Kay called an orderly and it took the orderly and three nurses to get Barney up and place him properly on his donut in the wheelchair, with his IV, Foley catheter, and CVP line. The realization that his legs were totally paralyzed seemed to distress him a great deal; the nurses could see it in his face. His chin quivered as he sat in his chair, but he quipped, "I'll be famous yet. The first actor ever to perform entirely from a wheelchair. Maybe I can play Franklin D. Roosevelt for the next twenty years."

However, Barney's twenty minutes in the wheelchair were unsuccessful. He couldn't explain it, but he became extremely uncomfortable. His face paled, his BP dropped, and the nurses called the orderly to help get Barney back to bed. Once he was settled, he just lay there speechless, shaking his head.

"It won't work," he told Hailey later. "I can't do it. I can't sit up in a chair."

Kay was standing in the doorway, Hailey was checking the CVP to make sure it would function properly since they'd had to manipulate the line twice in getting Barney up and down. "You going to just give up like that, Barney?" Hailey demanded. "Just give up without even trying? Man, you disappoint me. I thought you were a fighter. All that funny talk and all you are is a faker."

Smiling, he raised his hand and gave Hailey a peace sign. "You're a good girl, Hailey."

"You'll find out. I've a good mind to turn you over my knee."

"What for? I defy you to tell me just what you'd do if you turned me over your knee."

Hailey almost blushed.

"You're a good nurse," he said. "You're all good nurses. Now, can I have my tranquilizer? The blue one. I feel like blue."

Hailey looked at Kay, subdued. "O.K., Barney," she said, and walked out of his room with Kay.

They both knew then that Barney was no better off mentally than Harvey, because both men had given up on life.

Bobby Cross hadn't though. After his brush with septic shock three days after his admission to Trauma Recovery, Bobby began to recuperate rapidly. The chest tubes were removed first. Then the doctor ordered him weaned off the respirator. The weaning process for Bobby was typical. First, Buddy from respiratory therapy removed the respirator adaptor from the tracheostomy tube in Bobby's larynx and replaced it with a T-bar for fifteen minutes out of every hour. Patients on respirators became quickly dependent on the machine to do their breathing for them, and if the respirator was removed, they became anxious. Therefore it was necessary for the removal of the respirator to be done gradually. A T-bar was a plastic tube in the shape of a "T" which provided oxygen and humidity while Bobby was off the respirator. As the weaning process progressed, the time on the T-bar was increased gradually until he became adapted to breathing on his own again.

All Bobby's communication meantime, had been through his writing on a pad with a pen. Bobby had been in TRU three weeks when the respirator was removed forever, the tracheostomy tube removed from his throat, and he was able to speak. Now, the nurses almost wished he had the trach tube back in place because he was so full of questions.

He asked Kay, "I already know when you nurses say BP you mean blood pressure, but why do you always say two numbers? What do they mean?"

Kay told him that blood pressure meant three things: the force of the *contraction of the heart* to push blood through the vessels, the *amount* of blood pushed through the vessels, and the *resistance* of the vessels to the flow of blood. When the nurse pumps up the blood-pressure cuff, she told him, it exerts pressure on the brachial artery in the upper arm, and as the nurse listens for the pulse beat with the stethoscope over the artery in the bend of the arm, she slowly releases air from the cuff. She watches the blood-pressure mercury as it moves down the manometer. The first pulse beat she hears is the systolic pressure, the highest reading, normally about 90 to 140 millimeters of mercury. She continues to listen as the mercury continues to drop, and the last pulse beat she hears is the diastolic pressure, usually 50 to 100 millimeters of mercury.

Bobby said, "Oh."

Kay wondered if she'd explained in terms that were over his head, or whether she'd explained in too much detail.

Later he asked her, "How many pints of blood did I get altogether after I was shot?"

"As I recall, about thirty; some plasma, some whole

blood, some packed cells."

Bobby rolled his eyes as if wondering if he'd ever understand what all went on in this place. He raised his hands and said, "What's plasma, what's whole blood, what's packed cells?"

"O.K. Whole blood is just what it says, whole blood, like runs in your veins all the time. Plasma is the clear liquid that remains when the red blood cells have been removed. Packed cells are blood with the plasma removed. O.K.?"

"Why? Why did I get all the different kinds?"

"We use plasma only at first when we pick up a victim because there's no time to type and cross-match his blood, to check what type of blood he has, whether it's A positive or A negative or B positive or B negative or O or whatever. Plasma won't cause adverse reactions because the blood cells have been removed. But when you've lost a lot of blood we need to replace it with whole blood in order to replace all its components—plasma, blood cells, albumin, and so on—and to increase the fluid volume. When your blood volume is back to normal but you still need more blood cells because you're still sort of anemic, then we give you packed cells. Packed cells build up your hemoglobin and hematocrit without overloading your circulatory system. O.K., I know what you're going to ask, what's hemoglobin and what's hematocrit. Hemoglobin is the red blood cells' oxygen carrier. Hematocrit is the measurement used to determine the number of red blood cells in the blood."

Bobby grinned. "Overloading my circulatory system would cause high BP."

"Right."

"And a high reading on the CVP."

"Right."

"When I lost all that blood after I got shot, I had a low BP."

"Yes."

"And a low CVP."

"Yes."

"Know what, Ms. Carlton?"

"What?"

"I've decided I'm gonna be a doctor."

Happily, the day after his tracheostomy tube was removed, Bobby Cross, grinning and waving, was transferred from Trauma Recovery to the trauma ward via a wheelchair. Next day the nurses in Trauma Recovery received a dozen red roses from Bobby and his parents. It didn't happen often, only occasionally that a patient or his family sent flowers or candy or a card to the nurses who had nursed them back to health and, in many instances, had saved their lives. More often they received a thank you and most of the time, not even that. It was fortunate, then, that their rewards did not depend on the gratitude of a patient or his family; for the supreme reward was recovery.

"To you and only you I can tell the ballad of Billy Roy Ballew. Ethics bind Harry and me not to speak of our experiments to anyone. Besides, there's always the chance somebody will steal Ballew from us." Syd was sitting on the edge of the bed taking off his socks. He was the only one in the house who would be able to sit on the edge of the old high bed with his feet touching the floor.

Kay, propped amid pillows, watched him, a glass of red wine in her hand. If she sipped slowly, the wine would warm her and eventually relax her. If she took it too

191

quickly, it made her dizzy and sometimes upset her stomach.

"So I ask you not to repeat anything I tell you. It's hard to believe anyway." Syd continued to remove his clothes slowly, revealing more of his hard, lean body as he shed garment after garment. His wife observed him, becoming amused at his preoccupation with thoughts of his experiment, and his unawareness of the striptease he was performing. His wiry black hair was tousled. He had taken off his tie earlier, and the first two buttons of his shirt were undone, revealing the black hair curled on his chest. As he began to unbutton the cuffs of his shirt, he told her how Harry had hypnotized Ballew in their first session and had taken him back to the trauma of his birth and even to the embryonic phase. As Syd unbuttoned the front of his shirt, he told her about the second session when Ballew spoke in French and described the countryside in France. He was removing his undershirt as he described the third session when Billy Roy spoke in cockney English, assumed a furtive look, and hunched up in the chair saying, "Ah swear t' Gawd, Inspector. T'wasn't me wot stole the ol' laidy's purse atall. I seen the bloke wot done it, and like the laidy sed, t'was tall 'e was, and with a patch over 'is left eye. It is poor I am, but honest and wot shillin's I don't earn, I ask for koindly. I don't take purses from laidies, I don't." He had grinned, raised his brows, and reached his hand palm up toward Harry. "You wouldn't be wantin' to spare a penny for a poor man to buy hisself a cup o' tea now would ya?"

Kay said, "I find that hard to believe. Are you sure he's not pretending, Syd?"

By then Syd was bare-chested and stepping out of his trousers. "It's incredible, too incredible. But no, he's in a

192

trance, Kay. What would he have to gain by pretending, anyway? And, an uneducated man like him speaking perfect French and also English with a cockney accent? No, I doubt it. I've done a lot of studying along with this experiment, you know," he said laying his trousers on the chair nearby. "This guy's memory cells include genes of memory so sophisticated, they recall a language Ballew never spoke. True, his father came from France and he could have picked up much of the French language from him, but try to explain the cockney accent." Syd shook his head as he stood there in the dimly lit room in his undershorts. The room was large with an eleven-foot ceiling; it had an old bronze gaslight fixture with smoked glass globes and cloudy crystal prisms. Now electrified, it still put out a dim light. The antique four-poster, the old marble-topped dresser on one side of the room, the old Aubusson rug covering the floor were worth a fortune. And they were only samples of what the rest of the house contained. Syd wasn't aware of the room, however; his mind was back in the lab, remained there, just as it had these past three weeks, and just as Kay's mind remained at St. Luke's and *had* for over a year.

"Do you realize," Syd mused aloud, "the magnitude of this thing, Kay?"

She, a smile on her lips, only raised her brows, and her natural seductive look brought him suddenly back to the house on Sixty-second Street, to the bedroom, and finally to the present condition of his undress. He smiled, spread his hands over his chest and quipped, "Well, it can get even more magnitudinous, baby."

He went to her then, took her face in his hands, smiled, touched the corners of her mouth with his lips. "It's been weeks."

She nodded. "I know."

"Is it me, or you?"

"Both, I think."

"It can't be me. Not when I sleep in the same bed with you, baby." He kissed her lightly on the lips. "You've been asleep or tired or mad—"

"You're blaming it all on me and that's not entirely fair, Ssss—"

It wasn't entirely fair, but it was true, he thought as he kissed her and stretched out beside her. It was true because he burned and yearned for her even after she had fallen asleep—even when he reached out for her in the night only to have her roll away. It's the damned hospital, he thought as he caressed her silken hair, kissed the hollow of her throat, and felt the soft places under his hand. Too much pressure . . . bringing it all home with her . . . worry . . . He had felt her jump awake in the night, heard her sigh. So urgently had she responded to him in the past. But now, this minute, sluggishly . . . not really wanting to make love . . . letting him only to please him. Damned if he oughtn't to give up, to leave her alone tonight . . . until she felt better. That's what he *ought* to do. Next time.

CHAPTER X

Kay went daily to the nursery to check on Harrison who was progressing slowly and had gained two pounds in two and a half weeks. The O_2 cannula and the feeding tube had been removed and he was receiving formula by mouth. Because Ursala had worn down Dr. Paine's resistance, at seven every evening both Mr. and Mrs. Harrison, gowned, gloved, and masked, were allowed to hold and feed the baby in the seclusion of the curtained isolation nursery.

Meantime, Harrison with his blue-eyed charm and winsome ways, was winning nurses all over the hospital to his side. Eva Patterson, the obese, young, pink-cheeked L.V.N., who dominated the nursery with her breathless bluster and who initially had been unwilling to believe in the wisdom of fighting for Harrison's life, said to Kay, "You remember that Dr. Daizat said Harrison wouldn't even be able to feed himself if he grew up? Look, if my hand was where my elbow is, I could . . . reach my mouth like this." Patterson demonstrated, and sure enough, she was able to bring the bend of her elbow up to her mouth. It was simple. She demonstrated it with Harrison's dimpled hand and flexible wrist. His hands and feet could bend—flex and extend—because the tibial and femoral flexor and extensor muscles were normal, but neither his feet nor hands could rotate, a handicap to be sure. "But certainly not enough of one to cause him to be a hopeless invalid," Patterson maintained now.

Kay and Ursala already had figured all that out because they'd searched for any positive features in Harrison's malady from the beginning, which was why they persisted in believing that everything possible should be done to save his life.

Perhaps they were wise, perhaps not. Medical scientists had searched for ways to preserve the lives of infants born with malfunctions of the body and brain for years, and now that they had reduced the infant mortality rate to eighty percent of what it was fifteen years ago, a new dilemma had arisen; should they apply their newly acquired knowledge to preserving the lives of hopelessly malformed and severely mentally retarded infants, who would live to suffer physically and mentally and would cause their families innumerable heartaches? Ethically and morally, the doctors were bound to fight for any infant's life. Or were they? Studies were being done on how many infants were allowed to die who otherwise might have lived a useful life if efforts had been made to save them. The results were not conclusive yet, but they were frightening. Technically nobody—hospitals, communities, or parents—wanted to take the rap for allowing any infant to die who could be saved. So the buck stopped with the child's own physician. Ultimately, he was the one who had to make the decision of whether to take extraordinary measures to save the severely handicapped infant or not. He was, in such a case, omnipotent. But that omnipotence sometimes got modified by caring parents, conscience-stricken colleagues, or badgering nurses, and the doctor was prodded into doing something to save the infant's life.

In Harrison's case, Dr. Paine didn't feel omnipotent, only frustrated. He felt guilty when he strapped Harrison down with tubes and monitor leads to help him live, or made him go through the stress of surgery—a stress that surely was as frightening and uncomfortable for the infant as it was for an adult—knowing all the while Harrison would eventually die due to a defective immune system or a dozen other congenitally related maladies yet undetected.

Yet, Dr. Paine would feel guilty if he allowed Harrison to die too. He knew that if a doctor had a couple of nurses prodding him and overwrought parents pressuring him, and he couldn't make a decision, he could always bring in some of his colleagues to help share the guilt. That helped.

And Harrison rallied after his surgery like a real fighter. Even Dr. Paine caught himself smiling and letting those tiny, stubby fingers wrap around his own big one—until he saw Dr. Kreel's blue-eyed trauma nurse watching, or that bulldog-jawed nurse, Meuller, eying him suspiciously. Then he'd cut his smile off and pretend to be checking Harrison's reflexes or something instead.

Dilemmas. When Kay left the nursery each day her own dilemma of trying not to become too attached to Harrison was a thing she had to fight. She knew she was losing ground rapidly—in favor of Harrison.

After residing in CCU for five days, Ike Salter was taken to surgery where Dr. Pugh installed a permanent pacemaker. When Ike returned to CCU after the procedure, the unit's head nurse, Beasley, telephoned Kay, who took a break to pay him a visit. He was drowsy, but glad to see her, and after she spoke with him briefly, she left. And in the waiting room across the corridor from CCU, sat Cass. He rose from his chair when he saw Kay coming out of the unit, knocked over a cigarette stand, and while he juggled it, called, "Kay, wait!"

She paused and smiled, watching him try to figure out how the ashtray went on the stand. Finally he gave it up, laid the whole thing on the floor, and came to her.

It was the first time she had seen him since the Ranger had delivered Ike to St. Luke's. He looked more like himself now than he had that day. His face was the same as it had been three years ago, deeply tanned, eyes gray-blue, hair a little thinner perhaps, and perhaps he had gained a few pounds. When she had seen him earlier his denim jeans and shirt were soaked, his straw Western hat dripping. Now his hair was neatly combed, he wore a crisp, ivory-colored shirt, slim blue trousers, and as he came to her, ran his fingers through his hair. "Kay, I had to see you. Tried to come into Trauma Recovery but that big bruiser of a security guard outside the door told me no visitors were allowed in there." Cass grinned, shook his head. "I didn't want to tangle with him so I asked politely if he'd carry a message to you. He told me you were off for three days. Is it true no visitors are allowed in there?"

"It's true."

"Then I'll have to send messages in to you."

"Why?"

Cass spread his hands and said, "Well, I thought I'd invite you to lunch or something. For old times' sake."

Kay glanced at her watch. "You have exactly twenty minutes to buy me lunch."

His eyes brightened. "If you'll guide me to the cafeteria, I will. I'm lost in this place."

"All I have time for is the coffee shop. Come on."

Over a sandwich and coffee Cass gazed at her as he had in the old days, forgetting his coffee and his own drooping ham-salad sandwich. "So you think Ike will be all right now?"

Kay was feeling beautiful and light-hearted under his gaze—and a little guilty too, knowing that Syd, for all his love for her, his unselfishness, was horribly jealous of any man who showed her more than ordinary attention. But twenty minutes for old times' sake couldn't hurt anything and Cass had been almost her fiancé at one time, during a time when her feelings were all mixed up, when she needed affection and love, but was afraid of falling in love.

"A permanent pacemaker isn't the best thing in the world," she told Cass, "but it's a remarkable device and a lifesaver. It works like the temporary pacemaker except that it's installed under a flap of skin on the left side of Ike's chest. You know, it sends an electric current about sixty-six times a minute to initiate the heartbeat. The nurses in CCU will give Ike a booklet explaining how it works, with a list of precautions he should take when he goes home, also some warning signals and such. And Dr. Pugh watches his patients closely so it would be worth it for Ike to keep Dr. Pugh as his cardiologist even though he'll have to drive such a long way in to see him."

Cass wasn't hearing a word. Nor was he attempting to hide the wonder of seeing her again as evidenced by his saying, "Kay, you just came down out of the clouds. You'll never know how much I've daydreamed—" He paused, laid his untasted sandwich on his napkin, rested his arms on the small, square laminated table. "I've never remarried."

"I know," she said dropping her gaze from his face.

There was an awkward pause before he asked, "How long have you been married, Kay?"

"Two years, two months." Her eyes lifted to his.

"Are you happy?"

For a moment she stared at him, thinking she'd not dare tell Syd about this; then she said, "No. But it has nothing to do with my marriage."

Mesmerized by the blue eyes that had haunted him for three years, Cass asked, "Are you sure?"

"Yes. I'm very sure."

"Then I'll not ask to see you again even as a friend. It's your job that makes you unhappy?"

"Oh . . . more or less."

His eyes took on a pained look and he touched her fingers with his. "I offered you—"

"Cass, I remember what you offered." After a moment more of silence she said, "Ike tells me you're running for a seat in the state legislature."

He said, "I am. Somebody's got to represent the landowners in central Texas. The farmers and ranchers in eleven counties picked me. Fact is, a delegation of us went to see the governor yesterday, so look for an article about us in the newspaper and you'll see what I'm representing and why—without my taking up this valuable twenty minutes telling you." He took a deep breath. "How's Russell?"

"Growing tall, unlike his father, more like his grandfather, and wanting to become a doctor."

"A doctor?" Cass's eyes dulled. "On a schoolteacher's salary? Kay, you'll have to work at this gosh-awful job till you die an old woman—"

She stood up quickly. "You're getting personal now,

Cass. And it's time for me to get back to TRU."

He glanced at his wrist watch. "I've got five more minutes," he said looking hurt.

"I haven't. It'll take me five to get there from here."

As she tossed the wadded up wrappers of her sandwich into the waste container, he towered over her saying, "You've gotten harder, Kay—your voice, your face, your eyes. You aren't the same."

She smiled. "I've disappointed you then. So I'm sure you're glad that our—that *we* didn't work out."

"On the contrary," he said as he held the coffee-room door open for her. "If we had worked out, you'd be suntanned instead of pale as a ghost, soft-eyed like a doe as you used to be, dressed in denims all day instead of that shapeless scrub dress, and silk and satin things at night instead of . . . whatever you wear."

"That's enough, Cass."

"I've got five minutes, Kay," he said, "and I'm going to walk with you to Trauma Recovery and make the best of every minute."

"Why?"

"You know why."

"I love Syd, Cass."

"I wonder. He kept trying. I left to wait. I knew it would take time for you to get over Ken's death, like it took time for me to get over Jenny's."

"Don't wonder about my loving Syd, Cass, because I do."

"You thought you might love me once."

"Once."

"I could have married a dozen times."

"You should have."

"I didn't because I had hopes. I showed up at Preston

201

General after you had left—"

"I left a year after we broke up."

"And during that year I had Ike asking after you. Didn't he visit you several times when he was in town seeing Dr. Ellis?"

"Yes."

"When I asked about you in the ICU they told me you were married, where you'd moved to, and I told myself, 'Cass, she's gone.' Don't you see?"

"Yes, I see, but it doesn't matter."

They stepped onto the elevator and because there were others on it, Cass had to stand there hat in hand while the elevator door shut and it began its ascent. He bent down to her. "I told you it would take time," he said, and when he glanced to the side and saw the other passengers looking at him, he tightened his lips against his teeth, but his anger welled up into his face and he bent down to her again and said, "Damn it. I was giving you time."

The elevator door opened and Kay stepped out while Cass had to wait for other female passengers to step out, too, and he hurried and caught up to her just at Trauma Recovery's door. She paused and turned to him. "I understand that you were giving me time, but what you must realize is that I loved Syd, even then."

He straightened and said, "You *have* gotten hard, Kay." He nodded. "Yep. You used to push the dagger in gentle. But now it's more of a plunge and a twist."

Suddenly she felt sorry for him and relaxed, shook her head, but all she could say before she went into TRU was, "I'm sorry."

He would have followed her inside, but the monolith dressed in a security guard's uniform placed himself in front of him saying, "I wouldn't be for pursuin' the nurse, sir. Because where she is now, an outsider is forbidden to go."

Cass nodded, backed away, and said, "I know," and turned and sauntered down the corridor to the nearest exit.

While Kay was having lunch with Cass, Hailey was leaning against the wall in Leola's room, black arms folded across her ample, white-uniformed bosom saying, "So you *can't* keep a telephone number written down anywhere in your house. O.K., there's one place you can keep it where nobody can find it." She pointed to her head. "In your brain, Leola. You memorize that number. And you do it now. And every day you think about that number so it stays in your brain. 'Cause someday you just may need it."

Earlier, Anita had told her in terms no one else dared, "Look, Leola, like Kay said, nobody deserves to be beaten. And everybody deserves some privacy—even in marriage. There's a sex gap so neither husband nor wife can understand the other completely because they're poles apart—no pun intended—and nobody in either sex understands a man who beats his wife. And harder to understand is a wife who lets him get away with it."

The evening before, Yancy on the eleven to seven shift had said to her, "You like being a rug, Leola? No, of course you don't. Then stop being a rug. Sooner or later your boy's gonna grow up and if you're still alive and your husband starts slugging on you, he and that boy are gonna come to blows—then it won't be just you involved; it'll involve your kids."

Ginger Manning told her, "It's not necessary to have your husband put in jail. If you don't want that, you can secure a restraining order against him to keep him from bothering you, especially if you decide to separate from him." Ginger was remembering what the social worker had told the nurses at the in-service meeting, that wife-battering was considered simple assault and the husband, therefore, was usually not prosecuted.

Kay supposed the nurses' constant encouragement for Leola to put a stop to her husband's beating might be called brainwashing. And what they were actually doing was encouraging her to *leave* Parkman. Nursing school instructors would probably pull their hair if they knew what their former students were doing, she thought, and maybe what they were doing was wrong. But from their viewpoint there didn't seem to be any alternative. And like Ginger had said in report, Leola's mind was full of intimidating garbage, so she *needed* brainwashing. The plan of action taken by the nurses had originally been to let Leola vent her feelings, tell the secret hurts she'd endured for eight years. However, they couldn't avoid offering their opinions because her situation touched something very sacred and deep within their souls—pride in being a woman, and dignity.

All their concern seemed to help. When Leola found out that the nurses, who represented a cross section of women from all levels of society, were enraged at the thought of a man beating a woman, her eyes became brighter, her smile quicker, and it was then that she began to tell the nurses some of the plans she once had had for her future. She had wanted to become a fashion designer and had had two years of formal education toward a bachelor of arts degree with a major in fashion designing. Two days after she had told Kay about her husband's searching the dirty clothes hamper for incriminating evidence of her infidelity, Leola asked for a pad of paper and a pencil and began to sketch. The nurses, trying to appear casual although secretly they were gleeful, amply provided her with sketch pads and pencils bought at the dime store on their way to the hospital. On the day Kay had lunch with Cass, Leola ended up with six sketch pads from six different nurses.

Leola's surgical incision was healing well, her appetite was normal, and there was little abdominal pain now. The crisis period of two to three weeks was over and Leola would soon be moved upstairs to the trauma ward. A week after her surgery, Dr. Kreel had ordered her up in a chair t.i.d.—three times a day. Twice on day shift and once on three to eleven, the nurses helped Leola out of bed, maneuvering her to the chair in her room while manipulating the IV tubing and Foley catheter, and there she sat and had her lunch and sketched on her pad. The nurses were surprised at her talent, and their honest delight encouraged her even more.

As Hailey said, "You don't have to go home at all, Leola. You can go to the BWS center and have your cousin bring your kids there. But if you do decide to go home, you keep that number up in your head. And don't be forgetting it."

But nobody ever dreamed Leola would go home.

Kay, standing in the hallway, had been listening to Hailey's comments, and seeing Leola look up from her sketch pad and smile at her, she came into the room and looked at what she was sketching. It wasn't the classic, tall, thin model she had sketched, but an almost petite one in a full-skirted scoop-necked dress with slender sleeves to the wrist. The fabric seemed to have a sheen to it, and Kay said, "Blue. I see the dress in a medium blue and it's lovely, Leola."

Leola looked up at her smiling, "You think so? Because this is supposed to be you and this dress is the kind of thing you would look good in."

Flattered, Kay took the sketch Leola handed her as Hailey said, "She drew me in a tailored suit. I'm gonna find me a dressmaker to copy it, I'll tell you for sure. Now, can I go to lunch, Kay?"

"Has everybody else been now?"

"Everybody but me, and I'll bet what food's left is as cold as last night's biscuit."

After Hailey left, Kay and Anita had the unit to themselves because Jan was off duty. The unit was quiet with only the four patients. Days ago Dr. Worley had stopped shouting that he hurt and now sat propped up in bed wearing his bifocals, reading every word of the daily newspaper. He read all day every day from the front page to the comic strips, never commented, never cracked a smile, never spoke unless to answer a question; he didn't care for conversation at all and never appeared to notice anything that went on in his room. The nurses didn't like him very much because he wasn't friendly. In nursing school they were taught that, "All behavior has a reason," and therefore the nurses must not judge the character of a patient by the way he behaves. That was the ideal. In reality there were patients they liked very much and some they actually abhorred. Dr. Worley was somewhere in between. He couldn't have cared less. He was bent on recovery and no nonsense was necessary to bring it about either. Dr. Kreel had said only that day that Worley's descending colon seemed to be healing sufficiently and that surgery to suture the two ends of the colon together and close the stoma in his abdomen was imminent.

Kay left Leola's room and went to check Worley's IV since Hailey had reported that it was nearly out. Hailey had placed a new bag of D5W on the IV pole so all Kay had to do was pull the tubing from the used bag and insert it into the new.

"Certainly glad to see the sun today," she offered tentatively.

Dr. Worley glanced at her. "What say?"

"I said, it's good to see the sun today."

Dr. Worley looked puzzled, then looked over at the window where the blind was open letting the sun stream in, and as if seeing the window for the first time said, "Oh, yes. Yes, it is," and returned his attention back to his newspaper.

Kay shrugged mentally, marked the time the IV was hung on the tape stuck to the bag, adjusted the drip rate carefully. "There. Now you're all set."

Dr. Worley looked up from his paper. "I beg your pardon?"

"I said, you're all set now."

He looked puzzled again until Kay pointed to his newly hung IV. "Oh, yes, yes," he said nodding and bent his gaze back to the paper. Actually his gaze didn't bend, it tilted up so that he could read through the bottom part of his bifocals.

She left the room feeling . . . nothing, and went in to check on Harvey Chunn. His I FEEL LIKE SHIT sign still hung on the wall over the bed. As she looked closer, she saw that Harvey's IV bag was drained almost dry and that all the tubing hung down with catheter hub on the floor pouring fluid.

When she looked alarmed at Harvey, he smiled wryly.

"You were right. I only bled a little before it clotted. I can feel it on the sheet."

He'd pulled out his IV and there was a blood stain on his bed sheet the size of a teacup.

Kay rummaged in the dressings box on the shelf near his bed and, taking an alcohol pledget—a disposable alcohol-saturated pad sealed in foil—and a four-by-four gauze sponge, swabbed the crusted blood from the site where the IV catheter had been; then she pressed the four-by-four over the site. Only when she had finished did she look fully down on his face and ask, "Why?"

He shrugged. "Just wanted to see if what you said was true. Next time, I'll remove the tubing and leave the catheter in and see if air goes to my heart like I read in the book, or if I bleed to death out of the catheter like *you* said."

"I didn't say you'd bleed to death. Because we'll be watching you better than that." Kay gathered the equipment she'd need to start an IV from the equipment shelf. The nurses had decided to treat Harvey's threats with a respectful show of indifference. Yet to watch him closely because they knew he meant what he said in his threats. They did not humor or scold.

"You're not going to start another damned IV—" he began incredulously.

"I certainly am."

"Because I won't let you."

"Yes, you will."

"Why? Why do you have to start another IV?"

"Because the doctor wrote on your chart 'IVs D5W 1000 cc q. eight hours,' and that's what you're going to get."

"What's q. mean?"

"Every," she said turning the inside of his arm up. She examined it for a ropy vein, the kind a young man should have. There were several.

"Find a juicy one?"

"Three or four juicy ones," she said tying the tourniquet around his upper arm.

"Big enough to cut and let me bleed to death?"

"Maybe." She palpated one of the veins. Then tore open the package containing the needle with its catheter. She was aware that Harvey was watching as intently as a half-blind man could.

"This is gonna hurt like hell and I'm gonna yell," he warned.

"That's O.K. as long as you keep your arm still. Because if you move it when I stick the needle in I'll just have to stick you again." She swabbed the site she'd chosen with an alcohol pledget.

"You girls enjoy sticking me, don't you?"

"Not particularly."

"Yeah, you do, because you enjoy hurting men. All women enjoy hurting— Ouch, goddamn it! I hope you got it in the first time!"

"Was she pretty, Harvey?" Kay asked, releasing the tourniquet while the blood backed up in the catheter, indicating she was in the vein.

"Who? Oh shit! I hope you're in. Jamming the damned thing in all the way—"

"You know who."

"No, she wasn't pretty. Why is it all women want to know if she was pretty? As a matter of fact she was very plain. It was her brain I was attracted to and I mean it. She was smart, a Ph.D. in philosophy. Threw me over for a tennis coach." Harvey laughed angrily. "Can you imagine? A tennis coach."

"That's really pretty depressing." Kay was taping the hub of the catheter to his arm, carefully covering hub and several inches of the tubing with tape. It would be difficult for Harvey to peel off the tape and find the hub.

"Yeah." He fell silent a moment. Then, "I'm glad you didn't feed me that sick old line about how much better it is that I found out what she was like before I married her."

"I'm glad, too, then."

"Because we wouldn't have gotten married. Marriage is the pits."

"For some people, maybe."

"What about for you?"

"I'm married to a professor at the university, very happily."

"That's rare."

"No, it's not."

"It is. Nobody's happily married. Nobody. Nobody's *happy*. Never met a happy person in my life. All problems. How do we do it, anyway?"

"Do what, Harvey?"

"Keep on living."

"I don't know what you mean."

"How do we keep on living when life is nothing but crap, morning, noon, and night. Work, pay taxes, dodge traffic tickets, get shit on by other people, try to raise yourself up in the world and nobody will let you. Suffering, sickness, hurting. Nothing but crap and all we've got to look forward to is death. Sweet death. Sweet oblivion."

"Death may not be oblivion, Harvey."

"If it's not, even hell can't be worse than this." He fell

silent a moment as Kay began to stretch a clean bottom sheet over half of his mattress as he rolled to his side. Finally he asked, "Do you believe in God?"

"Yes."

"See any of this stuff about—about life after death? People who've been resuscitated and come back to tell how it was over on the other side?"

"Not really." She thought about Mr. Hinton at Preston General telling about seeing a light and mountains in the distance after having been resuscitated. Who could say what it meant? She couldn't tell Harvey, because she wanted to avoid talking about death with him, that there were times after a patient had died when she felt that the patient was not gone, that he was staying around awhile even after his body had been moved to the morgue. Still, there were other times when patients died that she felt they had departed instantly. But one common feeling she shared with most other nurses: that there was a personality that departed for other places. She had never met a nurse yet who did not believe in life after death. All she could tell Harvey at this juncture in his recovery was, "I do believe there is life after death, though, Harvey. And I believe in God."

She truly felt sorry for Harvey. Dr. Spade hadn't succeeded in changing his outlook. All he'd succeeded in doing was making him angry. Dr. Cash had ordered him up in a chair twice a day and he had refused. He and Barney refusing to get up in a chair. Both doctors had talked with them about it, threatened, cajoled, but both patients preferred to remain in bed. At the most, they allowed the nurses to roll the heads of their beds up some, and Barney didn't even like that. The nurses tried every day to get Harvey up in a chair, but he refused to cooperate. As Dr. Spade had written in his progress notes for that day, Harvey was a "very difficult patient."

"Are you sure you wouldn't like to sit up in a chair to rest your back, Harvey?" she asked. The nurses had already tried the Here-we-go-Harvey-you're-going-to-sit-up-in-the-chair-right-now approach and he had told them, "You wanna bet? The hell I am!"

"Yes, I'm sure I wouldn't like to sit up in a chair, Kay. I want to lie here and hope I sleep. Oblivion is what I want. Did you know my mind races constantly? I'll bet my IQ is 200 since I shot myself. Mind races! Tranquilizers would probably relax the ol' bod, but not the ol' brain. What I need is a sledge hammer. *Conk!* Right on my head. So please leave the room, Kay, so I can sleep. But beware. Next time I'm going to peel off this tape you put on me and pull the tube from the catheter hub, leave the catheter in, and hope I bleed to death quickly."

"I'll leave, but I'll be watching, Harvey."

"Sure. I know. But, honey, you can't be two places at once."

Anita was giving Barney a back rub when Kay went into his room. He was facing the door so he smiled as she entered. "I've been thinking, Carlton," he said. "I don't have to work the stage, I can be in the movies or on TV. I can be the millionaire who does nothing but sit in his wheelchair and dole out a million dollars every now and then." Tears fell to his pillow and Kay realized as the other nurses did, that in the fight for survival, Barney was losing. His mental outlook was becoming grim and it was affecting his recovery. He should be going up to the trauma ward by now, but Dr. Kreel said that as long as his vital signs fluctuated as they did, Barney would remain in TRU.

Two young men in the throes of despair; Barney pretending to joke about his handicaps, Harvey threatening suicide. It was enough to cause a pall of gloom to hang over TRU. Critical-care units were like living souls and had good days and bad. They experienced moods: apprehension, routine, tension, boredom. The mood of TRU lately was glum.

She felt the gloom in her bones as did the other TRU nurses, and during her three days off, it had never left her. Now, seeing hopelessness in Barney's homely face, she had to turn away lest he see her own despair. Both Barney and Harvey, caught up in their own hopeless futures, were becoming more and more self-involved, each unable to extend his thoughts beyond himself.

While Kay was looking over Barney's vital-sign sheet, Anita finished the back rub. Barney said, "How's the fellow doing who shot himself in the head?"

Kay looked up from Barney's chart, met Anita's gaze. Anita shrugged. "How did you know about that?" Anita asked.

Tears were still glistening in Barney's eyes as he answered, "His doctor, the big red-headed guy, Cash, he has a loud mouth. I heard him talking about it out at the desk."

Nurses never gossiped with patients about other patients, seldom even mentioned other patients, so Kay hesitated. To tell Barney how Harvey was could depress him more. On the other hand, the very fact that Barney had asked about Harvey was evidence that he could still extend his concern outside himself. "Harvey is very depressed."

"Dr. Spade's not working miracles on him either?"

213

She shook her head.

"That's—" Barney, who was still lying on his side facing the door, stopped speaking. Anita, who was washing her hands at the sink, froze. Kay turned to see what had caused their alarm. Standing at the nurses' station was Parkman. Sighing with impatience and tensing with apprehension, Kay went to the desk. She noticed Parkman's furtive glance around the unit; his eyes reflected anxiety. Wondering where Pasternak was, she said, "Mr. Parkman, visitors aren't allowed in here. I suggest—"

He pinned his intense glare upon her and said, "Are you and her the only nurses here?"

"At the moment, but—"

"O.K., I've come for Leola," he said softly. "Now I suggest you get her clothes together and her medicines because I'm taking her home."

Kay blurted, "You can't do that!"

Parkman grabbed her wrist and said, "Yes, I can. And I will. Now you do as I tell you so nobody gets hurt. I don't want to do any harm and I'm not doing anything wrong. I just want to take my wife home where she belongs."

Kay tried to pull her arm free of his grasp. "She's not well yet, Mr. Parkman. She's on IV medications."

"I called Dr. Kreel and he told me I couldn't take her home. But he's wrong. She needs to be home. She can be taken care of there just as good. This hospital's costing me plenty and the kids, they need their mother."

Parkman's ignorance and his obvious nervous or mental condition were evident in both his behavior and appearance. The pupils of his eyes were dilated, the sclera red, his complexion pale. "No, I won't help you,"

Kay said.

"You got no choice, lady," he said. Then he called to Anita, "You in there. Come here."

Anita obeyed seeing the horror in Kay's face, sensing something awful was going on.

"Go get Leola's clothes ready. Take out all those tubes and stuff. She's going home. And don't do anything funny," Parkman said, still speaking softly. He did not need to speak harshly because his expression, his awful eyes did that for him. To Kay he said, "You will stay here with me in case she does something funny." Then to Anita again, "Don't do anything funny, you understand?"

Kay's knees were threatening to buckle under her as she glanced at the clock. Another fifteen minutes before Hailey was due back from lunch. Desperately she hoped for someone to intrude.

Seeing her glance at the TRU door, Parkman said, "If you're hoping for that security guard, don't. I just saw him eating his lunch in the coffee shop." A piece of slick, dark hair had fallen over Parkman's forehead now; his eyes darted from the door to Kay to Leola's room to the clock and Kay sensed he was as scared as she was. Leola must not leave, she was too weak and needed her IV antibiotics, her pain medication, but she would never be able to make Parkman understand. "Mr. Parkman, please. This could do a great deal of harm to her. *Don't* pay your hospital bill or whatever, but let Leola stay."

"No way. I mean no harm to her or anybody else, nurse, but Leola belongs home with me. I can take care of her just fine."

Kay lost her temper. "Like you did before?"

He gripped her wrist harder, his face flushed. "You shut up. You don't know anything." Then to Anita he called, "Hurry up, nurse. Before I get mad."

Anita was taking her time, hoping as Kay was, that someone would come into the unit, see what was happening, and run for help. For a long moment while Kay stood frozen from fear and Anita was busy removing Leola's Foley catheter and monitor leads, all was silence in the unit.

Then from Barney's room came a booming, baritone voice, "Unhand the woman, villain! Or else I'll get out of this bed and see that you do. Let go of her *right now!*"

Parkman gave a start. Barney's stage voice was more convincing than his words, and for a moment he stared into Barney's room.

"Now, before I get you with these scissors, you scoundrel." Barney did sound convincing and Parkman stared as if fully expecting Barney to rise and come forth tubes and all, but since he made no move other than to raise himself off the bed with his arms, Parkman soon saw through his bluff and lost his consternation.

Meanwhile something occurred to Kay. She said to him, "I need to remind the other nurse to get Leola's medicines."

Parkman nodded impatiently. "Do it then. From here."

Kay called, "Anita. Don't forget Leola's meds. And especially don't forget the blue ones. The *blue* ones, Anita."

Blue? She saw Anita's unspoken question, read her thoughts even as they occurred; for nurses never referred to any medication by its color. *Blue? Oh, Code*

216

Blue. The CPR code. Sure! Hit the CPR button above Leola's bed. Of course!

Anita went carefully to the head of the bed, raised her hand full of tubes slowly—and pressed.

Kay shut her eyes and thanked God, knowing that once the CPR button was pushed, a buzzer would sound at the hospital switchboard and a light would flash over the letters T-R-U on the panel above the switchboard. In every corridor the switchboard operator's voice would be heard paging, "Code Blue, TRU. Code Blue, TRU. Code Blue, TRU." There was no paging speaker in TRU, however, but Kay knew the CPR button had been pressed because she saw the small, red CPR light blinking in each of the patient's rooms. In seconds five members of the highly trained CPR team would rush for TRU.

Meanwhile Barney was pretending to climb out of bed yelling, "I said let the nurse go and get out of here! All right, I'm coming after you, fiend!"

She felt the team before they entered. The floor vibrated under her feet and suddenly the door to TRU slid open and the CPR team thundered in. The sheer surprise of it caused Parkman to release her and stagger backward and Kay cried, "He's trying to take his wife out. There's no CPR."

While the three-man and two-woman team from ICU, CCU, and ER stood momentarily bewildered, the pneumatic doors slid open and Pasternak, sheepishly hoping to get a glimpse of the CPR, entered. He saw Parkman, saw the expression on Kay's face, saw the diorama of the CPR team frozen in the inaction of indecision, and realized what the situation was. Even before Parkman knew he was there, Pasternak clamped

217

his mighty paw on his shoulder.

"Out ya go, ya bastard. Quietly now, so as not ta disturb anybody else. Out with ya," he said and escorted Parkman unceremoniously out the door.

Kay sat down in the desk chair and for several moments experienced a tendency to faint. The CPR team plied her with questions about the cause of their confusion. Billy from ER suggested she have her wrist x-rayed because it looked swollen. Anita took care of a frightened Leola while Hailey, having heard the CPR page and run from the cafeteria, stood horrified for a while and finally brought Kay a cup of coffee.

When all the CPR team finally left, in possession of a real juicy tidbit with which to cultivate the hospital grapevine, Kay went to Leola and found her still crying. Anita was trying to comfort her. Leola said to Kay, "He's crazy. He loves me, but he's crazy."

Kay and Anita looked at each other.

"He's crazy, but he loves me. Maybe if I do go back to him, he will have learned his lesson and won't hit me anymore."

Kay had to bite her tongue to keep from venting all her frustration and fear on her patient. She could only say faintly to Anita, "I'll call Dr. Kreel." And with tears of fury still in her eyes, she said, "I'm glad you read me and pushed the button."

Anita, who had been avoiding Kay since their discussion about her being a lesbian, smiled. Her affection showed then, the affection she felt for a friend whom she admired as a professional. "Sure. What are friends for?" she said.

After Kay had notified Dr. Kreel of Parkman's attempt

218

to take Leola out of the unit, and listened to him vent his spleen and curse and swear that he'd have a CPR button installed at the nurses' station for the nurses' protection, she went in and thanked Barney for his attempts to rescue her. Barney was more depressed than ever. All he had been able to do was threaten and lay in his bed helpless.

Then she went in to see if Harvey had been disturbed by the commotion.

"I'm sorry if you were disturbed by all the confusion, Harvey."

"I was. And I helped you more than you think. Because it occurred to me that while that maniac had your attention, I could easily peel off this tape, remove the tubing from the catheter hub, and happily bleed to death. But I didn't. It even occurred to me to get up and help you, but you've got me all tied down with tubes and all this paraphernalia."

She smiled. "Thanks."

"Say, who was the idiot that kept yelling threats at that madman and not doing anything about it?"

Kay laughed for two reasons; first, that Harvey cared enough about what was going on to want to help, and second, because of the question itself. "That was Barney."

"The guy who got his ass shot off for fooling around with somebody else's wife?"

Shocked, Kay asked, "Who told you about that?"

"I overheard it. Yancy, that behemoth on night shift has a loud mouth. I overheard her talking about him in the kitchen. Paralyzed isn't he?"

"Yes, from the perineum down."

219

Harvey turned his face from her, folded his hands over his abdomen. "We've a-a-ll-ll got problems, haven't we?"

"Everybody. Some small, some large like Barney's."

"And poor ol' Harvey Chunn's. O.K., Kay, you've checked on me, now leave me alone. Provided there's no more dramatics in this paradise for vampires and prison wardens, I'll sleep. I hope. Oblivion. The poet sayeth, 'Sweet oblivion is what I truly seek, provided my IV's able to leak.'"

"That's awful, Harvey."

He smiled grimly. "Good afternoon."

Next, Kay checked on Dr. Worley who was reading *Newsweek* and never looked up when she entered his room. "Dr. Worley?"

He looked up from his magazine.

"I hope we didn't frighten you."

"I beg your pardon?"

"I hope the commotion at the nurses' station didn't bother you."

"Commotion? I wasn't aware of any commotion."

By the expression on Worley's face, and in view of his previous oblivion to anything that went on around him, Kay knew he was telling the truth.

"Well, I'm glad," she said and left the room.

Her reaction to fear and anxiety was delayed by about twenty minutes. As she left Dr. Worley's room, she felt suddenly dizzy. She leaned against the wall a moment, then feeling sick to her stomach, ran for the nurses' rest room next to the TRU kitchenette where she abruptly threw up in the toilet. She retched again and again until Hailey was there handing her a damp washcloth.

"Lord, Kay," Hailey said. "I don't blame you for being sick. If it was me he threatened, I'd still be shaking a week from now."

But while she retched Kay kept thinking, I won't tell Syd about this. I won't tell him I vomited. No, I won't tell him about that or anything else that's happened today. While she washed her face she wondered, If I did tell Syd about all this, would he be angrier at Parkman? Or Cass?

CHAPTER XI

There were usually two or three patients, who had been transferred to the ward from TRU, whom Kay liked to visit on her lunch break if she had the time. Now there was Bobby Cross, and there was Ike. She could never be sure when she visited Ike, however, that she wouldn't encounter Cass, so she minimized that risk by not visiting Ike every day. He seemed to understand and told her, "Kitten, Cass has a very reasonable nature, but you remember I told you once how he is. He don't buy just any ol' bull or farm implement. He waits. Then when he sees what he wants, he knows it right away and wastes no time going after it." Ike placed his hands in his lap. He was sitting in a chair by the window in his room, dressed in a green satin robe, his hair neatly combed, and Kay knew that beneath that robe the wound in the skin where the permanent pacemaker had been implanted was healing quickly. She'd peeked at his chart at the nurses' station on the ward and saw that he was adapting to the pacemaker mentally and that the device was doing its electronic duty. His heart was still being monitored by telemetry. Taped to his chest was a transistorized monitor. It sent signals of the electrical impulses of his heart to the monitor in CCU and the signals appeared on the oscilloscope at the nurses' station under the words, TELEMETRY: ROOM 362. Ike would be monitored for several more days until the crisis period of ten days had passed.

"But now," he went on, "you're happily married and Cass has no right to do any pursuin'. He's an honorable man and never has dallied with no married woman. But when it comes to you, Kitten, maybe he don't think too straight."

"Ike, he didn't do anything wrong. We just had lunch and discussed . . . discussed our past relationship and I firmly told him that I love Syd."

"But, Kitten, it didn't take. If it weren't for that mean-eyed security guard Cass says is standing outside the door where you work he's liable to go in to see you. That ain't right. Still, I can't help but believe Cass will do the right thing when it comes right down to it. His morals are as old-fashioned as yours." Ike grinned suddenly. "Now that wasn't quite true. They're *almost* as old-fashioned."

Kay couldn't help but feel she hadn't seen the last of Cass. And somewhere deep inside she was hoping she hadn't. Why? Because he offered security for her the same as always? No, not security, *escape*. Escape from what, nursing?

"How far is the nearest hospital, Cass," she had asked him once three years ago when he was telling her about his ranch.

"Forty mile or so," he had answered.

"What about my nursing, Cass?"

"Don't you see darlin'? You'll never have to work again," he had replied.

But nursing was her life. Once you practice nursing, she had often thought, it's in your blood. There was a shortage of nurses at St. Luke's and there was a shortage of nurses all over the United States while a large percentage of registered nurses remained unemployed. Among the reasons for that, the nursing journals said, were poor salaries, poor working conditions, burnout. Nurses were under too much pressure too long. Kay understood that, pondered it; often you work twelve straight days and always overtime. At best you may get every other weekend off. In nursing as in no other profession you're always subject to being yelled at by doctors and seldom were you ever supported by administration. One mistake, one medication error, and you could endanger a life; lawsuits for negligence were on the rise. You could never let your guard down. You occasionally did double shifts. Supervisors would have you work twenty-four hours straight sometimes if you didn't flat refuse, all because of the nursing shortage. When she thought about it, Kay wondered that there were any nurses left on the job at all—until she thought about it a little more. If she had her choice of professions to train for, she would still choose nursing.

For nowhere else was so much responsibility in your hands. Nowhere else could you bring comfort and hope to so many. And nowhere else were the rewards as immediate and gratifying. With varying degrees of intensity and devotion, every nurse on every ward in every hospital all over the world had one main goal in mind for those she cared for: *recovery*.

Still, even the highly dramatic CPRs were becoming routine to Kay. She no longer felt gratified to help bring a patient through a crisis. Her feelings of growing complacency, coupled with a tinderbox of emotional blowups, had been coming on now for about a year.

Burnout? Hers was more of a slow fizzle.

So, that day after she visited Ike, she went back to the unit. En route she tried to tear her mind away from an image that had begun to form of herself at a lovely writing desk, pen in hand, dressed in a long, satin gown. And, as in some lovely Victorian novel, there was a rap on the door, she looked up, and *he* walked in. But was he dressed in a suit and carrying a briefcase, or was he in Western jeans and cowboy boots? Infidelity, that's what the last image in her mind was and she hated herself for it. Hated herself because she knew she loved Syd.

She was so wrapped up in her own feelings that it was a shock to her when she returned to TRU to find Anita sitting in the kitchen, a cup of coffee in one hand, a cigarette in the other, her eyes red from crying over her problems.

Kay approached her. "Anita?"

Anita took a drag on her cigarette and blew smoke defiantly at the ceiling. She looked at Kay, her lips trembling, and said, "I knew there would be repercussions because somebody found out I'm a lesbian."

"What—?"

"It was Abby Jones wasn't it? Kay, she's scheduled me fourteen days straight and that includes the Fourth of July weekend on which I asked to be off. It was to be my only chance to visit my parents in Fort Worth. I told her weeks ago." Anita puffed again on her cigarette. "Not only that, she treats me with contempt. You've surely seen that."

Kay had. "I'll talk to her about the scheduling, Anita. Maybe she just goofed."

"Sure. She goofed, all right. Well, if she thinks I'm going to get mad and quit, she's wrong."

"She doesn't want that, she—"

"Doesn't she?" Anita ground out her cigarette and poured the rest of her coffee down the kitchen sink. "I'm taking my fifteen-minute break while Hailey watches Leola and Worley for me." Anita paused as she stood up. "You know that if I actually do get to take our fifteen-minute break, that rare privilege gets shorter and shorter and the on-duty hours get longer. I wake up at night and can't go back to sleep. Keep worrying about Leola or Barney or Harvey. Isn't that just great? Burnout, isn't it, Kay? You and me. Know what they say helps to prevent that? A change." Anita laughed. "Can you see me doing floor duty? I'd go crazy in a month. Labor and delivery? Ha! Nothing makes me madder than seeing those wimpy husbands full of fear and contrition because of what they got their poor wives into. OB? I *abhor* the whiny new mothers all thinking they're the goose that laid the golden egg. Nursery or pediatrics? Kids make me nervous. Surgery? I'm far too restless. CCU? I'd go to sleep and never wake up. Rotate from unit to unit? I'd feel insecure. Trauma Recovery would be worse than this." Anita stood up, tears were coursing down her cheeks. Kay was feeling ashamed of herself for wallowing in her own self-pity when there were other nurses around her who were going through the same thing. She put her arm around Anita.

"I don't know how to help, Anita. But I will get your schedule changed, I promise."

"Better watch out, Kay. Don't touch me. People will think we're in love."

Kay smiled. "There's a song—"

"There's a song for everything. Just like there's a how-to book for everything. My break's up." Anita put her hand on Kay's shoulder. "Thanks for listening. I feel better already."

As she watched Anita leave the kitchenette and enter Barney's room, Kay thought again, What we need in this hospital is a psychiatrist for the nurses, or some sort of sounding board. Maybe other professional men and women need that, too. Maybe other professions also experience burnout.

She went to the desk then and, after studying the schedule, called Abby Jones who was in the supervisor's office. Kay told her about how the schedule could be rearranged. Abby, in a bad mood, was reluctant to agree to the change, but finally assented. To Anita, Kay's interference on her behalf was really a super thing for her to do. To Kay it was routine like everything else.

But the routine of her private life was soon interrupted. Dr. and Mrs. Sydney Carlton had been sent an engraved invitation to a reception in honor of Abraham Truelove who was ambitious to climb the political ladder from practicing attorney to district judge. Ben said that Truelove was courting anybody who was in a position to influence a lot of people of voting age: the clergy, university professors, legislators, commissioners. At first, Kay didn't want to go. But the more she thought about dressing in a formal gown, doing her hair up, and taking an evening to mix with people socially, the more she liked the idea. Syd was game as always. He had a grace in social situations that reminded her of a professional skater's. He was at ease, could converse on any subject, or even argue any subject if it were necessary. Besides, he said, there'd be legislators there and it wouldn't hurt to get acquainted with a few in case he ever decided to apply for that state-government grant Uncle Ben had said was available for his research.

The only thing was, he was unusually good-looking so Kay had to deal with a jealousy problem because ladies flirted with him and fawned over him and she invariably came home in a foul mood.

He was even handsomer in a tux, though it embarrassed him to wear one. The entire time they were dressing for the reception he was making quips about feeling like a penguin, looking like an undertaker, resembling Dracula if he only had a cape. He even went so far as to stick two of her artificial fingernails on his upper incisors and pretend to bite her on the neck. He posed in front of the mirror when he had finished dressing, tugged at the cutaway coat, fingered his left cuff link, and liked what he saw, she could tell.

Meanwhile, she had back-combed her hair, piled it all on top of her head in a loose chignon, and stuck silver combs in the chignon. The blue lawn fitted neatly in the bodice; it should, she thought, for a hundred and seventy-five dollars—and fifteen dollars more for alterations. She frowned that the waist was too tight after all that. The skirt clung to her slender hips and flared out mid-hip, flattering for her figure since she wasn't tall. She had purchased the dress because it reminded her of the one Leola Parkman had sketched for her. She thought the high heels, which were higher and barer than she'd ever dared to wear before, helped her achieve a willowy look, until she asked Syd about it.

He looked at her, his eyes noticing all of her and he raised his brows and said, "Willowy?" Smiling the old Syd smile, he took her in his arms. "I never saw a willow look like *this*."

"Stop. You'll muss me."

"*Feel* like this either. Let's forget the tux rental, forget the social contacts, Kay baby, and let's stay home."

"Not on your life," she said pushing him away. "I'm going through with this now even if it harelips the governor."

Tilting his head, Syd said, "It just might. It just might." For the governor was to be one of the speakers at the reception.

The hostess, an influential friend of the Trueloves, claimed there were over two hundred people crowded into the Diamond Square Ballroom. Truelove proved to be a stout, balding fellow with a firm, warm handshake and a heavy Texas drawl. His wife was tall, attractive, and fiftyish. The governor himself was shorter but stouter than he appeared on TV, and the grouchy look which newspaper pictures always seemed to capture, had miraculously vanished.

After they had passed down the reception line Syd was taken over by a couple of university professors. Kay was quickly pulled into conversation with their wives and discovered she enjoyed just being a wife. They were unpretentious, home-loving, husband-pleasing ladies, the kind that mystified Kay because they seemed to lack much personal identity. Those who worked outside the home had jobs, they said, not careers. There was an important difference, they said. A job was something you did for pay until you paid off the boat and the camper or the kids' education. A career was something you did for your own gratification until you retired. Some of the ladies had finished their formal education and some of them hadn't. But Kay couldn't tell which were which. They were caught up in clubs, PTA, church activities.

They played bridge and golf. They bowled on leagues; they took painting lessons. They carried their lives with dignity and pride. Kay felt a mixture of feelings; pride in her own profession and disappointment that her career lacked any social status. Though she was highly trained and experienced in a technical profession, her social status was barely above that of a house servant.

What an eyeopener this potpourri of society was! More than once during the course of the evening, she heard, "You're a nurse, Kay? Oh *my!* I could never be a nurse; I have too soft a heart."

Rubbish, Kay thought. Do you think it takes a hard heart to care for people day after day, to ease their pain and hardships day after day, to see them recover and see them die? To bathe, feed, and dress them? Carry their excrement and endure the odors and sights of sickness and trauma? That's a hard heart? She frequently had to bite her tongue to keep from voicing it aloud.

After the last such statement by one of the professors' wives, which Kay ignored because she was enjoying the conversation of this group of amiable ladies and didn't want to spoil it, she felt a touch on her elbow and turned to see Cass smiling down at her. Shocked, she just stood there staring up at him.

"I didn't expect to see you here," he said and nodded a greeting to the other ladies in the group. Kay was shocked further to notice that many of the commissioners' and legislators' wives knew him. After exchanging a few embarrassed words with the ladies, he drew her away from the others and she went along hoping to prevent attracting any more attention to her and Cass than was necessary.

"It never occurred to me you'd be here, Cass," she

said. "But I should have known."

"It never occurred to me that you would be here either," he replied. They were standing apart from the crowd near a large, long bay window that overlooked the Colorado River which reflected the lights in its placid, if not prolific, waters. "But there I was deep in conversation with the mayor and four other gentlemen, when, lo, I looked up and beheld a neck—a slender neck with a wisp of chestnut-colored hair fallen from the hairdo on top. And I thought, An angel, a *special* angel, dressed in blue. Did you know it was possible for somebody to recognize somebody else just by seeing a neck?" Cass's blue eyes gleamed in the light coming from the myriad of chandeliers overhead. Dressed in a tux like the other men at the reception, he looked handsome but ill-at-ease, and she had to press her fingers to her lips to keep from giggling. She felt giddy anyway because somebody had put too much vodka in the Bloody Mary she had sipped at the beginning of the reception. She had barely tasted the champagne she was holding in her hand now.

She recalled an article she had read in the paper earlier in the week—about Cass, along with a dozen other farmers and ranchers, meeting with several legislators in a senate hearing room to demonstrate their support for some tax proposal or other. Cass had been quoted as telling the legislators, "I'd rather be inside a fence with a hot bull than be sitting here with you fellows." The article said Cass had complained that he was unused to that kind of danged suit, and his tie was strangling him, but the farmers and ranchers of eleven counties in the very heart of Texas were having problems with the proposed tax structure and needed help. Cass was the spokesman. Now he glanced around the large ballroom saying, "I don't see your husband. At least I don't recognize him. As I remember, he was tall, good-looking, with a personality sort of like—Burt Reynolds."

Now Kay did laugh. "He'll like that," she said. "Now, if you'll look over near the orchestra at that huddle of older gentlemen, you'll see Syd. He's the tall, young one. The others are university profs and I wish I knew what they're discussing because whatever it is, Syd isn't happy about it."

Cass looked. Then he said to Kay, "You're beautiful tonight, Kay. As your former suitor you have to allow me to say that."

"I don't have to, but I will." She sipped her champagne.

"Tell me what all you're doing now, how the last three years have been, what all you did."

She shrugged briefly and began.

Meanwhile Syd was furious. Every prof from the university who was in attendance at the reception was getting in on the conversation about Billy Roy Ballew. When Clay Borden had come up to him earlier and asked how his genetic-memory project was coming along, Syd had almost dropped his drink. The first thing he thought was that Harry had let the cat out of the bag, but by the time the others had surrounded him and besieged him with questions about the project, Syd began to realize that neither Harry nor himself were the ones who had spread the news about their research on genetic memory. It was ol' Billy Roy himself—bragging. He could see him now, stopping a professor on the campus walk: *Say there, rrrrr. How do I get to this here psychology building. I'm Dr. Carlton and Dr. Wyatt's project, you know, rrrrr. Flashes of memory*, rrrrrr.

Clay Borden, Ph.D.—Sociology 101 and 102 and Anthropology 301—was saying, "You realize, Sydney, that Ballew's speaking in French and also in cockney English, his appearance of being several different people just might be demonstrating a multipersonality neurosis? That's the way it appears to me." Syd knew Borden was referring to the neurosis in which the patient's personality splits into several separate personalities with different names and behaviors.

"Clay, you seem to know as much about what goes on in my private lab as Harry and I do," Syd said steadily while feeling his face flush with indignation.

"Your Mr. Ballew has a big mouth," Ashton Milsap offered. "He goes by the Forty-four Club after his sessions with you and as you know that's a campus hangout for upper classmen and a few stray profs. Besides, you can't keep this an absolute secret and why *should* you?"

"For Ballew's sake."

"Bah! Ballew loves the attention. Brags about being 'Louis, King of France reincarnated,' he calls it," offered Vernon Briggs—English 101, 102, 201, and no telling what the hell else.

Clay Borden said, "Sydney's concern with Ballew's privacy is a reflex action from his days as a registered nurse. To him, no doubt, Ballew is a patient instead of a subject."

"Nurse!" Milsap exclaimed.

"One thing, gentlemen," put in Dr. Coats—Micro 202, and Anatomy and Physiology—"How would you explain this Mr. Ballew's memories if he's a multipersonality neurotic?"

"Hallucinosis, naturally," Borden said.

Syd laughed incredulously. "You just said Ballew was a neurotic. Now he's a psychotic too. O.K., so he has flashes of memory that resemble hallucinations, but how do you explain those memories as described, in detail, under hypnosis?"

The professors looked at each other. Dr. Coats said, "Is hypnosis, necessarily, a truth serum?"

"A person under hypnosis cannot always be made to do something which is strongly against his will," said Borden. "But on the reverse side of the coin, can he *will* himself, even under hypnosis, to describe certain memory sequences he actually never had?"

The discussion went on. Syd, who was the expert on the experiment with Ballew, was actually the bystander. Amusing. They all knew more about it than he did. They reminded him suddenly of doctors. Professional jealousy was what it amounted to, each showing the others how much he knew about psychology, psychoanalysis, and psychiatry. And here all this time Syd had thought such intense professional jealousy was limited only to physicians!

What Syd decided not to tell them was that he and Harry had already dealt with the possibility of Ballew having a multipersonality, and of his memory sequences being hallucinations. But to be a multipersonality neurotic and have hallucinations or delusions that corresponded? Well, they had decided to do psychoanalysis on Ballew to see if he had any reason in his background to become a split-personality neurotic or a psychotic. But they realized that they were prejudiced already in favor of Billy Roy's sanity. What they needed was an objective, crackerjack psychoanalyst.

"What you need, Sydney," Clay was saying, "is to give Ballew a polygraph test to see if he's telling the truth, or thinks he's telling the truth. I first heard Ballew's tales yesterday; exaggerations like you never heard before. Talks just to hear himself. A bag of wind in my opinion."

Syd glared at Clay and said, "If that makes him a bag of wind, Clay, then maybe Harry and me ought to forget Billy Roy and concentrate on you." With that, he handed Clay his empty glass, excused himself, and started making his way among the crowd toward Kay. Because if he wasn't mistaken, the man she was talking to was the cowboy she almost married three years ago. Suddenly, his anger at the discussion about Ballew paled in the heat of his new fury. It took an eternity to shoulder, side-step, and excuse himself through the crowd. He was detained three times in his progress by professors' wives greeting him and squeaking cute nothings as he politely answered, excused himself, and went on. Meantime, Kay seemed to be enjoying herself—or her friend. Syd hadn't seen her that animated or happy in months. Jealousy seized him and held him in its viselike jaws; fury erased all reason, and all he wanted was to get to her, and get her away from the rancher he almost lost her to three years ago, then beat the hell out of the cowboy for grinning and touching her the way he was.

And Cass, honorable man that he was, wasn't entirely innocent. During the past week, he had convinced himself that Kay was unhappy, that her professor husband was spending too much time at the university doing no telling what—there were so many pretty coeds these days—and that her marriage was shaky at best, no matter how she denied it or declared she loved her husband. Cass was determined that when it fell apart, he would be available to help her pick up the pieces of her life and start all over again—as Mrs. Cass Carson.

He kept encouraging her to tell him about the last three years and he was jealous of every month she had spent since their parting. The more she told the more out of sorts he became, so that by the time Syd appeared suddenly beside them, the only one of the three who was enjoying everything was Kay.

Snapping black eyes looked exactly level into icy blue ones and neither man said a word. Kay's mouth fell open as she looked from one man to the other. At last she found her voice and said, "Uh . . . Cass, I'd like you to meet my husband, Syd. Syd, this is Cass Carson, Ike Salter's friend. Do you remember him? He visited Ike at Preston General when—"

"I remember him," Syd said never taking his eyes off Cass's face.

Cass said, "I think we met, more or less, three years ago."

She laughed and hiccuped inadvertently. "Oh! Well! I hadn't realized you two had actually met," she exclaimed too brightly. She said to Syd, "I was just telling Cass about the last three years, you know?"

"All about her work, actually," Cass told Syd without a smile.

"Yes," she chirped nervously. Somehow her voice had gotten squeaky or something; somebody had certainly put too much vodka in that innocent little Bloody Mary she'd drunk when she first got here. . . .

Syd took his eyes from Cass's face and said to her, "Now that you've renewed your acquaintance, I'm sure you're ready to go home, Kay."

"Home? So early? But we haven't heard the governor's speech or Abe Truelove's—"

Syd took the empty glass of champagne gently from her hand.

Cass was saying, "Home! But she's out for the evening dressed up in a fine dress, Carlton, and she—"

Syd looked back at Cass. "You noticed that, too, did you?"

"I sure did. And probably so has every other gent in the house. Your wife is an attractive woman."

"That's right, Carson. *My wife* is an attractive woman who gave you the boot three years ago, remember?"

"Syd!" Kay exclaimed in horror.

"I remember it vividly," Cass drawled ignoring her. "And I've got no intention of being on the toe end of that boot again. I was only talking with her. Nothing very personal—at least nothing for you to get all hot under the collar about."

"Syd," Kay said taking his arm, "let's go. People are staring."

Syd did not reply to Cass. His expression told Cass all that needed to be said and Kay pulled him away, away from Cass's cold glare. The two men kept *glaring* at each other and Kay imagined that everybody in the entire ballroom was staring. Humiliated and slightly dizzy, she held on to Syd till they were out in the drive where he gave the parking attendant his ticket; and while they waited for their car to be brought around, Kay said, "You made an utter fool of yourself, Syd. And you had no cause to do that."

"I had cause and you know it," he snapped. "In the first place I never saw you drink two drinks in one evening and it wasn't becoming to you, baby. In the second place, I didn't like the way that cowboy was looking at you."

"He's not a cowboy; he's a rancher and we were only talking."

"With him accidentally touching you all the while."

"Only my arm."

"Only your arm. He had no right to touch your arm."

"You were rude and uncouth."

"And he had his hands on you, to say nothing of his designs. So help me, Kay, I'd have beat hell out of him—"

"You'd have a hard time doing that."

"Think so? Don't bet on it, baby."

When the car arrived, he opened the door for her, she got in, and he accidentally shut it on her dress; down the street they went with her blue dress flapping under the door. She knew and didn't care. The evening was ruined so her dress might as well be ruined, too.

"What I want to know is how he came to be here. How long has he been around, Kay? You were both too easy and familiar to have just met after three years."

She said, "Are you accusing me of some clandestine affair?"

His hands gripped the wheel of the car as he contemplated that. Then he smiled grimly. "No, I guess not. Not you."

She sighed. "All right. I went on an emergency flight two weeks ago during the rain." She told him about picking up Ike Salter, of taking him and Cass to St. Luke's, of their talk in the coffee shop.

"And you didn't tell me. Why?"

"I didn't want you upset. Besides, you're never home anymore."

By then Syd was cutting in and out of traffic causing

her to gasp and grab the door handle. When he stopped for a traffic light, a car pulled up in the lane next to them and a man leaned out the window. "Why don't you look where you're going?" he shouted.

"Up yours, buddy," Syd yelled back.

Kay covered her face with her hand and they were silent the rest of the way home, both furious: he, because he was jealous and because she hadn't told him about meeting the John Wayne-type again; and she, because he'd ruined the evening and almost accused her of meeting Cass on the sly.

Once he pulled the car into the drive and stopped it, she got out and ran up the steps of the veranda holding her skirts. On the way she stepped out of one shoe, but went on inside anyway.

Ben, who had declined his invitation to Abe Truelove's reception, was relaxing in his Naugahyde recliner in the living room with a book in his hand and a pipe in his mouth. Russell was sprawled on the couch watching TV. Both turned their attention to Kay as she rushed in red-faced, slammed the door, gathered up her soiled skirts, and ran up the stairs. Syd came in, her shoe in his hand, slammed the door, and ran up the stairs two steps at a time. Ben and Russell looked at each other. Russell said in a monotone, "I'll bet they were the life of the party."

Ben, who loved Kay and Syd both and would defend both to the death, took out his pipe and said, "Well, they're both very spirited people, all right."

Russell gave him a look that conveyed to him that his statement was less than noncommittal so Ben returned to his book and hoped he'd eventually hear the slats hit the floor, even if it did shake the chandeliers downstairs. But he heard only their muffled voices.

"I'm going to bed because I've got a headache," Kay told Syd as she undressed. "So you can go on downstairs because I'm not going to fight with you."

He only glared at her and began to unbutton his coat. When she saw that he wasn't going to leave, she took her nightgown and went into the connecting bathroom, shut the door, and locked it. When she came out, he was dressed in a sport shirt and slacks, his beautiful tux thrown haphazardly into the chair by the window.

"Where are you going?"

"Outside," he said, "for a long walk."

She didn't answer, only climbed into bed as he opened the bedroom door and slammed it behind him. Seconds later, she heard the front door slam too.

She went to sleep without turning off the light. When she awoke after two A.M., the light was still on, but Syd was beside her, his back to her, lying very still.

She loved him, more than anything in the world; loved everything about him and should have taken more care at the reception to discourage Cass's attention. But the truth was, she had enjoyed the attention, felt beautiful. And it *was* a party. But she shouldn't have encouraged Cass's conversation. It could only lead to this— alienation from the man she loved. His hair was in a mess on his pillow. He never slept in pajama tops so his hard back was exposed above the sheet. She thought of his hairy chest, sensitive lips, the sleepy-little-boy look he must have on his face. She reached out and put her hand on the back of his neck, ran her fingers up into his hair. But though his flesh broke out in goose bumps, he didn't move. The little boy in him was pouting, still angry, still hurt.

"I love you," she said softly.

He didn't answer.

"I'm so unhappy when we fight."

He didn't respond.

She ran her hands over his arm, over his side, and moved closer to him, put her arms around him and held him close. "I do love you and only you and I *chose* you, remember?"

When he neither answered nor spoke, she gave up and started to withdraw her hand, but he caught it, held it firmly, turned over, and smothered her in his hot, humid embrace. He was not gentle this time, but neither did he hurt her. He caressed her hungrily, made love desperately, spent himself exhaustively, and lay quiet again on his back, having fulfilled his desire and hers, too.

He dozed, but still held her wrist in an iron-tight grip, as if unconsciously afraid to let go lest she go away from him forever.

After a while she tried to pull away, but his eyes flew open and he gripped her wrist tighter. "Syd, let me go. I have to go to the bathroom," she complained.

He turned his head toward her. "You go to the bathroom ten times a night. If I didn't know you were on the pill, I'd think you were pregnant."

"Well, I *am* on the pill. Now let me go."

When she came back to bed, he pulled her to him and said gently, "I'm sorry I was rough when we made love, but I'm not sorry I did what I did at the reception."

"You weren't rough."

"Sorry if I ruined your evening."

"Me, too."

"It's just that I love you Kay. Very much."

She took his head to her breast and held it there. "I know," she whispered.

"Anything else that's happened lately that you've kept from me, to keep from . . . upsetting me?" he asked. "Because if there is, I want to know. We promised to share everything. Is there anything you need to tell me?"

She thought about the commotion and fright Mr. Parkman had caused in TRU, of her threat to resign, of her vomiting in the nurses' bathroom, of her continuing discomfort over Barney's and Harvey's cases, her fear for Harrison. And she opened her mouth to tell him, closed it, opened it again. "No, Syd. Nothing. Not anything at all. Everything's just fine," she lied.

CHAPTER XII

After the eleven to seven shift gave report to the seven to three shift, the telephone rang at the nurses' station in TRU and Kay answered.

"Kay, this is Ursala," came the nurse's voice over the phone. "I take two days off and when I come back, what do I have? Harrison on O_2 again because of respiratory distress. Now Dr. Paine thinks he may have either hyaline membrane disease or something else is wrong with his heart. I say to Dr. Paine, 'What are you going to do for Harrison?' And you know what he said? He said, 'Meuller, what makes you so sure I can do *anything?*' Can you imagine? I truly think the bum would let Harrison die."

Kay sat down in the chair at the desk, her hand going to her head. "Has he called Dr. Daizat?"

"No, he has not. I said to him, 'Why haven't you called Dr. Daizat?' He said to me, 'Meuller, mind your own damned business.' He tells me to mind my own damned business. What *is* my business, Kay—to stand by and watch Harrison die?"

Kay told her when she took her lunch break she'd come by the nursery. Meanwhile, TRU was quiet. All four patients were able to help bathe themselves now with the nurses' help and Kay helped the others change the bed linen as usual. The doctors came in early, and one by one Kay read the doctors' progress reports on all four patients.

Patient   Moriah Morgan Worley

July 2—Vital signs stable. Will probably schedule for surgery for anastamosis of colostomy next A.M.
J. B. Kreel, M.D.

Patient   Harvey Piedmont Chunn

July 2—Still severely depressed but VS stable. Neuro signs stable. No further deterioration of vision. Will grant visiting privileges to one person daily beginning this A.M., if you have no objections, Dr. Spade. Is it feasible to begin administration of a tranquilizer or mood elevator now? Please call my office between 2 and 3 P.M. if possible for consultation. Thanks for your help.
Edwin Cash, M.D.

Patient   Leola Joy Parkman

July 2—Surgical wound resolving. VS stable. Pt. agitated today. Will keep in TRU a few more days for observation.
J. B. Kreel, M.D.

Patient   Barney Edwin Werger

July 2—VS remain unstable BP and widening pulse

> pressure. Detect deterioration of mentation, suggesting possible neurological complication. Will call Dr. Basehart on consult.
>
> J. B. Kreel, M.D.

July 2—Routine neuro exam reveals no neuropathy. Suggest psychiatrist for this pt. Thanks for consult, Dr. Kreel. Please note my name is spelled with EA.
>
> *Roland A. Baseheart, M.D.*

Deterioration of mentation? Barney did seem lethargic, but his low blood pressure had climbed back up to normal again just after Dr. Kreel had left the unit at 7:30.

The nurses in TRU were convinced Barney's problem was depression and depression only. Severe depression was a mental pain worse than most physical pains and just as debilitating. Barney's depression was not yet severe, but they all thought it was becoming so swiftly; so, apparently, did the doctors.

With that worry on her mind, Kay took her lunch break with Anita, leaving Hailey and Jan in TRU. They dropped in at the nursery. It was just before feeding time for the infants. To walk into a newborn nursery at feeding time was a riot. Eva Patterson huffed and puffed as she heaved herself between the rows of cribs, tiny rectangular cribs on wheels in which furious red infants squirmed. Each infant screamed on a different key of the treble cleft. All had their legs pumping, arms waving, eyes squeezed shut, and mouths open. It was dinner time and each baby demanded food. Before carrying the babies to their mothers, each had to be diapered and wrapped in a fresh receiving blanket if his or hers had been soiled.

Ursala and Patterson were diapering and blanketing while a third nurse was gathering and marking the prepackaged formulas for those infants who weren't breast-fed. The nurses couldn't hear each other speak because of the noise in the place, an inexplicably irritating noise which caused them to hurry to do whatever was necessary to hush that screaming. However, the nurses' attention was mixed with pathos which made some want to take the creatures up and hug them to their breasts. This was an inclination which Kay called instinct.

For the fun of it, Kay and Anita fell to helping diaper the infants. One huge, ten-and-a-half-pound girl was a note lower on the scale than her peers and her bellow was more irritating than that of the others. Kay had to laugh when big Eva Patterson finally lost her temper. She turned to the fat infant. "Oh hush up, you big, fat bag of blubber," Eva yelled irritably, then took up the infant and hugged her in a cushioned embrace. The nursery nurses then left, each pushing a cart with six tiny cells in it in each of which an infant yelled and squirmed. And down the corridors they went. Mothers could hear them coming even over the hospital noise and that of the room TV sets.

Meanwhile, Kay and Anita had been left in charge of NICU at their insistence. Each pulled on a clean gown over her scrub suit, tied on a mask, and went in to see Harrison in the NICU.

The nasal cannula had been inserted again into his tiny nostrils; he was paler than when Kay had seen him the day before. His sternal retraction wasn't severe, but it was noticeable. His eyes were shut. His vital signs were still being monitored. His heart rate was rapid, around

180. It seemed to Kay, by looking around at all the apparatus attached to him, that everything was being done for Harrison in terms of monitoring. She counted five tubes: IV, urinary catheter, oxygen cannula, cardiac monitor, and rectal temp probe. A feeding tube would probably be inserted through his mouth at feeding time. Harrison was partly awake, turning his head from side to side. His arms were tied to the sides of the warming crib to keep him from pulling out his tubes, but still he had caught the urinary catheter between his stubby toes and seemed to be trying to pull it out. Kay took the tube from between his toes before he did.

It did appear that everything was being done for him, but she thought surely there was something a specialist could do to help Dr. Paine. She felt sick, sick for Harrison, and she felt pain because of his struggles. She wanted to take him up in her arms, but she could only stroke the warm little head with its white peach-fuzz hair and put her gloved finger in his restrained hand.

"You should have a baby," Anita said to her. "Have a baby and quit this place while you've still got your sanity. But don't you dare! Please don't leave me with TRU."

Kay was thinking, If Harrison were mine, could I bear to see him suffer? There were other kinds of physical suffering besides pain and Harrison was experiencing one of them. If he were mine, would I wish him to pass on and be free of it forever? Or would I hold on to every hope that he would survive, expend every effort to see that everything was done for him even as he continued his pitiful struggle. She was beginning to receive some insight into what Dr. Paine had been experiencing all along with Harrison, and had probably experienced many times before: dilemma, frustration, indecision.

When Ursala and the others came back, Kay and Anita left reluctantly and went to the cafeteria, the prettiest and brightest place in the entire hospital. The cafeteria was large, new, and clean. One whole wall was constructed of huge, plate-glass windows overlooking a beautifully landscaped patio area. Large baskets of ferns and other tropical plants hanging in front of the windows added a tropical-paradise respite from the green tile floors and ivory walls of the dreary corridors. The steam table was long, displaying three choices of entrées, several hot vegetables, and beds of salads and fruits on crushed ice, all served by cafeteria help dressed in gold uniforms.

Hospital food was traditionally unpalatable. Preston General's had been unpalatable for years until right before Kay had resigned. At that time, the cafeteria had changed dieticians and under the management and supervision of a new young dietician, the fare had improved drastically. Syd said he'd believe it when he saw it.

St. Luke's cuisine was fair. The dietician had good days and bad. Sometimes one could identify the entrées and sometimes one couldn't. Today Kay thought she had chosen steak and mushrooms and it turned out to be liver and onions. But no matter. While Anita chattered about a rock concert she'd attended over the weekend, Kay's mind wandered to Harrison and his problems, then to Barney, then to Harvey. Harrison wasn't under her charge, but Barney and Harvey were and she felt terribly responsible for them. She thought about both men's reactions to Mr. Parkman's demands, and something about that kept pulling at her mind demanding attention. Something about the fact that both had showed a

248

willingness to help, however weak the willingness was, it was still there. So the plunge into despair was not complete for either of them. But neither were they improving mentally, which was no surprise. TRU, like other critical-care areas, had its maximum level of improvement. In critical-care units, patients improved only so far and then the improvement seemed to slow down or cease entirely until they were moved out to the regular ward, where recovery accelerated again rapidly. It almost never failed. She was in favor of transferring both Harvey and Barney to the ward and told Drs. Cash and Kreel so.

But Cash's objection to moving Harvey out was, he needed constant watching which the regular wards could not provide. Harvey had no family and no money to hire a private-duty nurse around the clock. His depressive state could be managed on the psychiatric floor, but not his head trauma. TRU was the only answer, at least for a few more days.

A few more days and Harvey could be beyond help, she was sure, due to his mental depression. When Harvey started to crash he'd do it suddenly—all vitals plummet like an airplane shot down.

Barney was different. He was unaccustomed to depression and his usual good humor kept dueling with his despair, causing his vital signs to fluctuate. She was as sure that the mental status of a patient influenced his physical state as she was of anything else in medicine. Dr. Kreel still refused to move Barney as long as his vital signs were unstable. It was his own unwritten code.

And neither man would try to help himself. Barney had attempted to get up in the chair only once and that had been a failure; he refused to try again. Harvey

249

refused to even think about it.

"... So I said to the giraffe, 'Giraffe, gee your neck is long.' And you know what he told me?"

Kay shook her head, still pretending to listen to Anita's prattle.

"He told me that *you haven't heard a word I've been saying*."

Kay smiled at her slowly. "I'm sorry, Anita. I really haven't."

"Worried about Harrison, aren't you? And Barney and Harvey and Leola."

Kay just looked at her.

Anita nodded. "You've got critical care-itis. I get it once in a while as you saw last week. Once a week I think I'm going crazy and swear I'm going to transfer to OB, geese or no geese. But do you know what I've started doing for it? I take a big dose of a medicine called 'play.' I go to concerts, movies, anything. Anything to take my mind off the hospital. Anything to remind me that there's something to life besides sickness and dying. Smoking helps. In the evenings I have a few cocktails; takes the edge off the worry. But I've found out the more I play the less likely I am to need the cocktails."

"OB has its problems too," Kay said half-heartedly.

"Tell me an area of this profession that doesn't. The regular ward's the worst. Too much confusion, too many doctors, too much staff to manage, too many patients. A ward nurse has got to be a plaster saint to put up with all of it—and have nerves of steel to boot." Anita ground out her second cigarette in the ashtray on the table.

"Why don't you quit and become a secretary or something?"

Anita put her cigarette case back into her purse.

250

"You're kidding, of course. I'll always be a nurse. So will you."

Kay nodded.

"But you'll go nuts if you keep worrying like you've been doing lately. I've been worrying, too, about Harvey and Barney mostly. One's a blind writer, the other's a paralyzed actor. Too bad we can't squash them together and throw away the messed up parts like we used to do with modeling clay when we were kids."

Kay regarded Anita. Something she had just said jarred the elusive solution in the back of her own mind. *Squash them together and throw away the—*

Suddenly the paging system clicked on overhead and the switchboard operator paged, "Kay Carlton to TRU stat. Kay Carlton to TRU stat."

Anita and Kay stared at each other.

"Barney," Anita said.

"Or a new admission," Kay said quickly pushing her chair away from the table.

"Or Harvey," Anita said standing up.

"Or Leola."

They shoved their trays through the window of the kitchen at the end of the steam table near the door and half-ran, half-walked down the corridor toward TRU.

Both Jan and Hailey were in Harvey's room when they hurried into the unit, and Kay didn't have to ask what had happened. Blood was everywhere—covering the sheets, the side rails, and had even spattered onto the tiled floor. Harvey had neatly peeled off the tape covering his IV intracath and disconnected the IV tubing from the catheter hub in his vein.

"Have you called Dr. Cash?" Kay asked Hailey.

"We've put in a call to his answering service, but he

251

hasn't called back yet."

"What're Harvey's vitals?"

"Normal except the pulse is a little fast as you can see on the monitor. He probably lost about 300 ccs at least. Kay, I'd just left the room. I don't see how—"

"Damn you, Harvey!"

The other nurses in the room paused in their fussing over Harvey and stared at Kay.

Harvey smiled wryly. "Another ten minutes, Kay, and oblivion would have been mine."

"Oblivion, hell, Harvey. The catheter would eventually have gotten clogged by a clot. You idiot!" She was out of control and knew it—all out of control—and the nurses knew it, too. Kay seldom cursed, seldom showed impatience with a patient. *Out of control*, flashed in her burning brain like a warning signal, so she left the room trembling more from fear of her loss of control now than of Harvey's attempted suicide.

At the nurses' desk she called the lab to come take a blood sample for a type and cross match in case Dr. Cash wanted to give him a unit of blood, and an H and H to determine his hemoglobin and hematocrit. Then she put in a call to Dr. Cash's answering service.

Dr. Cash did not have time to return the call, for he came into the unit in person just as Kay put down the receiver of the telephone.

She looked up as he entered. Dr. Cash, always half-irritated anyway, came to the nurses' station, red brows raised in a silent, irritated question. "It's Harvey Chunn. He pulled the IV tubing from his catheter hub," Kay told him.

Cash pursed his lips, shook his head, went in and took a look at the blood on the sheets, the floor, estimating the blood loss. Kay had followed him into the room and watched as he lifted the sheets and again looked at the floor. "Having a bad time, Harvey?" he asked.

"When have I ever *not* had a bad time, Doc?"

"Tried to do away with yourself again, eh?"

"Yeah, but it seems I blew it again."

Cash stood looking at Harvey, apparently at a loss as to what to do or say. "I guess, Harvey, I'll have to have the nurses restrain you. Tie your hands to the bedrail." He thought a moment, watched Harvey's stoic expression as he lay there with eyes shut, hands clenched at his sides. "Or I could tranquilize you down till you can't move."

"That sounds best, Doc."

"But there's always a day of reckoning, Harvey; a day when you've got to face your problems. You can't stay doped up forever."

"I'll worry about that later. Just dope me up now, Doc."

"Temporarily, maybe. Only until I figure out what to do with you. I don't usually give sedations to head-trauma patients. But in spite of your determination not to live, you've managed to survive the critical period." Cash appeared to want to say more, but he turned away suddenly in disgust instead.

"I ordered the lab to do a type and cross match," Kay said following him from the room, "in case you need to give him blood."

Cash glanced at her. "I didn't *order* a type and cross match."

"I know, but in here it's routine if—"

"Kreel's routine, not mine. Now you've added about sixteen dollars onto his hospital bill which was uncalled for. All I'm going to order is an H and H. I'm not going to give him blood. Maybe an injection of Imferon, iron to build up the blood, but I won't order a transfusion." Grumpily Cash went into the doctor's booth and shut the door to think and write orders and curse to himself.

As Cash sat down and picked up the dictaphone, the lab tech came in. Kay told him all that was needed was the H and H. She was feeling awful because of the way she had talked to Harvey. He needed TLC, not a dressing down. *I'll quit after work. Resign. I can't handle this anymore. I'll—*

The light over Barney's door came on and since the others were cleaning up the mess in Harvey's room, she answered the summons.

When she entered his room it was bright with sun pouring in through the half-pulled shade. He turned his face toward her.

"Hi Barney," she said affecting a smile. "What do you need?"

"Help me get up into a wheelchair, will you?"

"Wheelchair?" Her eyes darted around the room. Her spirits shot up like a rocket on the Fourth of July. "Just a second."

At Harvey's door she motioned for Hailey. "Barney says he wants up in a wheelchair."

Hailey dropped the wad of soiled sheets into a chair breathing, "Lord a-livin'!" and then hurried toward Barney's room. As Kay got the wheelchair from the storage alcove near the linen room, she could hear Hailey saying, "What set the burr under your tail, Barney?"

"No burr. And I wouldn't feel it if there was one. Just you and Carlton get me up. I'll help all I can. There's something I have to do."

Tug, tug, went the elusive solution as it tried to open

254

the door of her subconscious and get out into the light. *Too bad we can't squash them together and throw away the messed up parts—*

They lowered the bed to the level of the wheelchair seat and rolled the head of the bed up all the way. Together they shifted Barney, donut and all, over to the wheelchair, each nurse supporting one of his legs as they went. Once situated, they put his robe over his shoulders and looked at him expectantly.

Instead of Barney's face being pale now, it was scarlet. He said, "Now roll me to Harvey's room."

Hailey's eyes widened. "Barney, it's against the rules. We can't do it. Can't risk infection, you see, in case—"

"I don't have an infection. I'm aware that my temperature has been below normal like everything else about me." He turned to Kay. "I heard what happened in there. Roll me in there, will you?"

Absolutely against the rules to mix patients in TRU. And Dr. Cash was here and in a foul mood. He'd have their heads. *Too bad we can't squash them together and throw away the messed up parts—*

Kay hooked Barney's IV on the pole attached to the wheelchair, took a deep breath, and rolled him to the entrance of Harvey's room.

By then Harvey's bed linen had been changed and the nurses had cleaned up the blood on the floor. Anita had even started a new IV because the old one would have been contaminated once it was disconnected.

Harvey lay in his clean bed staring up at the ceiling, or at whatever a blind man, who could see only shadows and light, stared. Barney said, "Bastard!"

Harvey blinked, turned his face in Barney's direction. Jan and Anita paused in their fussing about the room to stare at Barney, then at Kay.

"Do you think you've got a monopoly on rejections?" Barney demanded.

Harvey's smile grew slowly. "You must be Werger. I recognize the dramatics. Good afternoon."

"Good afternoon, hell! A fine good afternoon for these nurses had you succeeded in doing away with yourself. They'd have all been fired. What kind of an ass are you anyway?"

"Grammatically you are incorrect, Werger. It's what kind of an ass *have* I? My answer is, 'Intact.' I don't fool around with married women."

"You *are* the ass, with no guts, and that's the worst kind, buddy. Do you think you have a monopoly on rejections? Man, I've been rejected a thousand times and it's not just the diarrhea of my brain they've rejected, but my entire body."

"You donating organs?"

"As a matter of fact I sacrificed one for experimental purposes."

Harvey paused before he replied, "You're *really* crippled, man."

"But I'm not trying to do away with myself."

"Congratulations."

The nurses were astonished that Harvey was as quick with one-liners as Barney. Barney did that to people. He'd affected the whole nursing staff that way.

"My name's not bastard, incidentally. It's Chunn, Harvey Chunn. I'm a writer. How do you do?"

"Through a colostomy, Chunn, for the rest of my life." Barney's mouth worked with mixed emotion. "What do you write, obituaries?"

"Staff writer for the *Evening Globe*. You've seen my name."

"Maybe in some graffiti on the wall of a cra—uh, a public rest room. Yeah, I've seen your name somewhere."

"Maybe it was in the credits of one of my TV plays. Dramatic plays, movie of the week. 'A Ticket for Tony' last January, and 'Tennessee' in April."

"Never heard of 'em."

"Yeah, well I never heard of you either. Barney Werger's a shitty name I'd never forget. Burned hamburger is what I picture when I hear that name."

"That's me. That's just about all that's left."

Harvey winced. "What are you doing in my room, anyway? Who invited you? Kay! Get him out. My new shot's beginning to work and I'm feeling sleepy."

"Going to trip out on downers, eh? Take the easy way?" Barney said, as if he hadn't been doing the same thing lately. "Yeah, Carlton, roll me out of here. This guy makes me sick."

"Ha!"

Well, Kay thought as Hailey rolled Barney down the hallway, that was a bummer. Or was it? And Dr. Cash, still dictating on the dictaphone in the doctors' booth hadn't witnessed the episode at all. She was thinking it was just as well.

"Barney, I'm sure you didn't help his ego any," Hailey told him as she and Kay got Barney back to his bed.

"Don't kid yourself, Hailey. The way I talked to Chunn is the only way you can get through his apathy to his gut. You have to shoot for a person's gut if you want to impress him. I know from experience. Now can I have my pain shot, please?"

Kay went in to check on Harvey. "Who the hell does he think he is, barging into my room calling me a bastard?" Harvey blinked, pondered, then said, "I *am* a bastard, you know. I did some investigating a few years ago and found out my mother was a whore. That's a real nice discovery. Never heard of 'A Ticket for Tony' and it played twice on CBS. Who does he think *he* is, Lionel Barrymore?" Harvey fell silent as Kay checked the new IV, and watched his pulse rate and arterial BP on the monitor on the wall above his bed. "That—that so-called actor, is he getting any better? I mean, will he ever get the feeling back in his— Will he ever use his legs again?"

"We don't know. Dr. Kreel thinks not."

"What the hell will a guy like him do for a living?"

"I don't know."

"Is he . . . getting along O.K.?"

"No."

"What's wrong?"

"What do you think? His life was acting. He acted in some local little-theater plays and dinner-theater plays all over the country. He'd even begun to act in off-Broadway productions. Drama was his major in college, and he was becoming well-known locally."

Harvey was silent, lying with his eyes closed, his hands relaxed and folded upon his abdomen. She was just beginning to think he had gone to sleep when he said, "We a-a-ll-ll-ll got problems."

"That's right, Harvey. And none of them are easy."

No, none of them are easy at all.

Since Mr. Parkman had attempted to take Leola out of

TRU, she had been restless and irritable. Immediately after he had been ejected from the unit, she had wept in fury and embarrassment. Then, as the hours passed, she became silent and meditative. Today, she was telling the nurses who came in to care for her, "He really *is* sorry, you know. Maybe he's learned his lesson and would be more patient with me."

"Patient with you for what, Leola?" Jan asked.

"Well, for whatever it is that I do that irritates him."

Jan, young and single, lived in an apartment with a roommate. After graduating from nursing school only two years ago, she'd spent one and a half years as staff nurse on the floor and six months in TRU. Big-boned, but tall and slender, Jan was a typical Swede. She'd never been married, would never understand anyone who would condone the abuse Leola had from Parkman. Of the four nurses on day shift in TRU, she was the least likely to be discerning in imparting what advice she did have. But on this occasion, she voiced what they had all wanted to say but ethically could not: "You should leave your husband, Leola."

The next day Jan was called into the nursing director's office and reprimanded for the advice she gave to Leola. Nobody knew how word of it got to Thompson; probably it was mentioned in report and Abby Jones told her about it, they decided. At any rate, the nurses passed the word from shift to shift, "Be careful what you advise Leola Parkman." Even if your advice might influence her to make a better life for herself.

At last Dr. Kreel wrote an order for Leola to be transferred to the trauma ward, and as Hailey and Jan got her ready to move, Kay took her vitals and recorded the transfer in the chart.

St. Luke's General Hospital

Patient *Leola Joy Parkman*
Hosp. No. *05621*   Ward *TRU*

NURSES' NOTES

Treatments and Medications	Nurse's Notes

6/6—7:30 Tetracycline 500 mg IV by AW

6/6—8:10 Dr. Kreel in. Left orders for transfer to ward. Transferred to room T-306 as per order. 350 ccs D5W IV infusing @ 8 gtts per min. V/S pulse 75; resp. 14, BP 140/80. In good spirits.
　　　　　　　K. Carlton, R.N.

In her new room on the ward Leola, once settled in her bed, took Kay's hand. She seemed a little frightened as she said, "Will I see you nurses from TRU again?"

Kay answered, "I'll be by to see you and so will the others, I'm sure."

"I want you to know that you nurses, and especially you, have given me the courage to try to make a life of my own with my children. And I have memorized the telephone number of the shelter for . . . for battered women." She smiled. "Me, a battered woman. Did you know I had never considered myself battered before?"

When Kay left the room she gave a brief report on Leola to the very apprehensive nurse in charge of the ward. The nurses had already been instructed by Dr. Kreel to watch out for Parkman and to limit his visits to thirty minutes twice a day, and to keep watch on the couple while he was visiting—a lot of responsibility on the nurses in charge and the nurses who would be assigned to Leola's care.

As she rode the elevator down to the second floor, it occurred to Kay once again what varied responsibilities nurses have. As a nurse you're a legal guardian, diagnostician, maidservant, medication dispenser, assistant surgeon, part-time respiratory therapist, lab tech, personal valet, manager, counselor, psychiatrist, bodyguard and friend. The pay was low, but the rewards were great.

I want you to know you nurses, and especially you, have given me the courage . . . was her personal reward for a few minutes counseling and a sore wrist. But it was reward enough.

CHAPTER XIII

Syd had written Dr. Grady Michaelson about Billy Roy Ballew, describing in a four-page typewritten letter his and Harry's sessions and their results. Michaelson was a psychoanalyst who had written a lengthy account in the *Psychology Today* journal entitled, "The Ballad of Seymour Coleridge." The account described how Dr. Michaelson had, through hypnosis, elicited sixteen separate personalities with sixteen different names from a severely neurotic patient.

Today a thick envelope lay in Syd's mailbox when he came to his office in the psychology building. The return address on the envelope was that of Dr. Grady Michaelson. Eagerly Syd unlocked his office door. As he went in he ripped open the envelope and sat down at his desk.

In the letter Dr. Michaelson stated that he was extremely fascinated by Ballew's case because it had been his suspicion for several years that the multipersonalities of Seymour Coleridge and others he had described, might be personalities from previous lives merged into the present life of the subject, personalities which mentally came to the contemporary neurotic's rescue. Syd's idea debunking reincarnation and theorizing genetic memory was a new and fascinating idea, Michaelson said. The doctor went on to write that he would indeed consider interviewing Ballew. In fact there was no need for Syd to send Ballew to California; Michaelson was just beginning a three-week vacation period with no plans and would be happy to meet Syd and Harry at the university and interview Ballew. He asked Syd to telephone him so that they could make further arrangements.

Smiling hugely, Syd picked up the receiver of the telephone, dialed 1 and the telephone number on Dr. Michaelson's letter.

Dr. Kreel hadn't left TRU since he had handed Kay the new trauma patient's History and Physical report. Most of the time Kreel dictated his operative notes and History and Physical reports. Today he'd written the H and P in longhand and then commenced to wander about the unit surveying the rooms and equipment while Kay read the report to acquaint herself more with the new patient. That morning Kreel had been busy. He had assisted Daizat in repairing the patient's ribs and was scheduled to perform surgery on Dr. Worley to reverse his colostomy later in the morning.

While Kreel sauntered around the unit lost in his own thoughts, sipping coffee he had taken from the nurses' coffee carafe in the TRU kitchen, Kay read the H and P on Mr. Jack Mackey Brunner.

St. Luke's General Hospital

Patient   Jack Mackey Brunner
Hosp. No.   09454   *Ward   TRU*

HISTORY & PHYSICAL

July 7—Admitted to Trauma Receiving at 5:45 A.M. by

district-six fire-department ambulance, 76-year-old male in respiratory distress. Police reported pt. was crossing street after buying newspaper at corner pharmacy and was struck down by automobile driven by teen-aged girl. Initial exam by Dr. Boweler in TR revealed possible fractured sternum and fractured ribs on the right. There were multiple abrasions and lacerations over much of the left side of his body, and numerous fresh contusions over much of his right side.

Abdominal tap was negative. Multiple abdominal and chest x-rays revealed simple fracture of the body of the sternum and compound fractures to the shafts of third, fourth, and fifth ribs on R side. R pleural effusion as result of puncture of pleura. Suffered slight concussion. (See TR admission sheet.)

Dr. Daizat assisted me in surgical clamping of third and fourth ribs to prevent further damage to lung. R pleural effusion relieved by chest tube in third intercostal space. Tracheostomy by Dr. Daizat. Pt. placed on respirator and admitted to TRU. (See op notes.)

Well-developed, well-nourished nonsmoker, retired for fifteen years from postal service. Has two sons and four daughters, all living within the city. Wife died in 1976 of breast cancer. Family claims pt. has been active and healthy most of his life with only occasional mild episodes of arthritis. On no medications except laxative for constipation. Takes this about twice a week. Father died of tuberculosis in 1909, mother died of unknown "kidney disease" in 1911.

CBC, lytes, sed rate within normal limits. VS are stable. No arrythmias have been noted on monitor.

J. B. Kreel, M.D.

Mr. Brunner had been admitted to TRU right at change

of shifts from OR. He was awake, alert, and stoically frightened. Dr. Daizat, who had performed a tracheostomy on Brunner, would manage the respirator and had sedated him lightly with morphine.

Although Brunner had arrived in TRU alert, he had refused to respond to any verbal stimuli. The usual neuro check proved that all neuro signs were normal. When Kay consulted his daughter in the TRU waiting room about his mental status, she was told that Brunner had always been alert and healthy, but that he was stubborn and didn't believe in doctors, hospitals, or illness, and was probably angry about finding himself in his present predicament.

He couldn't have answered verbally because of his tracheostomy, but he wouldn't respond any other way to their suggestions or questions. He stubbornly refused to nod or shake his head to yes-and-no questions.

But even so, Brunner with his snowy hair and his pathetic bruises and abrasions immediately captured the TRU nurses' hearts; whether he liked it or not he became each one's own grandfather. If there were ever nurses' pets in critical-care areas, they were usually the elderly patients.

Now Kay looked up from the History and Physical just as Dr. Kreel approached the nurses' station again.

He leaned on the desk, his blue eyes ablaze with some kind of private pleasure, and in his mild voice asked, "Carlton, is your jump suit freshly laundered, starched, and ironed?"

His easygoing smile was catching and Kay returned it. "It's never starched and ironed, Doctor, because the hospital laundry launders it. Besides, it's permapressed."

"Take a peek at your jump suits next time you go near

the nurses' lounge."

She looked at him wordlessly. He had a smug look, the same look he had had when the hospital had opened the new trauma ward on the third floor, or when the hospital had repainted the Ranger, or when he had acquired Korean War veteran helicopter pilot, Jerry Bergdorf, who was willing to live in a small brick house nearby to spend most of his day in the Ranger Control Center seeing to the vehicle's most intimate personal needs, and to be on call twenty-four hours every day. Or—

"I've ordered them ironed," he said. "My wife's idea."

She stared. "You're kidding. Why?"

"Are you familiar with the *Southwest Medical Journal?*"

She said, "I've heard of it."

"Well, the journal has hired a free-lance photographer to do a story on St. Luke's entire trauma program. I'm surprised you haven't heard. He's flown with Jerry on some routine transfers this week. Took a patient from here to the burn center in Galveston, and a critically ill child to Children's Medical in Dallas. They just got back from carrying twenty pints of blood to Alavord. The photographer was impressed with the Ranger's medivac equipment and its versatility, and especially its availability for routine ambulance services. I told him he hadn't seen anything yet, to wait till we have to make an emergency flight and he can see you girls in action. He's having fun swapping Vietnam and Korean war tales at the control station with Jerry, waiting for something to happen. So be prepared to look and act your best. Just in case."

"Are you kidding about ironing our jump suits?"

"As I said, take a look next time you pass the nurses' lounge."

The light came on over Harvey's door and since Anita was busy getting Dr. Worley ready for surgery, Jan was bathing Barney, and Hailey was taking Mr. Brunner's vitals, Kay rose to answer the light. She excused herself and went to Harvey's room. Kreel, still smiling smugly, sauntered out of the unit.

"Good morning, Harvey," she said to him. "What is it?"

He turned his face toward her. "I've been lying here thinking. What kind of S.O.B. is Werger to reprimand me for my behavior and call me a bastard?"

Astonished, Kay said, "Harvey, that was two days ago!"

"I've been doped up since then. Now that Cash has withdrawn the help, the more I think about that bastard's comments that day, the madder I get. Referred to my writing as diarrhea of the brain— What makes him think he can judge somebody's writing when he hasn't read any of it? Who's he to judge anyway—a two-bit actor starving to death—Kay? I want up in a wheelchair."

Kay hesitated only a fraction of a minute before she, smiling smugly, hurried out of Harvey's room to get a wheelchair. As she passed Room Five where Barney lay, she called Jan for help. When they rolled the chair into Harvey's room he was already sitting on the side of the bed.

"Hold it, Harvey," Jan said. "This is your first time up so you've got to take it slow."

"Feel dizzy?" Kay asked.

"Nope," he replied. The dressings had been removed

267

from his head weeks ago and only a small patch—a four-by-four gauze sponge—was taped to the surgical area on the back of his head. There was no dressing on the forehead now to cover the angry red vertical scar. His hair was growing out after having been shaved for the surgery, and was sticking out from his scalp about two inches in all directions, giving him a bizarre look.

While Jan lowered his bed to its lowest position, Kay felt Harvey's pulse to see how he was tolerating being up. Pulse rate was above normal, about eighty-five, but that was to be expected. She bent down and slipped on his house slippers which had been ready for this moment for three weeks. Harvey's CVP line and cardiac-monitor leads had been disconnected days ago which made him easier to manage. All Jan and Kay had to manipulate were his Foley catheter and IV. Kay hooked the urinary drainage bag onto the lower part of the wheelchair while Jan hung the IV to its pole attached to the chair's back. Jan then spread a sheet over Harvey's lap. With his shocked-looking hair and scraggly beard, which he would allow no one to comb or trim, and with an expression of indignation born out of hours of stewing because somebody had dared question his ability to write, Harvey sat stoically for the first time in over three weeks while Kay wheeled him from Room Two to Room Five, and just inside the door.

Barney had just had his bed bath and the head of his bed was rolled up all the way. He was prepared to settle down into the comfort of his pillows when Harvey suddenly appeared in the doorway of his room. Barney said, "Shakespeare, I presume?"

"You've got colossal nerve. You don't need any nerves below the belt, you've got enough above it to make up for

268

what got blown off. I mean, to judge somebody else's work when you haven't seen it!" Harvey blurted out with no preliminaries.

"I judge a book by its cover," Barney said, smiling.

Harvey's hands were gripping the arms of the chair. "You can't do that!" he exclaimed angrily. Then, tentatively, "What do you mean?"

"A play, any play, has an author. I've become astute over the years at judging a play by its author. If he's a bum, his play's a bummer. If he's well-heeled, his play's probably a dog, but he's being promoted by somebody in the theater hierarchy. If I never met him but his name is Mortimer J. Platypus, I know he's written a loser. Harvey P. Chunn sounds fishy to me."

Harvey said, "You're an egomaniac just like all the rest of the actors I've ever met. And I've met plenty. You'd have to be an egomaniac to demand the limelight with such nauseating consistency. And your humor smells too, like the asshole in your abdomen."

Barney's smile slowly ceased and his face reddened. "I think the bullet you put in your head must have improved your mind considerably. That was a good line, Chunn, aimed right at my gut. That's where you've got to aim, at the audience's gut."

"You're one to talk about guts—"

"At least I've got a few left—"

"Horseshit. I heard the nurses in here making your bed while you just lay there."

"How many times have you been up, Chunn? You haven't been up at all, have you? Just wanting to lie there till you figure out a way to do away with yourself. For no reason—rejection is no reason. Everybody that is anybody has been rejected before and after they became

269

famous; authors, playwrights, actors, Abraham Lincoln, Christopher Columbus, Jesus Christ, entire races and cultures—"

"I don't need to hear your half-baked sociology lecture. I'd be curious to hear you read some lines from a play, though—any play. Because I don't believe you acted in off-Broadway productions. That's a lie you conjured up to impress the nurses. Well, it doesn't impress me."

Harvey was very pale by now from the exhaustion of being up for the first time. His knees were trembling, but Kay could see that the plan that had been forming in the back of her mind for several days, the plan she hadn't been able to bring out of her subconscious until now, was on the brink of working, so she risked leaving him with Barney a moment longer.

Barney took the bait—or had Barney provided the bait himself? "I'll read some lines for you, Chunn. How about some of your own? Because maybe I don't believe you're a playwright. I still think you write obituaries for a living."

Harvey's jaw set. "I'll get my friend, Ernie, to bring a copy of my last play."

"One of the *many* that was rejected preferably."

"The best of the *two* that were rejected."

"Very well, have him bring it then so I can read and weep."

"Very well; Ernie's a her, a friend who does some of my typing."

"I was right. You're no playwright. Whoever heard of a writer who couldn't type?"

Because of Harvey's pallor and shortness of breath, Kay turned his wheelchair around to take him quickly back to his room, but Harvey said over his shoulder, "I can type; only Ernie's faster—and willing. And whoever the hell heard of an actor with no ass—"

The nurses were in a huddle at the desk pretending to be engrossed in vital-sign sheets, but actually they had been eavesdropping on Barney and Harvey. Neither man was fooling anybody with his pretentions of hostility toward the other. The interplay between them was a melodrama entitled *Empathy*. Cast of characters: crippled, cynical, comic actor played by Barney Edwin Werger; the blind, depressed, indignant writer played by Harvey P. Chunn; supporting actresses; the nurses of TRU.

Most of the time the daily hospital routine was truly as dramatic as the hospital soap operas on TV. Once in a while, it was more so.

While Kay and Jan were getting Harvey back into his bed, Dr. Daizat came into the unit and went into Mr. Brunner's room. Moments later he met Kay at the nurses' station saying, "I want to put an arterial line in Brunner while I'm here."

Kay nodded. She had anticipated that and had the arterial cutdown tray ready on the stand outside Brunner's door.

"How's Harrison?" she asked.

"Harrison is better," Daizat said, "but I don't think he'll be better for long. It's not hyaline membrane disease. We think it's a leakage in the anastamosis site of one or the other of the arteries in the heart, or one in the heart itself which we didn't find the first time, or something that's developed in his heart since. Tomorrow it might be another and the next day something else. We don't know what's wrong." Daizat shrugged, shook his

271

head. "Could be one of a dozen things, a dozen things. Who knows?"

Anita approached the desk now because she had heard Harrison's name mentioned. Kay's eyes had misted because she had noted that Daizat had lost hope for Harrison, or he had never had any to begin with, or maybe he did not *want* to have hope. He was like Dr. Paine and Dr. Pugh. They had to try because of the pressure from the parents and the nursery nurses and because of their own consciences and ethics. But they thought Harrison was doomed by some terminal malady, and his sentence of death was from a higher authority.

Anita said, "If I ever stop believing in God, Dr. Daizat, it will be because of things like what has happened to Harrison."

Daizat always had time to teach or explain things to the nurses. He who had come from a country where women were regarded as chattel and considered less important than donkeys, treated the nurses at St. Luke's as intelligent colleagues. Now he leaned on the desk, looked up at the ceiling, and began to verbalize one of his many philosophies. "God is a fantastic scientist!" he exclaimed. "I don't see Him as a remote deity. He's like you and me. Only He's a great inventor, a mechanical genius, a great chemist, superior physicist, a magnificent sculptor. He envisioned a man and worked out all the mechanics to make him live, all the intricacies of how to make him work, all the integral parts interacting . . ." He drew in his breath, his black eyes turned upon Anita as he shook his head for emphasis, ". . . with remarkable precision. We are able to build robots of metal and wires and transistors, and manage them by computer.

Ah, but *He* built us of soft tissue, vessels, organs, and the most sophisticated computer of all, the human brain. He's just more advanced in His technology than we are." The "Arab," as Abby Jones called him, reached back into the common history of Jews, Gentiles, and Arabs alike and came up with, "When the first two robots God created decided to ignore His admonition to abstain from eating the fruit of the tree of knowledge of good and evil, He said in effect, 'All right, my friends, then I leave it to you, with your new knowledge, to work the bugs out of my invention yourselves.'" Daizat shrugged, smiling beneath his bristly mustache. "And so you see we've tried to correct the mechanical flaws that show up now and then and to keep the independent robots running at peak performance, lo these many thousands of years."

The unit was so quiet! Barney and Harvey were sunk deep in their own thoughts. Dr. Worley had been taken to surgery moments earlier. Only Mr. Brunner's respirator's sighing broke the stillness as Daizat contemplated his own philosophy. A little awed, Kay and Anita watched him, for occasionally a doctor would offer a brief philosophical viewpoint on something pertaining to the workings of the human body and mind, but this was the first time they'd ever heard this one.

Kay's other questions about Harrison went unasked and unanswered, because Daizat jerked his head toward Room Three. "Let's do the arterial line, Carlton."

Near noon, the orderlies brought Dr. Worley back from OR where his colostomy had been closed, the two severed ends of his colon reconnected. If all went well, his GI tract would begin to function normally again in two or three days. When surgery was performed on the intestines, or when the intestines were handled during exploratory surgery, peristalsis almost invariably ceased. Peristalsis was the wormlike movement of the small and large intestines which caused digested and semidigested material to move through the twenty-three feet of small intestine and the five feet of large intestine toward the rectum for excretion. Therefore, the most important observation the nurses and doctors could make of a patient after abdominal surgery was to listen for bowel sounds, the gurgling and squeaking, usually heard only through the stethoscope, of intestinal fluid and gas. The second thing they watched for was the passing of flatus, or gas. A doctor checking on his patient after abdominal surgery, searched the patient's chart diligently—sometimes feverishly—for any observation the nurses might have made in the chart that the patient had passed flatus. The passing of flatus by an abdominal surgery patient was an occasion for great rejoicing by the nursing staff and an occurrence which provided the surgeon with a great deal of relief and pride in the fact that he had performed his operation well and that the patient was responding accordingly.

But one couldn't expect peristalsis to begin for Dr. Worley for several days yet. The nurses fussed over him as they did over a new admission but he had not been in the unit fifteen minutes before everybody realized the quiet that day was only the calm before the storm. The change began when Worley pulled out his nasogastric tube and began to cry, "I—hurt."

"Dr. Worley? Dr. Worley!" Anita said loudly to him, trying to penetrate the remaining haze of anesthesia to get to his reasoning. "Dr. Worley, you must leave the nasogastric tube in! Don't pull it out or you'll get sick to your stomach! And when you need something, use your nurse call bell. Here, I'll hook it right here on the bedrail so all you have to do is reach up and press the button when you want something. Don't shout, O.K.? You can have something for pain in about twenty minutes. You aren't due yet for a pain shot. If you need anything just push the call bell. Don't shout, O.K.?"

"I—hurt."

The respirator in Mr. Brunner's room continued to hiss and clunk. Harvey's IV infiltrated without his help, causing his arm to swell with fluid which had infused into his skin instead of into his vein; Barney's colostomy had leaked and the unit reeked with surgical prep and feces. Kay finished charting Worley's admission from OR and transcribing doctors' orders from the charts onto the Kardex, and went in to help clean Barney's bed. He lay depressed, silent with humiliation. Then she hurried in to suction Mr. Brunner's tracheostomy, a great gaping wound around the trach tube. Irritably, Kay found herself wondering for the hundredth time why Daizat, one of the best of thoracic surgeons always made such huge gashes for his tracheostomies.

She washed her hands again. The staff washed their hands a hundred times a day in TRU, always between patients, using a soapy Betadine solution that seemed to make their fingernails grow but their hands look older than their years. For six years Kay had washed her hands ninety times a day in Betadine solution; secretly she chalked up in the file of her brain the observation that those scrubs could be the reason critical-care nurses' hair had such beautiful sheens. . . .

275

By mid-afternoon, she found herself clenching her teeth with tension. She suddenly wanted to go home—just walk out and go home. Instead, she cried—for no reason, just began to cry. The tension isn't really that bad, she told herself. But it was nearing three o'clock and nobody had been able to take a lunch break. Anita was out of sorts because of her schedule again, Hailey was behind in her nurses' notes, and Jan was starting an IV for Harvey who was shouting, "Ow! Ouch, damn it!"

While Kay washed her hands after cleaning Mr. Brunner's trach with its bleeding gash, the telephone rang at the nurses' station. With paper towel still in hand, she hurried to the nurses' station and answered irritably, "Kay Strom, ICU!"

There was silence on the other end of the line, and then Kay, realizing what she had said corrected herself, "I mean, Kay Carlton, TRU."

"Kay? What's wrong?" came a breathless female voice over the line.

"Who is this?" Kay asked reddening.

"Beasley in CCU. Kay, Ike Salter just crashed. Just thought you'd want to know before you left for home."

Kay was silent, the blood draining from her face.

"He went into V-tach, pacemaker and all. He was still on telemetry so we saw it on our monitor and rushed in with lidocaine. They're doing CPR now."

"Oh God, no," Kay whispered.

"Sorry, Kay. Just thought you'd want to know."

Anita was at her side, put her arms around her, and said, "Harrison?"

"No. Ike Salter," Kay said dropping the receiver.

"The friend you and Walsh picked up in the Ranger?"

Kay nodded. "They're doing CPR. . . ."

"Go on, Kay. I'll give report for you."

Kay ran—forgot lab coat, just ran out the door of TRU, down the corridor to the elevator. Slowly the door of the elevator opened and she stepped inside. The doors moved so slowly to close. Impatiently she pushed the button for the third floor, once, twice, three times. Then the doors shut and the elevator began its slow ascent.

It's a nightmare and everything is gray, Kay thought. "No, no, no, no," she kept saying. Not *Ike*.

The elevator stopped and she waited for the doors to open. Slowly they opened; she rushed out. People stared as she ran down the corridor for the old building. Pacemakers initiated electrical impulses which caused the contraction of the heart muscle, but they could not stop V-fib or V-tach.

In the corridor outside Room 362 stood Cass. He had been in the waiting room when the code was called. He heard them call Code Blue, 362, and knew. He knew, too, when he saw Kay in her TRU greens running toward the room, her hair loose from its barrette, her face red, her cheeks wet, her eyes wide with fear.

"Kay!"

She went into his arms and he held her. "Kay, it's Ike!"

She nodded against his chest and pulled away. The door to Room 362 was shut, but a respiratory therapist came out, glanced their way, and ran down the corridor. A lab tech went in hurriedly and shut the door. Kay did not want to witness CPR on Ike. Not on *Ike*.

Cass's face was stricken with horror and grief, and she led him to the nearby waiting room. From there, they

277

could watch the door to Room 362. The friends held each other's hands in the waiting room for five minutes before Kay found her voice. "Were you in there?"

He shook his head. "Visiting hours begin at three and I was waiting here."

There was silence between them for a while.

"How long—" Cass began. "How long does it take?"

"Oh Cass, who knows?" Who knows? It depends on how quickly the heart dies, or how quickly it responds—ten minutes? They'll work and work and work. Thirty minutes at the very least. "Where's Ike's wife, Maydy?"

"At a hotel. She was resting so that she could come back tonight. The nurses have called her. She's coming by taxi. I should be down there to help her . . . but I can't bear to leave here." He shook his head. "They've only been married just three years—"

Kay looked at his face—ruddy, beaded with perspiration, distraught. Ike was his best friend, an old friend. Perhaps it was his helplessness, his aloneness, his fear and hurt that caused her for a moment to think that she loved him. He did not take his eyes from her face. It was as if from her he drew the strength to endure this awful moment of silence, of waiting. He held her hand, his thumb passing over her knuckles back and forth. She spoke a little, silly things like: he's strong, we have the best CPR teams in the country, he has a super doctor—while waves of horror and disbelief kept washing over her and she felt weary, weary of everything.

Then, suddenly, the page system clicked on overhead. "Code Blue TRU. Code Blue TRU. Code Blue TRU."

Kay shot to her feet. "My God, Cass! That's my unit!"

Incredulously he said, "Kay—"

Officially at 2:50 she was still on duty. And it didn't matter anyway, because TRU was her unit. And who— *who?*

The backup CPR team would come into play now. At a hospital as large as St. Luke's it wasn't unusual to have two CPRs going on at the same time.

"I have to go," she told Cass, backing away.

He held out his hand to her, his face registering shock and disbelief. "Kay!"

She turned around and ran back, back down the corridor toward the elevator. But she took the nearby stairs instead. She flew down, around, down, around, down to the second floor, and down the corridor. Who? Who in TRU? Barney? What had Harvey done now? Mr. Brunner?

The backup CPR team was thundering through the wide-open doors of TRU as Kay ran in. Room—Room Four. *Dr. Worley.*

Anita was on her knees on the bed beside Worley performing cardiac massage counting, "One, two, three, four . . ." Buddy from respiratory therapy was just taking over the ambu bag, the bag which pumped air and oxygen into the patient's lungs via a face mask. The lights were on at their brightest. The blue TRU crash cart was at the bedside. On top was the stereo-tape-player-looking defibrillator with its three-inch-diameter paddles attached.

The CPR team leader, a resident doctor from ER, commanded Anita to cease cardiac massage so that he could see the pattern on the monitor. Jan told Kay that one amp of lidocaine had already been given. The monitor continued to show V-tach. Worley had suddenly

279

gone into V-tach, then into V-fib within two seconds, then into respiratory arrest. Jan had defibrillated him once resulting in reversion from V-fib to V-tach, an improvement, but not good enough.

Kay was already at the crash cart and screwing the plunger into an amp of sodium bicarbonate. On the monitor, the blip showed V-tach.

"Recharge!" the team leader said.

A nurse from ICU who stood at the crash cart pushed the RECHARGE button of the defibrillator while another slapped the saline pads onto Worley's chest, one over the sternum, the other just below his left nipple. Saline pads were to prevent paddle burn.

"Stand back," the resident said as he took the paddles from the ICU nurse. He placed one paddle on each saline pad, pushed the button on its handles.

Thunk, thumped the defibrillator.

All eyes swung to the cardiac monitor. The blip had disappeared, but when it reappeared, the pattern was normal except for an occasional PVC.

"Another fifty milligrams of lidocaine," the resident said. Kay had already opened the package containing the prefilled syringe of lidocaine and handed it to Jan. As Jan pushed the lidocaine into the IV, Kay opened and tossed an amp of sodium bicarb onto the bed. In cardiac arrest, acidosis could cause death. Bicarb, hopefully, would counteract acidosis.

In seconds the lidocaine, thought to be a cardiac-muscle tranquilizer, seemed to eradicate the PVCs and the pattern on the monitor remained normal. The CPR team stood by watching, however, just in case. The longer the pattern stayed normal, the better chance it had of *remaining* normal.

Dr. Kreel appeared while everybody was watching the monitor and waiting, and was apprised of what had happened, of the treatment and medications given. Wordlessly he went to the head of the bed and lifted Worley's eyelids one by one. He nodded. "He's O.K." The ashen color of Worley's skin was already turning pink, and now his chest rose and fell with his own breathing. The resident had not chosen to intubate him, to insert an endotracheal tube in his trachea in order to attach a respirator. There hadn't been time. And Worley was doing his own breathing now.

The CPR team milled around. Mission accomplished— unless Worley fibrillated again. But after a few moments, one by one the team members left the room. The lab tech came in to draw blood for enzyme and electrolyte studies to determine whether Worley was acidotic or the bicarb had compensated or overcompensated. The respiratory therapist was drawing blood for arterial blood gases from Worley's other arm.

The monitor blip remained stable. Dr. Kreel was in a good humor. "Fine job you people did," he said strolling around the nurses' station. "You're the best CPR team in the Southwest. You nurses are the best in the world. I hear there's a CPR going on somewhere in the old building too. When it rains it pours. Now I've got to figure out why Worley did this. Carlton, let's keep Worley's heart steady. Hang a lidocaine drip and infuse it at the usual rate. I'd give my eyeteeth to know why he did this. Heart attack. Classic heart attack. I think you people blew the old IV site so you'd better start a new IV. When it rains it pours. . . ."

Hailey said to Kay, "How's your friend?"

Kay shook her head. "I don't know."

"Go on, honey, we'll give report and I'll hang the new IV and clean up the mess. The other shift's here now to take over. Go on to your friend."

Twenty minutes had passed since she had left Cass. Kay grabbed her lab coat and handbag from the nurses' rest room. Pulling on the lab coat, she ran down the corridor again, to the stairs, climbed up, up, then hurried down the corridor.

Cass was standing with Maydy as Kay approached slowly, afraid to hear what he had to say. She paused and he looked up at her. His face told what she didn't want to know.

She went to him slowly. "Cass?"

He did not answer and she wondered if it was anger or profound grief or both that she saw in his face.

It was Maydy, Ike's wife who said, "Kay, Ike's gone." She wept, she retained her poise a moment longer. "It was a heart attack. The doctor said it was probably massive." And then her composure crumbled. Cass took her on down the corridor. He did not look back. His look had not encouraged Kay to follow or to speak to him. She thought his expression might even have forbidden her to follow or to speak.

Only partially aware of persons coming from and going into Ike's room, she slumped against the wall. They moved slowly now, spoke softly. She knew how they felt. They felt defeated, even guilty. They were asking themselves what had gone wrong—what they could have done for Ike that they hadn't.

Kay pulled her handbag over her shoulder and started on down the corridor. *Cass, you never understood that I love my work. You called it a gosh-awful job when it was my life. You never understood why I chose it over an easier way*

*of life. And now I know why I couldn't love you. Because
you never would have understood.*

She didn't know whether it was the rain on her windshield or the water in her eyes that blurred her vision.
She only knew she was going home. And wished to God
she didn't have to go back to St. Luke's ever again.

CHAPTER XIV

Dr. Grady Michaelson was fiftyish, distinguished looking, an immaculate dresser, highly educated, just a shade egotistical, and exceedingly excited after his first encounter with William Royce Ballew.

"Son," Ballew told him, "what you need is to lift a few weights like me, *rrrrrrr*. It'll put some muscles in your arms and not so many in your head. Haw . . . haw . . . haw . . . haw."

After the interview, Michaelson was convinced that Ballew's memory experiences were real, but he wanted to do some in-depth psychoanalysis on him. Syd was a psychologist with clinical training, but Michaelson was a psychoanalyst by profession, an M.D., and was specialized in psychiatric medicine. Syd as a professor tended to observe Ballew from an academic viewpoint, while Michaelson observed him from a clinical one. After Ballew left the office and Michaelson, Syd, and Harry conferred in the psych lab, Michaelson confessed, "The reason I mentioned in my letter that I'm interested in Ballew's background is that as I said, I've analyzed certain individuals whom we scientists of the mind have come to believe are multipersonality neurotics, but I've come to suspect for some time now, that these individuals, because of some severe psychological trauma in their lives, actually have split into several different personalities. Now, don't judge me to be a kook, gentlemen, but—could these multipersonalities actually be manifestations of the personalities from whom the subject was reincarnated? What I mean is, the individual is reincarnated, say, sixteen times from sixteen different people over a period of perhaps two thousand years, and when the personality of the contemporary person comes under severe psychological duress, the personalities from whom the subject was reincarnated, emerge into his subconscious, coming to the rescue, so to speak. I believe as you do, Sydney, in genetic memory. But I have been thinking more in terms of genetic memory from a subject's previous existence."

"Your theory of preexisting personalities coming to the contemporary subject's rescue has at least one difficulty that I can see right away. In the case of your Seymour Coleridge, the personalities that emerged seemed to also be contemporary. In Ballew's case—"

"Not necessarily, Sydney," Michaelson interrupted. "Some of those personalities that emerged, seemed—rather quaint."

"In Ballew's case he described the building of a log hut in cockney English and the management of a coach-and-four in perfect French. Flashes of memory, brief but vivid, and neither had a conscious thought of Ballew. I don't believe in previous existence; I believe that genetic memory comes from ancestral genes."

Michaelson smiled. This was the kind of exchange he liked best, the exchange of ideas, new ideas, and Sydney Carlton's was the kind of mind he liked to challenge. "Yes, that's an interesting theory to be sure. I had not

285

considered it until you wrote about it. And it is a much more scientific approach than the reincarnation theory, I must admit. And that's what excites me. We have two new theories with which to deal in this case." Michaelson reared back in the desk chair beaming upon his less educated colleagues, who were sitting in the metal folding chairs before the desk. Harry Wyatt was just Carlton's helper in the game because Carlton had no expertise with hypnosis and no desire for any.

Earlier, Syd had played all the tapes of the hypnotic sessions with Ballew for Michaelson. The doctor couldn't have been more pleased, intrigued, or cooperative. Syd had wanted the best psychoanalyst in the country to interview Ballew and he had him, had baited him with the barest hint of Ballew's rare talent.

Michaelson began to tell of a special case of split personality he had analyzed, comparing it with Ballew. The hour grew late, but still the three doctors sat, discussing Ballew, and other subjects Michaelson had worked with. The more they discussed Ballew's case, the more convinced they became of Syd's theory of genetic memory.

In the meantime, Kay was home with Ben and Russell. Syd's supper, warming in the oven, was slowly drying out.

And Billy Roy Ballew was out drinking and bellowing tales to the boys in the bar; because it was against his principles to go home to the wife and kids till he had belted down a few and felt on his very best behavior.

The head of Barney's bed was rolled up all the way as he hunched over the bound screenplay lying open on his overbed table. To the nurses' horror he kept shaking his head over and over, turning pages of Harvey's script, shaking his head.

It was one of those shaky moments when the nurses were inclined to pass the buck. Anita had said maybe they ought not to have risked giving Harvey's script to Barney because Barney's rejection could cause unpredictable harm to Harvey's ego. Jan said she wanted no part in the scheme—she'd been in trouble for meddling once that week already—but she was interested in observing the situation from a distance. Hailey was in it up to her ears along with Kay. Kay had gone about it properly. She had told both Drs. Kreel and Cash what was going on between the two men and had asked permission to give Harvey's script to Barney. She had anticipated an argument, but neither doctor cared about her plans. Spade wasn't consulted because he was on a three-week vacation.

So Ernie, a slender, brown-eyed, elfin girl, brought Harvey the play script and he solemnly dispatched it by Kay to Barney.

For almost twenty-four hours now Harvey had been awaiting word from Barney about the script, which Kay saw was entitled, *Conterminous*, the story of a Greek sculptor who maintained a disdain for everything contemporary and wished for the old way of life. By now, Harvey was wild with anxiety. He had asked for a cigarette a dozen times and was told just as many times that smoking was not allowed in TRU. He asked for a cigar to chew on. Ginger Manning had to call Dr. Cash at six A.M. that morning for permission to give Harvey a cigar to chew on, then had to prevail on one of the respiratory therapists to find a cigar. Harvey had also been drinking coffee, cup after cup. His anxiety had affected the nurses too. Anita was in the kitchen—the only place in TRU where smoking was allowed—smoking one cigarette after another, and Kay was drinking her third cup of coffee. Hailey was quiet and sullen; Jan's eyes were wide and she was keeping as busy as possible. She was also keeping her distance. It was ten o'clock in the morning. The nurses on other shifts weren't at all sure the seven to three shift had done the right thing in giving Harvey's manuscript to Barney, but they had reserved expressing their opinions of it until they could see the results; then, Kay knew, they'd let seven to three know they'd really pulled a boner if the experiment went badly—or they would tell them that seven to three weren't the only ones who had egged Barney on to read Harvey's manuscript.

Meanwhile routine continued on for all of them. Dr. Worley, after his heart attack the day before, was quiet again and meditative. Dr. Kreel had no idea why Worley had had the heart attack only three hours after surgery, but cardiologist Dr. Pugh had told him it was caused by the stress of surgery. Now, Worley's vital signs and monitor blip were stable.

Barney's vitals had shot up. He had a slight temp, his pulse rate had increased, so had his BP. They were above normal, but they were *steadily* above normal.

At the moment, Hailey was patiently and judiciously trying to persuade Brunner to eat. She explained that just because the tracheostomy tube was in his trachea, that was no reason he couldn't eat. She told him that the esophagus, where the food passes from the mouth to the stomach, was a separate passageway from the trachea— the tube that runs from the larynx to the bronchi and to the lungs. There was a little balloon on the trach tube that kept food from going into the trachea, she told him.

But all of her explanations and cajolery were of no avail. Brunner seemed angry to be in his predicament. Never in his life had he ever been sick. *Never.* And to be carefully crossing a street simply to fetch his morning paper, and be mowed down by an automobile at dawn, was not fair. He was crushed. And a machine had to breathe for him. He had six grown children, all living, all devoted, waiting one or two at a time, or all together in the waiting room, wishing him well. But Brunner seemed determined to manage without all the hospital nonsense, or die trying. He didn't believe in all the paraphernalia around him. When it was a man's time to go, he should go. God had ordained it. None of this silly apparatus was going to make one whit of difference and he wasn't going to prolong his pain and fear by eating and staying alive.

"C'mon, Mr. Brunner. It's carrots," Hailey cajoled. "Sure, it's puréed carrots, but it's carrots. Open your mouth, Mr. Brunner, for ol' Hailey."

Brunner kept his teeth clenched tightly and allowed no expression to show on his face. When it was a man's time to go, it was time to go and there was no way out of it.

When Kay finally got around to going to Harvey's room again, he turned his head quickly toward her. "Kay?"

"Yes."

"Got any more coffee?"

"How about a glass of fruit juice instead?"

"I want coffee."

"Nervous about your script?"

"Just because that half-baked crippled actor's reading it?" Harvey paused. *"Is* he reading it?"

"Who, Barney?"

Harvey raised both hands into the air. "My God, *yes!*"

Smiling, Kay said, "I think so."

"You think so! Why don't you know? Don't you know every time somebody scratches his crotch in here?"

"Harvey, calm down."

"Get me up in a chair. A wheelchair, O.K.?"

"Sure. Let me get help."

But Kay had to go outside TRU to the closest ward for a wheelchair because Jan and Anita were already using TRU's. They were getting Barney into it, a slow tedious maneuver.

By the time Kay got back with the wheelchair, after an argument with the charge nurse on the pediatrics ward— each ward guarded its wheelchairs and other equipment from raiders from other units with threats of violence if the items weren't returned—Hailey had given up with Brunner and came to help her with Harvey. "Roll me to Werger's room," Harvey commanded when he was in the chair.

Kay heard Barney in the hallway say, "I can manipulate this baby buggy myself." She saw him run into the wall, but with a little help he wheeled himself down the hall and met Harvey halfway.

"Shakespeare, I presume?"

Harvey did not register surprise to hear Barney in the hallway. "You should know by now. You read slower than I did when I was two years old."

Barney tapped the script in his lap with the back of his hand. "Man, this . . . this . . ."

Harvey's knuckles whitened as he gripped the arm of the wheelchair as Barney sought for words to express himself.

. . . Nurses have no right to interfere in other people's lives, Kay was thinking. But Anita was reasoning that they weren't really interfering; they were letting things happen naturally. Nurses manage patients, but sometimes it's better to let them manage themselves, Hailey thought.

"This is the pits, Chunn," Barney said.

The nurses couldn't detect the wilting of Harvey's soul by his outward appearance; they could *feel* it. His mouth tightened.

"What I mean is, this is damned good. You've got a damned good story, fantastic characters, and a fresh theme. It's dramatic and well done, but it's the *pits*." Barney went on, "It's too heavy. Show this on television and everybody will blow their brains out."

Harvey spit tobacco juice into the paper cup the nurses had given him to carry, as if he were unconcerned. Only thing was, there was no spit, only pretense. "You're some critic."

"I think I am, and right now I'm *your* critic. I'm surprised, frankly, because this is good. I wouldn't have believed it. Only it needs humor, or some sort of *relief*. Something to soften it—a kid, or a kitten or somebody playing handball."

"Give me one word to describe the screenplay, the same word the studios gave me, and I'll believe you're an honest critic."

"It's too . . . *tedious*."

Harvey winced only slightly. "I believe you are an honest critic." His face registered fleeting pain. "A kid or a kitten or somebody playing handball . . ."

"Yeah."

"Well, I hate kids, despise cats, and never played handball."

"You game for specific suggestions?"

291

"No. I can either write or I can't. Thank you, Werger. Now I know specifically what's wrong. The tediousness needs relief, like one gets from sexual intercourse."

"Wrong. Your entire screenplay *is* the sexual intercourse, what it needs are a few orgasms. Pardon the crudity, Nurses."

"Hand me my script."

"Relief from the tediousness, just small snatches—"

"Give me my script."

Barney handed it to Hailey; she handed it to Harvey. Harvey said, "Somebody roll me back to my room." His voice was expressionless and contained a note of finality to it. The nurses looked at each other embarrassedly. Had the experiment failed?

"A real artist has got to believe in himself," Barney said to Harvey's retreating back. "No matter who says what about his work. He's got to believe in *himself.*"

Such things were not routine. Routine was hanging IVs, checking drip rates, giving medications, putting patients on bedpans, emptying bedpans and urinals and Foley catheter bags, giving bed baths, changing linen, seeing that patients had their deodorant, combing their hair, checking to make sure bowel movements were regular and urine output adequate, keeping watch on respirator settings, checking doctors' orders, calling the lab or x-ray or respiratory therapy for lab work or x-rays or treatments, checking wounds, cleaning and dressing wounds, giving oral care, emptying drainage canisters, suctioning tracheostomy tubes of collected secretions; and recording all of it—every detail. Nurses did this all many times a day, each shift doing the same thing, day in and day out until they saw a patient grow steadily stronger or steadily worse, or crash suddenly as Dr.

Worley had done. Routine in TRU never really got boring; it just got . . . tedious, like Harvey's screenplay. CPRs broke the monotony. New admissions broke the monotony. But once in a while patient interaction broke the monotony, too.

The nurses talked for a day and a half about the meeting of the minds in the hall of TRU. The day after Barney read Harvey's screenplay, he had the nurses get him up in the wheelchair, and roll him to the door of Harvey's room. It was Harvey's vitals that were fluctuating now. Instead of anger and self-contempt, he was complacent. He did not threaten suicide now. The nurses did not know whether he was deep in thought or willing himself to die, but whatever was going on in Harvey's poor head was a struggle.

Kay went quietly to stand behind Barney's chair ready to whisk him away. They could not risk any reprisals by Harvey or any further assaults by Barney.

Suddenly, in a deep baritone voice, Barney boomed, "Progress, Daren? What *is* progress? Man beats his brains out against the brick wall of progress and what are the results? His own slow but certain destruction."

Harvey's face had turned toward him. His beard trembled. "You haven't convinced me, Demetri. Look at *yourself*. Progress made you what you are."

"I am what I am because of the work of—" Barney raised his hands up before his face. "Because of *these*— these hands; and the eyes within my brain that are able to see as an artist sees—with his soul. Don't speak to me about progress. An artist was his own master in every century that's past—and still is."

Tears? Running down Harvey's cheeks?

"That's drama, Chunn. A meager sampling from two

professionals, you and me. Lines that stick in the mind and not in the craw."

"Who the hell are you to judge?" Harvey said softly.

"Lying there on your back! You should be writing."

"Revising, according to you."

"Yes, revising. This is too good to throw away."

"What about the tediousness?"

"All you need is light in your life. The tediousness will take care of itself."

"Light!" Harvey laughed bitterly. "You forgot, my friend. I'm blind."

"You've got a girl who can type—Ernie. I saw her once when she came into the unit. You were blind before you shot yourself. She's in love with you, friend. I could tell that in just the brief moment I saw her before she walked into your room, and from a distance of twenty feet."

"In love! Ernie? With *me?*" exploded Harvey. "You're—You've got—*balls!*"

Barney sighed. "Nope," he said. "Those got blown off with the old arse too, Chunn."

While Harvey in his partial blindness, in the world he'd closed himself into, digested this new information, Barney turned his chair around and Kay wheeled him back to Room Five. End Act I, Scene Three of *Empathy*.

The past two days, since Ike's death, Kay had moved slowly, grieving because of his death, grieving because of Cass's inability to understand that her own unit had needed her more than he did; feeling guilty, too, because that wasn't exactly true. The CPR team was adequate to handle Worley's CPR, and the TRU nurses were adequate to aid them. Still, there had been that thing called responsibility which she could not shirk when the

CPR was called for TRU, a responsibility she did not owe Cass but did owe her own unit. Her grief and Cass's final look at her kept returning over and over to her mind, even as she worked. At noon, she was still thinking about it as she was hanging a unit of packed cells for Dr. Worley. Dr. Kreel had ordered packed cells because Worley's hemoglobin and hematocrit were too low; but his fluid volume, according to his central-venous-pressure reading, was too high. To add another pint of whole blood could overload his system and cause more work on his now-damaged heart—and cause, if not another MI, at least congestive heart failure; his damaged and weakened cardiac muscle might be unable to push that volume of blood through his veins. With packed cells, Worley could get the benefit of red blood cells and not the overload of extra fluid.

The telephone rang just as she was regulating the flow rate of the cells. Red blood cells were tricky; run them too slowly and they clotted and wouldn't infuse. Yet, running blood in too fast could cause infusion reaction. A nurse had to watch a patient carefully for infusion reactions and take his vital signs every five minutes. When the telephone rang, Kay left Anita in charge of watching Worley and the transfusion, and hurried to answer the telephone.

It was Ursala. "Oh, Kay, Harrison's crashing and Dr. Paine's here. Dr. Daizat's here. Dr. Pugh's here and nobody's doing anything. They say there's nothing to do. What do they know? They think it's a leakage in his heart. But they don't want to do surgery and see, because they say he's too weak. What are we going to do? He'll die if they don't. I think they just don't want him to die when they're operating because it'll look as if they killed him.

Ah, they—none of 'em know *nothing*."

Kay didn't see how she could take a lunch break today. About half the time she couldn't because of some crisis going on in the unit. At noon, the doctors took off for two hours from their office practice and that's when they liked to do procedures. Before office hours they did surgery and made hospital rounds. After their offices closed at five, some of them made rounds again, but most of them went home. If one needed to do a cutdown or tracheostomy, he did it at noon. Today, there was no impending minor surgery; but five rooms were occupied in the unit and there was plenty to do.

Dr. Cash had ordered the nurses to ambulate Harvey in the TRU hallway b.i.d.—twice a day—and that took two nurses and about ten minutes each time. Dr. Kreel was going to help Dr. Hishu with some debridement on Barney's behind in preparation for his impending plastic surgery. Worley had to be watched closely for blood reactions, and Mr. Brunner had to be fed, even though he refused to eat. It was a typical day in TRU and Kay didn't see how she could spare the time to go to the newborn nursery.

But she did. At two P.M. she took a fifteen-minute break while all was quiet. Barney's gluteal area had been debrided, Harvey had been ambulated once in the morning and once at one o'clock. Dr. Kreel had ordered a feeding tube to be passed down Mr. Brunner's esophagus to his stomach since he refused to take food, and that was done. However, Brunner had already pulled it out twice. Dr. Worley had brightened everybody's day by beginning to pass flatus. The more flatus he passed, the more secure everybody became. To hold flatus back for the sake of discretion was not only impossible but painful to an injured colon and Worley did not like pain. When he broke wind, it was with reckless abandon and everybody could hear it all over the unit. Once, when Worley discharged a particularly loud report, Barney shouted, "Hello!" Hailey had sneaked a bottle of room deodorant into the room to make the air there more pleasant.

So, all being quiet, more or less, Kay hurried down the corridor for the newborn nursery, and when she arrived she was alarmed because she could see that all three of Harrison's doctors were still in the newborn ICU. She said nothing to Patterson as she slipped the gown over her scrub suit and tied on the mask; but Patterson, puffing, came to her. "Dallying is what they're doing. Yeah, they're working on him, but they're not doing what they should."

Kay went in, approached the crib where Harrison lay. Sternal retraction was very noticeable today; the tips of the baby's tiny fingers were cyanotic. Harrison already looked dead. Kay's hand flew to her mouth. The doctors were discussing autoimmune reactions, Harrison's probable lack of resistance to disease, the results of the x-rays taken earlier that morning, why the site of anastamosis was leaking. Discussing, only discussing. Weighing theories.

Kay looked at Ursala standing by white-faced and grim. Ursala shrugged, and Kay, emboldened by her growing lack of tact and concern for getting along with her so-called superiors—and even more so by her alarm for Harrison—asked Dr. Daizat the approachable, "Have you decided what you're going to do?"

He blinked. "Not yet. It's almost certain death if we try open heart surgery again. X-rays show there's a leak in the aorta where we attached the aorta to the left ventricle. We can't understand it. It's as if his body rejected the sutures; yet we know he has a *defective* immune system, one that's almost nonexistent."

"When are you going to do surgery?"

Dr. Paine turned quickly to her. "He just told you it's certain death if we do surgery," he snapped.

Not easily intimidated—not anymore—Kay snapped back, "And certain death if you don't."

Daizat smiled, shrugged, spread his arms wide in a supplicating gesture. "Why cost the parents an operating fee?" He dropped his shoulders when he saw her shock, became sympathetic. "Ah, it's hard to accept. But you must understand that the kid is doomed anyway. His immune system is almost nil and eventually—"

"A lot of kids have defective immune systems."

"But this one—" He indicated the deformed baby in the warming crib. "Ah, have a heart, Carlton. The parents, even if he lived through the surgery and we kept him alive for a few more years, the parents, do they deserve to struggle and learn to love the kid, to deal with his handicaps only to lose him?"

"The fact is," said Dr. Pugh when he observed Kay's forehead red with fury, her eyes narrowing in rage. "We're damned if we operate and damned if we don't. We can't decide what's right. We're weighing all probabilities—"

"You've been weighing the probabilities since ten o'clock this morning," Kay said. "How many probabilities do you have to weigh? And what have you gone to medical school for, Dr. Pugh—to operate on the most likely to succeed?" She looked at Daizat. "Just a day or so ago you said God had left it up to us to work the bugs out of the machinery, Dr. Daizat, and you're dropping the ball." To Dr. Paine she said, "If you doctors are undecided as to what to do—let Harrison die because he's a freak, or try to operate and have him die because of that—have you thought of asking his parents what *they* would prefer that you do?"

The doctors looked at each other, and Ursala and Kay looked at each other, too. Neither of them believed the doctors had thought of that solution. Great medical minds weighing one scientific factor against the other had never thought to ask the young parents. Actually, Kay didn't give a damn about what the parents wanted. There were parents who wanted their handicapped infants to die and that infuriated her, a cowardly shirking of a tremendous responsibility; but she knew what the Harrisons would want.

Dr. Paine turned slowly to face Kay. "You're from TRU, aren't you?"

She nodded.

"Then I suggest you go back to TRU; we don't need your hysteria in here at the moment."

Knowing what Dr. Paine was thinking—that she was one of Kreel's hoity-toity, know-it-all nurses from the trauma wing—Kay shook her head and said, "My break's not up yet."

He turned back to the others. Daizat had been wiping his forehead with his handkerchief and now folded it neatly and stuffed it into his back pocket. "Let's call the parents," he said.

It took Ursala thirty seconds to find the Harrisons' telephone number. Dr. Paine called them, told them the problem, hung up, turned around to face the huddle of nurses and doctors at the desk and said, "Let's operate."

*   *   *

Kay was aware as she gave report to the three to eleven shift that Harrison was at that moment being prepared for surgery. He would undergo surgery at about 3:30 and it would last several hours. She would have to go on home, but she knew it was going to be a long evening.

At the supper table Syd was in his best humor as he described Dr. Michaelson's theory and expressed the excitement he felt because of Billy Roy Ballew's case. Russell was always eager to hear the things Ballew said, since Syd had begun to share them with the rest of the family, and Syd was an excellent mimic.

He buttered his roll as he mimicked, "A few more years of studying, Dr. Michaelson, *rrrrrrr*, and your head will be swelled as big as the Goodyear blimp, *rrrrr*. What you and Harry need, son, is a good razor. Shave off some of that fuzz on your chin and glue it on that bald spot on top of your head. Haw . . . haw . . . haw . . . haw."

Russell laughed and Ben said, "Did you outline a plan as you had hoped?"

"We did," Syd answered. He looked at Kay. "This casserole is good, sweetheart. What's in it?"

Her thoughts came back to the subject at hand. "Just a recipe I thought up. I guess you could call it a noodle casserole."

"But what's in it?" Ben asked.

"Hamburger meat, noodles, mushrooms, sliced ripe olives, and grated cheese."

"With all that and served with a salad it sounds like a complete meal," Ben said. "Take long to fix?"

"What?"

"I said, did it take long to fix?"

"No."

"What's your plan for Ballew?" Russell asked Syd, bored with the deviation in the conversation.

Syd sipped his iced tea and said, "Well, first we're going to give Ballew a polygraph test, hoping to eliminate any doubts about the veracity of his answers to our questions. It's highly improbable that under hypnosis he could consciously fabricate an impersonation. But if there's any doubt at all, we need to eliminate it. Then we'll have another hypnotic session and try to bring out Louis Velours and the Englishman, Peterson, for Dr. Michaelson to observe. He'll have some questions prepared to ask Ballew—something in regard to a previous life he may have lived. I'll take the other route, try to establish a link between Velours, Peterson, and Ballew. I'll try to eliminate the reincarnation theory and go for—Kay?"

She had stood up. "I just thought of something I need to do."

He regarded her a moment, reading her thoughts as always. "Going to call the hospital?"

"Yes." She had told them about Harrison's surgery.

Yes, the three to eleven charge nurse of the newborn nursery said when Kay called. Harrison had survived the three-hour surgery, but he was in a very unstable condition. Vital signs were unstable; but at least he had survived. And the doctors were ecstatic. The nurse had overheard them saying they were going to go have a drink together to celebrate—taking their beepers along, of course, in case the nurses needed to call them. And Harrison's parents had cried with relief at Harrison's surviving the surgery.

Smiling, Kay went back to the table to listen to Syd tell about Ballew. They were delighted about Harrison, but more so because her mind came back to them, to her family—to her son Russell, a solemn quiet, intelligent boy of thirteen; to Uncle Ben, easygoing, loving; and to Syd who loved her more than life.

The day Ike died, when Syd heard about it from Kay, he secretly telephoned St. Luke's and obtained the name of the funeral home who had come for Ike's body. Then the next day, he telephoned the funeral home to find out the date and time of Ike's funeral. Tonight, when Kay went up to bed, Syd went with her, and once they were in their room together, while she did the things she always did to herself after her bath—putting moisture cream on her face, brushing her hair at the old-fashioned dresser— he approached her, put his hands on her shoulders, and said, "You want to go to Ike Salter's funeral?"

She was startled and when she did not answer, he said, "It's day after tomorrow at three o'clock. If you can leave work at noon, we can make it. I'll give the students in my afternoon class a walk."

She turned to look up at him, saw his love for her in his eyes, rose, and went into his arms. "Yes, yes, I want to go," she said. "I didn't know him except as a patient in the hospital at Preston General and at St. Luke's, but he was a friend."

"I know," Syd said resting his chin on top of her head.

July, deep in the heart of Texas, in the northern part of the hill country, was sweltering hot. Breezes from the Gulf of Mexico, some two hundred miles to the south, wafted up and caused the humidity to soar with the heat. However, with electric ceiling fans stirring the air, the stone church in the little town of Concho was cool. The church was packed when Kay and Syd arrived. They had been there only a short while before Cass came in with Ike's widow. If only he understood, Kay thought as she watched them pass down the aisle while the crowd in the church rose to stand in respect.

The service was brief and Kay and Syd filed by to view Ike, now only a wax figure of the man he used to be. The mouth was unsmiling, but the perpetual grin still showed in the deep lines around his eyes. She was glad for the bright, sunny day outside, for all its heat and humidity.

The cortège drove to a small cemetery outside Concho; south breezes were strong on the hill. Cass, Maydy, and several ranch hands gathered under the canopy. This was Kay's only glimpse of Cass's world, these ranch hands dressed uncomfortably in suits they weren't accustomed to, some only in clean shirts and jeans, all with Stetsons in hand. Four of them were Chicanos, two appeared to be Indians, four were white youths, one was a Negro. Ike had once been Cass's foreman and the ranch hands were probably a mixture of Cass's men and Ike's.

Syd and Kay stood to the side of the canopy under which the casket sat, and where Cass, Maydy, and the ranch hands stood. She could observe Cass's profile—Cass, who had lost his wife some thirteen years ago, and now his best friend; Cass, who had no one now. The minister was intoning the last words that would be said over Ike. A jet airplane roared up from the south going north, and a red-winged black bird called in a nearby mesquite tree, *"Pert Cheeter."*

Once, Cass turned his head slowly, as if he had known she was there, and looked at Kay, his blue eyes steady, unsmiling.

She smiled tentatively; he turned back to face the minister.

When it was over, Cass and Ike's multitudinous

friends gathered around him and Maydy, blocking out her view of him, and she and Syd went to their car parked on the road.

Going home, Syd held her hand on the seat beside him. A tumbleweed blew across the highway; the scent of new-mown grass was strong coming from the mowers scattered up and down the right-of-way. Syd said, "Baby, I've been wanting to talk to you about something. I wish you'd take a leave of absence for a while." When he saw her about to protest, he said, "Now let me finish. You've been caught up in your job too intensely, under the gun for too long. Few people can put up with that kind of tension for six years as you've done. And you deserve a vacation."

She sighed. "I can't yet. There's nobody to replace me."

"Yes, there is. As I said before—"

"Nobody's indispensable. Well, for the time being *I* am."

"You're tired, you're nervous, you're out of sorts. Our family life is next to nil and our sex life is worse than that. Kay—"

"You haven't been too available yourself and—"

"That's temporary."

"And if our sex life is nil it's because you come home too late for—"

"Your job goes on and on. I just think—"

"*You* think. I think, too. Yes, I need a vacation, but now's not the—"

"You need more than a vacation."

"Am I that bad?"

"I think you've got a lot of stamina but—"

"But what?"

304

"It can't last forever, sweetheart."

Kay leaned her head back on the seat. He was right, of course. Today before she had left the unit at noon, she had visited the newborn nursery to check on Harrison. He was "holding his own," Ursala had said. Still on O_2 and feeding tubes and monitors, Harrison was sleeping soundly. His vital signs were stable. She had noticed for the first time that he'd grown feathery blond eyelashes. The repaired cleft in his lip was only a red line now. Someday it would be only a tiny white line a quarter of an inch long and no wider than a hair.

The last three days Harvey, arm in arm with one of the nurses, had been ambulated in the hall and Barney would yell out his door when Harvey passed asking if he *really* needed a seeing-eye nurse. Harvey would quip something like, "Yeah, well, how did the nurses ever find a colostomy bag big enough for you since you're so full of it."

That morning Barney had been sitting by the window when Harvey had plodded past his door. "Hey, Chunn. The doctor says I'm going to get me a new gluteus tomorrow. And a new set of you-know-whats."

"Who's the poor doctor?"

"Hishu."

"Bless you," Harvey said. "Well, well. I was just getting used to the plastic rear idea. Now you'll have to help me remember the other for my next play."

"Remember it yourself."

"What a poignant focus for my new-found sense of humor."

"Your sense of humor needs help, all right, even if its just gas."

"Yeah, well your gas is worse than that guy's gas in

Room Four."

"Guy in Room Four? I thought those explosions were coming from you."

Harvey had had no reply and had passed on by, leaving Barney to laugh at his own joke.

She was smiling now, her eyes closed, and Syd said, "You couldn't be thinking of the hospital, could you?"

"I am."

"Tell me about it."

She did, all the way home, all one hundred ten miles, nothing but of Harvey and Barney and Harrison and Leola and Mr. Brunner. And when they pulled into the drive of their home, they were laughing because of Dr. Worley's excessive gas, and his uncompromising way of getting rid of it.

CHAPTER XV

Barney Werger went to surgery the morning Kay returned to work after Ike's funeral. Surgery was a scary experience for nearly every patient and Barney was no exception. Ginger Manning told the seven to three shift in report that he had spent the presurgery hours at the end of the night shift quipping and joking with the nurses. Everyone knew this was his way of releasing tension.

"One good thing about working on my behind," Barney told Kay when she went in to take his presurgery vital signs, "I won't have to have an anesthetic. I've got a built-in anesthetic from my stoma down." This was true.

"But you'll still have an anesthesiologist there to watch your vital signs, Barney, as you know," Kay said, wrapping the blood-pressure cuff on his upper arm.

"Yeah, and the position which I'm sure to be in during the surgery should help the anesthesiologist and me see eye to eye about things. Do you think he plays chess?"

She smiled, placed the earpieces of the stethoscope in her ears. "Maybe."

She could barely hear him because of the earpieces in her ears, when he said, "Or I could write a treatise entitled, 'The Reconstruction of Barney's Butt—the

Upside-down Story.'"

She pumped the cuff up smiling, watched the manometer gauge on the wall; the first thump of the pulse was on 134; T-H-U-M-P, THUMP, THump, thump, thump; the last audible thump was at 86. His BP was slightly high, but indicative of anxiety which was normal for a presurgery patient. She released the rest of the air in the cuff and removed the stethoscope.

"Or how about, 'Plastic Surgery, Sunny Side Up'?" Barney was saying.

Hailey was standing on Barney's other side waiting for Kay to finish taking the vital signs and had been giggling almost continuously as she stood with the preop check list in her hand. "All right, Barney. I know some of this stuff is silly to you, but we gotta check it off the list. Now you answer plain and simple, you hear?"

Barney folded his hands over his abdomen. "I'll try."

"O.K., do you have on your person any valuables like rings, watches, pins, billfolds—"

"I keep them in all the pockets of this flowery hospital gown I've been wearing for a month."

"Anything of value?"

"The only thing really dear to me was practically shot off along with my behind, Hailey."

Giggling, Hailey continued, "Have you removed all hearing aids, contact lenses, wigs, hair pieces, false teeth, partial plates? *Any* prosthesis?"

"Whatever's left is the real thing, Hailey."

"Did you empty your bladder?"

"The night shift put that catheter back in and saved me the trouble of wetting the bed."

"I forgot," Hailey said. "All you've got left then is your preop."

Barney considered that. "If that means what I think it means, that's still intact, yes. But it's only functional as plumbing."

"Preop is your medication before surgery," Kay told him. "You've got Demerol ordered and I'll give you that in a second."

Barney said, "I need it, Carlton. I've got a feeling . . . that I won't survive this."

"Barney, you aren't even going to have a general anesthetic. And all the doctors will be doing is grafting some tissue, maybe muscle and certainly some skin from your abdomen and perhaps your back, and reconstructing the nerves in the gluteal area and filling in with silicone. The most they plan to give you is Demerol and a few local anesthetics. And Dr. Hishu is a very good plastic surgeon, Dr. Cash is an excellent neurosurgeon, and Dr. Jerome is a very good anesthesiologist," Kay said. But she took his hand anyway. "I know. It's *still* scary."

Barney squeezed her hand. "Yeah," he said contemplatively. "I'll be glad when it's . . . all behind me."

Harvey came to the door on his first walk of the day, led by Jan, and said, "I want to wish you luck, Werger. I hope the operation on your one end doesn't adversely affect the other. Don't let them ruin your capacity for expounding audacious baloney."

Barney waved him away. "You can just call me Sitting Bullshit, Chunn."

Moments later Harvey seemed to watch as the orderlies wheeled Barney from his room down the hallway near Harvey's door and out the TRU doors. Ten minutes later Dr. Kreel came into the unit, walked down the hall, stopped at the nurses' station where Kay was

309

checking lab slips for treatments and said, "Cash's patient still in here?"

Kay looked up. "Yes."

"Why?"

Uh-oh, she thought, but said, "Harvey's made a couple of attempts to harm himself, Dr. Kreel, and has been very depressed. Also his vital signs haven't been exactly stable."

"But he's stable now, isn't he?"

"Yes."

"Well, we may need his room if we have a couple more trauma patients come in. You know the rule, always to keep one room vacant. And if two more come in—"

"There're three vacant."

"I know, but a bad automobile accident or chemical-plant explosion or something could fill this place up in seconds, as you know."

She didn't answer; she didn't have a chance because Dr. Cash, in a good humor for once, came briskly through the doors at that moment whistling, nodded to Dr. Kreel, and went in to see Harvey. Kay knew he was probably making his rounds quickly while they were preparing Barney for surgery, and it would be awhile before he would be needed in surgery for the nerve reconstruction. Kreel lingered at the desk, fiddling with the monitor screen, surveying the dressings cabinets near the nurses' station. Kay watched him out of the corner of her eye knowing he was up to something.

Finally Cash came out of Harvey's room and Dr. Kreel, the epitome of diplomacy, turned quickly to him before he could enter the doctors' booth and said, "That patient, Chunn, still having problems?"

Dr. Cash had Harvey's chart in his hands and, pausing

at the nurses' station, looked up and said defensively, "Not really, why?"

Kreel shrugged. "Just wondered. We try to transfer trauma patients out of here as soon as possible. Transferring patients out to make room for new ones takes time and sometimes a patient in serious trouble doesn't have that kind of time."

Cash's eyes had become dark as he stood there, chart open in his hands. "My patient has been in serious trouble, Braxton, and could have developed any number of complications—"

"I know. But he's been ready for transfer for a week now, and leaving him here any longer could be psychologically regressive for him, it seems to me."

"I know that and Andrew Spade is on the case and hasn't mentioned transfer," Cash said, his face almost the same color as his hair now. "You keep forgetting, I don't have my own critical-care unit. ICU isn't for him—or CCU or even surgical ICU. Where do you suggest I transfer him, Braxton?"

"The floor."

"He isn't ready for the floor."

Dr. Kreel turned to Kay. "What do *you* think, Carlton? Chunn's ambulating, isn't he? Vitals are stable?"

Kay replied, "He's ambulating and his vitals are stable, but—"

Kreel turned to Cash. "There, you see? The unit is full except for three rooms and a bad accident could fill them at any second."

Cash was eying Kay. "But what, Carlton?"

"Well . . ." Kay began flushing, "he needs close supervision yet." She never had become totally comfortable with irate doctors or when she was being put on the spot.

Cash threw down the metal-covered chart on the desk. "All right, Braxton. I'll transfer Chunn out to the floor. But remember, if he jumps out the third-floor window or develops neuro complications that the floor nurses don't catch, you can blame yourself."

"Blame—" began Kreel incredulously.

"I'm overdue in surgery," Cash said and stormed out of the unit without leaving med orders or transfer orders or any orders for Harvey, and Dr. Kreel told Kay, "I won't have to blame myself; he'll do that for me." Kreel appeared to want to say more about it, but ethics wouldn't allow it. Personal ethics. Doctors did not talk about each other—except to drop hints—to hospital personnel; only with other doctors did they express their opinions.

Kay was unconcerned about that, though; her immediate problem was that now she'd have to page Dr. Cash for orders for Harvey because his IV orders needed updating before they could give him any more, and his antibiotics needed to be renewed. Also, if Cash meant to have Harvey transferred out, she needed those orders too. She wanted to tell Dr. Kreel that Harvey did need close supervision yet, but he was right, too. All personnel knew that in the critical-care units a patient could progress just so far, then stopped progressing until he was moved out to the floor. Out there the patient's recovery was accelerated again up to a point and then did not improve again until he was discharged from the hospital. Actually, she was unsure what was right for Harvey and she resented each doctor trying to get her to side with him. She hated it, was sick of it, sick and—

The telephone rang on her desk. It was Walsh wanting to speak to Dr. Kreel. By the tone of her voice, Kay knew it must be an accident somewhere and Walsh needed Kreel's instructions before relaying the information on to Kay.

Kay handed the receiver to Kreel, rose, and went to Barney's room where Anita was making his bed. "Looks like an emergency call, Anita. So let me ask you to page Dr. Cash quick because he'll be in surgery in a minute and—"

"I heard the ruckus out there," Anita said rolling her eyes.

"I just want you to page Dr. Cash because we need med orders, IV orders, and transfer orders, O.K.?"

"O.K. Good luck."

Kay hurried back to the desk just as Kreel, beaming delightedly, put the receiver of the telephone down. "Auto accident on the Interstate, Carlton," he said. "The fire-department ambulances can't get there because of highway construction and a five-car pileup. Also the freeway's congested with work traffic. Officers say four people have been injured, but only one critically. So hop to, honey. And remember, the photographer is with Jerry. Now's your chance to shine!"

It normally took Jerry Bergdorf about five minutes to get the Ranger ready for takeoff so Kay and Marsha Walsh had learned to change into jump suits in five minutes. Sometimes they didn't have time to change, but it was better if they did. Jump suits didn't get in their way, were sterilized, and contained all sorts of pockets for emergency equipment. So Kay ran down the hall for the lounge near the Comstat booth.

Walsh was already in the lounge zipping up the front of

her suit. She said, "Look at this," indicating the neatly laundered suit. "Kreel told me he had the laundry iron these by hand, but I didn't believe it."

Kay smiled and found her jump suit. There were eight hanging on the numbered hangers between two sets of lockers. Her number was two. "Do I smell starch, or do I smell starch?" she said pulling off the top part of her surgical greens.

"You smell starch. I don't believe it. Have you seen the photographer?"

Kay threw the surgical top toward the canvas laundry bag. "No."

"He's about our age, thirty to thirty-five, red hair, beard. A real hunk of a man!"

"What have you heard about the accident?"

"Nothing," Walsh replied as she watched Kay slip into the jump suit; "except the cops say the critically injured one is squashed like a pancake. This is going to be one of those messy pickups. And us in starched jump suits! It's ridiculous!"

"Where on earth will we land if the freeway's jammed?"

"Right on the freeway, Comstat says. Cops are attempting to push back cars for the forty or fifty feet we need for a landing." Marsha was still watching as Kay zipped up her jump suit. "Look at you. Trim as a seal. Size eight. I don't believe it. *Nobody's* a size eight. It isn't fair. One of the best jobs in the hospital, got a handsome husband and a kid. And I didn't miss the stars in the eyes of that rancher the day we picked up Ike Salter, God rest his soul. It isn't fair."

"Cass is just a friend," Kay said lifting her hair out of the collar of the suit.

314

"He may be *just* a friend to you, honey, but you're not *just* a friend to him. He had soap-opera eyes when he looked at you if I ever saw any. It just ain't fair!" Marsha jerked open the door as Kay hurried out. "Two handsome hunks in a lifetime is too much, but two at the same time is ridiculous. My God, it just isn't fair!"

They ran through Trauma Receiving, out the door, and up the ramp to the Ranger, whose rotors were already whirling. Walsh leaped in first, then Kay. Kay shut and latched the door.

Jerry turned halfway around in his seat. "Marsha, you've met Boyett. Boyett, meet blue eyes."

Boyett? The photographer's face peered jovially around the medication cabinet behind the passenger's seat. His expression froze in disbelief, brightened, and he exclaimed, "Katy!"

"Hugh! Hugh Boyett!"

"Katy, my God."

She had been fastening her shoulder harness preparatory to lift-off and she clutched the hand he held out to her. "Hugh, I never dreamed the photographer was you!"

Jerry was singing, "Beeootiful, beeootiful brown eyes, beeootiful, beeootiful brown eyes, I'll never love blue eyes again—"

Hugh said, "Katy, lass. What . . . how—"

She laughed. Hugh Boyett, once her patient, nearly a lover. He had come into Preston General's ICU a mangled mass of flesh and bone after a plane crash, had been patched, mended, and wired together by surgeons, and nursed back to life by the nurses. Hugh had taught her not to be afraid to live or to love again; he had said once that he adored her.

There was no ring on the fingers of his left hand, which she still held.

"I don't believe this," Walsh was saying more to herself than anyone else. "I just don't believe it."

Today, the sensation of lift-off was both unpleasant and exhilarating; usually the exhilaration of lift-off was almost sensual. Kay glanced at her watch—10:46. She'd never become accustomed to the apprehension she always felt for Syd and Russell when there was an accident somewhere. Every call caused personal consternation. Is it Syd? Is it Russell? Uncle Ben? But Syd would be safely in his second class at the university and Russell safely at home rolling the newspapers for his route. St. Luke's receded swiftly below, then disappeared from sight.

Jerry was asking Hugh something and he had taken his attention from Kay for a moment. She shut her eyes, wondering why the motion of the helicopter was suddenly so unpleasant.

"Relax."

Kay blinked at Walsh.

"Relax, kid. Look at your hands," Marsha said in a whisper. "This guy bothering you?"

Kay's hands were clenched into fists. She made them relax and shook her head smiling. "No, Hugh's just a friend," she said forcing her mind to ignore the sensation of lift-off. Her tension never let up anymore. If it wasn't anxiety over doctors' quibbling, it was over the possibility of a patient doing himself in right in the unit, or a dozen other tension-provoking things. Life hadn't been easy back in Preston General, but the work at St. Luke's was worse. And you couldn't prevent what everybody called burnout by going to OB because there was tension there, too. She had heard the gossip at the cafeteria table just the week before about the nurses having been forced to call the security guard to eject a priest on the OB floor. A young girl had had an illegitimate baby and was giving it up for adoption. For the girl's protection, the nurses had been instructed by the obstetrician not to allow visitors to her room and not to give out her room number to anyone—or even to admit she was a patient at the hospital to anyone—in person or over the telephone. When they had denied any knowledge of the girl to the priest, he had gone up and down the OB corridor shouting her name. Somebody had said that because he was so intent on finding her, you'd think it was *his* child she was giving up for adoption. . . .

"Katy? Smile," Hugh said now.

The proboscis of a buglike camera was peering at her, and behind that was a shock of red hair. Click. And Hugh, smiling, appeared from behind the camera. "Tell me, Katy, how come you to be here of all places? I left you at Preston General."

"I married Syd. He's a professor at the university here."

Hugh nodded, studying her with his soft, blue eyes. "Ah, and so your dreams have come true."

Feeling the slight jolt of the copter as it hit a wind current, her hand went to her stomach. "M-more or less."

Hugh kept studying her and said, "Am I responsible—perhaps a little—for this?" He indicated the interior of the Ranger with a sweep of his hand.

"Maybe a little," she said. "You haven't married, Hugh?"

"No. As I told you once, Katy, marriage is not for me."

317

I'm a solitary man not given to stayin' home, tendin' gardens, and mowin' lawns. I could not abide the eternal comin' home evenin's and dandlin' babies on my knee. She had never believed that, and she was sure Hugh didn't either. His eyes were still upon her face and he asked her now as he had asked her then, "How free are you, Katy?"

Free enough, she had answered him then. *But not for this crippled man who adores you? No, Hugh, I'm sorry.*

But this was today, and this was under different circumstances. "How free am I?" she asked smiling and leaning her head back against the side of the copter. "I don't think I'm really very free at all." She indicated the interior of the Ranger with a sweep of her hand.

"Ranger I to Comstat," Jerry said into the microphone. "I have the site of the accident spotted below. There's a ring of flares and barely room to set her down. Stand by, Cal."

Kay gripped the side bar of the helicopter. Descent did not usually bother her; but today it did. She gritted her teeth, glad that Hugh had faced forward again. She felt nauseated, heard Walsh say softly, "You all right, Kay?"

Kay nodded, holding her breath while Jerry sang, "Ilene, come home tonight. Ilene, come home. The fire is lit and here I sit, waitin' fer you to come ho-ome."

The Ranger jolted a little. Kay opened her eyes and smiled weakly at Walsh. "Just a little nauseated," she said.

"Yeah, kid," Marsha whispered. "You should see your face. White with touches of green here and there." She glanced at the back of Hugh Boyett's head. "Don't let *him* see you act like this."

Through the copter's window, they could see the worst crowd of bystanders Kay had ever seen, and cars as far as the eye could see, some strewn askew upon the freeway, some balanced precariously on the embankment on either side of the freeway. There were scores of emergency vehicles, flashing lights on the overpass above the freeway and on the embankment; some police cars had been unable to reach the wreckage.

For Hugh's benefit Marsha said, "O.K., Kay let's go!" She jumped out of the Ranger first and pulled the stretcher out as Kay pushed. Carrying the stretcher, they ran below the whirling rotors to where the police directed them, to a huddle of officers on their knees some one hundred yards from two mangled vehicles. Kay got only a glimpse of them and of Hugh already crouching nearby, taking shots of the wreckage.

At first glimpse, the man under the army blanket appeared to be dead already. Kay's and Marsha's minds ticked off their assessments point by point: head trauma, battered skull; blood matted in his hair, on his face. Quickly Kay pressed her fingers to the bloody neck and found the carotid pulse, weak and rapid. Walsh had pulled back the blanket and they could see that the angle of the man's left arm demonstrated compound fractures of the tibia, also possible fracture of the sternum. Almost certain contusion of the heart; then, broken collar bone for certain, maybe fractured cervical vertebrae. One thing was certain, the victim was mangled and it would take a neurosurgeon, an orthopedic surgeon, a cardio-vascular surgeon—

Suddenly the victim shuddered and ceased to breathe. CPR in a case like this was the pits! Kay had begun to palpate his unfractured arm for an IV, but stopped that and reached for the ambu bag which Walsh had ready. Marsha had also carefully inserted an airway, a very trickly procedure because they suspected the victim suffered a fractured cervical vertebrae—a broken neck—and she could not tilt his head back to open the airway. Closed chest massage was out of the question because of the fractured sternum. The cessation of the victim's breathing could have been due to brain stem damage or cardiac arrest because of shock trauma.

Even while they were assessing the victim's injuries, they had been prepared for this emergency. Walsh had the portable defibrillator already out of the bag. It resembled a portable tape player and even contained a miniature monitor screen, but there was no time to place the leads. The absence of the victim's carotid pulse and the cessation of breathing told them all they needed to know. Walsh placed the paddles of the defibrillator on the victim's bared chest and shouted, "Stand back!" Then she pressed the button on the paddles.

Thud. The victim's body jumped; his arms flopped at his sides. Kay felt for the carotid. "He's perfusing," she said. "Pulse is steady."

The next step in stabilizing the patient for transfer to the copter was to offset shock by starting plasma and an IV. It was incredible to them how easily they could start an IV under these circumstances, whereas in the units, sometimes they failed. Something gave them extra perception in emergencies like this and both Marsha and Kay slipped the intracaths into each of the victim's arms. Marsha thrust the plasma bag into a police officer's hands and said, "Hold that!"

Kay, holding up the IV bag of Ringer's lactate in one hand, felt for the victim's carotid pulse with the other. She found it. The officer who had begun to breathe the victim with the ambu bag, kept pressing it, forcing air into his lungs. What was needed now was to get the victim to the Ranger and on a respirator.

"Pulse is still steady," Kay told Marsha.

Now came the tricky part. Beneath the mattress on the stretcher was a thin but strong sheet of pressed wood. Marsha directed the police to take it from the stretcher. She and Kay were certain the victim had multiple spinal injuries, so to prevent further injury they had to move him as little as possible. Slow process, awkward, and in this case, messy. Six sets of hands lifted him, keeping his spine as straight as possible, and slipped him onto the fracture board on the ground, painfully slow business, jolting and moving him as little as possible. It took all four policemen and both nurses to lift the victim lying on the fracture board, to the stretcher. He was a big man, burly with a hairy chest and big face, and he was heavy. After they had strapped him on the stretcher and placed sandbags from the storage pockets of the stretcher up and down both sides of his body from the top of his head to his feet, they pulled the stretcher up on its expanding legs and began to roll it carefully but quickly toward the copter. The faces of both nurses expressed the same impulse: *urgency*. This victim wasn't going to make it, but they had to try. The gaping crowd of bystanders was only a blur, and Hugh with his camera only a sound; *click, click-click, click.*

With the police officers' help, the nurses handed the stretcher into the copter to Jerry; he helped them pull it aboard and secure it. Hugh Boyett leaped into the Ranger and the passenger's seat. As Walsh shut the door, Kay told Jerry, "Get Comstat!"

Marsha was hanging the plasma while Kay hung the IV of Ringer's lactate on the IV hooks overhead; both were aware of the clicking of Hugh's camera. Marsha said, "Kay you report to Kreel, will you, while I get this guy on the respirator?" She had been breathing the victim with the ambu bag since boarding the Ranger.

Jerry said, "Ranger I to Comstat. Got that blue-eyed brunette wants a chat, Dr. Kreel."

"Go ahead, Ranger I," came J. Braxton Kreel's voice over the headset. Kay had to smile at the formality in Kreel's voice; she realized that Hugh had put a headset on and that Kreel had figured he might.

Kay said, "Multiple injuries, Dr. Kreel, crushed sternum, fractured clavicle and left tibia, possible abdominal injuries. Definite head trauma, laceration of the scalp, probably subdural hematoma. Probable spinal injuries, suspect fracture of the cervical vertebrae." She had come a long way as a nurse. In R.N. school they taught one not to diagnose; it was not a nursing function, nurses were just to give observations. In ICU, she had diagnosed, but didn't advertise it. In TRU she diagnosed and said so. "Pupils react slowly and unevenly, Doctor. He arrested, we defibrillated, and his pulse is now near 200, but steady. Weak, though. IV of plasma—" Her mind went suddenly blank. "IV of plasma and one of Ringer's lactate is infusing. Victim's being placed on respirator with face mask. We're afraid to intubate due to spinal injuries."

"Good work, Carlton." Dr. Kreel's voice came importantly over the headset. "But be sure to place sandbags on either side of his body and don't move his trunk or neck." They had already placed the sandbags, of course, and Kreel knew it. He was just putting on a good show for Hugh Boyett, now taking notes as fast as his hands could fly over the pad. "Get monitor leads on him so you can tell if he goes into cardiac arrest. I need to know whether he goes into respiratory arrest first, or cardiac arrest. It might help us decide about the location of the head injuries later. Get plasma in as fast as you can and the Ringer's, too. I want two units of plasma in by the time you get here. Got that?"

Kay glanced at Marsha smiling. "We got it, Doctor."

"O.K., if you need me I'm here."

"Right. Four, Doctor." She pulled the headset down around her neck. She hadn't noticed, but Jerry had already lifted off. Ranger I was airborne and moving rapidly.

Because the victim was unconscious, there was no way one could assess the severity of the brain or spinal-cord damage, except by reflexes. But they had no time for that except to note that the pupils of his eyes reacted very sluggishly and unevenly to light. Their job now was to keep him alive until they got to St. Luke's. His clothing, a plaid cotton shirt and brown trousers, were soaked with blood. So were the nurses' jump suits. The victim's pulse was weaker, but Walsh had the plasma bag encased in the blood pump which was forcing it into his veins rapidly. Kay took his BP again. Forty. Bad, really bad. Breathing was stertorous beneath the face mask which was held tightly to his face by Marsha, and there was a rattling down deep in his throat, an *rrrrr* with every expiration. Something jarred Kay's consciousness. She looked up at Marsha. "Did you remember to get his ID from the police?"

"A cop stuffed it in my pocket."

Both their eyes focused then on Kay's hands, shaking violently. Kay wrapped them around the victim's unfractured arm. "I can't stop shaking," she whispered to Marsha. Hugh, in the passenger's seat couldn't hear them because he still had the headset on.

Walsh flashed her a look. "I know."

Her "I know" and the look meant, You're washed up as a trauma team member, Kay. You've reached your limit of incompetence. Everybody has a limit of incompetence in critical care. Kreel called it the Pesky Principle.

Suddenly Kay's teeth were chattering. Critical-care personnel were always scared in CPRs and medical emergencies, but when a patient's life was at stake, their hours of training and experience always took over, causing a calm clearheadedness to steal over them so that they could perform efficiently and with calm precision— until they reached their limit.

The accident had not been too many miles from St. Luke's and already the Ranger was lowering onto the helipad, landing. Walsh threw open the door. Hands reached in for the stretcher. "Don't jolt him," Kay managed.

The stretcher left the copter; a team of four raced with it and the portable respirator down the ramp for Trauma Receiving, with Hugh Boyett limping beside them with his camera; *click click*. The limp, Kay thought vaguely, was all that was left to remind Hugh of his near-fatal accident three years ago, a limp and a horrible memory.

Walsh was unsympathetic about Kay's shakiness as they walked down the ramp toward Trauma Receiving. Her mind was on something else now—something that rankled her grass-widowed soul. "Three. Three men like that in a lifetime. Who are you, anyway, Cleopatra reincarnated? Jezebel? How many of these guys have you got, Kay? Won't tell, eh? It's not fair, damn it, not fair at all." Walsh took hold of her arm to stop her and said, "If you get pregnant, I'll never speak to you again." And then as they resumed their walk down the ramp, "It's not fair. It just ain't fair."

They changed quietly into their surgical greens and Kay went back to the unit. Anita met her at the door.

"Harvey's been transferred to a semiprivate room on the trauma ward," she said. "And Ursala says you'd better go to the nursery as soon as possible."

Kay didn't have to think about it. She turned and hurried for the newborn nursery.

In the NICU, Harrison lay dying. His three doctors were standing around the isolette. Ursala was grim with grief and fury. "Dr. Paine wrote 'No heroics' on Harrison's chart," she told Kay.

Trembling, Kay caught hold of Dr. Paine's arm. "Why no heroics on Harrison?"

Rudely, Paine shrugged off her grip.

Suddenly furious, she cried, "Why? When just a little effort on your part and he could live?"

Dr. Paine turned slowly and regarded her silently for a long moment. "A *little* effort?" he said softly. "We operated—open heart—twice. On a newborn, with a congenital heart defect and an abnormal immune system. We've been fighting a losing battle from the beginning."

"Fighting? I see nobody fighting," Kay said. "Nobody but Harrison."

The other doctors were staring at her, and because of her respect for Drs. Daizat and Pugh, she felt embarrassed and degraded.

Dr. Paine, still regarding her morosely said, "If you'll bother to take a look at Harrison, Nurse, you'll see that

325

he has stopped fighting, too."

She saw the depression then in Dr. Paine's face, in all their faces. Three who had tried—but had they tried hard enough?

The monitor blip above the isolette suddenly began to stretch out. *No heroics for Harrison. No CPR.* She would have taken him up and held him while he took his last breath, but Dr. Paine beat her to it. He turned from her suddenly, lifted the baby up in his big hands and held him while he took one, two, three gasps of air; then lay still.

Dr. Daizat turned away and left the unit. Dr. Pugh put his hand on Paine's shoulder, gripped it briefly, and left also. Kay couldn't see Dr. Paine's tears because of her own. But somehow, she knew they were there.

Ursala had disappeared, so Kay went back to TRU where she told the other nurses about Harrison. *I could never become a nurse because I have too soft a heart.* Bullshit and every other curse word there is in the world, Kay thought vehemently. Every nurse in TRU cried, cried as they went about their tasks of helping the others live, cried while they checked and prepared Room Six for the new victim who was now in surgery. They worked, they worried, they cried, and yes, they prayed. They always prayed. It was an ongoing prayer that really never ceased.

Barney had returned from his two-hour surgery and when Kay had gained control of her tears, she went to check on him. Still groggy from his Demerol, he did not notice her red and swollen eyes. "Well, Carlton, Doc Hishu says they'll do two more surgeries on my gluteus maximus, and then in about a month from now it'll all be complete and he'll remove the dressing on my backside, and behold—the unveiling of the great gluteus. There should be TV cameras here and reporters. Chunn can do the main story. Only thing wrong is, I'll be facing the wrong way." Barney was in good spirits again. Another two or three days and he'd be moved out of TRU, Kay was sure.

It was almost three o'clock and time for report when the orderlies brought the trauma victim into TRU. The four nurses set to work hooking up monitor leads, nasogastric suction, Foley catheter bag, while Dr. Markowitz's technician set up the traction. Crutchfield tongs had been applied to the victim's head, inserted through the bones of the skull like ice tongs. To provide traction to keep his neck extended, the technician attached a rope to the tongs and extended it over a pulley which he attached to the head of the bed. Apparently there were lower spinal injuries, too, and Kay wondered why Dr. Markowitz hadn't ordered the patient placed on a striker frame so that he could be turned easily. Even the spinal-injured patient must be turned to prevent decubiti or bed sores. She turned to ask the doctor about it; and he, anticipating her question, said, "He won't need a striker frame."

She saw Dr. Cash standing in the hallway and went to him. "What about the head trauma on this patient?" she asked, for he was holding the patient's chart and she couldn't see what had been done for him.

"Severe brain damage. No chance he'll ever gain consciousness. Has a flat EEG, of course, but an EEG at this point isn't reliable because sometimes in severe trauma like this a patient will register a flat EEG even though he regains consciousness later. In this case, he won't. If he survives another three days, we'll do another EEG. But he has severe brain-stem damage." That meant he'd never breathe on his own again. "There were three subdural hematomas and fractures of two cervical vertebrae. Extensive spinal-cord damage." Cash drew in a deep breath. "That's not to mention multiple fractures all over his body. What I'm trying to say is, no heroics on him, O.K.?"

"You'll have to put that on the chart."

"No, no, just pass it along from one shift to the other."

"I can't do that and I won't."

"Why?"

"Because we nurses are legally liable if you don't write it on the chart."

"Well, I'm liable if I do. His wife won't agree to 'No CPR.' She wants heroics done for him even though he's nothing but a vegetable, will never be anything but a vegetable, and probably won't survive the night anyway. And if he does survive the night, he'll die tomorrow. He's paralyzed, totally, and his brain is a scrambled egg. No heroics."

"If you don't put 'No CPR' on the chart, we'll have to do it, Dr. Paine," Kay said.

"My name is Cash."

Kay blushed. "Just the same—"

"All right. All right."

On the way home from his hell I'm going to stop by a liquor store and buy me a bottle of . . . of whiskey! Kay thought. She'd never bought a bottle of liquor in her life, but today . . .

At the nurses' station Dr. Cash was grimly scribbling on the new patient's chart and Kay went back into the patient's room to check the set up. IV of D5W was infusing slowly. A unit of whole blood was infusing as rapidly as they dared to infuse it. The monitor showed a rapid but regular heart rate. The MA-1 respirator sighed and clunked and pushed air into the tracheostomy in the patient's throat. His left arm was in a cast, he was encased in a spica cast from his waist down. If she could have his chart, she'd be able to see why he had had abdominal surgery, for there was a large abdominal dressing covering his abdomen. Probably a ruptured spleen; no telling what else. Anita was checking the reaction of his pupils to light. She shook her head. "No reaction at all."

Only then did a measure of sympathy begin to push through Kay's shell, the shell she'd had to form around herself when she'd begun to treat him, the shell every nurse or doctor has to form around him- or herself in order to be objective enough to function at saving a life. In a critical emergency, one had to momentarily banish sympathy, or at least hold it at bay and think of the human machine—fix the machine. Now she could let herself feel sympathy again.

On the patient's uninjured arm someone had wrapped a blood-pressure cuff. She pumped it up, listened for the BP. It was 90 over 42. Low. But that was to be expected until his fluid volume was increased. The Foley bag showed scant, concentrated urine, perhaps blood-tinged.

The patient was a big man, not flabby or fat, just big and muscular, with a protruding abdomen. His trunk was large, but his legs were almost thin, like some obese elderly person's—or like those of a cartoon character in the newspapers. His hair had been shaved and once the nurses had sponged the dried blood from the lacerations on his face, Kay could see the day-old beard on his jaw.

She turned and left the bedside more depressed than before and went to the nurses' station. The three to eleven crew was already there. One of the nurses was holding the new patient's chart and Kay took it from her without explanation, because she wanted to see the patient's name. She thought she already knew who he was. She was right. The new trauma patient, on whom Dr. Cash had just ordered no CPR, was William Royce Ballew.

CHAPTER XVI

"What you need, son, is to eat rare beefsteak once a day like me, *rrrrr*. Do you know how I got these muscles? Worked on the docks unloading freight at the port of Houston for twelve years, *rrrrr*. That's what both you perfessers ought to do. Eat rare beefsteak and work on the docks a few years. It'll make hair grow on your chest, *rrrrrr*."

Syd switched off the recorder and covered his mouth with his fist. For a long time he sat at the desk in his office thinking nothing, letting his mind remain a blank as long as possible. Then, little vignettes of painful memory began to flicker in his mind. They were punctuated by zigzag lightning flashes of disbelief, frustration, horror, despair, sympathy, regret—all the fiery demons that trouble the human mind at times like this.

William Royce Ballew had died early that morning. Syd, Harry, and Dr. Michaelson had sat up in the TRU waiting room along with Ballew's wife and two of his oldest children, drinking coffee, unable to believe what had happened to Ballew. Only Syd had sensed what the nurses felt for Ballew, something that went beyond ordinary sympathy, something that was empathy, combined with a determination to force someone to survive.

But Ballew had died at dawn and there was probably no CPR. Syd had waited for Kay to arrive at her usual hour. Grief overwhelmed him. The greatest hope for success in his studies of genetic memory had died with poor old crushed Billy Roy. Dr. Michaelson stayed awhile after Dr. Kreel came to tell Mrs. Ballew the bad news. When she and the children left, Michaelson shook hands with Harry and Syd and bade them good-by, assuring Syd that even though Ballew was gone, in their carefully taken notes and the recorded tapes of their sessions with him, his testimony for genetic memory lived on. "A trip to England and France to trace Ballew's ancestry would be required, and might give the answer to whether or not Ballew had inherited the memory of his forefathers," Michaelson had said. Harry had replied, "Syd, that trip abroad can be funded by the government grant that's available for your research." A trip to Europe for him and Kay to search for Ballew's genesis? That was little consolation now, though. What Syd was feeling at the moment was grief for Ballew as a man.

Suddenly his grief shifted to worry. He worried about Kay—worried because he had lost one thing of value to him. Grief spreads like a disease. . . . Maybe a trip would get her away from that scene. Lately she had become grim, tense, unhappy, tired, depressed. She had lost weight, seldom laughed. He was determined to do something, anything to make her leave St. Luke's for at least a year. Burnout was a danger to all nurses and a major reason for the national shortage of nurses. In critical care it just happened more often and quicker. He knew burnout when he saw it.

That John Wayne-type was right after all. He'd wanted to take her away from all of it. The cowboy's insight—or was it his selfishness—would have prevented this burnout of Kay's.

She arrived at the TRU waiting room early and, upon seeing Syd's face, knew Ballew had not survived the night. She came into his arms. "I'm so sorry, darling," she said against his chest.

A lump in his throat prevented him from replying. He took her chin in his hand and looked at her face, the face he loved, the full lips, the blue-green eyes. He wanted to say, "Baby, let's take a vacation. How about England or France?" Or, "Kay, why don't you go to Thompson today and resign?" Or, "Sweetheart, I love you for trying." But he couldn't. He simply kissed her forehead and said, "See you at four, Kay. I'll be home early."

She had only nodded and he had left, gone home, shaved, showered, dressed, and met his first class. Now he sat alone in his office. He looked up at the ceiling. *Billy Roy, if you can hear me, if there is such a thing as reincarnation* . . . Syd sniffed. Reincarnation; he almost, but not quite, wished he believed in it.

In TRU the body had just been removed from Room Six when Kay arrived for work, and the housekeeping ladies had descended with their buckets and disinfectant, their usual Chicano chatter absent; for they knew there had been a death in that room just an hour or so before, and so they worked in silence.

Dr. Kreel had already been there and written an order for Barney to be transferred to the floor—a surprise to Kay. After report she took up the receiver of the telephone and dialed Admitting, requesting that Barney be transferred to Room T-316, Harvey's room, if at all possible. Luckily, the room was unoccupied except by

Harvey, and Admitting agreed to transfer Barney there. Then Kay read the report on Ballew's decease. His vital signs had been unstable all evening. Then at nine o'clock his BP had dropped out. An Aramine drip had been hung in an effort to improve his blood pressure, but to no avail. Then a dopamine drip was hung for the same purpose, but to no avail. Still, Ballew hung on through the night with almost no blood pressure until 5:15 when he arrested. Ballew, with all his memory long gone, had never regained consciousness, of course.

Hailey rolled Barney out of TRU at ten o'clock. "Be sure you come to my room for the unveiling, Carlton," Barney admonished from the wheelchair. "In all your long and colorful career, you'll never see anything else like it, I promise."

"I hope not, Barney. And I will be by to see you. Hope you have a good roommate."

"I hope she's a blue-eyed blonde," he said making an hourglass shape with his hands. "Not that it would do me much good, but I can still look, can't I?"

Still smiling, Kay went in to check on Dr. Worley. Since his heart attack, he had been quiet, almost pensive, introspective, and he used the nurse call bell now when he needed something. Today Dr. Kreel had written an order for him to be transferred to the floor. Kay checked his IV saying, "Dr. Kreel ordered you to be transferred to the floor, Dr. Worley."

He looked up from the morning paper. "I beg your pardon?"

"We'll be moving you to the regular ward in about fifteen minutes," Kay said brightly.

"Oh, that's fine. Fine," he said. Then, nodding and sipping his decaffeinated coffee, he went back to reading his paper.

Considering that Harrison had died the day before and Ballew had died only that morning, Kay was in better spirits than she had expected. Probably because of a puzzling discovery she'd made while studying the calendar at home the night before while Syd was sitting up at the hospital. So, feeling rather cheerful, she went in to watch Hailey feed Mr. Brunner. Brunner had not been able to tolerate the feeding tube so the nurses had tried by various means to ooze food into his mouth. Hailey was using an asepto syringe, a large plastic one. She filled it with the puréed food, then stuck the tip into a space where Brunner had lost a bicuspid, and squirted. Brunner had no choice but to swallow for the first few days although, stoically, he was still determined not to cooperate. He had even resorted to removing the respirator from his tracheostomy occasionally. Luckily the nurses were able to set the warning signal on the respirator so that when he removed the tubing, a buzzer would sound and a nurse would go in, scold Brunner mildly, and put the tube back on the tracheal adaptor so that the machine could breathe for him again. He wouldn't look at the nurses or the doctors and he wouldn't communicate with anyone. He even defecated in his bed occasionally without indicating the need for a bedpan. The nurses tended to believe his injuries had affected his mental capacity because of his stubbornness and his refusal to communicate or cooperate. But despite their anger at some of his behavior, they couldn't help but regard him with special affection.

Hailey thought she had solved the problem of getting food down Brunner's throat, but recently he had figured out a way to work the food, which she squirted into his throat, to the front of his mouth and hold it. Hailey was furious by the time Kay entered the room.

While Kay watched, Hailey cajoled and pleaded to no avail, so Kay offered to try and Hailey gratefully let her.

Kay had tried before to feed Brunner. She'd spent many moments trying to get him to eat since he'd arrived as a patient in the unit. Now she sat down, and instead of using the syringe, she took a plastic spoon in hand. "Open up, Mr. Brunner," she said.

He stolidly kept his mouth shut.

"You've got four daughters and two sons out in the waiting room all anxious to hear if you've eaten or not. If you won't feed yourself at least open your mouth so *I* can feed you."

Brunner would not. And he would not look at her.

"Your vital signs are good, Mr. Brunner, and soon Dr. Daizat will take you off the respirator."

No response.

"O.K., so this isn't steak and mashed potatoes. At least it's vegetables and meat ground up. That's better than IVs, isn't it?"

No response and Kay was losing her patience swiftly. "If you don't eat, we'll have to install a tube into your intestines and feed you directly."

Not a flicker.

"Open up, now. I'm losing my temper."

No response.

She did lose her temper. "Mr. Brunner! All *right!* Don't you know we're only trying all this—" she said with a sweep of her hand to indicate the monitor, the respirator, the IVs, the food, "—all this to help you *live?*"

No response. But his eyes began to shine and when she

studied them closer, she saw that tears had appeared. She rose, pushed the bedside table up in front of him, placed the spoon and vegetables and grape juice within his reach, and left the room.

She went to the desk, but watched out of the corner of her eye. Just as she suspected, Brunner looked slowly around to see if anyone was watching, sneaked a few mouthfuls of puréed vegetables, and drank some of the grape juice. Then he pushed the table away and assumed his stoic demeanor again.

Why, that scoundrel! Kay had to smile. In report she'd tell the others to leave his food on the tray in front of him and leave the room. He'd probably sneak what he wanted and hope nobody would know the difference. Mr. Brunner, like everybody else, really *did* want to live. In spite of all the hospital nonsense and apparatus.

It was noon and TRU was quiet. Only Mr. Brunner was in the unit now. Dr. Worley had been transferred to the floor. An hour later a dozen red roses had been delivered to the TRU nurses' station. The card accompanying the roses read simply; "From Dr. Moriah M. Worley."

Kay took her break and went to see Ursala in the newborn nursery. Ursala had done her crying over Harrison and now it was time to get on with her work.

"Ah, I see a lot of these kids deformed physically and mentally, and sometimes one of them will steal away my heart like Harrison did," Ursala said misty-eyed. "But someday, you watch, there'll be a way to prevent birth defects. Dr. Paine says it'll be years yet. But what does he know? Miracles happen every day."

Miracles happen every day; miracles like Barney and Harvey.

When Kay visited their room, both were sitting by the window looking out over the hospital's beautifully kept front lawn three stories below. Or rather, Barney was looking and Harvey was enjoying the sun on his face and body.

"Can you believe it, Carlton?" Barney said when Kay came into their room. "There must be over five hundred rooms in this part of the hospital and who do I get stuck with for a roommate? *This* yokel!"

"I was here first, Werger. Who invited you?" Harvey said.

"You could have gotten somebody who snores all night and watches game shows on TV all day," Barney told him. Then to Kay he said, "We got to talking and decided maybe we ought to pool our resources. I haven't got legs, but I've got sensational ideas to help with Chunn's screenplays."

"Who said your ideas were sensational?" Harvey protested. "I don't think they're exactly sensational; they're little oases of absurdities in an otherwise intellectual drama." He looked at Kay. "It's stupid stuff like this buffalo joke—"

"At any rate, he's blind," Barney said. "He can push my wheelchair while I tell him where to push it. Figuratively speaking and literally speaking. Together we can make it, Carlton."

Harvey said shaking his head. "Not if all you've got to offer is stuff like that stupid buffalo joke."

"Ernie lives next door to Harvey. Don't you see? Harvey's thinking of asking her to move in with him— uh, hopefully under matrimonial circumstances—and I can rent her apartment next door. She can do the typing and the cooking for him and whatever else needs to be

338

done. I can be no threat to their relationship, unfortunately, unless these repaired nerves regenerate. And I'll help with the screenplays. Liven 'em up. Together we'll be another Rogers and Hammerstein—without the music."

When Kay left shortly, Harvey was still shaking his head and saying incredulously, "This stupid, *stupid* buffalo joke."

She left their room feeling as if the sun had shone on her, too, only deep down somewhere inside. She glanced at her watch. Thirty minutes of her lunch hour were left. She had plenty of time to visit Leola Parkman.

But when she came to Leola's private room there was no one there. The room had been cleaned and polished, the bed crisply made. Evidently, the former occupant had vacated it and it had been made ready for the next patient.

Puzzled, Kay went to the trauma ward's nurses' station where the usual chaos and confusion reigned supreme. The telephone was ringing. A ward clerk was taking off doctors' orders; two nurses in crisp, white uniforms and caps were conferring over a chart. A doctor stood beside the large, revolving cylinder where fifty metal-covered charts were kept, giving verbal orders to the charge nurse. A third nurse hurried past Kay carrying a tray of medications. A volunteer lady of the hospital auxiliary, dressed in a pink smock, was pushing a cart of canned fruit juices and soda pop down the corridor. A patient call bell made a "ding" sound on the intercom. The haggard nurse, sitting at the desk writing, paused, pushed the button on the intercom, and said, "Can I help you?"

The whining voice, which came over the intercom in reply, was drowned out by the ward clerk's telling whoever was on the telephone to call Admitting instead. When she had slammed the receiver down, Kay asked her, "What happened to Leola Parkman?"

The ward clerk replaced her glasses, which had been dangling on a chain around her neck. "Oh, honey! You're from TRU, aren't you? Boy! Did we have a mess! She left. Her husband checked her out AMA—against medical advice. I made him sign all the papers releasing the hospital and Dr. Kreel from any responsibility, though, I can *assure* you."

Kay choked out, "She went willingly?"

The clerk nodded emphatically. "She certainly did. All smiles, too. Waving and smiling. Can you believe it?"

Sick, Kay turned away. She *couldn't* believe it. Just couldn't! *That stupid,* stupid *woman!*

"Oh, by the way," said the ward clerk. When Kay turned back to face her again, she said, "Your name is Carlton? I can see by your name tag. Mrs. Parkman left you a note."

The ward clerk looked under one chart, then another, and another. She then checked under a stack of lab slips and a Kardex where she found the note, and handed it to Kay. Kay unfolded it.

Kay,
Tell the others I remember the number.
Leola Parkman

Yes, she might remember the number, but little good it would do her if he killed her first.

Kay left, too sick to go to lunch. Instead, she went back to TRU.

Hugh Boyett was waiting in TRU when she entered. He

had followed Dr. Kreel's instructions and was dressed in surgical greens. Kay laughed. "Look at you. You look like a surgeon!"

He had been prowling around the unit taking pictures, she knew, and had just sat down to entertain Hailey, Anita, and Jan with tales of Scotland. He rose beaming when he saw her. "Katy! My Katy!"

Three sets of eyebrows shot up, but Kay laughed. "We're twins!" she said coming to stand beside him; for both were dressed in identical surgical greens.

Hugh looked down at his suit, then over at hers where her breasts—fuller lately—gave shape to the shapeless shirt, and her behind—also fuller lately—enhanced the plainness of the trousers.

He shook his head slowly, his mouth forming a small "O." "No-oo, Katy, lass," he said softly. "For you've got a bit more sculpturin' to ye than I."

Sensing Kay's wish to speak to him alone, the other three nurses who'd been enjoying Hugh's Scottish brogue, which he stealthily brought out of mothballs whenever he wanted to impress someone or to get attention, left one by one.

He promptly instructed her to sit in front of the monitor screen where Mr. Brunner's lone blip bobbed, for he wanted to take her picture. "Now take a pen and pretend you're doing something," he told her. She obeyed, taking lab slips out and pretending to check them. *Click, click, click.* It occurred to her that this was Hugh's life—the click of the camera—and how thankful she was he was able to do it, because there had been a time . . .

"What a story this is going to make, Katy," he said, sitting in the desk chair next to hers. "I am not a writer and my story will mostly be in pictures. But it will be a terrific story in spite of my discomfort at waking those terrible memories . . . because of all the critical-care apparatus in here." He tilted his head, his eyes softening. "Ah, Katy . . ." Hugh straightened and said, "It will be an entire story of St. Luke's trauma facilities. I'll follow the rescue team from Comstat's booth to the Ranger, to the site of the accident, to the care of the patient in the helicopter, back to Trauma Receiving, to surgery, to Trauma Recovery. It will be the entire inside story, don't you see. And you, mostly you, as the main focus."

"Please no, Hugh. Focus on the patient."

Hugh smiled sadly, almost uncomfortably. "Unfortunately—"

"Yes, I know. Mr. Ballew didn't make it, but hundreds have. Someday I want to check and see just how many—"

"Eighty percent. I've already checked, Katy. Eighty percent more victims recover from critical injuries at St. Luke's than they did before the trauma units were established." He smiled and took both her hands in his. "Ah, Katy, what fun we could have together if you were single. It's too bad for me you're now married."

Smiling, she shook her head. "It's a good thing for *me* that I am."

Hugh left the unit moments later, kissed her hand, and in his fetching Scottish brogue said with a lilt, "I'll always be rememberin' ye, Katy. With ever a tug at me hearrrt."

When he was gone the nurses besieged her with questions about who he was, where she had known him before. She told them Hugh's story, all of it. Dr. Kreel had wanted Hugh to do the inside story and he would. For

Hugh had once been a trauma patient himself; he knew the *real* inside story.

Finally Hailey turned away to reenter Brunner's room and Jan returned to restocking the dressings cabinet. Anita, who stood by the desk, wordlessly handed Kay an envelope addressed to "Mrs. Kay Carlton in care of Trauma Recovery." As Anita walked away, Kay opened the envelope and slowly unfolded the single page. The handwriting was legibly masculine and bold.

> *Dear Kay,*
>
> *I just want to thank you and your husband for attending Ike's funeral. You'll never know what that meant to me. Maydy is doing well and so am I, considering.*
>
> *I was mad, Kay, because I needed you when Ike died that day, but I realize, too, you've got a duty at St. Luke's, more important than friendship or love, I reckon. Something I guess I'll never understand.*

Kay looked up, picturing Cass's grief-stricken face. "Few people do," she said aloud.

> *I realize I'm laying my life on the line to write this next, but if things don't work out with you and Syd— well, you know—*
>
> *Cass*

"You'll be waiting," she finished for him.

All was calm in the unit except for the housekeeping personnel who were clattering mops and buckets, wiping bedrails, chattering, and cleaning Dr. Worley's vacated room until it gleamed and smelled of disinfectant. Kay was still holding Cass's note when the telephone rang.

"Kay Carlton, TRU."

"Kay, this is Marsha," came Walsh's voice over the line.

Kay thought, Darn! Another emergency call. "What's up?" she asked.

"I don't want you to get scared, now, Kay. It's O.K., but your son, Russell, just came into TR. He has an injured—"

"Oh my God!" Kay exclaimed loudly and dropped into her chair, causing the other three nurses to hurry out of the rooms and stand by the desk.

"Kay, I promise. It's O.K.," Walsh continued. "He's just hurt his knee. Fell on some broken glass; but we thought you'd want to know he's here. Your husband—*Wow*—is here with him. So calm down, O.K.?"

Kay dropped the receiver and turned to Anita. "It's Russell. In TR." She stood up. "To hell with all this."

"Sure, go on," Anita said, alarmed. "And forget report. Do what you have to do. Need someone to go with you?"

Kay shook her head and bolted out the door. She was still trembling as she hurried down the corridor for Trauma Receiving. One more shock. Just one more shock and she'd go crazy—even if he wasn't hurt. Oh God, just one more shock. They could be deceiving her after all; it might be worse than Marsha said. Oh, God. Russell!

But Trauma Receiving was quiet and Syd took her hand just outside Trauma Room Two. "He's O.K. Just a lacerated knee that needs a few stitches."

Nevertheless, she went in to see for herself.

Russell was sitting on a treatment table in Trauma Room Two with Marsha standing beside him. A new resident doctor whom Kay had never seen before was sitting on the stool by the table, sorting through his sutures, vials of novacaine, Betadine prep, and syringes in the sterile pack on the Mayo stand. He was obviously nervous because he was under the direct, benevolent scrutiny of the director of the trauma units himself, J. Braxton Kreel.

"Hi, Mom," Russell said.

Kay took a deep breath. "How—"

"I fell down on my bike and cut my knee on a broken bottle," Russell said and winced as the resident sponged the knee with Betadine prep.

The wound was deep and bleeding and Kay could see the patella—the kneecap—through ragged edges of cutaneous and adipose tissue.

The resident threw a glance in Kay's direction. "Mrs. Carlton, will you please wait in the waiting room?" he asked irritably. "Your husband can stay because he says he was a nurse, but I just don't need anybody fainting in here."

Kreel burst out laughing. "Take another look at Mrs. Carlton, Boswell," he said jauntily. "*This* one is not going to faint."

When Dr. Boswell turned, he saw that Kay was wearing surgical greens.

"That outfit she's wearing can mean only four things at St. Luke's Boswell," Kreel went on laughingly. "It means she's either a surgical nurse, an OB nurse, a newborn nursery nurse, or she's a nurse in one of the trauma units. In her case, she's my number-two trauma nurse, my number-*one* Trauma Recovery nurse. She's seen it all," Kreel boasted. "She's seen twice the blood and guts you'll ever see as an internist, Doctor!" Kreel laughed again at young Dr. Boswell's red face, and turned to Syd. "Just how many years has she worked in a critical-care capacity?"

"Six."

"And two of those have been in the best trauma unit in the Southwest," Kreel bragged.

There seemed to be a buzzing somewhere in the distance, and the lights grew dim as Boswell bent to inject Russell's knee with a local anesthetic.

"Ow," Russell said.

The resident injected a little novacaine and then worked the needle around and injected a little more. He removed the needle, and while he rummaged around on the tray for the proper suture, Dr. Kreel was saying, "She's one of *my* nurses. These two girls right here have seen it all, seen everything. Treated everything."

Boswell's face was still red as he took a stitch in Russell's knee, tied it, sponged Russell's blood with a sterile four-by-four sponge, then continued to stitch, tie, and sponge.

Kreel went on, "She's seen more trauma in six years than you'll see in a lifetime, Dr. Boswell-well-well-well."

The buzzing was louder and her peripheral vision was narrowing, narrowing to that bloody knee. . . .

"My nurses are some of the most-most experi-experienced nurses-nurses-nurses in the entire-tire world-world-world-wor—"

The roaring engulfed her.

When she awoke, she knew exactly where she was—on the trauma-room treatment table—and exactly what had happened. She saw Dr. Kreel standing beside the table looking sheepishly down at her; she turned her head to see Syd. "I fainted, didn't I?" she asked.

Syd opened his mouth and when nothing came out, she looked at Dr. Kreel and said cheerfully, "I resign."

He blanched. "Now, Carlton, don't be hasty. It's different when it's your own kid who's hurt. Why, I remember not too long ago when one of my little girls bloodied her forehead—a deep laceration—my God, I went a little berserk!"

"But I still have to resign."

Kreel looked hurt. "You can't. Why, who would replace you?"

"Anita Wilson."

"Who'll replace Wilson?"

"Somebody. There's always somebody."

While she sat up with Syd's help, Dr. Kreel said, "I'll tell you what, Carlton. Get Jones, your supervisor, to give you three days off. I'll order it. Get yourself some sun, get some rest, enjoy your family, read a good book. Then see how you feel."

"I'll still have to resign."

"Bah," he said. "You take that three days off like I said." He started for the door. "Why you'll even feel better by tomorrow morning; you just wait and see if I'm not right."

When they were alone, Syd said, "You never fainted completely before, baby."

"I know. How's Russell?"

"Waiting to go home. They're putting a dressing on his knee now."

"Let's go home."

She met Walsh outside the room with Russell. "This is a good kid," she said. "Smart too. Wish he was mine." She paused, and while Syd went to the trauma admitting desk to pay his sixty-five dollars for the use of the trauma room, Walsh asked, "How do you feel, Kay? You really conked out. Just dropped like a ton of bricks."

"I feel fine."

"You sure? Because you're still pale."

"I'm sure."

Marsha narrowed her eyes at Kay. "If you are what I think you are, don't speak to me. It isn't fair. None of this with you is fair at all."

They drove Russell home, mostly in silence. But once they were alone in their bedroom with Russell downstairs showing his bandaged wound to Uncle Ben, Kay sat down on their bed and held her arms out to Syd.

He went down on his knees and buried his face between her breasts and she held his head, running her fingers through his hair. "I'm sorry about Billy Roy, Syd. We tried."

"I know, baby."

"There never was any hope for him."

After a moment of silence Syd said, "Kay, you've got to ignore Kreel and resign immediately. That's what you've got to do."

"I know I do."

He raised his head to look at her. "You do?"

"Sure I do."

He stared. "Why?"

"Well . . ." She paused. "I've been . . . you know . . . busy. Lost track of time, and so have you. I forgot my pills I guess a dozen times or more. Menstrual periods all mixed up . . . until lately."

His face paled. "Lately?"

"We seldom have had time to make love and you

348

hadn't noticed—"

"My God and I thought it was— And you didn't tell me?"

"It occurred to me, but my cycle was so messed up—"

"That frequent urination—"

"Even my nipples are already discoloring." She laughed. "But you didn't notice. And only last night did it occur to *me* that I should check the calendar—"

"My God! Some nurses we are!" He laughed, stared at her in disbelief. "We, of all people—"

"There are no absolutes in medicine."

He laughed, still regarding her with awe.

"Don't tell anybody that we didn't know all along, Syd. It's too embarrassing."

He gathered her into his arms. "My God, me a—"

The bed gave way suddenly with a resounding crash and the prisms on the overhead chandelier tinkled as they laughed, held each other, and laughed some more.

"Uncle Ben will think we're making love." She laughed.

"So? Maybe we will."

"I'll resign tomorrow. Give my two weeks' notice."

"Promise? Because if you don't I'll do it for you. Me a—"

"I promise."

"No emergency calls either during the two weeks you have left."

"O.K. Anita can go on those."

"No lifting or pulling on patients, do you hear me?"

"Yes, Dr. Carlton."

He held her, still shaking his head incredulously. "Take a year off. Take forever off. You've done enough

349

nursing for a lifetime."

"Maybe. Maybe not. Nursing gets in your blood, you know."

"I know. But at this point what do you really want to do?"

She looked up at the ceiling, pondered, and said, "Right now I'm not sure. But probably I'll go back after the baby is born, maybe in a month. Maybe in a year. Maybe . . . someday."

Syd smiled down at her, remembering another day and another time when he had thought along those same lines. "In the meantime, baby, maybe we'll take a trip to England and France, and you'll be—"

"I'll just be Mrs. Carlton, maybe start redecorating this beautiful old house while I enjoy my children, and you and Uncle Ben. And eventually . . ." She looked at him again smiling. "Eventually, who knows? Maybe I'll even write that book."

WHITEWATER DYNASTY BY HELEN LEE POOLE